DREAMS *of* GODS *and* MONSTERS

LAINI TAYLOR

First published in America in 2014 by Little, Brown and Company

First published in Great Britain in 2014 by Hodder & Stoughton
An Hachette UK company

First published in paperback in 2015

12

A CIP catalogue record for this title is available from the British Library.

B format paperback 978 1 444 72275 8
A format paperback 978 1 444 72276 5
eBook 978 1 444 72274 1

Printed and bound by Clays Ltd, Elcograf S.p.A

Hodder & Stoughton policy is to use papers that are natural, renewable
and recyclable products and made from wood grown in sustainable forests.
The logging and manufacturing processes are expected to conform to
the environmental regulations of the country of origin.

Hodder & Stoughton Ltd
338 Euston Road
London NW1 3BH

www.hodder.co.uk

For Jim,
for the happy middle

Once upon a time,
an angel and a devil pressed their hands to their hearts

and started the apocalypse.

1

Nightmare Ice Cream

Nerve thrum and screaming blood, wild and churning and chasing and devouring and terrible and terrible and terrible—

"Eliza. *Eliza!*"

A voice. Bright light, and Eliza fell awake. That's how it felt: like falling and landing hard. "It was a dream," she heard herself say. "It was just a dream. I'm okay."

How many times in her life had she spoken those words? More than she could count. This was the first time, though, that she'd spoken them to a man who had burst heroically into her room, clutching a claw hammer, to save her from being murdered.

"You... you were screaming," said her roommate, Gabriel, darting looks into the corners and finding no sign of murderers. He was sleep-disheveled and manically alert, holding the hammer high and ready. "I mean... really, *really* screaming."

"I know," said Eliza, her throat raw. "I do that sometimes." She pushed herself upright in bed. Her heartbeat felt like cannon fire—doomful and deep and reverberating through her entire body, and though her mouth was dry and her breathing shallow, she tried to sound nonchalant. "Sorry to wake you."

Blinking, Gabriel lowered the hammer. "That's not what I meant, Eliza. I've never heard anyone sound like that in real life. That was a horror-movie scream."

He sounded a little impressed. *Go away*, Eliza wanted to say. *Please.* Her hands were starting to tremble. Soon she wouldn't be able to control it, and she didn't want a witness. The adrenaline crash could be pretty bad after the dream. "I promise, I'm fine. Okay? I just..."

Damn.

Shaking. Pressure building, the sting behind her eyelids, and all of it out of her control.

Damn damn damn.

She doubled over and hid her face in her bedspread as the sobs welled up and took her over. As bad as the dream was—and it was *bad*—the aftermath was worse, because she was conscious but still powerless. The terror—the terror, *the terror*—lingered, and there was something else. It came with the dream, every time, and didn't recede with it but stayed like something a tide had washed in. Something awful—a rank leviathan corpse left to rot on the shore of her mind. It was remorse. But god, that was too bloodless a word for it. This feeling the dream left her with, it was knives of panic and horror resting bright atop a red and meaty wound-fester of *guilt.*

Guilt over what? That was the worst part. It was...dear god, it was unspeakable, and it was immense. Too immense. Nothing worse had ever been done, in all of time, and all of space, and the guilt was hers. It was impossible, and with any distance from the dream Eliza could dismiss it as ridiculous.

She had not done, and nor would she ever do . . . *that*.

But when the dream entangled her, none of it mattered—not reason, not sense, not even the laws of physics. The terror and the guilt smothered it all.

It sucked.

When the sobs finally subsided and she lifted her head, Gabriel was sitting on the edge of her bed, looking compassionate and alarmed. There was this pert civility about Gabriel Edinger that suggested a better-than-fair chance of bow ties in his future. Maybe even a monocle. He was a neuroscientist, probably the smartest person Eliza knew, and one of the nicest. Both of them were research fellows at the Smithsonian's National Museum of Natural History—the NMNH—and had been friendly while not quite *friends* for the past year, until Gabriel's girlfriend moved to New York for her postdoc and he needed a roommate to cover the rent. Eliza had known it was a risk, cross-pollinating life hours with work hours, for this exact reason. *This*.

Screaming. Sobbing.

It wouldn't take much digging for an interested party to ascertain the . . . depths of abnormal . . . upon which she'd built this life. Like laying planks over quicksand, it sometimes seemed. But the dream hadn't troubled her for a while, so she'd given in to the temptation to pretend she was normal, with nothing but the normal concerns of any twenty-four-year-old doctoral student on a tiny budget. Dissertation pressure, evil lab-mate, grant proposals, rent.

Monsters.

"I'm sorry," she said to Gabriel. "I think I'm okay now."

"Good." After an uncomfortable pause, he asked, brightly, "Cup of tea?"

Tea. Now there was a nice glimpse of normal. "Yes," Eliza said. "Please."

And when he ambled off to put on the kettle, she composed herself. Pulled on her robe, rinsed her face, blew her nose, regarded herself in the mirror. She was puffy, and her eyes were bloodshot. Awesome. She had pretty eyes, normally. She was accustomed to getting compliments on them from strangers. They were big and long-lashed and bright—at least when the whites weren't pink from sobbing—and several shades lighter brown than her skin, which made them seem to glow. Right now, it chilled her to note that they looked a little . . . crazy.

"You're not crazy," she told her reflection, and the statement had the ring of an affirmation often uttered—a reassurance needed, and habitually given. *You're not crazy, and you're not going to be.*

Deeper down ran another, more desperate thought.

It will not happen to me. I'm stronger than the others.

Usually, she was able to believe it.

When Eliza joined Gabriel in the kitchen, the oven clock read four AM. Tea was on the table, along with a pint of ice cream, open, with a spoon sticking out. He gestured to it. "Nightmare ice cream. Family tradition."

"Really?"

"Yeah, actually."

Eliza tried, for a moment, to imagine ice cream as her own family's response to the dream, but she couldn't. The contrast was just too stark. She reached for the carton. "Thanks," she said. She ate a couple of bites in silence, took a sip of tea, all the while tensed for the questions to begin, as they surely must.

What do you dream about, Eliza?

How am I supposed to help you if you won't talk to me, Eliza?

What's wrong *with you, Eliza?*

She'd heard it all before.

"You were dreaming about Morgan Toth, weren't you?" Gabriel asked. "Morgan Toth and his pillowy lips?"

Okay, so she hadn't heard *that*. In spite of herself, Eliza laughed. Morgan Toth was her nemesis, and his lips were a fine subject for a nightmare, but no, that wasn't even close. "I don't really want to talk about it," she said.

"Talk about what?" Gabriel asked, all innocence. "What is this 'it' you speak of?"

"Cute. But I mean it. Sorry."

"Okay."

Another bite of ice cream, another silence cut short by another non-question. "I had nightmares as a kid," Gabriel offered. "For about a year. Really intense. To hear my parents tell it, life as we knew it was pretty much suspended. I was afraid to fall asleep, and I had all these rituals, superstitions. I even tried making offerings. My favorite toys, food. Supposedly I was overheard offering up my older brother in my place. I don't remember that, but he swears."

"Offering him to who?" Eliza asked.

"*Them*. The ones in the dream."

Them.

A spark of recognition, hope. Idiotic hope. Eliza had a "them," too. Rationally she knew that they were a creation of her mind and existed nowhere else, but in the aftermath of the dream, it was not always possible to remain rational. She asked, "What were they?" before she quite considered what she was doing. If she wasn't going to talk about *her* dream, she shouldn't be prying into *his*. It was a rule of secret-keeping, in which she was well-versed: Ask not, lest ye be asked.

"Monsters," he said with a shrug, and just like that, Eliza lost interest—not at the mention of monsters, but at his *of course* tone. Anyone who could say *monsters* in that offhand manner had definitely never met hers.

"You know, being chased is one of the commonest dreams," Gabriel said, and went on to tell her about it, and Eliza kept sipping tea and taking the occasional bite of nightmare ice cream, and she nodded in the right places, but she wasn't really listening. She'd thoroughly researched dream analysis a long time ago. It hadn't helped before, and it didn't now, and when Gabriel summed up with "they're a manifestation of our waking fears," and "*everyone* has them," his tone was both placating and pedantic, as though he'd just solved her problem for her.

Eliza really wanted to say, *And I suppose* everyone *gets pacemakers when they're seven years old because 'manifestations of their waking fears' keep sending them into cardiac arrhythmia?* But she didn't, because it was the exact kind of memorable factoid that gets regurgitated at cocktail parties.

Did you know that Eliza Jones got a pacemaker when she was seven because her nightmares gave her cardiac arrhythmia?

Seriously? That's insane.

"So what happened to you?" she asked him. "What happened to your monsters?"

"Oh, they carried off my brother and left me alone. I have to sacrifice a goat to them every Michaelmas, but it's a small price to pay for a good night's sleep."

Eliza laughed. "Where do you get your goats?" she asked, playing along.

"Great little farm in Maryland. Certified sacrificial goats. Lambs, too, if you prefer."

"Who doesn't? And what the hell's Michaelmas?"

"I don't know. I pulled that out of the air."

And Eliza experienced a moment of gratitude, because Gabriel hadn't pried, and the ice cream and tea and even her irritation with his scholarly jabber had helped to ease the aftermath. She was actually laughing, and that was something.

And then her phone vibrated on the tabletop.

Who was calling her at four AM? She reached for it…

…and when she saw the number on the screen, she dropped it—or possibly *flung* it. With a *crack* it hit a cabinet and bounced to the floor. For a second she had hope that she'd killed it. It lay there, silent. Dead. And then—*bzzzzzzzzzzzz*—not dead.

When had she ever been sorry not to have broken her phone?

It was the number. Just digits. No name. No name came up because Eliza had not programmed *that number* into her phone. She didn't even realize that she remembered it until she saw it, and it was like it had been there all along, every moment of her life since…since she'd escaped. It was all there, it was all right there. The gut-punch was immediate and visceral and undiminished by the years.

"All right?" Gabriel asked her, leaning down to pick up the phone.

She almost said *Don't touch it!* but knew this was irrational, and stopped herself in time. Instead she just didn't reach for it when he held it out to her, so he had to set it down on the table, still buzzing.

She stared at it. How had they found her? How? She'd changed her name. She'd *disappeared*. Had they known where she was all along, been watching her all this time? The idea horrified her. That the years of freedom could have been an illusion...

The buzzing stopped. The call went to voice mail, and Eliza's heartbeat was cannon fire again: burst after burst shuddering through her. Who was it? Her sister? One of her "uncles"?

Her mother?

Whoever it was, Eliza had only a moment to wonder if they'd leave a message—and if she'd dare to listen to it if they did—before the phone emitted another buzz. Not a voice mail. A text.

It read: *Turn on the TV.*

Turn on the . . . ?

Eliza looked up from the phone, deeply unsettled. *Why?* What did they want her to see on the TV? She didn't even have a TV. Gabriel was watching her intently, and their eyes locked in the instant they heard the first scream. Eliza almost jumped out of her skin, rising from her chair. From somewhere outside came a long, unintelligible cry. Or was it inside? It was loud. It was in the building. Wait. That was someone else. What the hell was going on? People were crying out in...shock? Joy? Horror? And then Gabriel's phone started to buzz, too, and Eliza's unspooled a sudden string of messages—*bzzz bzzz bzzz bzzz bzzz*. From friends this time, including Taj in London, and Catherine, who was doing fieldwork in South Africa. Wording varied, but all were a version of the same disturbing command: *Turn on the TV.*

Are you watching this?

Wake up. TV. Now.

Until the last one. The one that made Eliza want to curl up in fetal position and cease to exist.

Come home, it said. *We forgive you.*

2

The Arrival

They appeared on a Friday in broad daylight, in the sky above Uzbekistan, and were first sighted from the old Silk Road city of Samarkand, where a news crew scrambled to broadcast footage of . . . the Visitors.

The *angels.*

In flawless ranks of phalanxes, they were easily counted. Twenty blocks of fifty: a thousand. *A thousand angels.* They swept westward, near enough to earth that people standing on rooftops and roads could make out the rippling white silk of their standards and hear the trill and tremolo of harps.

Harps.

The footage went wide. Around the world, radio and television programs were preempted; news anchors rushed to their desks, out of breath and without scripts. Thrill, terror. Eyes round as coins, voices high and strange. Everywhere, phones began to ring and then cut off in a great global silence as cell towers overloaded and crashed. The sleeping slice of the planet was awakened. Internet connections faltered. People sought people. Streets filled. Voices joined and vied, climbed and crested. There were brawls. Song. Riots.

Deaths.

There were births, too. Babies born during the Arrival were dubbed "cherubs" by a radio pundit, who was also responsible for the rumor that all had feather-shaped birthmarks somewhere on their tiny bodies. It wasn't true, but the infants would be closely watched for any hint of beatitude or magical powers.

On this day in history—the ninth of August—time cleaved abruptly into "before" and "after," and no one would ever forget where they were when "it" began.

* * *

Kazimir Andrasko, actor, ghost, vampire, and jerk, actually slept through the whole thing, but would afterward claim to have blacked out while reading Nietzsche—at what he later determined was the precise moment of the Arrival—and suffered a vision of the end of the world. It was the beginning of a grandiose but half-assed ploy soon to fritter to a disappointing ending when he learned how much work was involved in starting a cult.

* * *

Zuzana Nováková and Mikolas Vavra were at Aït Benhaddou, the most famous kasbah in Morocco. Mik had just concluded bargaining for an antique silver ring—*maybe* antique, *maybe* silver, definitely a ring—when the sudden hubbub swept them up; he shoved it deep in his pocket, where it would remain, in secret, for some time.

In a village kitchen, they crowded in behind locals and watched news coverage in Arabic. Though they could understand neither the commentary nor the breathless exclamations all around them, they alone had context for what they were seeing. They knew what the angels were, or rather, what they weren't. That didn't make it any less of a shock to see the sky full of them.

So many!

It was Zuzana's idea to "liberate" the van idling in front of a tourist restaurant. The everyday weave of reality had by this time become so stretched that casual vehicular theft seemed par for the course. It was simple: She knew that Karou had no access to news of the world; she had to warn her. She'd have stolen a helicopter if she had to.

* * *

Esther Van de Vloet, retired diamond dealer, longtime associate of Brimstone and occasional stand-in grandmother to his human ward, was walking her mastiffs near her home in Antwerp when the bells of Our Lady began to toll out of time. It was not the hour, and even if it had been, the tuneless clangor was overwrought, practically hysterical. Esther, who didn't have an overwrought, hysterical bone in her body, had been waiting for something to happen ever since a black handprint had ignited on a doorway in Brussels and scorched it out of existence. Concluding that this was that something, she walked briskly home, her dogs huge as lionesses, stalking at her sides.

* * *

Eliza Jones watched the first few minutes on a live feed on her roommate's laptop, but when their server crashed, they hurriedly dressed, jumped in Gabriel's car, and drove to the museum. Early though it was, they weren't the first to arrive, and more colleagues kept streaming in behind them to cluster around a television screen in a basement laboratory.

They were stunned and stupid with incredulity, and with no small amount of rational affront that such an event should dare to unfold itself across the sky of the natural world. It was a hoax, of course. If angels *were* real—which was ridiculous—wouldn't they hew a little less closely to the pictures in Sunday school workbooks?

It was too perfect. It had to be staged.

"Give me a break with the harps," said a paleobiologist. "Overkill."

This outward certainty was undercut by a real tension, though, because none of them were stupid, and there were glaring holes in the hoax theory that just grew more glaring as news choppers dared to draw closer to the airborne host, and the broadcast footage became sharper and less equivocal.

No one wanted to admit it, but it looked . . . real.

Their wings, for one thing. They were easily twelve feet in span, and every feather was its own lick of fire. The smooth rise and fall of them, the inexpressible grace and power of their flight—it was beyond any fathomable technology.

"It could be the broadcast that's faked," suggested Gabriel. "It could all be CG. *War of the Worlds* for the twenty-first century."

There were some murmurs, though no one seemed to actually buy it.

Eliza stayed silent, watching. Her own dread was of a different breed than theirs, and was... far more advanced. It should be. It had been growing all her life.

Angels.

Angels. After the incident on the Charles Bridge in Prague some months earlier, she'd been able to maintain a crutch of skepticism at least, just enough to keep her from falling. It might have been faked, then: three angels, there and gone, no proof left behind. It felt, now, as though the world had been waiting with held breath for a display beyond all possibility of doubt. And so had she. And now they had it.

She thought of her phone, left intentionally behind at the apartment, and wondered what new messages its screen held in store for her. And she thought of the extraordinary dark power from which she'd fled in the night, in the dream. Her gut clenched like a fist as she felt, beneath her feet, the shifting of the planks she'd laid across the quicksand of that other life. She'd thought she could escape it? It was there, it had always been there, and this life she'd built on top of it felt about as sturdy as a shantytown on the flank of a volcano.

ARRIVAL + 3 HOURS

3

Choice of Life Skills

"Angels! Angels! Angels!"

This was what Zuzana cried out, leaping from the van as it fish-tailed to a halt on the dirt slope. "Monster castle" loomed before her: this place in the Moroccan desert where a rebel army from another world was hiding out to resurrect its dead. This mud fortress with its snakes and reeks, its huge beast soldiers, its pit of corpses. This ruin that she and Mik had escaped in the dead of night. Invisible. At Karou's insistence.

Karou's very freaked out and persuasive insistence.

Because . . . their lives were in danger.

And here they were back again, honking and hollering? Not exactly survival instincts in action.

Karou appeared, gliding over the kasbah wall in her wingless way, graceful as a ballerina in zero gravity. Zuzana was in motion, sprinting uphill as her friend dropped down to intercept her.

"Angels," Zuzana breathed, brimming with the news. "Holy hell,

Karou. In the sky. Hundreds. *Hundreds*. The world. Is freaking. Out." The words spilled out, but even as she heard herself, Zuzana was seeing her friend. Seeing her, and reeling back.

What the hell . . . ?

Car door, running feet, and Mik was at her side, seeing Karou, too. He didn't speak. No one did. The silence felt like an empty speech bubble: It took up space but there were no words.

Karou . . . Half of her face was swollen purple, scraped raw and scabbing. Her lip was split, puffy, her earlobe mangled, stitched. As for the rest of her, Zuzana couldn't tell. Her sleeves were pulled all the way down over her hands, clasped in her fists in an oddly childlike way. She held herself tenderly.

She had been brutalized. That much was clear. And there could be only one culprit.

The White Wolf. *That son of a bitch.* Fury blazed in Zuzana.

And then she saw him. He was stalking down the hillside toward them, one of many chimaera alerted by their wild arrival, and Zuzana's hands tightened into fists. She started to step forward, ready to plant herself between Thiago and Karou, but Mik caught her by the arm.

"What are you doing?" he hissed, pulling her back against him. "Are you crazy? You don't have a scorpion sting like a real *neek-neek*."

Neek-neek—her chimaera nickname, courtesy of the soldier Virko. It was a breed of fearless shrew-scorpion in Eretz, and as much as Zuzana hated to admit it, Mik was right. She was more shrew than scorpion, half-*neek* at best, and not nearly as dangerous as she might wish.

And I am going to do something about that, she resolved then and there. *Um. Right after we don't die here.* Because . . . *hell.* That was a lot of chimaera, when you saw them all together like that, charging down a hillside. Zuzana's *neek-neek* courage shrank up in her chest. She was glad for Mik's arm around her—not that she had any delusion that her sweet violin virtuoso could protect her any better than she could protect herself.

"I'm starting to question our choice of life skills," she whispered to him.

"I know. Why aren't we samurai?"

"Let's be samurai," she said.

"It's okay," Karou said, and then the Wolf was upon them, closely flanked by his entourage of lieutenants. Zuzana met his eyes and tried to look defiant. She saw scabbed scratch marks on his cheeks and her fury flared anew. Proof, as if there had been any doubt as to Karou's attacker.

Wait. Had Karou just said, "It's okay?"

How was this okay?

But Zuzana had no time to ponder the matter. She was too busy gasping. Because behind Karou, taking shape out of the air and filling it with all the splendor she remembered, was...

Akiva?

Well, what was *he* doing here?

Another seraph appeared beside him. The one who'd looked really pissed off on the bridge in Prague. She looked pretty pissed off now, too, in a focused, come-any-closer-and-I'll-kill-you kind of way. Her hand was on the hilt of her sword, her gaze fixed on the gathering chimaera.

Akiva, though, looked only at Karou, who...did not seem surprised to see him.

None of them did. Zuzana tried to make sense of the scene. Why weren't they attacking one another? She thought that was what chimaera and seraphim *did*—especially *these* chimaera, and *these* seraphim.

Just what had gone down at monster castle while she and Mik were away?

Every chimaera soldier was present now, and though surprise may have been absent, hostility was not. The unblinkingness, the concentration of malice in some of those bestial stares. Zuzana had sat on the ground laughing with these same soldiers; she had danced chicken-bone puppets for them, teased them and been teased in return. She liked them. Well, some of them. But right now, they were terrifying without exception, and looked ready to tear the angels limb from limb. Their eyes flicked to Thiago and away as they waited for the kill order they knew must come.

It did not come.

Realizing she'd been holding her breath, Zuzana let it out, and her body unwound slowly from its flinch. She caught sight of Issa in the crowd and gave the serpent-woman a very clear *what the hell?* eyebrow. Issa's answering look was less clear. Behind a brief smile of unreassuring reassurance, she looked tense and highly alert.

What is happening?

Karou said something soft and sad to Akiva—in Chimaera, of course, damn it. *What did she say?* Akiva responded, also in Chimaera, before turning to direct his next words to the White Wolf.

Maybe it was because she couldn't understand their language, and so was watching their faces for clues, and maybe it was because she had seen them together before, and knew the effect they had on each other, but Zuzana understood this much: Somehow, in this crowd of beast soldiers, with Thiago front and center, the moment belonged to Karou and Akiva.

The two of them were stoic and stone-faced and ten feet apart, currently not even looking at each other, but Zuzana had the impression of a pair of magnets pretending not to be magnets.

Which, you know, only works until it doesn't.

4

A Beginning

Two worlds, two lives. No longer.

Karou had made her choice. "I am chimaera," she had told Akiva. Was it only hours earlier that he had "escaped" the kasbah with his sister, to fly off and burn the Samarkand portal? They were to have returned and burned this one, too, sealing Earth and Eretz off from each other forever. He had wondered which world she would choose? As if she had a choice. "My life is there," she had said.

But it wasn't. Surrounded by creatures she had enfleshed herself and who, almost without exception, scorned her as an angel-lover, Karou knew it wasn't life that awaited her in Eretz, but duty and misery, exhaustion and hunger. Fear. Alienation. Death, not unlikely.

Pain, certainly.

And now?

"We can fight them together," Akiva said. "I have an army, too."

Karou stood rooted, scarcely breathing. Akiva had been too late. A seraph army had already pushed through the portal—Jael's ruthless Dominion, the Empire's elite legion—and so this was the unimaginable offer Akiva made to his enemy, to the astonishment of all, his own sister included. *Fight them together?* Karou saw Liraz turn an incredulous look on him. It was a good match for her own reaction, because one thing was sure: If Akiva's offer was unimaginable, Thiago's acceptance of it was unfathomable.

The White Wolf would die a thousand deaths before he would treat with angels. He would tear the world down around him. He would see the end of everything. He would *be* the end of everything before he would consider such an offer.

So Karou was as astonished as the rest—though for a different reason—when Thiago . . . *nodded.*

A hiss of surprise came from either Nisk or Lisseth, his Naja lieutenants. Aside from some pebbles discharged downhill by the lashing of a tail, that was the only sound from the soldiers. In Karou's ears, blood pounded. *What was he doing?* She hoped he knew, because she really didn't.

She stole a glance at Akiva. None of the grief or disgust, the dismay or the love that had shown on his face the night before was in evidence now; his mask was in place, and so was her own. All her turmoil had to stay hidden, and there was plenty of it to hide.

Akiva had come back here. *Can no one stay escaped from this damned kasbah?* It was brave; he had always been that, and reckless. But it wasn't only himself he jeopardized now. It was everything she was trying to achieve. The position he was putting the Wolf in: to come up with yet another plausible excuse not to kill him?

And then there was her own position. Maybe that was what flustered her the most.

Here was Akiva, this enemy whom she had fallen in love with twice, in two separate lives, with a power that felt like the design of the universe and maybe even was, and it didn't matter. She stood at Thiago's side. This was the place she had made for herself, for the sake of her people: at Thiago's side.

Moreover—*though Akiva didn't know this*—this was the Thiago she had made for herself: one she could bear to stand with. The White Wolf was...not himself these days. She had sealed a better soul into the body she despised—*oh, Ziri*—and she prayed to everything in the infinite array of gods of two worlds that no one would figure it out. It was a wrenching secret, and felt every moment like a grenade in her hand. Her heartbeat slipped in and out of rhythm. Her palms were clammy.

The deception was massive, and it was fragile, and it fell most heavily by far to Ziri to pull it off. To dupe all these soldiers? Most of them had served for decades with the general, some few for centuries, through multiple incarnations, and they knew his every gesture, every inflection. Ziri had to *be* the Wolf, in manner and cadence and in chill, suppressed brutality—to *be* him, but, paradoxically, a *better* him, one who could guide their people toward survival instead of dead-end vengeance.

That could only happen by degrees. The White Wolf wouldn't just wake up one morning, yawn and stretch and decide to ally with his mortal enemy.

But that was exactly what Ziri was doing right now.

"Jael must be stopped," he stated as a matter of fact. "If he succeeds in procuring human weapons and support, there will be no hope for any of us. In that, at least, we have common cause." He kept his voice low, conveying absolute authority and not a second's concern with how his decision would be received. It was the Wolf's way, and Ziri's impersonation was flawless. "How many are they?"

"A thousand," replied Akiva. "In this world. There will, no doubt, be a heavy troop presence on the other side of the portal."

"This portal?" asked Thiago with a jerk of his head toward the Atlas Mountains.

"They entered by the other," said Akiva. "But this one could be compromised, too. They have the means to discover it."

He didn't look at Karou when he said this, but she felt a flare of blame. Because of her, the abomination Razgut was a free agent, and he could easily have shown the Dominion this portal, as he had shown it to her. The chimaera could be trapped here, cut off from their retreat to their own world while their seraph enemies closed in on them from both sides. This safe haven she had led them to could so easily become their grave.

Thiago took it in stride. "Well. Let's find out."

He looked to his soldiers, and they looked back, wary, parsing his every move. *What is he up to?* they would be wondering, because it simply couldn't be what it seemed. Soon he would order the angels killed. This was all part of some strategy. Surely.

"Oora, Sarsagon," he commanded, "choose teams for speed and stealth. I want to know if there are Dominion at our door. If there are, keep them out. Hold the portal. Let no angel through alive." A wolfish smile conveyed pleasure at the thought of dead angels, and Karou saw some of the wariness leave the soldiers' faces. This made sense to them, if the rest didn't: the Wolf, relishing the prospect of seraph blood. "Send a messenger once you're certain. Go," he said, and they did, Oora and Sarsagon picking their teams with quick, decisive gestures as they moved through the gathering. Bast, Keita-Eiri, the griffons Vazra and Ashtra, Lilivett, Helget, Emylion.

"Everyone else, back to the court. Be ready to leave if the report is favorable." The general paused. "And ready to fight if it isn't." Again he managed, with no more than the shadow of a smile, to hint that he would prefer the bloodier outcome.

It was well done, and a little hope wicked into Karou's anxiety. Action was best, orders given and followed. The response was immediate and unfaltering. The host turned and moved back up the hill. If Ziri could maintain this unassailable demeanor of command, even the surliest of the troops would hustle to meet his approval.

Except, well, not quite everyone was hustling. There was Issa, moving defiantly against the tide of soldiers to come down the hill, and then there was the matter of Thiago's lieutenants. Except for Sarsagon, who had been given a direct order, the Wolf's entourage remained clustered around him. Ten, Nisk, Lisseth, Rark, and Virko. These were the same chimaera who had conspired to get Karou alone at the pit with Thiago—with the exception of Ten, who had made the mistake of taking on Issa and was now as much Ten as Thiago was Thiago—and she hated them. She had no doubt they'd have held her down for him if he'd asked, and could only be glad that he hadn't thought it necessary.

Now their lingering was ominous. They hadn't followed Thiago's order because they believed themselves exempt from it. Because they expected to be given other orders. And the way they were regarding Akiva and Liraz left no doubt what they assumed those would be.

"Karou," whispered Zuzana, at Karou's shoulder. "What the hell is going on?"

What the hell *wasn't* going on? All the collisions Karou thought she'd averted in the past days had boomeranged around to crash into one another right here. "Everything," she said, through gritted teeth. "Everything is going on."

The monstrous Nisk and Lisseth with their hands half-upraised, ready to flare their hamsas at Akiva and Liraz, weaken them and go in for the kill—or *try*. Akiva and Liraz, unflinching in the face of it, and Ziri in the middle. Poor sweet Ziri, wearing Thiago's flesh and trying to wear his savagery, too—but only the face of it and not the heart. That was his challenge now. It was more than his challenge. It was his *life*, and everything depended on it. The rebellion, the future—whether there would *be* one—for all the chimaera still living, and all the souls buried in Brimstone's cathedral. This deception was their only hope.

The next ten seconds felt as dense as folded iron.

Issa reached them at the same moment that Lisseth spoke up. "What orders, sir, for *us*?"

Issa embraced Mik and Zuzana, and shot Karou a look that glittered with some bright meaning. She looked excited, Karou saw. She looked *vindicated*.

"I've given my order," Thiago told Lisseth, cool. "Was I less than perfectly clear?"

Vindicated? About *what*? Karou's mind leapt at once to the previous night. After she had dismissed Akiva with a cool finality she certainly didn't feel, and sent him away for what she'd guessed would be the last time, Issa had told her, "Your heart is not wrong. You don't have to be ashamed."

Of loving Akiva, she'd meant. And what had Karou's answer been? "It doesn't matter." She'd tried to believe it: that her heart didn't matter, that she and Akiva didn't matter, that there were worlds at stake and *that* was what mattered.

"Sir," argued Nisk, Lisseth's Naja partner. "You can't mean to let these angels live—"

Let these angels live. That this could even be in question: Akiva's life, and Liraz's. They had come back here to warn them. The real Thiago wouldn't have hesitated to gut them for their trouble. Akiva didn't know this wasn't the real Thiago, and he'd come back anyway. For her sake.

Karou looked to him, found his eyes waiting for hers, and met them with a sting of clarity that was the final dissolution of the lie.

It mattered. *They* mattered, and whatever it was that had made them not kill each other on Bullfinch beach all those years ago... mattered.

Thiago didn't answer Nisk. Not with words, anyway. The look he turned on him scythed the rest of the soldier's words into silence. The Wolf had always had that power; Ziri's appropriation of it was startling.

"To the court," he said with soft menace. "Except for Ten. We will have words about my... expectations... when I'm done here. Go."

They went. Karou might have enjoyed their shame-faced retreat, but that the Wolf turned his gaze on Issa next, and on her. "You, too," he said.

As the Wolf would. He had never trusted Karou, but only manipulated and lied to her, and in this situation he absolutely would dismiss her along with the rest. And just as Ziri had his part to play, she had hers. In secret she might be the guiding strength of this new purpose, anointed by Brimstone with the Warlord's blessing, but in the eyes of the chimaera army, she was still—at least for now—the girl who had stumbled back blood-soaked from the pit.

Thiago's broken doll.

They could only work from the starting point they had, and that was the pit—gravel, blood, death, and lies—and she had no choice in this moment but to uphold the charade. She nodded her obedience to the Wolf, and it was acid in the pit of her belly to see Akiva's eyes darken. By his side, Liraz was worse. Liraz was contemptuous.

That was a little hard to take.

The Wolf is dead! She wanted to scream. *I killed him. Don't look at me like that!* But of course, she couldn't. Right now, she had to be strong enough to look weak.

"Come on," Karou said, urging Issa, Zuzana, and Mik forward.

But Akiva didn't let it go so easily. "Wait." He spoke in Seraphic, which none but Karou would understand. "It's not him I came to talk to. I would have sought you alone to give you the choice if I could. I want to know what *you* want."

What I want? Karou quelled a ripple of hysteria that felt dangerously like laughter. As if this life bore any resemblance to what she wanted! But, given the circumstances, *was* it what she wanted? She'd scarcely considered what it might mean. An alliance. The chimaera rebels actually joining with Akiva's bastard brethren to take on the Empire?

Simply put, it was crazy. "Even united," she said, "we would be massively outnumbered."

"An alliance means more than the number of swords," Akiva said. And his voice was like a shadow from another life when he added, softly, "Some, and then more."

Karou stared at him for an unguarded second, then remembered herself and forced her eyes down. *Some, and then more.* It was the answer to the question of whether others could be brought around to their dream of peace. "This is the beginning," Akiva had said moments earlier, his hand to his heart, before turning to Thiago. No one else knew what that meant, but Karou did, and she felt the heat of the dream stir in her own heart.

We are the beginning.

She'd said it to him long ago; he was the one saying it now. This was what his offer of alliance meant: the past, the future, penitence, rebirth. Hope.

It meant everything.

And Karou couldn't acknowledge it. Not here. Nisk and Lisseth had halted on the hill to peer back at them: Karou the "angel-lover" and Akiva the very angel, speaking quietly in Seraphic while Thiago just stood there and let them? It was all wrong. The Wolf they knew would have had blood on his fangs by now.

Every moment was a test of the deception; every syllable uttered made the Wolf's forbearance less tenable. So Karou dropped her gaze to the baked, stony earth and rounded her shoulders like the broken doll she was supposed to be. "The choice is Thiago's," she said in Chimaera, and tried to act her role.

She tried.

But she couldn't leave it at that. After everything, Akiva was still chasing the ghost of hope. Out of more blood and ash than they had ever even imagined in their days of love, he was trying to conjure it back to life. What other way forward was there? It *was* what she wanted.

She had to give him some sign.

Issa was holding her elbow. Karou leaned into her, turning so that the serpent woman's body came between herself and the watching chimaera, and then, so quickly that she feared Akiva might miss it, she raised her hand and touched her heart.

It pounded in her chest as she moved away. *We are the beginning*, she thought, and was overcome by the memory of belief. It came from Madrigal, her deeper self, who had died believing, and it was acute. She bent into Issa, hiding her face so that no one would see her flush.

Issa's voice was so faint it almost seemed like her own thought. "You see, child? Your heart is not wrong."

And for the first time in a long, long time, Karou felt the truth of it. Her heart was not wrong.

Out of betrayal and desperation, amid hostile beasts and invading angels and a deception that felt like an explosion waiting to happen, somehow, here was a beginning.

5

Getting-Acquainted Game

Akiva didn't miss it. He saw Karou's fingertips brush her heart as she turned away, and in that instant it all became worth it. The risk, the gut-wrench of forcing himself to speak to the Wolf, even the seething disbelief of Liraz at his side.

"You're mad," she said under her breath. "*I have an army, too*? You don't *have* an army, Akiva. You're *part of* an army. There's a difference."

"I know," he said. The offer wasn't his to make. Their Misbegotten brethren were waiting for them at the Kirin caves; this much was true. They were born to be weapons. Not sons and daughters, or even men and women, just weapons. Well, now they were weapons wielding themselves, and though they had rallied behind Akiva to oppose the Empire, an alliance with their mortal enemy was no part of this understanding.

"I'll convince them," he said, and in his exhilaration—*Karou had touched her heart*—he believed it.

"Start with me," hissed his sister. "We came here to warn them, not to join them."

Akiva knew that if he could persuade Liraz, the rest would follow. Just how he was supposed to do that, he did not know, and the White Wolf's approach forestalled him trying.

With his she-wolf lieutenant by his side, he strode forward, and Akiva's exhilaration withered. He flashed back to the first time he had ever seen the Wolf. It had been at Bath Kol, in the Shadow Offensive, when he himself was just a green soldier, fresh from the training camp. He'd seen the chimaera general fight, and more than any propaganda he'd been raised on, the sight had forged his hatred of the beasts. Sword in one hand, ax in the other, Thiago had surged through ranks of angels, ripping out throats with his teeth like it was instinct. Like he was *hungry*.

The memory sickened Akiva. Everything about Thiago sickened him, not least the gouge marks on his face, made certainly by Karou in self-defense. When the general came to a halt before him, it was all Akiva could do not to palm his face and slam him to the ground. A sword to his heart, as had been Joram's fate, and then they could have their new beginning, all the rest of them, free of the lords of death who had led their people against each other for so long.

But that he could not do.

Karou looked back once from the slope, worry flashing across her lovely face—still distorted by whatever violence she'd refused to divulge to him—and then she moved away and it was just Thiago and Ten facing Akiva and Liraz, the sun hot and high, sky blue, earth drab.

"So," said Thiago, "we may speak without an audience."

"I seem to recall that you like an audience," said Akiva, his memories of torture as vivid as they had ever been. Thiago's abuse of him had been performance: the White Wolf, star of his bloody show.

A crease of confusion flickered and vanished at Thiago's brow. "Let us leave the past, shall we? The present gives us more than enough to talk about, and then, of course, there is the future."

The future will not have you in it, thought Akiva. It was too perverse to think that if this somehow came to pass, this impossible dream, the White Wolf should ride it through to its fulfillment and still be there, still white, still smug, and still the one standing at Karou's door after everything was fought and won.

But no. That was wrong. Akiva's jaw clenched and unclenched. Karou wasn't a prize to win; that wasn't why he was here. She was a woman and would choose her own life. He was here to do what he could, whatever he could, that she might have a life to choose, one day. Whoever and whatever that included was her own affair. So he gritted his teeth. He said, "So let's talk of the present."

"You've put me in a difficult position, coming here," said the Wolf. "My soldiers are waiting for me to kill you. What I need is a reason not to."

This riled Liraz. "You think you could kill us?" she demanded. "Try it, Wolf."

Thiago's regard shifted to her, his calm unruffled. "We haven't been introduced."

"You know who I am, and I know who you are, and that will serve."

Typical Liraz bluntness.

"As you prefer," said Thiago.

"You all look alike anyway," drawled Ten.

"Well then," said Liraz. "That might make our getting-acquainted game more difficult for your side."

"What game is that?" inquired Ten.

No, Lir, thought Akiva. In vain.

"The one where we try to figure out which of us killed which of you in previous bodies. I'm sure some of you must remember *me*." She held up her hands to show her kill tally, and Akiva caught the one nearest him, closed his own marked fist over it, and pushed it back down.

"Don't flaunt those here," he said. *What's wrong with her?* Did she truly want this to degenerate into a bloodbath—whatever "this" was, this tenuous and almost unthinkable pause in hostilities.

Ten growled a laugh as Akiva pushed his sister's hand back down to her side. "Don't worry, Beast's Bane. It's not exactly a secret. I remember every angel who's ever killed me, and yet here I stand, speaking to you. Can the same be said of the very many angels I've killed? Where are all the dead seraphim now? Where's your brother?"

Liraz flinched. Akiva felt the words like a punch to a wound—the specter of Hazael raised casually, viciously—and when the heat around them surged, he knew it wasn't only his sister's temper but his own.

Here it was, then, a restoration to the natural order: hostility.

Or... not.

"But it wasn't a chimaera who slew your brother," said Thiago. "It was Jael. Which brings us to the point." Akiva found himself the focus of his enemy's pale eyes. There was no taunt in them, no subtle snarl, and none of the cold amusement with which he had regarded Akiva in the torture chamber, all those years ago. There was only a strange intensity. "I've no doubt we're all accomplished killers," he said softly. "It was my understanding we stood here for a different reason."

Akiva's first feeling was shame—to be schooled in coolheadedness by Thiago?—and his next was anger. "Yes. And it wasn't to argue for our lives. You need a reason not to kill us? How about this: Do you have somewhere better to go?"

"No. We don't." Simple. Honest. "And so I'm listening. This was, after all, your idea."

Yes, it was. His mad idea, to offer peace to the White Wolf. Now that he stood face-to-face with him, and Karou nowhere near, he saw the absurdity of it. He had been blinded by his desperation to stay near her, to not lose her to the vastness of Eretz, enemies forever. So he had made this offer, and it was only now, belatedly, that he saw how truly strange it was that the Wolf was considering it.

That the Wolf was looking for a reason not to kill him?

It had felt like aggression, that statement, like provocation. But was it, possibly, candor? Could it be the truth, that he wanted this peace but needed to justify it to his soldiers?

"The Misbegotten have withdrawn to a safe location," Akiva said. "In the eyes of the Empire, we are traitors. I am patricide and regicide, and my guilt stains us all." He considered his next words. "If you seriously mean to consider this—"

"This is no ruse on my part," Thiago broke in. "I give you my word."

"Your word." This from Liraz, served on a bare crust of a laugh. "You'll have to do better than that, Wolf. We've no reason to trust you."

"I wouldn't go that far. You're alive, aren't you? I don't ask thanks for it, but I hope it's perfectly clear that it's no matter of chance. You came to us half-dead. If I'd wanted to finish the job, I would have."

There could be no arguing with that. Indisputably, Thiago had let them live. He had let them escape.

Why?

For Karou's sake? Had she pled for their lives? Not...

...*bargained* for them?

Akiva looked up the slope where she had gone. She stood in the arched entrance to the kasbah, watching them, too distant to read. He turned to Thiago, and saw that his expression was still devoid of cruelty or duplicity or even his customary coldness. His eyes were open, not heavy-lidded with arrogance or disdain. It made a marked change in him. What could account for it?

One explanation occurred to Akiva, and he hated it. In the torture chamber, Thiago's rage had been that of a rival—a *losing* rival. Beneath the age-old hatred of their races had burned the more personal wrath of an alpha for a challenger. The humiliation of the one not chosen. Vengeance for Madrigal's love of Akiva.

But that was absent now—as absent as the reasons for it. Akiva was no longer his rival, no longer a threat. Because Karou had made a different choice this time.

As soon as this idea came to Akiva, Thiago's lack of malice seemed hard proof of it. The White Wolf was sure enough of his place that he didn't need to kill Akiva. Karou, oh godstars. Karou.

If it weren't for their bloody history, if Akiva didn't know what lurked in Thiago's true heart, it would seem an obvious match: the general and the resurrectionist, lord and lady of the chimaera's last hope. But he *did* know Thiago's true heart, and so did Karou.

It wasn't old history, either, Thiago's violence. Karou's downcast eyes, her tremulous uncertainty. Bruises, gouges. And yet the creature standing before Akiva now seemed the White Wolf's best self: intelligent, powerful, and sane. A worthy ally. Looking at him, Akiva didn't even know what he should hope for. If Thiago was *this*, then an alliance stood a chance, and Akiva would be able to be in Karou's life, if only at the edges of it. He would be able to see her, at least, and know that she was well. He would be able to atone for his sins and have her know it. Not to mention, they might stand a chance of stopping Jael.

On the other hand, if Thiago was *this*—intelligent, powerful, and sane—and he stood shoulder-to-shoulder with Karou to shape the destiny of their people, what place was there for Akiva in that? And more to the point, could he bear to stand by and see it?

"And there is something else," said Thiago. "Something I owe you. I understand that I have you to thank for the souls of some of my own."

Akiva narrowed his eyes. "I don't know what you're talking about," he said.

"In the Hintermost. You intervened in the torture of a chimaera soldier. He escaped, and returned to us with the souls of his team."

Ah. The Kirin. But how could anybody know that Akiva had done that? He hadn't let himself be seen. He'd summoned birds, every bird for miles around. He just shook his head now, prepared to deny it.

But Liraz surprised him. "Where is he?" she asked Thiago. "I didn't see him with the others."

Had she been looking? Akiva flickered a glance her way. Thiago's glance more than flickered. It sharpened, and settled on her. "He's dead," he said after a pause.

Dead. The young Kirin, last of Madrigal's tribe. Liraz made no reply. "I'm sorry to hear it," Akiva said.

Thiago's gaze shifted back to him. "But thanks to you, his team will live again. And to return to our purpose, was not his torturer the very angel we now must oppose?"

Akiva nodded. "Jael. Captain of the Dominion. Now emperor. We're standing here while he gathers his strength, and while your word means nothing to me, I'll trust one thing: that you would stop him. So if you believe your soldiers can distinguish one angel from another long enough to fight Dominion beside Misbegotten, come with us, and we'll see what happens."

Liraz, to Ten, added coldly, "We wear black, and they wear white. If that helps."

"It all tastes the same," was the she-wolf's laconic reply.

"Ten, please," said Thiago in a warning voice, and then, to Akiva, "Yes, we will see." He nodded a promise, holding Akiva's eyes, and the sanity was still there, the cruelty still absent, yet Akiva couldn't help remembering him ripping out throats, and he felt himself at the precipice of a very bad decision.

Revenant soldiers and Misbegotten, together. At best, it would be miserable. At worst, devastating.

But in spite of his misgivings, it was as if there was a brightness beckoning to him—the future, rich with light, calling him toward it. No promises made, only hope. And it wasn't just the hope kindled by Karou's subtle gesture. At least, he didn't think so. He thought that this was what he had to do, and that it wasn't stupid, but bold.

Only time would tell.

6

Beast Exodus

Karou had overseen one transfer of this small army from world to world already, and it had not been the best of times. Then, with a preponderance of wingless soldiers and no way to transport them from Eretz, they'd had to take multiple trips, and still Thiago had opted to "release" many of them, gleaning souls and bringing them along in thuribles. "Deadweight," he had deemed the bodies—exempting of course his own and Ten's, and some other of his lieutenants, who had ridden astride larger, flying revenants.

This time, Karou was relieved to line everyone up in the court and determine that what "deadweight" remained could be managed by the rest, and no releasing would be required.

The pit had been fed its last body.

She saw it from the air one last time as the company took flight, and it had a kind of magnetic hold on her gaze. It looked so small from up here, down its winding path from the kasbah. Just a dark indentation in the rolling dust-colored earth, with some mounds of excavated dirt standing near, shovels stuck in them like pickets. She imagined she could see scuff marks where Thiago had attacked her, and even dark patches that could be blood. And on the far side of the mounds, discernible to no one save herself, was another disturbance in the dirt: Ziri's grave.

It was shallow, and she'd blistered her hands on the shovel doing even that much, but nothing could have made her tip the last natural Kirin flesh into the pit with its flies and putrescence. She hadn't escaped the flies and putrescence so easily, though. She'd had to lean over the edge of that soupy, crawling darkness with Ziri's gleaning staff to gather the souls of Amzallag and the Shadows That Live, murdered by the Wolf and his cronies for the crime of taking her side.

She wished she could have them on her side again instead of in a thurible, stashed away, but in a thurible they'd have to remain—for now. For how long? She didn't know. Until such a time as was yet impossible to imagine: some time after all of this, and better than all of this, when the deception wouldn't matter anymore.

Should such a time ever come to pass.

It will come to pass if we bring it to pass, she told herself.

Thiago's scouts had reported no seraph presence within a several-mile radius of the portal in Eretz, which was a relief, but not one Karou could trust. With Razgut in Jael's hands, nothing was certain.

It felt wrong to be leaving—to be *fleeing*—with what was set in motion, but what else could they do? They currently numbered only eighty-seven chimaera—eighty-seven "monsters," in the eyes of this world, and possibly "demons," if Jael succeeded in selling his charade of holiness. They were too few to defeat him or drive him back. If they attacked him now, they would not only lose, they would help him in his cause. One look at these soldiers Karou had made and humans would be shoving rocket launchers into Jael's hands.

With Akiva's Misbegotten, though, at least they stood a chance.

Of course, that was its own hornet's nest: the alliance. Selling it to the chimaera. Treading the razor's edge of deception to manipulate a rebel army into acting against its deepest instincts. Karou knew that every step forward would meet resistance from a large contingent of the company. To shape the future, they would have to win at every pace. And who constituted "they"? Along with herself and "Thiago," only Issa and "Ten"—who was actually Haxaya, a soldier less evil but just as hotheaded as the real Ten had been—were in on the secret. Well, and now Zuzana and Mik.

"What's with you?" Zuzana had asked, incredulous, as soon as they'd left Akiva and Thiago to their negotiations. "Chumming with the White Wolf?"

"You know what 'chumming' is, don't you?" Karou had replied, evasive. "It's throwing blood in the water to attract sharks."

"Well, I meant 'being chummy,' but I'm sure there's a metaphor in that somewhere. What did he do to you? Are you all right?"

"I am now," Karou had said, and though it had been a relief to disabuse her friends of their notion of chumming, it had given her no pleasure to tell them the truth about Ziri. Both of them had cried, which had been like a pull-chain to her own tears, no doubt shoring up her appearance of weakness in the eyes of the company.

And that she could live with, but dear gods and stardust, Akiva was another matter. Letting him believe that she was "chummy" with the White Wolf? But what was she supposed to do? She was closely watched by the entire chimaera host. Some eyes seemed simply curious—*Does she still love him?*—but others were suspicious, eager to damn her and weave conspiracies out of her every glance. She couldn't give them ammunition, so she'd kept away from Akiva and Liraz at the kasbah, and tried now not even to glance in their direction, off the formation's far flank.

Thiago rode at the head of the host astride the soldier Uthem. Uthem was a Vispeng, horse-dragon aspect, long and sinuous. He was the largest and most striking of the chimaera, and on his back, Thiago looked as regal as a prince.

Nearer Karou, Issa rode the Dashnag soldier Rua, while right in the middle of everything, incongruous as a pair of sparrows clinging to the backs of raptors, were Zuzana and Mik.

Zuzana was on Virko, Mik on Emylion, and both were wide-eyed, clinging to leather straps as the chimaera's powerful bodies heaved beneath them, climbing the air. Virko's spiraling ram's horns reminded Karou of Brimstone. He was felid in body, but immense: crouching cat muscle, like a lion on steroids, and from the back of his thick neck bristled a ruff of spikes, which Zuzana had padded with a wool blanket that she'd complained smelled like feet. "So my choice is to breathe feet the whole way or spear my eyeballs out on neck spikes? Awesome."

Now she roared, "You're doing that on purpose!" as Virko banked hard left, causing her to slide cockeyed in her makeshift saddle of straps until he banked the other way and righted her.

Virko was laughing, but Zuzana wasn't. She craned her neck looking for Karou and hollered, "I need a new horse. This one thinks he's hilarious!"

"You're stuck with him!" Karou called back to Zuzana. She flew nearer, having to veer around a pair of overburdened griffons. She herself was weighed down by a heavy pack of gear and a long chain of linked thuribles, many dozens of souls contained within. She clanked with every movement, and had never felt so graceless. "He volunteered."

Indeed, if Zuzana hadn't been so light, it may not have been possible to bring the humans along. Virko was carrying her in addition to his full, allocated load, and as for Emylion, two or three soldiers had wordlessly taken up some of his gear so that he could manage Mik, who, though not large, wasn't the weightless petal Zuze was. There had been no question of leaving his violin behind, either. Karou's friends, it was clear, had won real affection from this group in a way she herself had not.

From most of them anyway. There was Ziri. He might not look like Ziri anymore, but he *was* Ziri, and Karou knew...

She knew that he was in love with her.

"Why don't you have a pegasus in this company?" Zuzana demanded, paling as she eyed the ever-more-distant ground. "A nice docile flying horse to ride, with a fluffy mane instead of spikes, like floating on a cloud."

"Because nothing is more terrifying to the enemy than a pegasus," said Mik.

"Hey, there's more to life than terrifying your enemies," said Zuzana. "Like not plunging a thousand feet to your death—*aaah!*" She shrieked as Virko suddenly dipped to pass beneath the smith Aegir, who was heaving hard to bear a sack of weaponry airborne. Karou seized a corner of the bag to help him and together they rose slowly higher as Virko drew ahead.

"Better be good to her!" she called after him in Chimaera. "Or I'll let her turn you into a pegasus in your next body!"

"No!" he roared back. "Not that!"

He straightened out, and Karou found herself in one of those in-between moments when her life could still surprise her. She thought of herself and Zuze, not so many months ago, at their easels in life-drawing class, or with their feet up on a coffin-table at Poison Kitchen. Mik had just been "violin boy" then, a crush, and now here he was with his violin strapped to his pack, riding with them to another world while Karou threatened monsters with resurrection vengeance for misbehavior?

For just a moment, in spite of the burden of the weapons bag, and the thuribles, and her pack—not to mention the anvil weight of her duty and the deception and the future of two worlds—Karou felt almost light. Hopeful.

Then she heard a laugh, bright with casual malice, and from the corner of her eye, caught sight of the flick of a hand. It was Keita-Eiri, a jackal-headed Sab fighter, and Karou saw at once what she was about. She was flashing her hamsas—the "devil's eyes" inked on her palms—toward Akiva and Liraz. Rark, alongside her, was doing the same, and they were laughing.

Hoping the seraphim were out of range, Karou risked a look in their direction just in time to see Liraz break mid-wingbeat and swing around, fury clear in her posture even at a distance.

Not out of range, then. Akiva reached for his sister and restrained her from rounding on their assailants.

More laughter as the chimaera made sport of them, and Karou's hands gripped into fists around her own marks. She couldn't be the one to put a stop to this—it would only make things worse. With clenched teeth she watched Akiva and Liraz draw even farther away, and the growing distance between them seemed a bad omen for this brave beginning.

"Are you all right, Karou?" came a hiss-accented whisper.

Karou turned. Lisseth was drawing up beside her. "Fine," Karou said.

"Oh? You look tense."

Though of the Naja race like Issa, Lisseth and her partner, Nisk, were twice Issa's weight—thick as pythons beside a viper, bull-necked and burly, but still deadly quick and equipped with venomous fangs as well as the incongruity of wings. It was Karou's own doing, all of it. *Stupid, stupid.*

"Don't worry about me," she told Lisseth.

"Well, that's difficult, isn't it? How can I not worry about an angel-lover?"

There had been a time, a very recent time, when this insult had carried a sting. Not anymore. "We have so many enemies, Lisseth," said Karou, keeping her voice light. "Most of them are our birthright, inherited like a duty, but the ones we make for ourselves are special. We should choose them with care."

Lisseth's brow creased. "Are you threatening me?" she asked.

"Threatening you? Now, how did you get *that* out of what I just said? I was talking about making enemies, and I can't imagine any revenant soldier being dumb enough to make an enemy of the resurrectionist."

There, she thought as Lisseth's face went tight. *Make of that what you will.*

They were moving along all the while, steady in the air in the middle of the company, and now the density of bodies before them parted, revealing Thiago astride Uthem, doubled back into their midst. The company re-formed around them, their progress slowing.

"My lord," Lisseth greeted him, and Karou could practically see the tattle forming in her thoughts. *My lord, the angel-lover threatened me. We need to tighten our control over her.*

Good luck with that, she thought, but the Wolf didn't give Lisseth—or anyone—a chance to speak. In a voice pitched just loud enough to carry, while scarcely seeming to be raised, he said, "Do you think because I ride ahead I don't know how my army acquits itself?" He paused. "You are as the blood in my body. I sense every shudder and sigh, I know your pain and your joy, and I certainly hear your laughter."

He swept the encircling soldiers with a look, and jackal-headed Keita-Eiri wasn't laughing when his gaze came to rest on her.

"If I wish you to antagonize our... *allies*... I will tell you. And if you suspect that I have forgotten to give you an order, kindly enlighten me. In return I will enlighten you." The message was for everyone. Keita-Eiri was just the unlucky focus of the general's chilling sarcasm. "How does that arrangement strike you, soldier? Does it meet your approval?"

Her voice thin with mortification, Keita-Eiri whispered, "Yes, sir." Karou felt almost bad for her.

"I'm so glad." The Wolf raised his voice now. "Together we have fought, and together endured the loss of our people. We have bled and we have screamed. You've followed me into fire, and into death, and into another world, but never perhaps into anything so seeming strange as this. Refuge with seraphim? Strange it may be, but I would be so disappointed if your trust failed. There is no room for dissent. Any who cannot abide our current course can leave us the moment we pass through the portal, and take their chances on their own."

He scanned their faces. His own was hard but lit by some inner brilliance. "As regards the angels, I ask nothing of you but patience.

We can't fight them as we once did, trusting to our numbers even as we bled. I don't ask your permission to find a new way. If you stay with me, I expect *faith*. The future is shadowed, and I can promise you nothing beyond this: We will fight for our world to the last echo of our souls, and if we are very strong and very lucky and very *smart*, we may live to rebuild some of what we've lost."

He made eye contact with each in turn, making them feel seen and counted, valued. His look conveyed his faith in them—and more, his trust in *their* faith in *him*. He went on: "This much is plain: If we fail to thwart this pressing threat, we *end*. Chimaera end." He paused. His gaze having come full circle to Keita-Eiri, he said, with caressing gentleness that somehow made the rebuke so much more damning: "This is no laughing matter, soldier."

And then he urged Uthem forward and they cut their way through the troops to resume their place at the head of the army. Karou watched as the soldiers silently moved back into formation, and she knew that not one of them would leave him, and that Akiva and Liraz would be safe from errant hamsa strikes for the remainder of the journey.

That was good. She felt a flush of pride for Ziri, and also of awe. In his natural flesh, the young soldier had been quiet, almost shy—the opposite of this eloquent megalomaniac whose flesh he now wore. Watching him, she had wondered for the first time—and maybe it was stupid that she hadn't thought to wonder it before—how being Thiago might change him.

But the thought subsided as soon as it came. This was Ziri. Of all the many things Karou had to worry about, his being corrupted by power was not one of them.

Lisseth, however, was. Karou looked to her, still hovering near in the air, and saw calculation in the Naja's eyes as she watched their general resume his place.

What was she thinking? Karou knew there wasn't a chance in hell of Thiago's lieutenants leaving the company, but god, she wished they would. No one knew him better, and no one would watch him more closely. As for what she'd told Lisseth about making an enemy of the resurrectionist, it hadn't been a joke or an idle threat. If anything was certain for revenant soldiers, it was that if they went into battle often enough, eventually they'd be in need of a body.

Bovine, thought Karou. *A big slow cow for you.* And the next time Lisseth shot her a glance, she thought, almost merrily, *Moo*.

7

A Gift from the Wild

The chimaera had ridden high over the peaks now. The kasbah was behind them, the portal just ahead, though Karou could barely make it out. Even up close it presented as a mere ripple, and you had to dive through it on faith, feel its edges feather open around you. Larger creatures did best to fold back their wings and hit it with speed, and if they went just a fraction too high or low they'd feel no resistance and overshoot it, remaining right here in this sky. That didn't happen now, though. This company knew what they were doing, and vanished through the crease one by one.

It took time, each looming shape winking out into the ether.

When it came Virko's turn, Karou called, "Hold on!" to Zuzana, and she did, and they careened through the cut. Emylion and Mik went next, and Karou didn't like having her friends out of her sight, so she nodded to the Wolf, who had circled around to see everyone through, and with one last deep breath of Earth air, she dove.

Against her face, the feather touch of whatever unknowable membrane it was that held the worlds distinct, and she was through.

She was in Eretz.

No blue sky here; it arched white over their heads and darkened to gunmetal gray on the single visible horizon, all the rest lost in a haze. Beneath them was only water, and in the colorlessness of the day it rippled almost black. The Bay of Beasts. There was something terrifying about black water. Something pitiless.

The wind was strong, buffeting the host as it fell back into formation. Karou pulled her sweater closer around her and shivered. The last of the host pushed through the cut, Uthem and Thiago last of all. Uthem's equine and draconic elements were indistinguishably supple, green and rippling and seeming to pour into the world out of nothingness. The Vispeng race not naturally being winged, Karou had gotten creative in order to preserve his length: two sets of wings, the main pair like sails and a smaller set anchored near his hind legs. It looked pretty cool, if she did say so herself.

The Wolf had bowed his head through the portal, and as soon as he was through, he sat up to take stock of his circling troops. His eye came quickly to rest on Karou, and though he paused on her only briefly, she felt herself to be—*knew* herself to be—his first care in the world, this or any other. Only when he knew where she was, and was satisfied that she was well, did he turn to the task at hand, which was to guide this army safely over the Bay of Beasts.

Karou found it difficult to turn away from the portal and just leave it there, where anyone might find it and use it. Akiva was to have scorched it closed behind them, but Jael had changed their plan. Now they would need it.

To return and start the apocalypse.

The Wolf once more took the lead, turning them eastward, away from the gunmetal horizon and toward the Adelphas Mountains. On a clear day, the peaks would have been visible from here. But it wasn't a clear day, and they could see nothing ahead but thickening mist, which had its pluses and its minuses.

In the plus column, the mists gave them cover. They wouldn't be sighted from a distance by any seraph patrols.

In the minus, the mists gave anyone cover... and anyone—or any*thing*—would not be sighted from a distance by themselves.

Karou was in a central position in the pack, having just come alongside Rua to check on Issa, when it happened.

"Sweet girl, are you bearing up?" Issa asked.

"I'm fine," Karou replied. "But *you* need more clothes."

"I won't argue with that," Issa replied. She was actually wearing clothes—a sweater of Karou's, slit wide at the neck to accommodate her cobra hood—which in itself was unusual for Issa, but her lips were blue, and her shoulders were drawn up practically to her ears as she shivered. The Naja race hailed from a hot climate. Morocco had suited her perfectly. This cold mist, not so much, and their frigid destination even less, though at least there they would be sheltered from the elements, and Karou remembered geothermal chambers in the lower labyrinth of the caves, if all was as it had been years ago.

The Kirin caves.

She had never been back to the place of her birth, home of her earliest life. She had planned to return, once upon a time. It was where she and Akiva were to have met to begin their rebellion, had the fates not had other ideas.

But, no. Karou didn't believe in fate. It wasn't fate that had murdered their plan, but betrayal. And it wasn't fate re-creating it now—or at least this twisted shadow-theater version of it, fraught with suspicion and animosity. It was will.

"I'll find you a blanket or something," she told Issa—or started to tell her. But in that moment, something came over her.

Or *at* her.

At all of them.

A pressure in the lowering mists, and with it a seizure of certainty. Karou shrank down and threw back her head to look up. And it wasn't only her. All around her in the ranks, soldiers were reacting. Dropping, drawing weapons, spinning clear of...something.

Overhead, the white sky seemed near enough to touch. It was a blank, but there was a rush in Karou's blood and a thrum like a sound too low for hearing, and then, sudden and looming, fast and massive, pushing before it a wind that flicked the soldiers aside like toys to a tide, something.

Big.

On them and blotting out the sky, fast and past, skimming the heads of the company. So sudden, so *there*, so huge that Karou couldn't make sense of it, and when it surged past, it touched her, and the trail of its air-warping weight seized and spun her. It was like an undertow, and the chains of her thuribles flew wild, entangling her, and for that dark spinning instant she thought of the black surface of the water far below, and thuribles splashing into it—souls consumed by the Bay of Beasts, and she fought for control of herself...and just like that was released, adrift in a weird calm of aftermath. Her chains were wound tight and tangled but nothing was lost, and all it took now was a glance to see what it was—what *they* were, oh. *Oh*—before the dense white day swallowed them again, and they were gone.

Stormhunters.

The biggest creatures in this world, save whatever secrets the sea held deep. Wings that could shelter or shatter a small house. That was what had brushed her: a stormhunter wing. A pod of the great birds had just glided right over the company, and a single wingbeat from the lowermost had been enough to scatter the chimaera from their formation. Before there was any space in Karou's head for marvel, she did a frantic accounting of the host.

She found Issa clinging to Rua's neck, shaken but otherwise fine. The blacksmith Aegir had dropped the bundle of weapons—all of them lost to the sea. Akiva and Liraz were still in their place far ahead, and Zuzana and Mik were up ahead, too, not far, but safely clear of the whiplash from that wingbeat. They looked no worse than mildly ruffled, but thoroughly slack-jawed with the marvel that Karou was still staving off—and the ranks were closing back in, not one of them so stoic as wasn't gaping after the great shapes already vanished into the haze. Everyone was fine.

They'd just been buzzed by stormhunters.

In her earliest life, Karou had been a child of the high world: Madrigal of the Kirin, the last tribe of the Adelphas Mountains. Amid the peaks the massive creatures ranged, though no Kirin, or anyone else that Karou had heard of, had ever seen a stormhunter *so close*. They couldn't be hunted; they were utterly elusive, too fast for pursuit, too canny to surprise. It was believed that they could sense the smallest changes in air and atmosphere, and as a child—as Madrigal—Karou had had reason to believe it. Seeing them from afar, adrift like motes in the slanting sun, she would take off after them, eager for a closer sight, but no sooner would her wings beat her intention than theirs would answer and carry them away. Never had even a nest been found, an eggshell, or even a carcass; if stormhunters hatched, if stormhunters died, no one knew where.

Now Karou had had her closer sight, and it was thrilling.

Adrenaline was coursing through her, and she couldn't help herself. She smiled. The glimpse had been too brief, but she'd seen that a dense fleece covered the stormhunters' bodies, that their eyes were black, big as platters and filmed by a nictitating membrane, like Earth birds. Their feathers shone iridescent, no single color but all colors, shifting with the play of light.

They seemed like a gift from the wild, and a reminder that not everything in this world was defined by the everlasting war. She gathered herself in the air, untangling a thurible chain from around her neck, and glided up to Zuzana and Mik.

She grinned at her friends, the pair of them still stunned, and said, "Welcome to Eretz."

"Forget a pegasus," declared Zuzana, fervent and wide-eyed. "I want one of those!"

8

Bruise the Sky

"More stormhunters," said the soldier Stivan from the window, stepping aside for Melliel.

It was their cell's only window. Four days they had been in this prison. Three nights the sun had set and three dawns risen to illuminate a world that made less and less sense. Bracing herself, Melliel looked out.

Sunrise. Intense saturation of light; glowing clouds, a gilded sea, and the horizon a streak of radiance too pure to look at. The islands were like the scattered silhouettes of slumbering beasts, and the sky... the sky was as it had been, which is to say, the sky was *wrong*.

If it had been flesh, one would say it was bruised. This dawn, like the others, it was revealed to have set forth new blooms of color overnight—or rather, of *dis*color: violet, indigo, sickly yellow, the most delicate cerulean. They were vast, the blossoms or bleeds. Melliel didn't know what to call them. They were sky-filling, and would spread by the hour, deepen and then pale, finally vanishing as others took their place.

It was beautiful, and when Melliel and her company were first brought here by their captors, they assumed that this was just the nature of the southern sky. This wasn't the world as they knew it. Everything about the Far Isles was beautiful and bizarre. The air was so rich it had body, fragrance seeming to carry in it as easily as sound: perfumes, birdcalls, every breeze as alive with darting songs and scents as the sea was with fish. As for the sea, it was a thousand new colors every minute, and not all of them blues and greens. The trees were more like a child's fanciful drawings than they were like their staid and straight cousins of the northern hemisphere. And the sky?

Well, the sky did this.

But Melliel had gleaned by now that it was *not* normal, and neither was the stormhunter gathering that grew by the day.

Out there over the sea, the creatures were grouped in ceaseless circlings. Blood Soldier of the Misbegotten, Melliel, Second Bearer of that Name, was not young, and in her lifetime she had seen many stormhunters, but never more than a half dozen in one place, and always at the sky's farthest edge, moving in a line. But here were dozens. Dozens interweaving with more dozens.

It was a freakish spectacle, but even so, she might have taken it in stride as some natural phenomenon if it weren't for the faces of their guards. The Stelians were on edge.

Something was happening here, and no one was telling the prisoners anything. Not what was wrong with the sky or what drew the stormhunters, and not what their own fate was to be, either.

Melliel gripped the window bars, leaning forward to take in the full panorama of sea and sky and islands. Stivan was right. In the night, the stormhunter numbers had surged again, as if every one of them in the whole of Eretz were answering some call. Circling, circling, as the sky bled and healed itself and bruised anew.

What power could bruise the sky?

Melliel let go of the bars and stalked back across the cell to the door. She pounded on it and called, "Hello? I want to talk to someone!"

Her team took notice and began to gather. Those still sleeping woke in their hammocks and put their feet on the floor. They were twelve altogether, all taken without injury—though not without confusion over the manner of their capture: a blinking stupefaction so entire that it felt like a breakdown of brain function—and the cell was no dank dungeon but only a long, clean room with this heavy, locked door.

There was a privy, and water for washing. Hammocks for sleeping, and shifts of lightly woven cloth so they might remove their black gambesons and stifling armor if they chose—which, by now, all of them had. Food was plentiful and far better than they were used to: white fish and airy bread, and what fruit! Some tasted of honey and flowers, thick-skinned and thin and varicolored. There were tart yellow berries and husked purple globes that they hadn't figured out how to open, having understandably been deprived of their blades. One kind had sharp spines and hid custard within; they grabbed for that one first, and there was one that none of them could stomach: a queer kind of fleshy pink orb, nearly flavorless and as messy as blood. Those they left untouched in the flat basket by the door.

Melliel couldn't help but wonder which, if any, was the fruit that had so enraged their father the emperor when it appeared by mystery at the foot of his bed.

There came no answer to her call, so she knocked again. "Hello? Someone!" This time she thought to add a grudging "please" and was irritated when the key turned at once, as though Eidolon—of course it was Eidolon—had only been standing there waiting for the *please.*

The Stelian girl was, as usual, alone and unarmed. She wore a simple cascade of white fabric fastened over one brown shoulder, with her black hair vine-bound and gathered over the other. Engraved golden bands were spaced evenly up both slim arms, and her feet were bare, which struck Melliel as embarrassingly intimate. Vulnerable. The vulnerability was an illusion, of course.

There was nothing about Eidolon to hint that she was a soldier—that any of the Stelians were, or that they even had an army—but this young woman had been, unmistakably, in command when Melliel's team was... intercepted. And because of what had happened then—Melliel still couldn't wrap her mind around it—and though they were a dozen war-hardened Misbegotten against one elegant girl, no thought entered their heads of attempting escape.

There was more to Eidolon—as there was more to the Far Isles—than beauty.

"Are you well?" asked that elegant girl in the Stelian accent that could soften the sharpest of words. Her smile was warm; her Stelian fire eyes danced as she greeted them with a gesture—a kind of cupping and proffering of her hand, a sweep of her gold-banded arm to take in the lot of them.

The soldiers murmured responses. Male and female alike, they were all in some fashion fascinated by this mysterious Eidolon of the dancing eyes, but Melliel regarded the gesture with suspicion. She had seen the Stelian... do things... with just such graceful gestures, unaccountable things, and she wished she'd keep her arms at her sides. "We're well enough," she said. "For prisoners." Her own accent was coming to sound vulgar to her, compared to theirs, and her voice gruff and grizzled. She felt old and ungainly, like an iron sword. "What's happening out there?"

"Things that would better *not*," Eidolon replied lightly.

It was more than Melliel had gotten out of her before. "What things?" she demanded. "What's wrong with the sky?"

"It's tired," said the girl with a shimmer in her eye that was like the sparking of a stirred fire. So like Akiva's eyes, Melliel thought. Every Stelian they had seen so far had them. "It aches," added Eidolon. "It is very old, you know."

The sky was old and tired? A nonsense answer. She was toying with them. "Is it something to do with the Wind?" Melliel asked, thinking the word with a capital letter, to distinguish it from every wind that had ever come before.

Indeed, calling it a "wind" was like calling a stormhunter a bird. Melliel's team had been nearing Caliphis when it hit them, seizing them like so many shed feathers and sucking them back the way they'd come, along with every other sky-borne thing in its path—birds, moths, clouds, and, yes, even stormhunters—as well as many things that the surface of the world had not been gripping as tightly as it might, like trees' entire blossom bounties, and the very foam off the sea.

Powerlessness, reeling miles of it. They'd been caught and carried—eastward first, beating their wings to get control of themselves, and then... the lull. Brief and far too still, it had given them just time to gasp before the full force came on again and sent them reeling again, westward now, back to Caliphis and beyond, where it finally released them. Such force! It had felt as though the ether itself had dragged a deep breath and expelled it. The phenomena had to be linked, Melliel thought. The Wind, the bruised sky, the gathering of the stormhunters? None of it was natural or right.

Eidolon's expression of mild loveliness went flat, no shimmer in her eyes now. "That was not wind," she said.

"Then what was it?" Melliel asked, hoping this unexpected candor would persist.

"*Stealing*," she said, and seemed poised to withdraw. "Forgive me. Was there anything else?"

"Yes," said Melliel. "I want to know what will be done with us."

With a viper-quick turn of her head, Eidolon made Melliel flinch. "Are you so eager to have something *done* with you?"

Melliel blinked. "I only want to know—"

"It is not decided. We get so few strangers here. The children should like to see you, I think. Blue eyes. Such a wonder." She said it with admiration, staring right at Yav, the youngest of the company, who was very fair. He blushed to his blond roots. Eidolon turned back to Melliel with a contemplative look. "On the other hand, Wraith has requested that you be given to the novices. For practice."

Practice? At what? Melliel wouldn't ask; since coming into contact with these people, she had seen such things as hinted at magic unimaginable. Those arts were long lost in the Empire, and filled her with horror. But Eidolon's eyes were merry. Was she joking? Melliel was not consoled. *So few strangers*, the Stelian had said. Melliel asked, "Where are the others?"

"Others?"

Not at all sure she wanted to press, Melliel replied, "Yes," and tried to sound stalwart. It was her mission, after all, to find out. Her team had been dispatched to trace the emperor's vanished emissaries. Joram's declaration of war on the Stelians had been answered—with the basket of fruit—so it had clearly been received, but the ambassadors had never returned, and several troop detachments had likewise gone missing in the quest for the Far Isles. In their days here, Melliel and her team had seen or heard no hint of other prisoners. "The emperor's messengers," she said. "They didn't come back."

"Are you sure of that?" asked the girl. Sweetly. Too sweetly, like honey that masks the gall of poison. And then, with deliberation, her eyes never leaving Melliel's, she knelt to take a fruit from the basket by the door. It was one of the pink orbs the Misbegotten couldn't abide. Fruit they might have been, but the things were essentially meaty sacks of red juice, off-puttingly mouth-filling, and *warm*.

The girl took a bite, and in that instant, Melliel would have sworn that her teeth were points. It was like a veil yanked askew, and behind it, Eidolon of the dancing eyes was a savage. Her delicacy was gone; she was... *nasty*. The fruit burst and she tipped back her head, sucking and licking, to catch the thick juice in her mouth. The column of her throat was exposed as red overspilled her lips, streaking down, viscous and opaque, to the white cascade of her dress, where it bloomed like flowers of blood, nothing but blood, and still she sucked at the fruit. The soldiers recoiled from her, and when Eidolon lowered her head again to stare at Melliel, her face was smeared with hungry red.

Like a predator, Melliel thought, raising its head from a hot carcass.

"You brought us your flesh and blood along with your animus," said Eidolon with her dripping mouth, and it was impossible now even to recall the graceful girl she had seemed but a moment ago. "What did you mean by coming here, if not to give yourselves to us? Did you think we would keep you just as you are, blue eyes and black hands and all?" She held up the skin of the sucked-empty fruit and dropped it. It hit the tile floor with a slap.

She couldn't mean…No. Not the fruit. Melliel had seen things, yes, but her mind would not admit *that* possibility. Simply no. It was a hideous joke. Her disgust emboldened her. "It was never our animus," she said. "We don't have the luxury of choosing our own enemies. We are soldiers." *Soldiers*, she said, but she thought: *slaves*.

"Soldiers," said Eidolon with scorn. "Yes. Soldiers and children do as they're told." A curl of her lip, surveying the lot of them, and she said, "Children grow out of it, but soldiers just die." *Just. Die.* Each word a jab, and then the door flew open untouched and she was on the other side of it without having moved, standing in the corridor. She had done this before: made time seem to stutter and strobe, steps lost along the way like seconds sliced out and swallowed.

Swallowed like that clotting red juice that wasn't blood, that couldn't be blood.

Melliel forced herself to say, "So we're to die?"

"The queen will decide what is to be done with you."

Queen? This was the first mention of a queen. Was it she who had sent Joram the basket of fruit that had seen fourteen Breakblades swinging from the Westway gibbet and a concubine flushed out the gutter door in a shroud?

"When?" Melliel asked. "*When* will she decide?"

"When she comes home," said the girl. "Enjoy your flesh and

blood while you can, sweet soldiers. Scarab has gone away hunting." She sang the word. "Hunting, hunting." A snarl of a smile, and again Melliel saw that her teeth were points...and again saw that they were not. Strobing time, strobing reality. What was true? A crack and strobe and the door was closed, Eidolon was gone, and...

...and the room was dark.

Melliel blinked, shook off a sudden heaviness and looked around her. Dark? Eidolon's words still echoed through the cell—*hunting hunting*—so it could only have been a second, but the chamber was dark. Stivan was blinking, too, and Doria and the rest. Young Yav, barely jumped up from the training camp and still with a boy's round face, had tears of horror in his blue, blue eyes.

Hunting hunting hunting.

Melliel spun to the window and, with a push of her wings, thrust herself at it and looked out. It was as she feared. It was no longer dawn.

It was no longer *day*. The black of night hid the sky's bruises, and both moons were high and thin, Nitid a crescent and Ellai but a crust, together giving off just enough light to brush the edges of the stormhunters' wings with silver as they tilted in their ceaseless circles.

Hunting, came Eidolon's voice—echo or memory or phantom—and Melliel steadied herself against the wall as an entire lost day raced through her and was stripped away, every stolen minute, she felt with a shudder, bringing her nearer to her last. Would they die here, the lot of them? She couldn't—or wouldn't—believe Eidolon about the fruit, but the memory of its dense flesh between her own teeth still made her want to gag.

These people might be seraphim, but there the kinship began and ended, and in Melliel's mind the shape of their mysterious queen—*Scarab?*—began to warp into something terrible.

Hunting hunting hunting.

Hunting *what*?

ARRIVAL + 6 HOURS

9

LANDFALL

At 15:12 GMT, with the whole world watching, the angels made landfall. There was a period of hours, while the formation's flight path carved due west from Samarkand, over the Caspian Sea and Azerbaijan, when their destination was a mystery. Across Turkey the westward path held, and it was not until the angels crossed the 36th meridian without turning south that the Holy Land was eliminated from contention. After that, the money was on Vatican City, and the money was not wrong.

Keeping to the formation in which they'd flown, in twenty perfect blocks of fifty angels each, the Visitors alighted in the grand, winged plaza of St. Peter's Basilica, Rome.

The scientists, grad students, and interns who'd gathered in the basement of the NMNH in Washington, D.C., watched the screen in silence as, in baroque regalia befitting his title—His Holiness, Bishop of Rome, Vicar of Jesus Christ, Successor of the Prince of the Apostles, Supreme Pontiff of the Universal Church, Primate of Italy,

Archbishop and Metropolitan of the Roman Province, Sovereign of the Vatican City State, Servant of the servants of God—the Pope stepped forth to greet his magnificent guests.

As he did, there came a shift in the first and central phalanx. It was difficult to make out details. The cameras were in the air, hovering in helicopters, and from this high vantage point, the angels looked like a living lace of fire and white silk. Exquisite. Now one of them stepped forward—he seemed to be wearing a plumed silver helm—and in one liquid movement, all the rest went down on one knee.

The Pope approached, trembling, his hand raised in blessing, and the leader of the angels inclined his head in a very slight bow. The two stood facing each other. They appeared to be talking.

"Did... the Pope just become the spokesman for humanity?" inquired a stunned zoologist.

"What could go wrong?" replied a dazed anthropologist.

Eliza's colleagues had put together an ad hoc media center by grouping a number of televisions and computers in an empty outreach classroom. Over the course of several hours, the tenor of their commentary had shifted almost entirely away from hoax theory toward the more unsettling realms of... *If it's true,* how *is it true, and what does it* mean, *and... how do we make it make sense?*

As for the television commentary, it was inane. They were bandying biblical jargon around like there was no tomorrow—which, *hey,* maybe there wasn't! *Ba-dum-bum.*

Apocalypse. Armageddon. The Rapture.

Eliza's nemesis, Morgan Toth—he of the pillowy lips—was using an altogether different vocabulary. "They should treat it like an alien invasion," he said. "There are protocols for that."

Protocols. Eliza knew exactly what he was getting at.

"That would go over well with the masses," said Yvonne Chen, a microbiologist, with a laugh. "*It's the Second Coming! Scramble the jets!*"

Morgan gave a sigh of exaggerated patience. "Yes," he said with the utmost condescension. "Whatever this is, I would appreciate some jets between it and me. Am I the only non-idiot on the planet?"

"Yes, Morgan Toth, you are," Gabriel piped up. "Will you be our king?"

"With pleasure," said Morgan, sketching a slight bow and flipping back his artfully overlong bangs on the way up. He was a small guy with a handsome face set atop skinny, sloping shoulders and a neck about the circumference of Eliza's pinkie. As for the puffy lips, they existed in a state of snide smirk, and Eliza was constantly plagued by urges to bounce things off them. Coins. Gummy bears.

Fists.

The two of them were grad students in Dr. Anuj Chaudhary's lab, both recipients of highly competitive research fellowships with one of the world's foremost evolutionary biologists, but from the day they met, the animosity Eliza felt for the smug little white boy had felt like nausea. He'd actually laughed when she told him the name of the scruffy public university she came from, claiming to have thought she was joking, and that was just the beginning. She knew he didn't believe she'd earned her spot here, that some form of affirmative action must account for it—or worse. Sometimes, when Dr. Chaudhary laughed at something Eliza said, or leaned over her shoulder to read some results, she could see Morgan's nasty assumptions in his smirk, and it enraged her. It dirtied her—and Dr. Chaudhary, too, who was decent, and married, and also old enough to be her father. Eliza was used to being underestimated, because she was black, because she was a woman, but no one had ever been quite so vile about it as Morgan. She wanted to shake him, and that was the worst of it. Eliza was *mild*, even after everything, and the rage itself enraged her—that Morgan Toth could *alter* her, bend her like a wire by the sheer awfulness of his personality.

"I mean, come on," he said, gesturing at the TV screens. The helmed angel and the Pope still appeared to be speaking. Someone had gotten a camera closer to the action, on the ground with them now, though not near enough for audio. "What are those things?" Morgan demanded. "We know they're not 'celestial beings'—"

"We don't *know* anything yet," Eliza heard herself say, though the last thing she wanted to do—dear god, the irony—was argue on behalf of *angels*.

Only Morgan could provoke her like this. It was like his voice—belligerent spiked with obnoxious—triggered an autonomic impulse to argue. All he had to do was take a position and she'd feel an immediate need to oppose it. If he declared affection for light, Eliza would have to defend the dark.

And she really, really didn't like the dark.

"Are you even a scientist?" she asked him. "Since when do we decide what we know before there's even any data?"

"You're making my point for me, Eliza. Data. We need it. I doubt the Pope's going to get it, and I don't hear the president demanding it."

"That doesn't mean he's not. He said every scenario is being considered."

"Like hell it is. I suppose if a flying saucer descended on the Vatican, they'd clear a landing strip for it in the middle of St. Peter's freaking Square?"

"It's *not* a flying saucer, though, is it, Morgan? Can you really not see how this is different?" She knew there was no point arguing with him, but it was maddening. He was pretending not to grasp the intense sensitivity of this situation out of some notion that it marked him as superior—like he was so far above the masses that their concerns were quaint to him. *How primitive your customs are! What is this thing you call "religion"?* But Eliza knew that this was a whole different kind of threat than a flying saucer would have been. An alien landing would unify the world, just like in a science fiction movie. But "angels" had the potential to splinter humanity into a thousand sharp shards.

She should know. She'd been a shard for years.

"There aren't many things that people will gladly kill and die for, but this is the big one," she said. "Do you understand? It doesn't matter what *you* believe, or what *you* think is stupid. If the powers that be pull any of your 'protocol,' it's not going to be pretty out there."

Morgan sighed again, steepling his fingertips to his temples in an attitude of *Why must I endure such mental frailty?* "There is no scenario in which it's going to be 'pretty'. We need to be in control of the situation, not falling to our knees like a bunch of bedazzled peasants."

And here Eliza had to bite the inside of her cheek, because she hated to agree with Morgan Toth, but she agreed with that. She'd been fighting that fight for years—to never again fall to her knees, never again be knocked to them and held down, never again be forced.

And now the sky opened and *angels* poured in?

It was kind of hilarious. She wanted to laugh. She wanted to pound her fists against something. A wall. Morgan Toth's smirk.

She imagined how he would look at her if he knew where she came from. *What* she came from. What she'd *run* from. He would achieve a threshold of disdain unmatched in human history. Or more like fascinated, disgusted *glee*. It would make his year.

She decided to shut up, which Morgan took as a victory, but still she had a sense, from the fishy glint of his glare, that she should have shut up sooner. *People with secrets shouldn't make enemies*, she warned herself.

And, clear and unbidden, as if in response, from some deep layer of memory, arose her mother's voice. "People with destinies," it said, "shouldn't make plans."

"Oh my goodness!" came a perky trill from one of the embarrassing newscasters, drawing Eliza's attention back to the row of TVs. Something was happening. The Pope had turned aside to issue orders to underlings, and now, lugging cameras and microphones, a news team approached at a lurching run.

"It looks like the Visitors are going to make a statement!"

10

Tilt to Panic

The angel wore a helmet of chased silver topped with a crest of white plumes. It resembled a Roman centurion's helmet, with the addition of an overlong nasal guard—a narrow strip of silver that projected from the visor all the way to his chin, effectively bisecting his face. This concealed his nose and all but the corners of his mouth, while leaving his eyes, cheekbones, and jawline exposed.

It was a strange choice, especially considering that the rest of the host was bareheaded, their beautiful faces unobstructed. There were other odd things about the angel, too, but they were harder to assess, and his statement was soon to eclipse them all. Only later would the analysis of his posture begin, and his oddly bloated shadow, his mushy, lisping voice, and the whispering that was audible in his long pauses, as though he were being fed lines. Details would start to catch up with the general impression of *wrongness* he made—like a sticky residue on your fingers, except that it was on your mind.

But not yet. First, his statement, and the instant worldwide tilt it precipitated: straight to panic.

"*Sons and daughters of the one true god,*" he said—but . . . he said it *in Latin*, so that very few people understood him in real time. Around the whole sphere of planet Earth, amid prayers and curses and questions uttered in hundreds of languages, billions scrambled to find a translation.

What is he saying???

In the lag time before translations went wide, the majority of the human race experienced the angel's message first by witnessing the Pope's reaction to it.

It wasn't comforting.

The pontiff paled. He took a stagger step backward. At one point he tried to speak, but the angel cut him off without a sideward glance.

This was his message for humanity:

"*Sons and daughters of the one true god, ages have passed since we last came among you, though you have never been far from our sight. For centuries we have fought a war beyond human ken. Long have we protected you in body and soul while shielding you even from knowledge of the threat that shadows you. The Enemy that hungers for you. Far from your lands have great battles been fought. Blood spilled, flesh devoured. But as godlessness and evil grow among you, the might of the Enemy increases. And now the day has come that their strength matches ours, and will soon surpass it. We can no longer leave you innocent of the Shadow. We can no longer protect you without your help.*"

The angel took a deep breath and drew out a pause before finishing heavily.

"The Beasts . . . are coming for you."

* * *

And with that the riots began.

ARRIVAL + 12 HOURS

11

Breeds of Silence

Akiva stood stoic. The words he had just spoken seemed to hang in the air. The atmosphere in the wake of his pronouncement, he thought, was like the pressure in the path of the stormhunters' plunge—all air siphoned toward an onrushing cataclysm. Arrayed around him in the Kirin caves were two hundred and ninety-six grim-faced Misbegotten, all that remained of the Emperor's bastard legion, to whom he had just made his unthinkable proposal.

Pressure was building, the weight of the air defying the thin altitude. And then…

Laughter. Incredulous and uneasy.

"And will we all sleep head to toe, beast-seraph-beast-seraph?" asked Xathanael, one of Akiva's many half brothers, and not one he knew well.

Beast's Bane wasn't known for jokes, but surely *this* was a joke: the enemy coming to shelter with them? To join with them?

"And brush each other's hair before bed?" added Sorath.

"Pick their nits, more like." Xathanael again, to more laughter.

Akiva suffered an acute physical memory of Madrigal sleeping by his side, and the joke was not funny to him. It was all the less funny *here*, in the echoing caves of her slaughtered people, where, if you looked closely, you could still make out the blood tracks of dragged bodies on the floor. What would it be like for Karou to see that evidence? How much did she remember of the day she was orphaned? Her first orphaning, he reminded himself. Her second was much more recent, and his fault. "I think it would be best," he replied, "if we kept separate quarters."

The laughter faltered and gradually faded. They were all staring at him, faces caught between amusement and outrage, unsure where to settle. Neither end of that spectrum would suit. Akiva needed to bring them to a different place altogether: to acceptance, however reluctant.

Right now it felt very remote. He'd left the chimaera company in a high-mountain valley until he could make it back to bring them to safety. He very much wanted to bring Karou to safety—and the rest of them, too. This impossible chance would never come again. If he failed to persuade his brothers and sisters to try it, he failed the dream.

"The choice is yours," he said. "You can refuse. We have removed ourselves from the Empire's service; we choose our own fight now, and we can choose our allies, too. The fact is that we've shattered the chimaera. These few who survive are the foes of yesterday's war. We face a new threat now, not just to us, though indeed to us, but to all of Eretz: the promise of a new age of tyranny and war that would make our father's rule look soft by comparison. We must stop Jael. That is primary."

"We don't need beasts for that," said Elyon, stepping forward. Unlike Xathanael, Akiva did know Elyon well, and respected him. He was among the older of the bastards left living, and not very old at that, his hair barely beginning to gray. He was a thinker, a planner, not given to bravado or unnecessary violence.

"No?" Akiva faced him. "The Dominion are five thousand, and Jael is emperor now, so he commands the Second Legion as well."

"And how many are these beasts?"

"These chimaera," replied Akiva, "currently number eighty-seven."

"Eighty-seven." Elyon laughed. He wasn't scornful, but almost sad. "So few. How does that help us?"

"It helps us eighty-seven soldiers' worth," said Akiva. *For a start*, he thought, but didn't say. He hadn't told them yet that it was true the chimaera had a new resurrectionist. "Eighty-seven with hamsas against the Dominion."

"Or against us," pointed out Elyon.

Akiva wished he could deny that the hamsas would be turned on them; he still felt the sickness of their furtive palm flashes as a dull ache in the pit of his belly. He said, "They have no more reason to love us than we do them. Less. Look at their country. But our interests, for now at least, align. The White Wolf has given his promise—"

At the mention of the White Wolf, the company lost its composure. "The White Wolf lives?" demanded many soldiers. "And you didn't kill him?" demanded many more.

Their voices filled the cavern, bouncing and echoing off the high, rough ceiling and seeming to multiply into a chorus of ghostly shouts.

"The general lives, yes," confirmed Akiva. He had to shout them down. "And no, I didn't kill him." *If you only knew how hard that was.* "And he didn't kill me, either, though he easily could have."

Their cries died away, and then the echoes of their cries, but Akiva felt as if he'd run out of things to say. When it came to Thiago, his persuasion ran dry. If the White Wolf were dead, would he be more eloquent? *Don't think of him,* he told himself. *Think of her.*

He did.

And he said, "There is the past, and there is the future. The present is never more than the single second dividing one from the other. We live poised on that second as it's hurtling forward—toward what? All our lives, it's been the Empire propelling us—toward the annihilation of the beasts—and that has come and gone. It belongs to the past, but we're still alive, less than three hundred of us, and we're still hurtling forward, toward *something,* but it's not up to the Empire anymore. And for my part, I want that something to be—"

He could have said: *Jael's death.* It would have been true. But it was a small truth overshadowed by a greater one. In his memory dwelt a voice deeper than any other he had ever heard, saying, "Life is your master, or death is."

Brimstone's last words.

"Life," he told his brothers and sisters now. "I want the future to be *life.* It isn't the chimaera who stand in the way. They never did. It was Joram, and now it's Jael."

When it's a question of greater and lesser hates, Akiva knew, the more personal hate will win, and Jael had gone far to ensure himself that honor. The Misbegotten didn't yet know, though, how far.

Akiva held the news to himself for a moment, not wanting to tell it. Feeling, more than ever, at fault. Finally, he laid it like a corpse atop their hard silence.

"Hazael is dead."

There are breeds of silence. As there are breeds of chimaera. *Chimaera* essentially meant nothing more specific than "creature of mixed aspect, creature *not seraph*." It was a term that took in every species with language and higher function that lived in these lands and was not an angel; it was a term that would never have existed if the seraphim had not, by their aggression, united the tribes against themselves.

And the silence that preceded Akiva's news, and the silence that followed it, were no more kin to each other than a Kirin to a Heth.

The Misbegotten had, in the last year, been pared to a sliver of itself. They had lost so many brothers and sisters that those who remained could have drowned in the ashes of those who had died. They were bred to expect it, though this had never made it any easier, and in the last months of the war, when the body count crested to levels of hollow absurdity, a shift had occurred. Their fury had been growing—not merely over the losses but the expectation that they, being nothing but weapons, would not grieve. They grieved. And by any hallmark, Hazael had been a favorite.

"He was killed by Dominion in the Tower of Conquest. It was a setup." Speaking of it, Akiva was right back *in* it, seeing it, and the way that, in the extraordinary radiance of *sirithar* come to him too late, he had watched his brother die. He didn't tell the rest: that Hazael had died defending Liraz from Jael's unbearable plans for her. It was hard enough for her without it being known by all.

"It's true that I killed our father," he said. "It's what I went there to do, and I did it. Whatever you might have heard, I did not kill the crown prince, nor would I have. Nor the council, the bodyguards, the Silverswords, the bath attendants." All that blood. "All of that was Jael's doing, and all of it his plan. No matter how it fell out that day, he was going to lay it to me, and use it as pretext to exterminate us all."

Throughout the telling, the silence continued to evolve, and Akiva felt in it a loosening, as of fists relaxing their grips on sword hilts.

Maybe it was news to them that their lives would have been forfeit no matter what Akiva did that day, and maybe it wasn't. Maybe that wasn't what mattered. These two names—Hazael and Jael—could have served as their poles of love and hatred, and together combined to make this real, all of it. The ascendancy of their uncle, their own exile, even the fact of their own *freedom*—still so alien to them, a language they'd never had opportunity to learn.

They might do anything now. Even . . . ally with beasts?

"Jael won't expect it," said Akiva. "It will anger him, to begin with. But more than that, it will *unsettle* him. He won't know what to expect next, in a world where chimaera and Misbegotten join forces."

"And neither, I wager, will we." In Elyon's voice, Akiva thought, there was a tone of musing, as if the unknown beguiled as much as it alarmed him.

"There's something else," said Akiva. "It's true that the chimaera have a new resurrectionist. And you should know, before you decide anything, that she was willing to save Hazael." His voice caught. "But it was too late."

They digested this. "What about Liraz?" asked Elyon, and a murmur went around. Liraz. She would be their touchstone. Someone said, "Surely *she* hasn't agreed to this."

And Akiva said a blessing for his sister, because he knew that he had them now. "She's with them, encamped and awaiting my word. And you can imagine—" He softened for the first time since arriving and calling them together; he allowed himself to smile. "That she would rather be here with you. There isn't time to hash it over. Jael won't wait." He looked first to Elyon. "Well?"

The soldier blinked several times, rapidly, like he was waking up. Furrowed his brow. "A détente," he said, in a tone of warning, "can only be as strong as the least trustworthy on either side."

"Then let it not be our side," said Akiva. "It's the best we can do."

The look in Elyon's eyes suggested he could think of better, and that it began and ended with swords, but he nodded.

He nodded. Akiva's relief felt like the passage of stormhunters reshaping the air.

Elyon gave his promise, and the others did, too. It was simple, and slight, and as much as could be expected for now: that when the wind delivered up their enemies, they would not strike first. Thiago had made the same promise on behalf of his soldiers.

Soon they would all learn what promises were worth.

12

A Warm Idea

"You know what I might do?" Zuzana asked, shivering.

"What might you do?" inquired Mik, who was seated behind her, his arms wrapped all the way around her and his face tucked into the crook of her neck. That was the warmest part of her body right now: the crook of her neck, where Mik's breath was making its own microclimate, a few lovely square inches of tropical.

"You know that scene in *Star Wars*," she said, "where Han Solo slits open that tauntaun's belly and shoves Luke inside so he won't freeze to death?"

"Aw," responded Mik, "that's so sweet. You're going to tuck me into a fresh, steaming carcass to warm me up?"

"Not you. *Me*."

"Oh. Okay. Good. Because the thing *I* always think after that scene is that the guts are going to cool off fast, and personally, I'd rather be cold and *not* covered in wet tauntaun guts than—"

"Okay then," said Zuzana. "No need to get graphic."

"It's called a Skywalker sleeping bag," Mik continued. "A woman in America tried it in a horse."

Zuzana made a choking noise. "*Stop now.*"

"Naked."

"Oh *god*." She pulled forward so she could swing her face around to look at him. Immediately the microclimate of her neck began to drop in temperature. *Good-bye, tiny tropics.* "I did not need that in my mind."

"Sorry," said Mik, contrite. "I have a better idea, anyway."

"A *warm* idea?"

"Yeah. I was just working up my nerve when you distracted me with *Star Wars*."

The chimaera army, plus themselves and Liraz—Akiva having flown on ahead to get the high sign from *his* army, fingers crossed—was encamped in a sheltered valley in the mountains. *Sheltered* being a relative term, and *valley*, too. One thought of meadows and wildflowers and mirror lakes, but this looked like a moon crater. They were out of the worst of the wind, anyway; it was calm enough to get fires going, though they didn't have a lot of fuel, and the wood that someone—Rark? Aegir?—had chopped with a battle-ax was a stingy burner, throwing off popping green sparks and smelling disagreeably like the decades of cabbage buildup in Zuzana's aunt's Prague flat.

Seriously, that smell had no business existing in two worlds.

Zuzana wondered what idea Mik might have that called for nerve. "Will it impress me?" she asked.

"If it works? Yes. If it doesn't, and I come right back here looking sheepish or . . . um, looking *stabbed*, don't mock me, okay?"

Looking *stabbed*? "I would never mock you," Zuzana said, and she meant it in the moment. "Especially when there's a stabbing risk. There's not really, is there?"

"I don't think so. Humiliation, for sure." He took a deep breath. "Here I go." And then his body was gone from behind hers, leaving her fully exposed to the elements, and Zuzana realized that she hadn't actually been cold before, but now she was. Like climbing out of a tauntaun, covered in wet—

Ugh.

"What's Mik doing?" Karou asked, hopping down from the stone buttress that shielded them—sort of—from the wind. She'd been pacing up there, watching out for Akiva under the pretext of standing guard. The sun was going down, and Zuzana didn't think they expected the seraph back for a while yet, but she hadn't bothered pointing this out to her friend.

"I don't know," she replied. "Something brave, to keep us from freezing to death." Immediately she regretted the complaint.

Karou winced. "I'm sorry we're not better prepared, Zuze," she said. "You should have stayed. It was so stupid of me to let you come."

"Shush. I'm not sorry, and I'm not actually freezing to death or I'd climb into the blanket pile with Issa."

There was a huddle around some of the colder-blooded members of the company, and all spare blankets—including Zuzana's stinky neck-spike pad—had gone to that cause. Zuzana had a fleece on, at least, and Mik a sweater. They were lucky that they'd left all their things at the kasbah when they escaped, or they wouldn't even have had those.

"Where's he going?" Karou asked. Mik had set off in the opposite direction from the resting chimaera. "He's not . . . he wouldn't . . . *Oh.* He *is.*" There was dread and awe in her tone.

Zuzana shared both. "What's he thinking?" she hissed. "Abort. *Abort.*" But it was too late.

With his hands shoved deep into his jeans pockets and shuffling his feet like a terrified hobo, Mik approached . . . Liraz.

Zuzana rose to her feet to watch. The angel stood by herself at the farthest edge of this rock trench from the chimaera, looking every bit as pissed off as she had back at the kasbah, and on the Charles Bridge, too. Maybe *more* pissed off. Or maybe that was just her face? Zuzana had yet to witness evidence that the angel could look any other way. In flight, she and Mik had amused each other by coming up with personals ads for members of the company, and Liraz's had been something like: *Hot, perpetually pissed-off angel seeks living pincushion for scowl practice and general stabbiness. No kissing.*

Mik was not going to be that pincushion. Zuzana realized it was the "hot" part—literally—that he was after. It was crazy. And doomed. No way was Liraz coming over here to keep the huddled masses warm with her wings. Her fiery, lovely, toasty wings.

Mik was talking to her now. Gesturing. He made the universal sign of *brrr*, and then, right after, spread his arms like wings, and gestured back whence he'd come, putting his hands together in a plea. Liraz looked, saw Zuzana and Karou watching. Her eyes narrowed. She returned her attention to Mik, but only briefly, and looked at him—*down* at him; she was tall—with flat disinterest. She said nothing, didn't even bother to shake her head, just turned her back on him like he wasn't even there.

How dare she? "I'll tauntaun *her*," Zuzana muttered.

"What?" said Karou.

"Nothing."

Mik was coming back, sheepish but not stabbed, and though his mission had failed—what had he thought, that Liraz could possibly care about their comfort?—it had been marvelously bold. The chimaera, for all their monstrosity, were more approachable than she was.

"My hero," Zuzana said without a hint of mockery, and, taking Mik's hand, led him back over to the meager fire to set about conjuring up some more neck tropics.

13

Together

The sun set. Nitid rose, followed by Ellai, and Karou enjoyed her friends' wonder at their first sight of the sister moons, even if they were just slivers tonight. They were gifted another glimpse of storm-hunters, too, though this one from more like the usual distance. The temperature dropped further, and the huddles of chilled creatures tightened. They cooked, ate. Oora told a story with a haunting, rhythmic refrain.

Liraz still stood aloof, as far as she could get from the beast huddles, and as Karou tucked her fingers into her armpits for warmth, the waste of the angel's wing heat seemed positively profligate, akin to pouring out water in the desert. She couldn't exactly blame Liraz, though, after the hamsa flashes she had endured on the journey. Well, she *could* blame her for being rude to Mik; Mik didn't have hamsas, and really: *Who could be mean to Mik?* Even the worst among the chimaera couldn't manage that. And look at Zuzana! Not for nothing was her chimaera nickname *neek-neek*, and yet Mik turned her to honey. So far, Liraz alone had proven immune to the Mik effect.

Liraz was special. Specially antisocial. Spectacularly, even. But Karou felt responsible for her, left in their midst as...what? An ambassador of sorts? No one could be worse suited to the role. There had been that moment before Akiva left, when his gaze had cut across the distance to Karou. No one could do that like Akiva could, burn a path across space, make you feel seen, set apart. They still hadn't spoken since leaving the kasbah, or even stood near each other, and she'd been cautious with the direction of her glances, but that one look had said many things, and one of them was a plea to look after his sister.

She didn't take it lightly. As far as she'd been able to tell, no one was tormenting Liraz, and she hoped they wouldn't be so stupid, with Akiva not here to hold her back.

When will he get here?

Down below, the fires popped their green sparks and belched their cabbage stinks, emitting paltry warmth, and Karou paced the ridge, keeping an eye over the chimaera on one side, scanning for Akiva on the other. Still no hint of wing-glimmer in the deepening darkness.

How was he faring? What if he came back with bad news? Where would the chimaera go, if not to the Kirin caves? Back to the mine tunnels where they'd hidden before taking shelter in the human world? Karou shuddered at the thought.

And at the thought of facing the enormity of the angel invasion alone.

And of the loss of this chance.

She realized how much, in so short a time, she had come to rely on the idea of this alliance, crazy as it was, and all that it meant for this company—for both meeting their basic needs and giving them purpose. The chimaera needed this. *She* needed it.

Also, she was freezing her butt off in the open while the Misbegotten enjoyed the comforts of her ancestral home? Which, if she recalled correctly, had *hot springs*?

Oh hell no.

She heard the faint scritch of claws on stone, the only hint of the White Wolf's gait, and turned to him. He carried tea, which she gratefully accepted, wrapping her fingers around the hot tin cup and holding it right up to her face to breathe the steam.

"You don't have to be up here in the wind," he said. "Kasgar and Keita-Eiri have the watch."

"I know," she said. "I can't sit still. Thanks for the tea."

"You're welcome."

"Where did you send the others?" she asked. From up here, she'd seen him talk with his lieutenants and then send four teams of two back the way they'd come.

"To fan out around the eastern reaches of the bay," he said. "Keep their eyes to the horizons. One from each pair will rendezvous here in twenty-four hours, and then at twelve-hour intervals after that, so we'll know it's clear before we leave the mountains."

She nodded. It was smart. The Bay of Beasts was seraph territory. *Everywhere* was seraph territory now, and they had no idea what the rest of the Empire's forces were doing, or where they were doing it. The mountains provided some shelter, but to return to the human world, they'd have to be out in the open for as long as it took their combined numbers to file back through the portal one by one.

"How do you think it's going?" he asked, his voice very low.

Karou glanced down toward the company, scattered below them against the edges of the broad rock hollow. Her anxiety was on high alert, but no one was looking at them, and anyway, distance and darkness must render them silhouettes, and the wind carry their voices away. "Good, I think," she said. "You're doing so well." At being Thiago, she meant. "It's a little eerie."

"Eerie," he repeated.

"Convincing. A few times I almost forgot—"

He didn't let her finish. "Don't forget. Not ever. Not for a second." He drew in breath. "Please."

So much behind that word. *Please don't forget I'm not a monster. Please don't forget what I gave up. Please don't forget me.* Karou was ashamed for having voiced her thought. Had she meant it as a compliment? How could she imagine he would take it as one? *You're doing so well acting like the maniac I killed.* It sounded like an accusation.

"I won't forget," she told Ziri. She recalled her brief moment of worrying that wearing the Wolf's skin might change him, but when she made herself look at him now, she knew there was no danger of that.

His eyes weren't Thiago's, not now. They were too warm. Oh, they were still the Wolf's pale eyes, of course, but more different than Karou would have thought they could be. It was unreal how two souls could look out through the same set of eyes in such drastically different fashion, seeming to reshape them entirely. Absent the Wolf's hauteur, this face could actually look kind. Of course, that was dangerous. The Wolf never looked kind. Courtly, yes, and polite. Composed in a mimicry of kindness? Sure. But *actual* kind? No, and the difference was drastic.

"I promise," she said, dropping her voice low, so that it was almost inaudible beneath the coursing of the winds. "I could never forget who you are."

He had to lean nearer to catch her words, and didn't move away after, but replied in the same secret tone, near enough that her ear felt the stir of his breath, "Thank you." His tone was as warm and un-Thiago-like as his eyes, and laced with yearning.

Karou turned abruptly back toward the darkness, buying herself some space. Even Ziri's spirit couldn't alter the Wolf's physical presence enough that his nearness wouldn't make her shudder. Her wounds still ached. Her ear throbbed where those teeth had torn it. And she didn't even have to close her eyes to remember how it had felt, being trapped beneath that body's weight.

"How are you holding up?" he asked, after a silent moment.

"I'm okay," she said. "I'll be better once we know." She nodded into the night as if the sky held the future—which, she supposed, if Akiva was flying back to them, it did, one way or another. Her heart suddenly squeezed. How deep was the future? How far did it go?

And who was in it with her?

"Me, too," said Ziri. "At least, I'll be better if the news is good. I don't know what to do if this plan fails."

"Me, neither." Karou attempted a brave face. "But we'll think of something if we have to."

He nodded. "I am hoping to see . . . the place where I was born."

So hesitant in his words. He'd been a baby when they lost their tribe, and had no memories of life before Loramendi. "You can call it home," Karou said. "At least, to me you can."

"Do you remember it?"

She nodded. "I remember the caves. Faces are harder. My parents are blurs."

It hurt to admit this. Ziri had been a baby, but she'd been seven when it happened, and there was no one else left to remember. The Kirin existed only as long as her memory held on to them, and they were mostly gone already. She hunched around a pang of conscience. Would she forget Ziri's face, too? The thought of his body in its shallow grave haunted her. The way the dirt had caught in his eyelashes, then her last glimpse of his brown eyes before she'd covered them over. The blisters on her hands still stung from her desperate burying; she couldn't feel that pain without seeing his face slack in death. But soon enough, she knew, it would lose its clarity. She should draw him—*alive*—while she still could. But she couldn't show him if she did. He had a way of reading too much into small gestures, and she didn't want to give him hope. Not the hope he wanted, anyway.

"Will you show me around, when—*if*—we get there?" he asked.

"We won't have much time," she said.

"I know. But I hope there's *some* time to be alone, even for a little while."

Alone? Karou tensed. What did he think, that they would find themselves alone?

But he tensed, too, on seeing her expression freeze. "I don't mean alone with you. I mean, not that I wouldn't . . . but I didn't mean that. Just—" He took a deep breath, let it out hard. "I'm just tired, Karou. To not be watched, and not worry that I'm making some misstep, for just a little while. That's all I meant."

Oh god, how selfish was she, thinking only of herself? The pressure on him was so great, crushing, and she couldn't even stand the thought of being alone with him? Couldn't even *pretend* to stand it?

"I'm so sorry," she said, miserable. "For all of this."

"Don't be. Please. I won't say it's easy, but it's worth it." He looked and sounded so earnest. Again, the expression was utterly foreign to the Wolf's face and voice, reshaping both, and managing even to tinge the general's untouchable beauty with *sweetness. Oh, Ziri.* "For what we might accomplish," he added. "Together."

Together.

Karou's heart mutinied, and if there had been a shadow of doubt remaining, it wouldn't have survived this surge of clarity. Her heart was half of a different "together"—a dream begun in another body, and, contrary to the lie she'd been telling herself for months, apparently not ended in it.

She forced a smile, because it wasn't Ziri's fault, and he deserved better from her, but she couldn't make herself say the word—*together.*

Not to him, anyway.

* * *

Ziri saw the strain in Karou's smile. He wanted to believe it was because she was forced to look at him through this body, but... he knew. Just like that. If he hadn't known absolutely before this moment, it was his own fault, not hers, and it settled in him now.

No hope here. No luck friction, not for him.

He bid her good night, left her there pacing on the ledge—watching for the angel to return—and felt, as he walked away, the features of this face slip back into their habitual expression. There was a minor twist at the corners of the lips to convey amusement—the cruel kind. But it wasn't Ziri's. He was not amused. Karou was still in love with Akiva? The real Thiago would have been disgusted, furious. The fake Thiago was only heartbroken.

He was also jealous, and it made him sick.

He felt the loss of his body more keenly than ever, not because it would have made a difference to Karou, but because he wanted to fly—to be free even for a little while, to exhaust his wings and lungs, smash himself against the night and let his sorrow show on this face that wasn't even his own—but he couldn't even do that. He didn't have wings. Just fangs. Just claws.

I could howl at the moons, he thought with a scrape of despair, and where his hope had been, in that space of new cold, he placed another that did little to warm it.

It had nothing to do with love; there was no use wasting hope on love. That was a matter of luck, and the only reason he'd ever had to call himself lucky was left to rot in a shallow grave in the human world. "Lucky Ziri"—what a joke.

His new hope was simply to be Kirin again, someday. To live through this—and not be found out, and not burned as a traitor for deceit, and not left to evanesce. He still counted it true, what he had told Karou just now: that it was worth it, his sacrifice, if it could help lead the chimaera toward a future free of the White Wolf's savagery.

But beyond that, Ziri's hope was modest. He wanted to fly again, and be rid of this hateful body with its mouthful of fangs, its jagged claws.

If anyone ever did love him, he thought bitterly, it might be nice to be able to touch her without drawing blood.

14

The Longest Five Minutes in History

Liraz felt . . . guilty.

It was not her favorite feeling. Her favorite feeling was *the absence of feeling*; anything else led to turmoil. Right now, for example, she found herself angry at the source of her guilt, and, though aware that this was an improper emotional response, she could not seem to *unfeel* it. She was angry because she knew she was going to have to do something to . . . assuage the guilt.

Damn it.

It was the human with his damned imploring eyes and his shivering. What did he mean, asking her to keep him warm—and his girl—as if they were *her* responsibility? What were they even doing here, traveling with beasts? It wasn't their world, and they weren't her problem. This guilt was stupid enough, but oh, it got worse.

It got stupider.

Liraz was also angry at the chimaera, and not for the reason that would have made sense. They were not, for a miracle, aiming their hamsas at her. She hadn't felt their magic drill its sick ache through her for the entire time that they'd been encamped here. And *that* was why she was angry. Because they weren't giving her a reason to be angry.

Feelings. Were. Stupid.

Hurry up, Akiva, she thought to the night sky, as if her brother might rescue her from herself. Small chance of that. He was a wreck of feelings, and that was another reason for fury. Karou had done that to him. Liraz could imagine her fingers around the girl's neck. No. She'd twist her ridiculous hair into a rope and strangle her with that.

Except, of course, that she wouldn't.

She would give Akiva five more minutes to arrive, and if he still didn't come, she would do it. Not strangle Karou. The other thing. The thing that she had to do to put a halt to this absurd spillage of *feelings.*

Five minutes.

It was her third five minutes already. And each "five minutes" was probably more like fifteen.

Finally, heavily, Liraz started walking, inwardly cursing Akiva with every step. She'd given him the longest five minutes in history, and he still hadn't arrived to put a stop to this. The camp was asleep, save for a griffon on guard duty, up on a pinnacle. He wouldn't be able to tell what was happening from up there.

The Wolf had come down from prowling the ledge a half hour ago, and retreated to one of the fires—fortunately, one of the farther ones. His eyes were closed. Everyone's were. As far as Liraz had been able to determine, no one was awake.

No one would even know what she'd done.

She was silent, prowling slowly. She arrived at the proper . . . beast huddle . . . and surveyed it with distaste for a moment before stepping near. The fire was a sad thing, producing almost no heat. There was the pair of humans, sleeping curled into each other like twins in a womb. *Fetal*, she thought. *Pathetic*. She stared at them for a long moment. They were shivering.

She looked around once, quickly.

Then she knelt beside them and opened her wings. It was within a seraph's basic power to burn low or high; a simple thought, and the heat intensified. Within seconds, the warmth spread to the whole huddle, but it took a while, Liraz noted, for the shivering to taper off. She herself had never known cold. It gave every appearance of unpleasantness. *Weak*, she thought, still watching the human pair, but there was another word lurking, defying it. *Fearless*.

They slept with their faces touching.

She couldn't wrap her mind around it. Liraz had never been that close to another living soul. Her mother? Maybe. She didn't remember. She knew that something in the sight made her want to cry, and so, she thought, she should hate it, and them. But she didn't, and she wondered why, watching them and keeping them warm, and it was a while before she lifted her eyes to look around the fire. She had wondered something else: whether Akiva and Karou had shared . . . this? This fearless nearness. But where was Karou? There was Issa, the Naja, resting peacefully, it seemed, but to Liraz's deep dismay, she saw that Karou was not among these sleepers.

So where *was* she?

Her heart slammed, and she just knew. *Godstars. How could I have been so careless?* Suffused with dread—oh, and dread made her angry—Liraz tipped back her head and looked up, and there, of course, was Karou, right above her, perched on the rocky ledge—

How long has she been there?—knees tucked up to her chest, arms wrapped around them tight. Awake? Oh yes. Cold, clearly. Watching.

Intrigued.

At the moment that their eyes met, Karou cocked her head to one side, a sudden birdlike motion. She didn't smile, but there was an open warmth in her look that seemed to reach out toward Liraz.

Who wanted to send it right back at her on the end of an arrow.

And then, simply, Karou tucked her face against her knees and settled in to sleep. Liraz didn't know what to do with herself, caught in the act. Back away? Burn everyone?

Well, maybe not that.

In the end, she stayed where she was.

But by the time the chimaera host was awakened and Akiva's return made known—with good news: the Misbegotten promise was given—Liraz was up, and no one knew what she'd done but Karou. Liraz thought of warning her not to tell anyone, but feared that caring that much about it just broached a whole new level of vulnerability and gave Karou even more power over her, so she didn't. But she *did* glare at her.

"Thank you," Akiva said quietly when they had a moment by themselves.

"For what?" Liraz demanded, squinting at him as if he might somehow know how she'd passed the last hours.

He shrugged. "For staying here. Keeping the peace. It couldn't have been fun."

"It wasn't," she said, "and don't thank me. I might be the first one to draw my sword, once I have backup."

Akiva wasn't fooled. "Mm hmm," he said, suppressing a smile. "Hamsas?"

"No," she grudgingly admitted. "Not a touch."

His brows went up in surprise. "Amazing."

It *was* amazing. Liraz grimaced, remembering her absurd anger about it—what did they mean, leaving her in peace like that? It was odd, though. It was *off*. But saying so would just sound foolish, and maybe it was. Akiva looked hopeful. Liraz hadn't seen him look like that . . . ever. It squeezed her heart—a bad and good feeling. How could a feeling be both bad *and* good? Akiva was happy; that was the good. Hazael should be here; that was the bad.

"Did you tell them?" she asked Akiva. "About Haz?" She was strumming at the bad ache in an effort to blot out the good.

Akiva nodded, and she saw with a mixture of guilt and petty triumph—but mostly guilt—that she'd blotted out his hopeful look, too, lacing it with pain. "Can you imagine how much easier this would all be, if he were here?"

Instead of me, thought Liraz, though she knew that wasn't what Akiva meant. *She* meant it, though. Maybe she'd been acting on Hazael's behalf in the night, sharing her fire, but it was feeble compared to what he would have brought to this bizarre communion of beasts and angels. Laughter and helpless grins, a swift breaking down of barriers. No one could hold out long against Haz. Her own gift, she thought with an inward shudder, was very different, and unwelcome in the future they were trying to build. All she was good at was killing.

For so long it had been a source of pride and boasting, and though the pride was gone, she would wear her boasts forever. Her sleeves were pushed all the way down, as they always were now, hiding the truth of her tally—the awful truth that it wasn't just her hands that were marked. She might have shoved her hands in the chimaera's faces back at the kasbah, but she hadn't flaunted the full and terrible truth.

The campfire tattoos, the columns of five-counts—each one made up of four fine lines with a strike-through—were not confined to her hands. Up her arms they climbed, giving her flesh the look of black lace. No one else had a count like hers. No one.

It ended at the elbows, frittering away in one incomplete count: two fine lines that were the last two kills she'd had the stomach to record. Before Loramendi.

Loramendi.

She'd been having a recurring dream since then, in which, possessed of the belief that they would grow back *clean*, she...cut her arms off.

Just how she accomplished this, the dream never made clear. Oh, the first arm was easy, sure. The second was the puzzle her mind skipped blithely over.

How, exactly, does one cut off both of her own arms?

The point was, they didn't grow back. Or at least, she always woke up before they could. She would lie there blinking, and she could never get back to sleep until she imagined an ending, one in which the fountaining blood from her stumps arranged itself into growth—bone, flesh, fingers—solidifying until she was whole again. Whole, and also unmarked.

A clean start.

A fantasy.

She'd never told anyone but Hazael, who had diverted her for a half hour after by trying to solve the puzzle of dual self-arm-severing, ending up sprawled on his back and declaring it impossible. She hadn't told Akiva because, well, he wasn't there. After Loramendi, he had left them, and even though he'd come back, he was in a world of his own. Take right now, for example. He was looking past Liraz, and she didn't have to follow his gaze to know at whom. He was staring; she snapped her fingers in front of his eyes.

"A little subtlety, brother? The chimaera will take it out on *her* if they think there's still something between you two. Haven't you heard what they call her?"

"What?" He looked genuinely surprised. "No. What do they call her?"

"Angel-lover."

She saw his eyes brighten, and rolled her own. "Don't look happy. It doesn't mean she loves you. It only means they don't trust her." She was scolding him as if *she* were the one who understood these things—or *cared*. What little Liraz knew of feelings was more than enough, thank you, but . . . well, she wasn't going to go talking about it or anything, but there was something in the good half of this ache in her heart that made her want to curl her wings around it and guard it from the cold.

ARRIVAL + 18 HOURS

15

Familiar Terror

Eliza didn't sleep the night of the Arrival. She could feel the dream perched on her shoulder, and knew what would happen if she did, but that wasn't the primary reason. No one was sleeping. The world had been stirred by a hot poker, and sparks of crazy were flying. The news in the wake of the angel's address was a horror show of riots and sectarian violence, Rapture cult vigils and mass baptisms, looting and suicide pacts and—*oh hell*—animal sacrifice. There were also, of course, the all-night Armageddon theme parties, the drunk frat boys in demon costumes pissing off rooftops, the women offering themselves up to have the angels' babies.

Predictable human idiocy.

There were ecstasy and fury, and there were desperate pleas for reason, and there were fires, so many fires. Madness, thrill, gloating, panic, noise. The NMNH was on the National Mall, and right outside, thousands were passing by, marching on the White

House, not so much united in a message to the president as just wanting to be part of something on this momentous night. What kind of something remained to be seen. Some carried votives, others megaphones; a few wore crowns of thorns and dragged enormous crosses, and more than a few guns were tucked into pockets or waistbands.

Eliza stayed in.

She didn't go home, for fear that someone would be waiting for her there. If her family had her phone number, no doubt they also knew where she lived. And where she worked, too, but there was security at the museum. Security was good.

"I'm going to stay here," she told Gabriel. "I have some work to catch up on." It wasn't entirely a lie. She had DNA to extract from a number of butterfly specimens on loan from the Museum of Comparative Zoology at Harvard. The clock was ticking on her dissertation, but she didn't imagine anyone would fault her for taking the day off, under the circumstances. She wondered if anyone in the world had gotten anything done today—besides Morgan Toth, anyway. He'd stalked off in disgust after the angel delivered his message, and spent the rest of the afternoon in the lab, as if he could prove, by contrast to his own calm, what fools the seven-odd-billion other humans on the planet were.

He'd finally left, though, to Eliza's relief, and she had the lab to herself. She locked herself in, kicked off her shoes, and tried to focus her thoughts.

What did it mean? What did it all *mean*?

There was a thrum at the base of her skull that felt like caged panic and the onset of a headache. She popped some Tylenol and curled up on the sofa with her laptop to watch the speech again. Again, the angel made her skin crawl before he even opened his mouth and slurred out his wet words. Not that you could see his mouth when he did. Why the helmet? It was so odd. You could see most of his face, but that central piece cut it in half, and the effect was jarring—combined with the fact that his eyes weren't exactly pools of warmth. They were startlingly blue, flat and cruel.

And then there was the way he hunched slightly forward, occasionally shifting his weight as though he were adjusting a load on his back, though there was nothing there.

Was there?

Nothing she could see, anyway. Eliza turned up the volume. There was that *whispering.* It filled his pauses, but she couldn't make out anything but the eerie, papery sound of it. Where was it coming from?

She watched the speech a few times through, listening to the Latin and not referencing the translation, just staring at the angel and trying to put her finger on the disparate elements of wrongness. But all the while she was doing it, she knew she was avoiding the real issue, which was his message.

CNN had been the first to replay the speech with captions, and when Eliza had read them for the first time, a chill had seeped into her and settled, beginning to transform her to ice.

. . . the Enemy that hungers . . . flesh devoured . . . the Shadow . . . the Beasts.

She made herself put on the captioned version now, unconsciously tracing the small scar at her collarbone. She didn't have the pacemaker anymore. They'd removed it when she was sixteen—not because the terror had ever abated; her body had just grown strong enough to bear it.

The Beasts are coming for you.

Ice, from the inside out. Chills and terror. *The Beasts are coming.* It was familiar terror.

Because it was the dream.

16

What Promises Are Worth

The Kirin caves.

Today, two armies would meet. Soldiers raised to hate one another, who had never looked on one another but with the urge—and intent—to kill, and who, for the most part, had never once attempted to overrule that urge. The chimaera had a small head start. They'd had Akiva and Liraz to practice at not killing, and so far, so good.

The Misbegotten hadn't been tested, but Akiva believed that his brothers and sisters would keep their promise to not strike first. Although the Kirin caves and the mountain that held them were still in the distance, he imagined that he could feel the clench of two hundred and ninety-six jaws as they ground down on every instinct, every lash of lifelong training.

"A détente can only be as strong as the least trustworthy on either side," Elyon had warned, and Akiva knew it was true. Of the Misbegotten, he believed there was no weak link. A link of chain was, in fact, their sigil, signifying that each soldier was part of a whole, and that their strength was in their unity. The Misbegotten did not make promises lightly.

And the chimaera? He watched them in flight, taking it as a good sign that they'd left off the petty flashing of hamsas with which they'd begun the journey. As to trust, that was a long way off; hope would have to do in the meantime. *Hope*. He smiled at the unconscious conjuring of Karou's name.

Karou. She was one of many in the formation, and smaller than most, but she filled Akiva's sight. A snap of azure, a glitter of silver. Even burdened by thuribles, she was as fluid in flight as an air elemental. Around her coursed dragon-things and centaurs set on wings, Naja and Dashnag and Sab, Griffon and Hartkind, and she shone in their midst like a jewel in a rough setting.

Like a star in the cupped hands of night.

What would it be like for her here? Artifacts of her tribe were everywhere in the caves: their weapons and utensils, pipes and plates and bracelets. There were musical instruments with rotted strings, and mirrors she must have looked in when she wore another face. She had been seven when it happened. Old enough to remember.

Old enough to remember the day she lost her entire tribe to angels—and still she had saved his life at Bullfinch. Still she had let herself love him.

We are the beginning, he heard inside his head, and it felt like prayer. *We always have been. This time, let it be* more *than a beginning.*

* * *

Karou saw the shadowed crescent in the face of the mountain ahead and an ache gripped her heart. Home. Was it? She'd said it to Ziri:

home. She tested it now, and it felt true. No more air quotes around it. Of everywhere she had lived in her two lives, only here had she belonged without question—neither refugee nor expat but blood daughter, her roots deep in this rock, her wings kin to this sky.

She might have grown up here, free. She might never have known the way the great cage of Loramendi cut all light to confetti and cast it to the rooftops by the stingy handful—never a full bath of sun or moon on your face but that it was slashed through by the shadows of iron bars. She might have lived her life in this effulgence of mountain light.

But then she would never have known Brimstone, Issa, Yasri, Twiga.

Her parents would be alive. They would be *here*.

She would never have been human, or tasted that world's rich and decadent peace, thrived in its friendships and art.

She would have children of her own by now—Kirin children, as wild in the wind as she had once been. A Kirin husband.

She would never have known Akiva.

At the moment that this thought flickered unbidden into her mind, she saw him. He was flying, as he had been, with Liraz, off the formation's right flank. Even at this distance she felt the jolt of his eyes meeting hers, and a whole new set of *might haves* unspooled in her.

She might have made this flight eighteen years ago, instead of dying.

So much to rue, but to what end? All unlived lives cancel one another out. She had nothing but *now*. The clothes on her back, the blood in her veins, and the promise made by her comrades. If only they would keep it.

Remembering Keita-Eiri's casual malice, she was far from confident. But there was no time to worry.

They were here.

* * *

As planned, Akiva and Liraz entered first. The opening was shaped like a moon crescent, many tall Kirin-lengths in height, but narrow, so that no more than several bodies could attempt entrance at once. There were niches high and low for archers, now unoccupied. The Kirin had been archers of renown. Misbegotten were trained in all weapons, but not generally armed with bows. Why should they be? They were the bodies sent in first to break steel on beasts. Let more precious flesh hang back and fire the arrows.

It was the steel that Akiva looked to when he scanned the assembly of soldiers, and here is what he saw:

The hands of his brothers and sisters hung awkward, because they were deprived of their usual place atop their sword pommels. That was where a swordsman rested his hand, but to illustrate their promise, the Misbegotten—all two hundred and ninety-six of them—refrained from it, lest the pose seem threatening. Some had hooked their thumbs in their belts; others clasped hands behind backs or crossed arms over chests. Uneasy, unnatural poses all.

The moment was come, and it was massive. A host of revenants was bearing down on them—such a sight as all had seen, and they had only survived it before by greeting it with gut-screams and steel. Steel without fail. To not draw now felt like madness.

But no one drew.

Akiva's pride in them in that moment was ferocious. He felt

enlarged by it, and charged by it, and he wished he could go to each one and embrace them in turn. There was no time for that now. After, if all went well. As it would. As it *must*. Elyon stood ahead of the rest, so Akiva and Liraz crossed to him.

Through the narrow crescent, the entrance "hall" to the Kirin caves revealed itself to be a series of connected caverns stair-stepping deeper into the mountain. At some time long ago, the walls had been opened up and shaped to create one continuous space, but it was still in every way rough and cavernous, complete with fanglike stalactites overhead—hiding more niches for archers; this was a fortress, not that it had saved the Kirin. The floor was of uneven rock, in which the in-billowing snow and rain caught and gathered in puddles and froze. Though the sky was clear today, there was ice on the floor, and frost plumes where each soldier's breath met the air.

The seraphim were silent, poised. The growing noise, already kicking off echoes, was not coming from them. Akiva turned on his heel and watched with the rest as the chimaera army entered.

First came a felid, petite and graceful, with a pair of griffons. All were light in their landings, though burdened with gear, thuribles included. Astride one of the griffons rode Thiago's wolf-aspect lieutenant, Ten, who slid to her feet and stalked forward, eyes making a bold sweep of the angels, to take a position facing them. The others followed her, and fell into the beginning of a line. One army facing another. It made Akiva nervous; it looked too much like battle formation, but he couldn't very well expect the chimaera to turn their backs on their foes.

More came in, and he saw a pattern emerge: the least fearsome first, the least unnatural, and with breathing space between groups so that the seraphim could accustom themselves by degrees to the presence of their mortal enemy. With each landing of two or three creatures, the formation took shape. Somewhere in the middle, the humans were delivered, and the kitchen women, and Issa, who slipped with liquid grace from the back of her Dashnag mount to incline her head and shoulders in a sinuous bow of greeting to the angels. She was beautiful, her manner more courtesan than fighter. Akiva saw Elyon blink, and stare.

As for Karou, the angels could have no idea what to make of *her*—gliding in wingless, absent beast aspect, and trailing her gemstone-blue hair. No one would recognize her for what she was: a Kirin come home. But Akiva saw the taut sculpt of her expression and knew that she was living a barrage of memory. He watched her eyes sweep the cavern and wished he could be with her.

He watched her when he should have been watching the rest. Both sides.

There must have been tells, if only he had been watching.

Eighty-seven was not a great many, as Elyon had previously observed, and they were short even that number, with the scouts Thiago had dispatched. Soon the bulk of the chimaera were on the ground. The Misbegotten had heard, of course, that these chimaera rebels were a breed apart. When their first round of strikes had hit the slave caravans in the south, they were whispered to be phantoms, the curse of Brimstone's dying words come back to haunt them. Now they saw them clearly. These beasts were winged—most—and overlarge, the biggest among them with a gray cast to their flesh that made them seem half-stone, or iron. In flew a pair of Naja who bore but passing resemblance to Issa; if Elyon blinked at *them*, it was for a different reason altogether, and far less pleasant. There were bull centaurs with hooves as broad as platters, Hartkind whose massive antler racks bristled more points than Joram's whole trophy room.

It came to Akiva that his father's barbarous trophies—chimaera heads mounted on walls—would have exploded with the Tower of Conquest and dispersed with everything else, and he was glad. He hoped they'd vaporized. He still didn't understand what he'd done that day, and even doubted at times that it *was* he who had done it. Whatever it was, it had been epic, and a failure—coming too late to save Hazael, while letting Jael get away with his life. Unfocused energy, pointless violence.

Thoughts too grim for a moment like this. Akiva shook them off. Saw Thiago's Vispeng mount out in the sky, dipping toward the crescent. They would be the last. All the other chimaera had landed; the two armies stood facing each other, tense and alert, each biting their promise between their teeth.

Or their lie.

Akiva realized that he'd been expecting this success, because he was unsurprised by it. He was pleased—or a greater word for pleased. Moved. Grateful, to the full reach of his soul.

The détente held.

...

Until it didn't.

17

Hope, Dying Unsurprised

From the rough center of the chimaera formation, Karou's view of the cavern was cropped by the larger soldiers surrounding her, but she had a clear line on Akiva and Liraz, standing apart from the rest with one of their brothers.

Here we are, Karou was thinking. Not "home"; she meant something else. Yes, it was home, and the memories were vivid, but that was the past. This…this was the threshold of *a future*. The Wolf was still in the air; she was aware of his approach behind her, but she was watching Akiva. He had done this, and she felt the marvel within herself, fluttering, like butterflies or hummingbird-moths or…like stormhunters. This was big.

Could it really happen?

It *was* happening. When she and Akiva had breathed their first thoughts of this dream to each other, they had wondered if any of their kin and comrades could be brought around. Not all, they'd always known, but some. *Some, and then more.* And here in this cavern were the *some.* Here were the beginnings of *more.*

Karou's eyes were on the angels—her eyes were on Akiva—and so . . . she witnessed the precise moment when it all fell apart.

Akiva *recoiled.* For no visible reason, he flinched as if struck. So, too, Liraz and the brother beside her, and though Karou wasn't looking directly at the greater throng of Misbegotten, she saw the wave of movement sweep over them, too. The fluttering inside her died. And she knew that this alliance had been doomed the day Brimstone dreamt up the marks.

The hamsas.

Who? Damn it, *who?*

It didn't matter if it was one chimaera or all of them. It was a trigger well and truly pulled. A flicker of a second, and everything changed. Just like that, the charge in the cavern went from tension to release—uncoiling of muscle and will—and *relief,* to shake off this madness imposed on them and fall back to the way they had ever dealt with each other.

There would be blood.

Karou's panic screamed inside her. *No. No!* She was in motion. A leap and she was airborne, over the heads of the army, and she was looking to see: Who had done it? Who had begun it? No one was standing with hands out-held. Keita-Eiri? The Sab looked alert, alarmed, her hands clenched in fists; if she had done this, she had done it like a coward, like a *villain,* picking a fight that must kill so many. . . .

Zuzana and Mik. Karou's heartbeat stuttered. She had to get her friends out.

Her look swept backward, an arc that took in the collective

crouch to pounce, the baring of fangs, the first instant of soldiers giving in to instinct.

And she saw Thiago, still in the air. Uthem, with his head stretched forth on his long neck, suspending his beautiful length from his two sets of wings. And she saw a streak in her peripheral vision. A second later she registered the *twing* that had preceded it…

As the arrow pierced Uthem's throat.

* * *

From the first sick touch of magic, the single word *no* pounded in Akiva's head. *No no no no no no!*

And then the arrow—

The Vispeng screamed. It was the scream of horses dying, and the sound filled the cavern, it entered them all, and the creature was falling. It collapsed out of the air, the chimaera host leaping clear beneath it as it came in reeling to pitch headlong onto the rock floor. The impact was violent. Eyes rolling wild, its neck whipped and lashed, the arrow splintering as its long, gleaming body torqued, hurling its rider off before finally scudding to a sickening stillness.

Thus was the White Wolf delivered to the feet of the Misbegotten: flung right to them over the ice-slicked floor as, at his back, his army sent up a roar.

Akiva saw it all through a veil of horror. Had the chimaera planned this treachery? The hamsas had come first, of that he was certain.

But the arrow. Where had it come from? Overhead. Akiva's eye caught flickers of movement amid the stalactites, and his horror was joined by fury at his brothers and sisters. The ferocious pride he had felt in them vanished. All those hands hovering clear of sword hilts—it was an empty show when archers hid overhead with bowstrings stretched taut. And as for the hands, they wouldn't hover for long.

The White Wolf was on his knees. Teeth bared in grim smiles on both sides. Dead center in the seraph formation, a hand reached. The movement cascaded. It was like choreography. A split second and one hand became three became ten became fifty, and Akiva's own uncoiling reaction was too slow, and desperate. He raised empty hands in supplication, heard Liraz give a hoarse cry of, "*No!*"

There was only this second. A *second*. Hands on hilts. In one second a tide turns, and a tide cannot be unturned. Once those swords sang free of their sheaths, once those winched beast muscles unwound, this day would run as red as the Kirin's last and fill this cavern once again with blood, to all of their sorrow.

A flash of azure. Akiva's eyes met Karou's, and her look was unbearable.

It was hope, dying unsurprised.

And for the third time in his life, Akiva felt within himself the chrysalis of fire and clarity—an instant, and then the world changed. As if a muting skin were peeled back, all was laid before him: steady and crisp-edged, gleaming and *still*. This was *sirithar*, and Akiva was poised inside a moment.

Had he told his brothers and sisters that the present is the single second dividing the past from the future? In this state of calm, crystal brilliance—the gathering violence slowed to a dream—there was no division. Present and future were one. Every soldier's intention was painted in light before him, and Akiva saw it all before it happened. In those strokes of light were swords drawn.

Hands hewn off, collected in heaps, hamsas and kill tallies mingled, seraph hands and chimaera, scattered.

Foretold by light, this beginning died, just like the last, and a new beginning took its place: Jael would return to Eretz and find no rebel force to fight through—neither chimaera nor bastards to oppose him but only their blood frozen to red ice on this cavern floor, because they'd been so kind as to kill each other for him. The way would be open, and Eretz would suffer. Akiva saw all of this, the grand, echoing, world-shaking shame of it, and he saw... in the tilt toward chaos... in the seconds still to come, how Karou would unsheathe her moon blades.

She would kill today, and perhaps she would die.

If this second was allowed to turn.

It must not be allowed to turn.

In Astrae, Akiva had loosed from his mind a pulse of rage, frustration, and anguish so profound that it had exploded the great Tower of Conquest, symbol of the Empire of Seraphim. He couldn't fathom what it was, or how he'd done it.

And, still unfathoming, he felt another pulse slip loose from that same unfamiliar place within him.

It went out and was gone from him, whatever it was—*what was it?*—and it took *sirithar* with it, so that Akiva was thrust back into the ordinary flow of time—fast, dim, and loud. It was like passing from a mirror-smooth lake into rapids. He staggered a step, robbed of the brilliance that had seized him, and he could only watch, unbreathing, to see what his magic would wreak.

And to see if it would matter.

18

A Candle Flame Extinguished by a Scream

All those seraphim, hands to hilts, and chimaera in the coiled instant before the spring.

Thiago was on his knees in the gap between armies—he would be the first to die. Karou's hands reached for her own blades, and within her was still the hollow scream of *No!* If there had been time to think in that second—that second that was as full of *intent* as any second had ever been, as full of the promise of blood—she would not have believed any power could stop it. Her hope had died with the angels' first recoil.

Her hope had died. She thought. She wouldn't have believed there could be a depth of despair beneath this one. But then it hit her.

Sudden and devastating. It dragged her under.

The certainty of *ending.* Seeing the angel blades ready to slide free and slash, hearing the snarl of chimaera ready to tear the future apart with their teeth, it was as if every shred of thought or feeling that had ever or would ever exist was stamped out and replaced by this . . . this . . . this bitter smear of pointlessness.

Dead end, it shrieked, *and for what?*

The despair was entire, complete as a possession, but fleeting. It released her, and was gone, but it left Karou gutted, guttered, feeling for all the world like . . .

. . . a candle flame extinguished by a scream.

And in the aftermath of its enormity she might have been nothing more than the curl of smoke left to drift and disperse at the end of all things—at the evanescence of the world itself.

Dead end, and for what?

Dead end. Dead end.

And her hands failed to finish what they had begun. She didn't draw. She couldn't. Her blades stayed slung at her hips as she dragged in a breath, almost surprised by the feeling—that there was life still in her, and air to breathe.

One second.

Another breath, another second.

She was in the air and she let herself drop, landing in a sagging crouch to fall to her knees, and her mind was still an echo of *No!* as she became aware that, around her . . . nothing was happening.

Nothing. Was happening.

Bunched beast muscles had fallen slack. Tally-blacked hands were frozen on sword pommels; seraph blades caught the light, many half-drawn, and halted there.

The two bloodthirsty armies had just . . . stopped.

How?

The moment seemed very long. Karou, dulled by the immensity of her despair, scarcely knew what to make of it. She had felt the moment tilt and hurl them toward disaster. How was it that they had all simply *stopped*? Had she misread the tilt, the disaster? Had it all been posturing on both sides, just rattling of swords? Could it be as simple as that? No. No, she was missing something. Around her there was mute confusion, slow blinking, and drags of breath as hoarse as her own. She tried to shake off her fog.

And then she saw, in the no-man's-land between facing armies, the White Wolf rise to his feet. All eyes fixed on him, hers, too, and the fog began to abate.

Could it be... had this somehow been *his* doing?

She rose. It was difficult to move. Her despair may have gone, but it had left its heaviness draped over her, thick and bleak. She saw that the Wolf's knees were bloodied from the impact of his fall; Uthem lay dead, and the pool of his blood was spreading. Thiago had risen just as the blood overtook him, and it pooled now around his wolf feet, slicking their white fur and spreading onward, toward the first file of angels. Uthem was large; there was a lot of blood, and the Wolf made a dramatic picture standing in it, all in white but where his own blood blossomed at his knees and brow. And his palms.

His palms were bloody, and he held them pressed together. It looked like prayer, but it was clear what it meant. Instead of attack, he held his hamsas blind, ink eye to ink eye. He held his power in check, and himself. A soldier dead on the ground, and no reprisal from the vicious White Wolf? It was a powerful gesture, but Karou still didn't understand. How had it halted three hundred Misbegotten in mid-draw?

Thiago spoke. "I pledge on the ashes of Loramendi that I and mine come to you for coalition, not for blood. This makes a bad beginning, and was no plan of mine. I will discover who among us has raised a hand against my express command. That soldier, whoever it may be, has broken *my word*." This he spoke low in his throat, his voice rough-edged with disgust, and a shiver trilled down Karou's spine.

Thiago turned, sweeping the gathering of his soldiers with a slit-eyed look. "That soldier," he said, peering into the heart of his army, "courted the death of this entire company today, and will be disciplined."

The promise was raw; they all knew what he meant by it. His gaze was deliberate and piercing, and lingered several times on particular soldiers, who withered beneath it.

He turned back to the Misbegotten. "There is reason to risk our lives, but we are no longer that reason to one another. A bad beginning may still be a beginning." He was vehement. He sought Akiva then; Karou felt him waiting for the angel to step in and help him put the pieces of this truce back together. She waited, too, sure of him—Akiva had brought them here; he must have words to mend this moment—but the pause dragged out a brief, strained silence.

Something was wrong. Even Liraz was squinting at Akiva, waiting. Karou felt a stab of concern. He looked unsteady, even ill, his broad shoulders bowed by some strain. What was wrong with him? She'd seen him look like that before; she'd *made* him look like that, but this couldn't be the effect of the hamsas, could it? Why should they hit him harder than the rest?

With evident effort, he said, finally, "Yes. A beginning," but there was a hollowness to his voice, compared with the Wolf's rich tone and strong words, even as he went on to say, "a very bad beginning. I regret this death, and . . . deeply I regret our readiness to cause it. I hope it can be put right."

"It can and will," replied the Wolf. "Karou? Please."

A summons. Karou felt spotlighted; fear darted erratic in her veins, but she gathered her will and moved. All focus shifted to her as she threaded her way through the host, straight to Uthem's side. She was standing in his blood. A nod from Thiago and she knelt, unslung the gleaning staff from across her back and lowered it into position, thurible swaying on its chain. A switch alongside the shaft activated a wheel lock similar to a friction-wheel mechanism in an antique pistol; it ignited the incense chamber in the thurible with a report like a snap of metallic fingers. An instant later, a sulfurous tang effused from it.

She felt Uthem's soul respond. It felt like gray skies and signal fires, the breaking of waves. Impressions flickered and faded as his soul slipped into the thurible and was safe. A half turn to lock it, a flick to extinguish the incense fuse, and she rose from her kneel, taking care to keep her hamsas from flashing any magic at the angels.

All eyes were on her. She glanced to Thiago. They hadn't talked about this, but it felt right. She said, "I have never resurrected a seraph, but as long as we are fighting on the same side, I will. If you wish it, though you may not. Think it over; it's your choice. My offer, my promise. And something else." One by one, she met the eyes of the rank of angels directly before her. "I might not look like it," she said, "but I am Kirin, and this is my home. So please step aside and let us enter."

And they did. They didn't exactly leap to it, but they parted, clearing the way for her. She looked back, found Issa in the throng. Zuzana and Mik, wide-eyed. Akiva's presence was like a flare in the periphery, calling to her, but she didn't look to him. She stepped forward. Thiago fell in beside her. The host came behind them, and the

Misbegotten let them pass. With blood on their boots, Karou and Thiago led their army inside.

* * *

"How did he do that?" Liraz breathed.

The question jolted Akiva, finally, out of his post-*sirithar* torpor. "How did who do what?"

"The Wolf." She looked stunned. "I was sure we were done. I *felt* it. And then..." She shook her head as if to clear it. "How did he stop it?"

Akiva stared at her. She thought *Thiago* had stopped it?

He gave a hard laugh. What else could he do? He knew that a pulse had gone out from him—not explosive this time—and whatever it had carried with it, he had felt the soldiers' collective intention sever. *He* had done it. He had stopped this slaughter from happening, and... no one had any idea, not even Liraz, and certainly not Karou.

While he had reeled in his magic's blowback, barely able to string a coherent sentence together, the Wolf had risen to the occasion and claimed the moment, and managed to earn himself even Liraz's awe? What then must Karou be feeling for him? Akiva watched her disappear down the passage at the head of her army, the White Wolf at her side—a striking pair they made—and all he could do was laugh. It ground like glass in his chest. *Perfect*, he thought. What a perfect backhand from... what? Fate, the godstars? *Chance?*

"What?" demanded Liraz. "Why are you laughing?"

"Because life's a bastard," was all Akiva could say.

"Well then," was his sister's flat reply. "I guess we fit right in."

19

The Hunt

Across Eretz, a pulse of magic surged. There was no Wind to presage it this time, no sound or stir, so nearly everyone who felt it—and *everyone* felt it—believed it theirs alone, their own despair. It was a wave of raw emotion so potent that, for an instant, it carved out every other feeling and took its place, in its brief passage colonizing every thinking creature—every *feeling* creature—with the absolute conviction of *the end*.

Its passage was swift and bleak; it raced across land and sky and sea, and no creature was immune to it, and no material nor mineral barrier to it.

Far faster than wings could have carried it there, it swept through Astrae, the capital of the Empire of Seraphim, and just as fast was gone again. In its silent aftermath, no citizen connected it with the shattering of their great Tower of Conquest.

But at the site of the Tower's husk, inside the vast and twisted metal skeleton that was all that remained of it, there stood five angels who did. Seraphim they were, but not citizens of the Empire. They'd come from afar, hunting—*hunting hunting hunting*—and now, in unison, like compass needles spun by the same magnet, they turned south and east. This overwhelming despair was trespass and violation; they knew it was not their own, and each paused just long enough to sound the depths of its appalling power before thrusting it away. Another taste from the unknown magus who plucked at the strings of the world.

"Beast's Bane," they'd heard him called in the harsh rumor-whispers of this craven city. Murderer and traitor, chimacra-killer, bastard and father-slayer. He had done this.

Now, with eyes the color of fire, the five Stelians fixed on the distant Adelphas Mountains.

And Scarab, their queen, spread her wings and said, with perfect wrath, through sharpened teeth, "On with the hunt."

20

Warp

In the Far Isles it was night, and the new bruise that blossomed in the sky would not be visible till dawn. It wasn't like the others. Indeed, it soon engulfed the others—all of them lost in its dark sprawl. From horizon to horizon it spread, deeper than indigo, nearly as black as the night sky itself. It was more than color, this bruise. It was warp, it was suction. It was concavity and distortion. Eidolon of the dancing eyes had said the sky was tired, and ached. She had downplayed the matter.

The sky was failing. The stormhunters didn't need to see it blacken. They *felt* it.

And started to scream.

21

Nitid's Hands

The Kirin caves weren't so much a village within a mountain as a series of them, connected by a network of passages radiating out from a massive communal space. A collaboration between nature, time, and hands, the space was raw and flowing, unplanned and improbable. A wonder. Overall, the impression was of a miraculous accident of geology, but in truth it was a miraculous accident of geology that had been shaped over hundreds of years by generations of Kirin adhering to a simple aesthetic: "Nitid's hands." They were the tools of the goddess, and their duty, as they saw it, was not to stand out or aggrandize themselves, but to copy—as it were—her style.

Scarcely a detail anywhere announced itself as "made." There were no corners, and even the stairs could almost have been naturally occurring—asymmetrical and imprecise.

It was dark, but not perfectly. Light wells admitted sunshine and moonlight, amplified by hidden hematite mirrors and crystal lenses. And it was never silent. Intricate channels conducted the wind throughout, carrying fresh air and making an eerie, ever-present ambient sound that was part dark and stormy night and part whalesong.

Walking through, Karou experienced it all in a rush of old and new experience that was like the convergence of two swift rivers: Madrigal's memory and Karou's marvel, merging at every step. Entering the grand central cavern, she at once remembered it and was struck breathless by the sight of it, stopping dead to throw back her head and stare.

She remembered the swoop of Kirin wings overhead, the calls and laughter and music, the flurry of festivals and the ordinariness of everyday life. She had learned to fly in this cavern.

It was immense, several hundred feet in height, so vast that echoes got lost and only sometimes found their way back. Screens of stalagmites stood up from the floor in undulating walls—dozens of feet high, hundreds of thousands of years forming, but it would be millions before they ever joined with their counterparts high overhead. The walls were veined with ore, glinting with gold, and terraced in places into niches that reminded her of honeycomb, or the balconies in an opera house. This was where the seraph soldiers had made their camps, looking down on the central space where orderly fire rings showed signs of recent use.

"Wow," she heard Zuzana murmur behind her, and when she turned to glance back, she glimpsed the Wolf's face as he swallowed hard, struggling against overwhelming emotion. There was no one to see; all the host came behind them, so only Karou witnessed the look of yearning and loss that briefly overtook his features.

"Come on," she said, and crossed the cavern.

Together, the chimaera and Misbegotten numbered somewhere

near four hundred, which was probably more than the number of Kirin who had lived in this mountain in the tribe's heyday, but there was room enough for all, and room enough to keep them separate. The seraphim could have the grand cavern; it was cold here. Her breath came out in clouds. Deeper down, the villages were warmed by geothermal heat. She made for a passage that would lead them to one. Not her own. She wanted to leave that one in peace, visit it alone, on her own time, if ever such a time came.

"This way."

22

The Abyss's Mad Gawk

"A whole chocolate cake, a bath, a bed. In that order." Zuzana ticked off three wishes on her fingers.

Mik nodded in appreciation. "Not bad," he said. "But no cake. I'll have goulash from Poison Kitchen, with apple strudel and tea. Then, yes: a bath and a bed."

"Nope. That's five. You used up your wishes on food."

"My whole meal is my first wish. Goulash, strudel, tea."

"Doesn't work that way. Wish fail. I win. You and your full belly will just have to watch while I take my magnificent hot bath and sleep in my wondrously soft warm bed." Hot bath, soft bed—what a delirious fantasy. Zuzana's aching muscles pleaded with her for mercy, but it was out of her power. They had no wishes; this was only a game.

Mik's eyebrows lifted. "Oh. I have to watch you bathe, do I? Poor me."

"*Yes*, poor you. Wouldn't you rather bathe *with* me?"

"Indeed." He was solemn. "Indeed I would. And the wish police will have a hard time keeping me out."

"Wish police." Zuzana snorted.

"Wish police?" said Karou from the doorway.

They were in a series of small caves that Zuzana understood had constituted a family dwelling in the days of the Kirin. With four rooms, shaped with the flow of the rock, it was kind of like an apartment inside a mountain. It had its amenities—some kind of natural heat, and even a rock closet with a sluice hole that strongly suggested a toilet (though Zuzana wanted confirmation of that before proceeding)—but there was no apparent bath, or beds. There were some piled furs in the corner, but they were gross and old, and Zuzana was pretty sure that a variety of otherworldly vermin were living out rich, multigenerational sagas in them.

There was a whole complex of dwellings like this arranged around a kind of village "square"—a much smaller version of the extraordinary cavern they'd passed through on the way here. The soldiers were getting settled, not that there was much to settle. Well, Aegir the smith had work to do, and Thiago had gone off with his lieutenants to do whatever it is war types do before an epic battle. Zuzana could wrap her mind around none of that, and didn't want to. Not the truth about "Thiago," and not the epic battle, either. If she tried, she started to shake and her mind switched channels on her, like it was flipping around looking for the kids' programming or—ooh!—Food Network.

Speaking of food, while Mik was scouting out the best spot for "resurrection headquarters," Zuzana had taken a few minutes to help the funny little furred chimaera women, Vovi and Awar, set up a temporary kitchen and organize the supplies they'd brought from Morocco. It didn't do any harm to get in good with the food-providers, and she *may* have gotten a few dried apricots in the bargain.

A couple of months ago, if someone had told her she'd get excited about a few dried apricots, she'd have given them the eyebrow. Now she thought she could probably use them as currency, like cigarettes in prison.

"We're playing Three Wishes," she told her friend. "Cake, hot bath, soft bed. How about you?"

"World peace," said Karou.

Zuzana rolled her eyes. "Yes, Saint Karou."

"Cure for cancer," Karou went on. "And unicorns for all."

"Bluh. Nothing ruins Three Wishes like altruism. It has to be something for yourself, and if it doesn't include food, it's a lie."

"I did include food. I said unicorns, didn't I?"

"Mmm. You're craving unicorn, are you?" Zuzana's brow furrowed. "Wait. Do they have those here?"

"Alas, no."

"They did," said Mik. "But Karou ate them all."

"I am a voracious unicorn predator."

"We'll add that to your personals ad," said Zuzana.

Karou's eyebrows shot up. "My personals ad?"

"We might have been composing personals ads on the way here," she allowed. "To pass the time."

"Of course you were. So what was mine?"

"Well, we couldn't write them down, obviously, but I think it was something like: *Beautiful interspecies badass seeks, um . . . non–mortal enemy for uncomplicated courtship, long walks on the beach, and happily ever after?*"

Karou didn't respond right away, and Zuzana saw that Mik was giving her a disapproving look. *What?* she replied by way of eyebrow. She'd left out the "genocidal angels need not apply" part, hadn't she? But then her friend dropped her face into her hands. Her shoulders started shaking, and Zuzana couldn't tell if it was from laughter or sobs. It had to be laughter, didn't it? "Karou?" she asked, worried.

Karou lifted her face back up, and there were no tears, but there wasn't a whole lot of mirth, either. "Uncomplicated," she said. "What's *that* like?"

Zuzana glanced at Mik. *This* was what uncomplicated was like. It was wonderful. Karou didn't miss the glance. She smiled at them, wistful. "Just know how lucky you are," she said.

"I do," said Mik.

"I *definitely* do," agreed Zuzana, quickly, and with a little more gusto than was really her style. She still felt so... *off.* Oh, hungry, dirty, and tired, most definitely—hence her three wishes—but this went way beyond that. For a minute there, back in the entrance cavern, she'd felt like she was staring at the end of the freaking world.

What the hell was *that?*

When she was a kid, she'd had this favorite doll—well, it was a duck, actually—and she had apparently rendered it quite vile with the depredations of her toddler adoration, including, as her brother Tomáš liked to remind her, her habit of sucking on its eyes. She'd found it comforting, the hard clicky smoothness of them against her tiny teeth.

Less than comforting had been her parents' campaign to persuade her that *this could kill her.* "You could choke, darling. You could stop breathing."

But what did that really mean to a toddler? It was Tomáš who had driven the message home. By...choking her. Just a little. Brothers, so helpful in matters of death demonstration. "You could die," he'd said cheerfully, his hands around her throat. "Like this."

It had worked. She'd understood. Things can kill you. All kinds of things, like toys, or older brothers. And as she'd grown up, that list had just gotten longer and longer.

But she'd never felt it this powerfully before. What was that Nietzsche quote that Goth poet-types love so much? *When you look into the abyss, the abyss also looks into you?* Well, the abyss had looked into her. No. It had gawked; it had *glared.* Zuzana was pretty sure it had left scorch marks on her soul, and it was hard to imagine ever feeling normal again.

But she wasn't going to go complaining to Karou about every fear and freak-out. She had *wanted* to come here. Karou had warned her it would be dangerous—and okay, the warning in the abstract was a little bit like telling a toddler about choking, minus the demonstration...but she was here now, and she didn't want to be the crybaby in this gang.

And as for *lucky*? "I'm lucky I'm even alive," she announced. "When I was little, I sucked on duck eyeballs."

Mik and Karou just looked at her, and Zuzana was glad to see Karou's wistfulness give way to bemused concern. "That's...interesting, Zuze," she ventured.

"I know. And I don't even try. Some people are just interesting. *You*, though, with your drab, ordinary life. You should get out more. Try new things."

"Uh-huh," said Karou, and Zuzana was rewarded with a glimpse of that elusive mirth. "You're right. So dull. I'll take up stamp collecting. That's interesting, isn't it?"

"No. Unless you're pasting them onto your body and wearing them as clothes."

"That sounds like someone's semester project at school."

"It totally does!" Zuzana agreed. "Helen would do it. But she'd make it a performance. Start out naked with a big bowl of stamps so people could lick them and paste them on her."

Karou finally laughed outright, and Zuzana felt pride of accomplishment. *Laugh achieved.* Maybe she couldn't make Karou's life—or love—less complicated, and maybe she didn't have any helpful hints when it came to, oh, angel invasions or dangerous deceptions or armies that clearly just wanted to start killing each other, but she could do this at least. She could make her friend laugh.

"So what now?" she asked. "The angels throw a magnificent banquet in our honor?"

Karou laughed again, but it was a dark sound. "Not exactly. Next is the war council."

"War council," repeated Mik, sounding a little dazed, as Zuzana most definitely felt. Dazed and far, far out of her depth. She imagined that every hair on her body was still standing on end from the weird, electric horror of the past hour. Seeing Uthem die? That was a first for her. She'd had to walk through *his blood*, and while that hadn't seemed to fuss the soldiers (as cool as if they waded through blood every morning to get to breakfast), it *had* fussed her, though she'd barely had time to process it. She'd been so . . . *spun* by her own paralyzed terror, and what she was now thinking of as "the abyss's mad gawk."

Karou gave a hard exhale. "That *is* why we're here." On *here*, she made a quick scan of the room and added, "Strange as it is."

And Zuzana felt even more out of her depth, trying to imagine what it meant to her friend, being back here. She couldn't, of course. This was the site of a massacre. Maybe it was the echo of the abyss that brought it on, but she imagined walking up to her own family's house and finding it deserted, the beds decayed and no one there to greet her—*ever*—and she sucked in a little breath.

"Are you all right?" Karou asked her.

"I'm fine. More to the point, are *you* all right?"

Karou nodded, smiled a little. "Yeah, I am, actually." She raised her torch and looked around. "It's weird. When I lived here, it was the world. I didn't know that everyone didn't live inside mountains."

"It's pretty amazing," Zuzana said.

"It is. And you haven't even seen the best part yet." Karou looked sly.

"Ooh, what? Please tell me it's a cave where cupcakes grow like mushrooms."

Score another laugh for Zuzana.

"No," said Karou. "And I don't have any cake, either, and I'm afraid the bed situation can't be helped, but . . ." She paused, waiting for Zuzana to figure it out.

Zuzana did. *Could it be?* "Don't tease me."

Karou's smile was pure; she was happy to give happiness. "Come on. I think we can spare a few minutes."

23

The Whole Point

The thermal pools were as Karou remembered, but also not at all as she remembered, because in her memories, there were Kirin here. Whole families, bathing together. Old women gossiping. Children splashing. She could feel her mother's hands working selen root into a lather on her head, and she even remembered its herbal smell, mingling with the sulfur odor of the springs.

"It's beautiful," said Mik, and it was: the water a chalky pale green, the rocks like pastel drawings, rose and sea foam. It was intimate but not small, not one pool but a cluster of joined baths fed by a gentle cascade, and the ceiling seemed to ripple, ashimmer with growths of crystal and curtains of pale pink darkmoss, so named because it grew in the dark, not because it was.

"Look over here," said Karou, and held out her torch, leading the way to the place where the cavern wall was pure, polished hematite. A mirror.

"Wow," breathed Zuzana, and the three regarded their reflections, side by side. They looked bedraggled and reverent. The curved surface warped them, and Karou had to move around to gauge what of the distortion of her face was from the funhouse mirror effect, and what was left over from her beating. The attack seemed ages ago, but her body knew differently. It had been two days, and her face was not recovered. Her psyche wasn't, either. In fact, the mirror distortion struck her as fitting: an outward manifestation of the inner warp she was trying to keep hidden.

They peeled off their clothes and slipped into the water, which was hot and very soft, so that within seconds of immersion, their limbs felt as smooth as doll porcelain, their hair like swansdown. Karou's and Zuzana's drifted like mermaid coils on the eddying surface.

Karou closed her eyes and sank beneath the surface, head and all, and let the moving water draw the tension out of her. If she were to play Three Wishes honestly, she might wish she could drift off as if this were Lethe, the river of oblivion, and take a nice long break from armies and doom. Instead, she washed and rinsed and climbed out. Mik politely faced away as she dressed in clean clothes. "Clean," that is, if dipped in a Moroccan river and dried on a dusty rooftop counted as clean.

"You probably have an hour on the torch," she told her friends, leaving them one and taking the other. "Can you find your way back?"

They said they could, so Karou left the pair to their perfect, uncomplicated enjoyment of each other, and tried not to be too jealous as her feet carried her back up toward the humming enmity of the armies.

"There you are."

She'd rounded a bend, nearing the hivelike center of the village, and there was Thiago. *Ziri.* When they saw each other, a flash of feeling transfigured him. He hid it quickly, but she saw it, and knew it. It was love inseparable from sadness, and it made her heart ache for him. "I'm with you," she had told him back at the kasbah, so he wouldn't feel so alone in his stolen body. But he *was* alone. She wasn't with him, even when she was. And he knew it.

She made herself smile. "I was just coming to find you." That was true, in any case. "Has anything been decided?"

He sighed and shook his head. He was unkempt, something the Wolf never was, except perhaps immediately after battle. His hair was in disarray, his brow dark with dried blood from his crash landing, and his knees and hands, scraped and bloodied, looked like meat. He cast a glance around and beckoned Karou through a doorway.

Only for an instant did she stiffen and want to demur. *He's not the Wolf,* she told herself, preceding him into the small chamber. It was dark, musty. Karou closed the door and made an arc with her sputtering torch to confirm that they were alone.

Alone. Was this what Ziri had hoped for, back in the night, just this small sad slice of time to let his Wolf posture fall slack? He sagged against a wall, plainly exhausted. He said, "Lisseth proposed we choose a scapegoat for a show execution."

"What?" Karou cried. "That's awful!"

"Which is why I said no, unless she wished to volunteer herself."

"I wish."

"She declined." He gave a wry, tired smile, then pitched his voice low. "They're still waiting for this to make sense. For me to reveal the true plan, which must, of course, involve slaughter."

"Do you think they suspect anything?" Karou asked, anxious, her voice a secret murmur like his. She wished she could speak to him in Czech as she could Zuzana and Mik, and not have to worry about being overheard.

"Something, yes. But I don't think they're near the truth."

"They better not get near it."

"I'm acting like I have an endgame that I just haven't shared with them, but I don't know how long that will hold. I was never in his inner circle. What if he told them his plans, and this secrecy looks wrong to them? As for this problem..." He lifted his hands to his head and drew in a sharp breath at the contact of injury to injury. "What *would* the Wolf do? He would do nothing. He would give the seraphim no one, and stare them down for asking."

"You're right." The image came to Karou easily, of the contempt the Wolf would hold in his eyes, facing his foes. "Of course, he really *would* be orchestrating a slaughter."

"Yes. But this is our tactic, in all of this: to begin believably, where he would, but not follow where he would take it. I'm giving the angels no one, and no apology. It's a chimaera matter, and that's the end of it."

"And if it happens again?" Karou asked.

"I'll see that it doesn't." Simple, heavy, full of threat and regret.

Karou knew that Ziri wanted no such responsibility, but she remembered his words in the air—"We will fight for our world to the last echo of our souls"—and the way he'd stood between two blooded armies and held them apart, and she didn't doubt that he could rise to any occasion. "Okay," she said, and that was the end of it.

A silence unspooled between them, and with the matter decided, the quality of "alone" changed. They were two tired people standing in the flickering dark, a tangle of feelings and fears—love, trust, hesitation, sorrow.

"We should get back," Karou said, though she wished she could give Ziri his peace for a while longer. "The seraphim will be waiting."

He nodded, and followed her to the door. "Your hair is wet," he said.

"There are baths," she told him, opening the door, remembering that he wouldn't know that.

"I can't say that doesn't sound good." He indicated the blood-caked fur of his feet, his raw-meat hands. There was the wound where his head had smashed the cave floor, too. She stepped closer to him, reached up to touch it; he winced. A good goose egg had risen under the dark, crusted blood.

"Ouch," she said. "Are you having any dizziness?"

"No. Just throbbing. It's fine." He was scrutinizing her face in return. "You're looking a lot better."

She touched her cheek, realizing the pain had gone. The swelling, too. She touched her torn earlobe and found that the flesh had knit itself together. *What?*

With a little gasp, she remembered. "The water," she said. It came back to her like a dream fragment. "It has some healing properties."

"Really?" Ziri looked down at his raw hands again. "Can you show me the way?"

"Um." Karou paused awkwardly. "I would, but Zuzana and Mik are in there." She blushed. It was possible that Zuzana and Mik were too tired to act like Zuzana and Mik, but with the restorative waters, it was likely that her friends would be making use of their hour of solitude, in, um, Zuzana-and-Mik fashion.

Ziri was not slow to take her meaning. He blushed, too, and the humanity that flooded his cold, perfect features was extraordinary. Ziri wore this body so much more beautifully than Thiago had.

"I'll wait," he said with a low, embarrassed laugh, avoiding Karou's eyes, and she laughed, too.

And there they were, in the doorway, blushing, laughing their embarrassed laughs, and standing too close—her hand drawn back from his brow but her body still curved toward his—when someone came around the bend in the passage and stopped dead.

Dear gods and stardust, Karou wanted to yell. *Are you kidding me?*

Because of course, of course, it was Akiva. The wind music had drowned out his footsteps. He was not ten feet away, and as skilled as he was at concealing those flares of sudden feeling, he did not entirely succeed in concealing this one.

A jerk of disbelief in his halt, a creep of color across his cheeks. Even, Karou was sure, an unguarded intake of breath. On stoic Akiva, these small signs were equivalent to reeling from a slap.

Karou stepped away from the Wolf, but she couldn't undo the picture they had made in that second. She'd felt her own flare of feeling at the sight of Akiva, but doubted that he could have detected it in her laughing, blushing face, and now, to make matters worse, there was the guilt of discovery, as if she had been caught in some betrayal.

Laughing and blushing with the White Wolf? As far as he knew, it *was* betrayal.

Akiva. The pull to fly to him was its own kind of gravity, but it was only her heart that moved. Her feet stayed rooted, heavy and guilty.

Akiva's voice was cold and quick. "We've selected a representative council. You might do the same." He paused, and on his face played the reverse process as that on the Wolf's. As he stood looking at the pair of them, his humanity retreated, and he was as Karou had first seen him in Marrakesh: soul-dead. "We're ready when you are."

Whenever you're done blushing by torchlight with the White Wolf.

And he turned on his heel and was gone before they could reply.

"Wait," said Karou, but her voice came out weak, and if he heard her over the wind music, he didn't turn back. *We could tell him*, she thought. *We could have told him the truth.* But the opportunity was lost, and it was as though he took the air with him. For a long second, she couldn't breathe, and when she did, she tried her best to make it sound measured and normal.

"I'm sorry," said Ziri.

"For what?" she asked with poor false lightness, as if he hadn't seen and understood everything. But of course he had.

"I'm sorry that things can't be different. For you." For her and Akiva, Karou understood that he meant, and—dear Ziri—he was sincere. The Wolf's face was vivid with his compassion.

"They can be," she said, somewhat to her own surprise, and in place of her guilt and her quiet torment, she felt resolve. Brimstone had believed it, and so had Akiva, and . . . the fiercest happiness in her two lives had been when *she* had believed it. "Things *can* be different," she told Ziri. And not just for her and Akiva. "For all of us," she said, summoning a smile. "That's the whole point."

24

Cue Apocalypse

Several hours later, Karou had entirely forgotten what that smile felt like.

Things can be different, sure. But first, you have to kill a whole lot of angels and probably mess up human civilization forever. And oh, you may well lose anyway. You might all die. No big deal.

It wasn't a surprise, exactly. It wasn't as if anyone was calling this meeting a "peace council."

It was one for the history books, no question about that. High in the Adelphas Mountains, which had ever stood as the main land bastion between the Empire and the free holdings, the representatives of two rebel armies faced one another. Seraphim and chimaera, Misbegotten and revenants, Beast's Bane and the White Wolf, not enemies today but allies.

It was going about as well as could be expected.

"I am in favor of the clear course." This was Elyon, the brother who had stepped into Hazael's place by Akiva's side. He and two others—Briathos and Orit—stood for the Misbegotten alongside Akiva and Liraz. With Thiago and Karou were Ten and Lisseth.

"And the clear course is?" inquired the Wolf.

Elyon said, as if it were evident, "We close the portals. Let the humans deal with Jael."

What?

This was not what Karou had been expecting. "No," she blurted, though it wasn't her place to respond.

Liraz objected at the same moment, and their words collided in the air. *No.* Positioned dead across the table from each other, they met eyes, Liraz's narrow, Karou's carefully neutral.

No, they would not close the portals between the worlds, trapping Jael and his thousand Dominion soldiers on the other side for humans to "deal" with. On this they might agree, though for different reasons.

"Jael will be dealt with by me," said Liraz. She spoke quietly, tonelessly. It was unnerving, and had the effect of sounding incontrovertible, like a fact long established. "Whatever else happens, that much is certain."

Liraz's reason was vengeance, and Karou didn't fault her for it. She had seen Hazael's body, as she had seen Liraz grief-torn and bereft, and Akiva at her side, just as anguished. Even from within Karou's own black well of grief that night, the sight had gutted her. She wanted Jael dead, too, but it wasn't her only concern.

"We can't put this on humans," she said. "Jael is *our* problem."

Elyon was ready with a response. "If what you tell us of humans and their weapons is true, it should be easy work for them."

"It would be if they saw them as enemies," she said. Jael's "pageant" was a stroke of cunning. "They will worship us as gods," Jael had told Akiva, and Karou didn't doubt he was right. She said to Elyon, "Imagine your godstars unfasten themselves from the sky and come down to stand before you, living and breathing. How exactly would you 'deal' with them?"

"I imagine that I would give them whatever they asked for," he replied, adding, with damnable, faultless logic, "which is why we must close the portals. Our first concern must be Eretz. We have enough to deal with here without picking a fight in a world not our own."

Karou shook her head, but his words had knocked hers askew, and for a moment she could find none. He was right. It was imperative that Jael not succeed in bringing human weapons into Eretz, and the simplest way to stop him would be to close the portals.

But it was unacceptable. Karou couldn't simply dust humanity off her hands and turn her back on an entire world, especially considering that Jael's pageant traced directly back to her. *She* had brought the abomination Razgut to Eretz and turned him loose with such dangerous knowledge as he possessed—of warcraft, religion, geography—and he had gifted it to Jael. She had brought this down on the human world as surely as if she'd match-made that pair of foul angels herself.

In the second that she searched for words, she scanned for support around the stone table and met Akiva's gaze. It was like a kick to her heartbeat, that burning stare. He was blank; whatever he was feeling toward her—disgust? disappointment? bone-deep, baffled hurt?—it was hidden.

"Shutting a door is one way of solving a problem," he said. He stared straight at Thiago. "But not a very good way. Our enemies do not always stay where we put them, and tend to come back on us unlooked for, and all the more deadly for it."

There was no doubt that he was referring to his own escape and its consequences. The Wolf didn't miss his meaning. "Indeed," he said. "Let the past be our teacher. Killing is the only finality." A glance at Karou, and he added with a very small smile, "And sometimes, not even that."

It took the rest of them a second to realize that Beast's Bane and the Wolf were in agreement, icy agreement though it was.

"It would be too uncertain," Liraz said to Elyon. "And too unsatisfying." They were simple words, and chilling. She had an uncle to kill, and she planned to enjoy it.

"Then what do you propose?" asked Elyon.

"We do what we do," said Liraz. "We fight. Akiva destroys Jael's portal so he can't summon reinforcements. We take the thousand out there, and then we come home by the other portal, close it behind us, and deal with the rest of them here in Eretz."

Elyon chewed on this. "Setting aside for the moment 'the rest of them,' and the impossible odds there, the thousand in the human world makes nearly three to one, their favor."

"Three Dominion to one Misbegotten?" Liraz's smile was like the love child of a shark and a scimitar. "I'll take those odds. And don't forget, we have something they don't."

"Which is?" inquired Elyon.

With a glance first to Akiva, Liraz turned to regard the chimaera. She didn't speak; her look was resentful and reluctant, but its aim was clear: *We have beasts*, she might have said, her lip a subtle curl.

"No," said Elyon at once. He looked to Briathos and Orit for support. "We've agreed not to kill them, that's all, though we would have been within our rights to do it after they broke the truce—"

"*We* broke the truce, did we?" This from Ten. Haxaya, rather, who seemed to be enjoying the deceit, in a way only she could. Karou knew her true face. She'd been a friend, long ago, and her aspect wasn't lupine, but vulpine, not so different than this, really—only sharper and more feral. Haxaya had claimed once that she was just a set of teeth with a body behind it, and the way she smiled Ten's wolf jaws was like a taunt. *I might eat you*, she seemed to be thinking, most of the time, including now. "Then why is it *our* blood that stains the cavern floor?" she demanded.

"Because we're quicker than you," said Orit, all disdain. "As if you needed further proof of it."

And with that, Ten was ready to launch herself over the table at her, teeth first and truce be damned. "Your archers are the ones who should answer for this, not us."

"That was defense. The instant you showed hamsas, we were free of our promise."

Really? Karou wanted to scream. Had they learned nothing? They were like children. Really freaking deadly children.

"*Enough.*" It wasn't a scream, and it wasn't Karou. Thiago's snarl was ice and command, and it tore between the facing soldiers and set both sides rocking back on their heels. Ten dipped her head to her general.

Orit glared. She wasn't beautiful like Liraz, like so many of the angels. Her features were ill-defined, her face full, and her nose had been broken some long time ago, smashed flat at the bridge by blunt force. "You decide what's enough?" she asked Thiago. "I don't think so." She turned to her kin. "I thought we were in agreement that we wouldn't proceed unless they proved their good faith. I don't see good faith. I see beasts laughing in our faces."

"No," said Thiago. "You don't."

"Pray you never do," added Lisseth helpfully.

Thiago continued as though she hadn't spoken. "I said I would discipline any soldier or soldiers who defied my command, and I will. It's not to appease you, and you won't be audience to it."

"Then how will we know?" demanded Orit.

"You'll know," was the Wolf's reply, as heavy with threat as his earlier pronouncement to Karou, but without the tint of regret.

Elyon was not satisfied. To the others, he said, "We can't trust them at our sides in battle. We can fight Jael without mixing battalions. They follow their command, and we our own. We keep apart."

It was Liraz who, with a considering look at the chimaera, said, "Even one pair of hamsas in a battalion could weaken the Dominion and give us an edge."

"Or weaken us," argued Orit. "And blunt our edge."

Karou had glanced at Akiva, and so she saw a spark light his eyes—the vividness of a sudden idea—and when he spoke up, cutting in abruptly, she expected him to give voice to it, whatever it was. But he said only, "Liraz is right, but so is Orit. It may be early yet to speak of mixing battalions. We'll leave that question for now," and as the talk moved deeper into the attack plan, Karou was left wondering: *What was that spark? What was the idea?*

She kept looking at him and wondering, and she had to admit she hoped it might be some way out of all this, because it was becoming clearer to her with every passing moment that, in one thing at least, the seraphim and chimaera were united. It was in their mutual unconcern, in the midst of their plotting, for the effect this attack would have on humans.

Karou tried to give voice to it as the war council wound on, but she couldn't make her concerns register. Liraz, it seemed to her, pointedly talked over her each time, and if their interests had earlier met in that one loud *no*, they had now diverged radically. Liraz wanted Jael's blood. She didn't care who it spattered.

"Listen," Karou said, urgent, when she sensed that their accord was becoming a settled thing. And it was a miracle that this council could find accord, but it felt like a *bad* miracle. "The instant we attack, we become part of Jael's pageant. Angels in white attacked by angels in black? Never mind what humans will make of chimaera. They have a story for this, too, and in their story, the devil *is an angel*—"

"We don't have to care what humans think of us," said Liraz. "This is no pageant. It's an ambush. We get in and we get out. Fast. If they try to help him, they become our enemy, too." Her hands were flat on the stone of the table; she was ready to push off and launch herself right this instant. Oh, she was ready for a bloodbath.

"This prospective enemy that you appear to be taking lightly," said Karou, "has. . . ." She wanted to say that they had assault rifles and rocket launchers and military aircraft. Small detail that the languages of Eretz couldn't begin to communicate these things. "Weapons of mass destruction," she said instead. That translated just fine.

"So do we," replied Liraz. "We have *fire*." Her tone was so cold that Karou stopped short.

"What do you mean by that?" she asked, her voice pitching high in her anger. She knew all too well what Liraz meant, and it stunned her. She had stood in the ashes of Loramendi. She knew what seraph fire could do. Could this be the same Liraz who had used her heat to warm Zuzana and Mik in their sleep, threatening to use it to burn a world?

Akiva stepped in. "It won't come to that. They are not our enemy. Our directive must be to cause as little collateral damage as possible. If humans become Jael's puppets, they do so in ignorance."

It was cold comfort. *As little collateral damage as possible.* Karou fought to keep her face blank as her mind rebelled. Literally or not, the human world was dry kindling to a flame like this. *Apocalypse,* she thought. This was something special even for *her* résumé of disaster, which had grown pretty fantastical over the past few months. *It's a good thing there are only two worlds for me to worry about destroying,* she thought. Except that, oh hell, there probably *were* more. Why not? One world, and you can call it a fluke—an excellent accident of stardust. But if there were two worlds, what chance that there were *only* two?

Step right up, worlds, thought Karou, *get your disaster here!* She cast again around the table, but she was surrounded by warriors in the midst of a war council, and everything that had been decided here could be filed under "*Of course, idiot. What did you* think *was going to happen?*" Still, she tried. She said, "There is no acceptable level of collateral damage."

She thought she saw a softening in Akiva's eyes, but it was not his voice that answered her. It was Lisseth's, just behind her. "So worried," she said in a nasty hiss. "Are you chimaera, or are you human?"

Lisseth. Or, as Karou now liked to think of her: future enjoyer of cud. It took every ounce of her self-restraint not to turn, look the Naja in the face, and say, "Moo." Instead she replied in a fact-stating tone, and with only the merest hint of condescension, "I am a chimaera in a human body, Lisseth. I thought you understood that by now."

"She understands perfectly. Don't you, soldier?" This was Thiago, half-turned to look at the Naja with warning in his eyes. She would get a dressing-down later, Karou thought. The Wolf could not have been clearer, before this council, that they were to present a united front, no matter what. It struck her as telling that Lisseth couldn't manage to follow that order.

"Yes, sir," Lisseth said, managing a reasonably deferential tone.

"And humans aside," Karou continued, "what about us? How many of us will die?"

"As many as necessary," responded Liraz from across the table, and Karou wanted to *shake* the gorgeous ice queen angel of death.

"What if none of it is necessary?" she demanded. "What if there's another way?"

"Certainly," said Liraz, sounding bored. "Why don't we just go and ask Jael to leave? I'm sure if we say please—"

"That's not what I meant," Karou snapped.

"Then what? Do you have another idea?"

And, of course, Karou didn't. Her grudging admission—"Not yet."—was bitter.

"If you think of any, I'm sure you'll let us know."

Oh, the slice of her gaze, that sardonic, dismissive tone. Karou felt the angel's hatred like a slap. Did she deserve it? She darted a glance at Akiva, but he wasn't looking at her.

"We're through here," announced Thiago. "My soldiers need rest and food, and we have resurrections to perform."

"We fly at dawn," said Liraz.

No one objected.

And that was it.

Thought Karou as the council broke up: *Cue apocalypse.*

Or . . . maybe not. Watching Akiva walk out without so much as a glance her way, she still had no idea what spark had leapt in his eyes, but she wasn't going to rely on him or anyone else to stand up for the human world. For her own part, she wasn't giving in to carnage this easily. She still had some time.

Not much, but some. Which should be fine, right? All she had to do was come up with a plan to avert the apocalypse and somehow convince these grim and hardened soldiers to adopt it. In . . . approximately twelve hours. While deep in a trance, performing as many resurrections as she could.

No big deal.

ARRIVAL + 24 HOURS

25

You, Plural

From the council, Akiva retreated to the room he had claimed for himself and closed the door.

Liraz paused outside it and listened. She raised her hand to knock, but let it fall back to her side. For almost a minute she stood there, her expression flickering between longing and anger. Longing for a time when she had stood between her brothers. Anger for their absence, and for her need.

She felt . . . exposed.

Hazael on one side, Akiva on the other; they had always been her barriers. In battle, of course. They had trained together from the age of five. At their best, they'd fought like a single body with six arms, a mind shared, and no one's back ever open to an enemy. But it wasn't only in battle, she knew now, that she'd used them for shelter like walls to stand between. It was in moments like this, too. With Hazael gone and Akiva in a world of his own, she felt the wind from all sides, as if it could buffet her apart.

She wouldn't ask for company. She shouldn't have to ask, and it hurt her that Akiva clearly didn't need what she needed. To shut himself away with his own grief and misery, and leave her out here?

She didn't knock on his door, but squared her shoulders and walked on. She didn't know where she was going, and she didn't particularly care. It was all filler, anyway—every second up until the one when she held her sword to her uncle's heart and slowly, slowly pushed it in.

Nothing would stop that from happening, not humans and their weapons, not Karou's frantic concerns, not pleas for peace.

Not anything.

* * *

Akiva wasn't grieving. The images that haunted him—his brother's body, Karou laughing with the Wolf—had been locked away. His eyes were closed, his face as smooth as dreamless sleep, but he wasn't sleeping. Nor was he exactly awake. He was in a place he had found years earlier, after Bullfinch, while he recovered from the injury that should have killed him. Though he hadn't died, and had even recovered full use of his arm, the wound to his shoulder had never stopped hurting, not for a second, and this was where he was now.

He was inside the pain, in the place where he worked magic.

Not *sirithar.* That was something else entirely. Any magic that he had made on purpose, he had made—or perhaps *found*—here. In the beginning it had felt like passing through a trapdoor down into dark levels of his own mind, but as time went on, as he grew stronger and pushed deeper, the sense of space was ever-expanding, and he began to awaken afterward vague and off-balance, as though he had come back from somewhere very far away.

Did he make magic or did he find it? Was he within himself or without? He didn't know. He didn't know anything. With no training, Akiva went on instinct and hope, and tonight, minute by minute he questioned both.

In the middle of the war council, the idea had come to him in a sudden flare that felt like revelation. It was the hamsas.

He wasn't delusional about the likelihood of the two armies achieving accord anytime soon. He'd known this would be fraught, but he also knew that the best use of their collective strength was in a true alliance, not just a détente. Integration. However they hit the Dominion—in mixed battalions or segregated—they would be outnumbered. But Liraz had been right: Hamsas in every unit would weaken the enemy and help balance the scales. It could mean the difference between victory and defeat.

But he couldn't very well expect his brothers and sisters to trust the chimaera, especially considering their poor beginning. The hamsas were a weapon against which they had no defense.

But what if they *did* have a defense?

This was Akiva's idea. What if he could work a counterspell to protect the Misbegotten from the marks? He didn't know if he could—or even if he *should*. If he succeeded, would it cause more strife than it resolved? The chimaera wouldn't be pleased to lose their advantage.

And...Karou?

Here's where Akiva lost perspective. How could you tell if your instincts were just hope in disguise, and if your hope was really desperation parading as possibility? Because if he succeeded, along with the chance for a true alliance between their armies came another, more personal one.

Karou would be able to touch him. Her hands, full against his flesh, without agony. He didn't know if she wanted to touch him, or ever would again, but the chance would be there, just in case.

* * *

Seraphim and chimaera had both posted guards at the mouth of the passage that joined the village and the grand cavern, with the intention of keeping the soldiers apart. There was a sense of lurking and skulking, the possibility of enemies around every corner. It was impossible to relax. Most on both sides felt trapped by the rough ceilings and windowless walls of this place, the skylessness, the impossibility of escape—especially for the chimaera, knowing that the Misbegotten were encamped between themselves and the exit.

They rested and ate and salvaged what weapons they could from Kirin arsenals long ago looted by slavers. Aegir melted down pots and tools to make blades, and his hammering joined the noises of the mountain. Some soldiers were put to work refletching old arrows, but there wasn't activity to occupy the bulk of the host, and their idleness was dangerous. No open aggression flared, but the angels, angry that no beast had been punished for oath-breaking, claimed they felt the sickness of hamsas pulsing through the walls at them.

The chimaera, however mindful of their general's clear commands, may have found more occasions than necessary to wearily lean, palms pressed to rock in support of their weight. That the magic of the hamsas passed through stone was unlikely, but it wasn't for lack of trying. "The black-handed butchers," they called the Misbegotten, and spoke in murmurs of hacking off their marked hands and burning them.

And then, atop the general confusion and compounding it, was the despair that had carved each of them hollow, and which still echoed in them like a fading drumbeat, beast and angel alike. None spoke of it, each holding it a private weakness. These soldiers may never have felt despair as profound as the one that had passed through them earlier, but they had certainly felt despair.

Like fear, it was always, always suffered in silence.

* * *

"Well?" asked Issa when Karou returned, alone, to the village. She'd lagged behind Thiago, Ten, and Lisseth, having had quite her fill of their company, and Issa had come up to meet her at the turning of the path. "How did it go?"

"About how you'd expect," Karou replied. "Bloodlust and bravado."

"From everyone?" Issa probed.

"Pretty much." She avoided Issa's eyes. It wasn't true. Neither Akiva nor Thiago had displayed either of those things, but the result was the same as if they had. She rubbed her eyes. God, she was tired. "Brace for a full onslaught."

"It's to be attack, then? Well. We'd better get to work."

Karou let out a hard breath. They had until dawn. How many resurrections could they possibly perform by then? "What good is a handful more soldiers in the face of a fight like this?"

"We do what we can," said Issa.

"And this is all we can do? Because warriors make our plans."

Issa was silent a moment. They were still at the outskirts of the village, at a hairpin turn in the rock passage around the other side of which the dwellings began, the path continuing down toward the "square." "And if an artist were to make our plans?" asked Issa gently.

Karou clenched her teeth. She knew she'd given the war council no alternative to consider. She remembered Liraz's mockery: "Why don't we just go and ask Jael to leave?" If only. *And the angels all went quietly home and no one died. The end.*

Fat chance of that.

"I don't know," she admitted bitterly to Issa, starting down the path with heavy steps. "Do you remember that drawing I did once, for an assignment? I had to illustrate the concept of war?"

Issa nodded. "I remember it well. We talked about it long after you had gone."

Karou had drawn two monstrous men facing each other across a table, and in front of each was an enormous bowl of...people. Writhing tiny limbs, wretched tiny grimaces. And the men were digging in with forks—each into the other's bowl—frenzied with hunger, pitching bite after bite *of people* into their gaping mouths.

"The idea was that whoever emptied the other's bowl first won the war. And I drew that before I even knew about Eretz, the war here, or Brimstone's part in it."

"Your soul knew," said Issa. "Even if your mind didn't."

"Maybe," Karou allowed. "I kept thinking about that drawing in the war council, and our part in all of this. We cheat the bowl. We keep filling it back up, and the monsters keep stabbing their giant forks in, and because of us, there's always more for them to eat. We never lose but we never win, either. We just keep on dying. Is that what we do?"

"It's what we *did*," corrected Issa, placing her cool hand on Karou's arm. "Sweet girl," she said. She was so lovely, her face as sweet as a Renaissance Madonna's. "You know that Brimstone had greater hopes of you."

In the chimaera tongue, the pronoun *you* has a singular form and a plural, and here, Issa used the plural. *Brimstone had greater hopes of you, plural.*

You and Akiva. Karou remembered Brimstone telling her—*Madrigal*-her, in her prison cell, just before her execution—that the only way he could keep on doing what he did century after century was by believing that he was keeping the chimaera alive.... "Until the world can be remade," Karou said softly, echoing what he had told her then.

"He couldn't do it," said Issa, just as softly. "And the Warlord couldn't. Certainly Thiago never could. But you might." Again, you plural.

"I don't know how to get there," she told Issa, like the sharing of a terrible secret. "We're here, chimaera and seraphim, together but not really. Everyone still wants to kill each other and probably will. It's not exactly a new world."

"Listen to your instincts, sweet girl."

Karou laughed, slappy with fatigue. "What if my instincts are telling me to go to sleep, and wake up when it's all done? Worlds fixed, portals closed, everyone on their proper side, Jael defeated, and no more war."

Issa only smiled and said, "You wouldn't want to sleep through this, love. These are extraordinary times." Her smile was beatific until it turned mischievous. "Or they will be, once *you* figure out how to make them so."

Karou smacked her lightly on the shoulder. "Great. Thanks. No pressure."

Issa pulled her in for a hug, and it felt like a thousand past Issa hugs that had always had the power to infuse her with strength—the strength of the belief of others. She had Brimstone's belief in her, too.

Did she still have Akiva's?

Karou straightened back up. They were almost back to "resurrection headquarters," the chambers Zuzana and Mik had chosen. She saw the green flicker of skohl torches through the open door. From farther down the path came the sounds of the host and the waft of cooking smells. Earth vegetables, couscous, flat bread, the last of their skinny Moroccan chickens. It smelled good, and Karou didn't think it was just because she was starving. It gave her a thought.

Listen to your instincts? How about to her stomach instead? It wasn't a plan or a solution; just a small idea. A baby step. "Tell Zuze and Mik I'll be right there," she told Issa, and went in search of the Wolf.

26

Bleed and Bloom

At around seven AM, more than twenty-four hours after waking up screaming, Eliza gave in to exhaustion and was plunged straight into the dream.

It began, as it always did, with the sky. *A* sky, anyway. To look at, it was simply a blue expanse, a speckling of clouds, nothing special. But in the dream, Eliza knew things. Felt them and knew them in the way of dreams, without consideration or doubt. This wasn't fantasy or figment, not while she was in it. It was like wandering past the cordon of her known mind into some place deeper and stranger but no less real.

And the first thing Eliza knew was that this sky *was* special, and that it was very, very far away. Not Tahiti-far. Not China-far. A kind of far that defied what she knew of the universe.

She was watching it, breath held, waiting for something to happen.

Hoping it wouldn't.

Dreading it would.

Like *remorse*, the words *hope* and *dread* were wholly inadequate to describe the intensity of the feelings in the dream. Ordinary hope and dread were like avatars to these—mere digestible representations of emotions so pure and terrible they would annihilate us in real life, rip open our minds and drive us mad. Even in the dream it felt like it would blast Eliza apart—the savage, unbearable pressure of this suspense.

Watch the sky.

Will it happen?

It can't. It mustn't.

It mustn't it mustn't it mustn't.

A choking sob built in her throat. A prayer cut through her hope-despair, plangent as a pull from a violin, a single word drawn out—*please*—so long and pure it would go on until the end of time—

—which might not be long at all.

Because the world was about to end.

Over and over again, prey to the dream, Eliza had been forced to watch it happen. The first time, she was seven, and she'd dreamt it countless times since, and no matter that she knew what was coming, she was plunged every time into the moment of horror when hope was still just within grasp—

—and then snatched away.

A blossoming in the blue. It started small: barely visible, a disruption in the sky, like a water droplet in an ink wash. It grew quickly and was joined by others.

The sky, it bled and bloomed. Pinwheels of color radiated out and out, horizon to horizon, joining and blending and merging like a kaleidoscope of stains. The sky . . . failed. It was beautiful to behold, and it was terrible. *Terrible and terrible and terrible forever, amen.*

This was how the world would end. *Because of me. Because of me. Nothing worse has ever been done. In all of time, in all of space. I don't deserve to live—*

The sky would fail, and let them in. *Them*. Chasing, churning, devouring.

The Beasts are coming for you.

The Beasts.

Eliza fled from them, in the dream. She wheeled and fled, and her panic and guilt were as ravenous as the horror that was coming behind her. Somehow, it was her fault. *She* would do it. She would be the one to let them in.

Never. I will never—

"What the hell? Did you *sleep* here?"

Eliza gasped awake and there was Morgan before her, framed in the doorway, his hair a freshly shampooed flop down over his forehead, boy-band style. His pouty mouth was twisted with distaste. Dear god, only the dream could make Morgan Toth and his sneer seem benign by contrast. The way he was looking at her, you'd think he'd caught her in the middle of some lewd act, rather than dozing on a couch, fully dressed.

Eliza sat up straight. Her laptop screen had gone dark. How long had she been out? She clicked it closed, wiped her mouth with the back of her hand and was glad to find it droolless.

No drool and no screaming, but there was a pressure on her chest that she understood was a scream in the making. It would have burst out right here in the lab if Morgan hadn't woken her, bless his horrid little self.

"What time is it?" she asked, standing up.

"I'm not your alarm clock," he said, moving past her toward his preferred sequencer. There were two hulking DNA sequencers in the lab and Eliza had never been able to determine a difference between them, but she knew of Morgan's preference for the one on the left and so, whenever possible, she tried to arrive first and claim it before he could. Of such petty victories is a day made sweet. Not today, though.

Given that it began with the dream and continued with exhaustion, that the world was falling apart, that her family had tracked her down and were out there, somewhere, *and* that she was stuck in yesterday's clothes, Eliza didn't imagine the day held much in the way of sweetness.

She was wrong; it did. But it held a lot of other things, too, and was soon to veer wildly from any possible expectation she might have had of it.

Wildly.

It began a couple of hours later with a knock that made Eliza look up from her work. She'd been having a hard time concentrating anyway, data swimming before her eyes, and she was glad of the distraction. Dr. Chaudhary answered the door. He'd come in not long after Morgan and had kept his commentary on world events brief. "Strange days," he'd said with a lift of his eyebrows before heading into his office. No chatterbox, Anuj Chaudhary. A tall Indian man in his fifties with a prominent hooked nose and thick hair turning silver at the temples, he had a genteel English accent and the manners of a Victorian gentleman.

"May I help you?" he asked the two men at the door.

One look at them, and Eliza felt transported into a TV show. Dark suits, regulation haircuts, bland features made even blander by a schooled lack of expression. Government agents. "Dr. Anuj Chaudhary?" asked the taller of the two, flipping out a badge. Dr. Chaudhary nodded. "We'd like you to come with us."

"Just now?" Dr. Chaudhary asked, as calmly as if a colleague had popped in with an offer of tea.

"Yes."

No explanation, and not a single extraneous word to soften the edges of their demand. Eliza wondered if government agents took a course in being cryptic. What was this about? Was Dr. Chaudhary in some kind of trouble? No. Of course not. When government agents came into laboratories and said, "We'd like you to come with us," it was because they needed the scientist's expertise.

And Dr. Chaudhary's expertise was molecular phylogenetics. So the question was . . . what DNA did they want analyzed?

Eliza turned to Morgan and found him watching the exchange with creepy, blazing avidity. *Alien invasion protocol*, thought Eliza. As soon as he felt her eyes on him, he turned with a smirk and said, "Maybe I'm not the only non-idiot on the planet after all," in a way that clearly singled *her* out as chief among idiots.

Which only made it incredibly sweet—here it was, her one taste of sweetness in a dark day soon to get much darker—when Dr. Chaudhary asked the agents, "May I bring an assistant?" and, getting a terse nod, turned . . . to her.

To *her*. Preciously, gloatingly sweet, almost too good to be true. "Eliza, if you wouldn't mind accompanying me?"

From the sound Morgan made, Eliza could almost have believed that the air was expelled from his lungs by way of every orifice in his head, and not just his mouth and nose. His ears and eyes had to be in on it, too, cartoon-style. It was that fully committal, a scathing hiss of disbelief, injustice, *scorn*.

"But Dr. Chaudhary—" he began, but Dr. Chaudhary dismissed him, brusque and businesslike.

"Not now, Mr. Toth."

And Eliza, sliding off her stool, paused just long enough to say, under her breath, "Suck it, Mr. Toth."

"That's what *I* should say to *you*," he replied, acid and furious, sliding a narrowed-eyed glance of insinuation toward Dr. Chaudhary. Eliza froze, experiencing the weird sensation of her palm going white-hot and rigid with the urgency to slap him across the face. Mindful of the agents and her mentor watching, she mastered the urge, but her hand felt heavy with the unspent slap.

Well, it was some consolation to be the one gathering equipment at Dr. Chaudhary's behest, and then the one following the agents out the door, leaving Morgan to expend his violent little-boy outrage alone.

There was a car waiting. Sleek, black, government. Eliza wondered what agency the men were with. She hadn't been able to read their badges. FBI? CIA? NSA? Who had jurisdiction over . . . angels?

Dr. Chaudhary motioned Eliza into the car first, then slid in beside her. The door clicked closed, the agents climbed in front, and the car drew out into traffic. As the distance grew between herself and the museum, Eliza's triumph faded, and worry began to overwhelm it. *Wait*, she thought, *let's think this through*.

"Um, excuse me. Where are we going?" she asked.

"You'll be briefed on arrival," was the response from the front seat.

Okay.

Arrival *where?*

It had to be Rome.

Didn't it?

Eliza flicked a glance to Dr. Chaudhary, who gave a minor shrug and lift of eyebrows. "This should be illuminating," he said.

Illuminating? Would it be? Were they really going to get access to the Visitors?

She had a brief image of herself stepping up to do a cheek swab on one of them, and she felt the tug of hysteria. Who would have guessed, after all that she'd turned her back on, that *science* would be bringing her face-to-face with angels? She had to swallow a laugh. *Hey, Ma, look at me!* God. It was only funny because it was so preposterous. She had chosen her own path, as different from her past as it could possibly be, and where did it lead her?

One of the biggest events in the history of humanity, and she would be there...sticking a Q-tip in an angel's mouth? *Open up.* Another burble of hysteria, choked down and covered up with a throat-clearing. Eliza was going to analyze angel DNA. If they *had* DNA. And they would, she thought. They had physical bodies; they had to be made up of something. But what would it look like? What resemblance would it bear to human DNA? She couldn't begin to imagine, but she believed that it was how this mystery would be solved. At the molecular level.

She would know what they were.

In the spinning of her mind, her exhaustion and anxiety and the weight of the dream still perched on her shoulder—like a carrion bird, biding its time—her thoughts kept flipping around to face her. It was like chasing someone, all out, and then just at the moment you reach out to catch them, they whirl on you, savage, and grab you by the throat.

She would find out what the angels were. That was Eliza in control of her thoughts. She would find out, the way she was trained to find out. Nucleotides in sequence, and the world and the universe and the future would all fall neatly into sense. Phylogeny. Order. Sanity.

Then the thought spun around and seized her, forced her to look at it, and it wasn't what she'd thought she was chasing. It had madness in its eyes.

It wasn't: *I will know what the angels are.*

What Eliza was really thinking was: *Will I know what* I *am?*

27

Just Creatures in a World

When Karou joined Zuzana, Mik, and Issa, she discovered that they'd been busy while she was in the war council: preparing the space, unpacking the trays, cleaning and sorting teeth. Zuzana had even taken a stab at laying out some necklaces—still unstrung, pending Karou's inspection.

"These are good," said Karou after careful study.

"Will they work?" asked Zuzana.

Karou looked them over further. "This is Uthem?" she asked, indicating the first. A row of horse and iguana teeth with tubes of bat bone—doubled, for the two sets of wings—along with iron and jade for size and grace.

"I figured he was a given," said Zuzana.

Karou nodded. Thiago would need Uthem to ride into battle. "You have a knack for this," she told her friend. The necklace wasn't perfect, but it was pretty close—and pretty amazing considering how little experience Zuzana had.

"Yep." No false humility from Zuze. "Now you just have to teach me the magic to actually translate them to flesh."

"Don't tempt me," Karou said with a dark laugh.

"What?"

"There's this story where a man is fated to serve as ferryman across the river of the dead for eternity. There's one catch, only he doesn't know it. All he has to do is hand his pole to someone else, and he hands them his fate, too."

"And you're going to hand me your pole?" asked Zuzana.

"No. I am *not* going to hand you my pole."

"How about we share it?" Zuzana proposed.

Karou shook her head, in exasperation and wonder. "Zuze, no. You have a life to live—"

"And presumably I will *be* living while helping you?"

"Yes, but—"

"So let's see here. I can either do the most amazing, astonishing, unbelievable, magical thing that anyone has ever heard of—*ever*—and, after all this war stuff is all over, help you resurrect a whole population of women and children and, like, build a race of creatures back to life, at the beginning of a new era for a world no one else even knows exists. Or... I can go home and do puppet shows for tourists."

Karou felt a smile twitch her lips. "Well, when you put it like that." She turned to Mik. "Do you have something to say about this?"

"Yes," he said, serious—and not mock-serious, but *serious*-serious. "I say let's discuss the future later, after 'all this war stuff,' as Zuze put it, when we know there's going to *be* a future."

"Good point," said Karou, and turned toward the thuribles.

Best-case scenario was a dozen resurrections, and that was pretty optimistic. The question was: Who? *Who are the lucky souls today?* Karou pondered, and as she sifted through the thuribles, she started a "yes" pile, a "maybe" pile, and an "oh Jesus, you stay dead" pile. No more Lisseths in this rebellion, and no more Razors with his sack of spreading stains. She wanted soldiers with honor, who could embrace the new purpose and not fight against it at every turn. There were a handful of obvious choices, but she hesitated over them, contemplating how they would be received.

Balieros, Ixander, Minas, Viya, and Azay. Ziri's former patrol—the soldiers who had defied the true Wolf's order to slaughter seraph civilians, flying instead to the Hintermost to die defending their own folk. They were strong, competent, and respected, but they had disobeyed the Wolf's order. Would their resurrection seem suspicious, another tick mark in a growing column of Things Thiago Would Never Do?

Maybe, but Karou wanted them; she'd take the blame. She wanted Amzallag and the Shadows That Live, too, but she knew that would be a push too far. She kept their thurible apart, a kind of totem for a brighter day. She would give them their lives back as soon as she could.

Balieros's team she put in the "yes" pile. There was a sixth soul with them. Brushing against her senses, it felt like a knife of light through trees, and though it was unfamiliar to Karou, she remembered Ziri telling her about the young Dashnag boy who'd joined their fight and died alongside the others.

It made no sense to choose an untrained boy as one of a mere dozen resurrections before a battle like the one ahead, but Karou did it anyway, with a feeling of defiance. "Resurrectionist's choice," she imagined herself telling Lisseth, or, as she now thought of the poisonous Naja woman: *future cow.* "You have a problem with that?" Anyway, the Dashnag wouldn't be a boy anymore. Karou didn't have juvenile teeth, and even if she did, this was no time for youth. So he was going to wake up and find himself alive, fully grown, and winged, in a remote cave in the company of revenants and seraphim.

Should be an interesting day for him. A part of Karou's mind kept telling her it was a terrible idea, but something about it felt right. Dashnags are formidable chimaera, few more fearsome, but she didn't think it was that so much as the purity of his soul. A knife of light. Honor and a new purpose.

"Okay," she told her assistants. "Here we go."

The hours vanished like time-lapse. Thiago came in somewhere in the middle to take over the tithing—he'd been to the baths, Karou saw, and was clean of crusted blood, his wounds beginning to heal—and together he and Karou added fresh bruises to those all but faded from their arms and hands. They didn't make it to a dozen ressurrections. Nine bodies came into being in under six hours, and they had to stop. For one thing, there was no space for more bodies. These nine pretty well filled the room. For another, Karou's exhaustion was making her dopey. Loopy. Useless. Done.

Apparently Zuzana was feeling the same. "My kingdom for caffeine," she mumbled, making prayer hands up at the ceiling.

When, however, in the next second, Issa entered with tea, Zuzana was not grateful. "*Coffee*, I meant *coffee*," she told the ceiling, as if the universe were a waiter that had gotten her order wrong.

Regardless, they drank the tea, silently surveying their work. Nine bodies, and all that remained now was to transfer souls to them. Karou let Mik and Zuzana handle this part, since her arms were trembling, and every movement sent a coordinated assault of aches and throbs rushing up them. She leaned against the wall with Thiago and watched Zuzana go down the line of new bodies, placing a cone of incense on the brow of each new head.

"Did you extend the invitation?" she asked the Wolf.

He nodded. "They consulted, and eventually accepted. Made it seem like a favor to us, mind you. *Reluctantly we agree to eat your food, but don't expect us to enjoy it.*"

"They said *that?*"

"Not in so many words."

"Well," said Karou. "It's pride. They might pretend not to, but they will enjoy it."

This had been her small idea, her baby step: to feed the seraphim. Someone, Elyon or Briathos, had let slip in the war council that the Misbegotten, having fled in a hurry from their various postings around the Empire, had already expended what small stores of food they'd managed to bring with them. Feeding them—nearly three hundred of them—would expend the chimaera's stores, too, but it was a gesture of solidarity for the sake of the alliance. We eat together and starve together. We are in this together.

And maybe someday we'll even live together. Just creatures in a world. Why not?

The rasp of the lighter—a little red plastic lighter with a cartoon face on it, entirely at odds with the seriousness of its task, not to mention out of place in this world—and Zuzana lit the incense cones, one by one down the line. The scent of Brimstone's revenant incense slowly filled up the rock chamber, and first Uthem, then the others, came alive.

Karou's emotions were complex. There was pride: in herself, and in Zuzana, too. The bodies were well-made, strong and proud, and not monstrous or exaggerated the way her kasbah resurrections had been. These were more in Brimstone's style, and she felt nostalgia and longing, too, for him.

And bitterness.

Here was a refill for the bowls. More meat for the grinding teeth of war.

Just creatures in a world, she had thought, moments earlier, and she wondered now, watching them stir to life: Could that ever be true?

28

Angel-Lover, Beast-Lover

As they had led the host down the winding passage to the isolated village, so now did Karou and Thiago lead them back up. The Misbegotten were already present in the grand, echoing central cavern that served as gathering place. They had, quite conspicuously, claimed the far half of the cavern, leaving the other half to the chimaera. Together but not, as though a line were drawn right down the center.

The food was carried in, great bowls of couscous spiked with vegetables, apricots, and almonds. The small quantity of chicken was stretched thin across all that food so that an actual morsel was rare, but its flavor was there, and there were discs of bread baked on a hot rock—more bread than Karou had ever seen in one place in her life. As vast a quantity as it looked, however, it went fast, and the eating even faster.

"You know what would be good now?" Zuzana whispered, when

the sounds of spoons on plates had mostly quieted. "Chocolate. Never attempt an alliance without chocolate."

Karou couldn't imagine that the Misbegotten, roughly treated as they had been their entire lives, had much experience with dessert.

"Absent that," Mik suggested, "how about music?"

Karou smiled. "I think that's a great idea."

He got out his violin and set about tuning it. Since they had come into the cavern, Karou had been watching for Akiva while pretending not to. He wasn't here, and she didn't know what to think. She didn't see Liraz, either; only several hundred unfamiliar angels, and every last one of them held their faces blank and grim. This wasn't inappropriate—it was the eve of the apocalypse, after all—but neither was it comfortable. Karou felt the détente to be as insubstantial as it had been on their arrival, and that all of these soldiers would as soon slit one another's throats as break bread together.

Mik began to play, and the seraphim took notice. Karou watched them, scanning those fierce and beautiful faces one by one, wondering at the soul of each. Gradually, she thought the music began to have an effect on them. The grimness didn't quite go out of their faces, but something softened in the atmosphere. You could almost feel the long, slow, gradual exhale that sapped the tension from several hundred sets of shoulders.

At dawn they would fly back to the human world. What was happening there? she wondered. How had Jael presented himself, and how had he been received? Were they scrambling to provide him with weapons? Even now training him to use them? Or were they skeptical? Some would be, but who would be louder? Who was *always* louder? The righteous.

The fearful.

"Karou," whispered Zuzana. "Translation needed."

Karou turned to her friend, who was back to learning Chimaera vocabulary from Virko just as she had at mealtimes at the kasbah. "What's he saying?" she asked. "I can't figure it out."

Virko repeated the word in question, and Karou translated. "Magic."

"Oh," said Zuzana. And then, with a furrowed brow: "Really? Ask him how he knows?"

Karou duly asked.

"We all felt it," Virko replied. "Tell her. At the same moment."

Karou blinked at him. Instead of translating, she asked, "You all felt what at the same moment?"

He met her eyes. "The end," he said. Simple. Eerie.

A chill went down Karou's spine. She knew exactly what he was talking about, but she asked anyway. "What do you mean, 'the end'?"

"What did he say?" Zuzana wanted to know, but Karou was fixed on Virko. An understanding was settling in her like something that had been hovering and darting just out of reach and had finally grown too tired to be wary.

Virko looked around at the company, gathered in small and large groups, some with eyes closed listening to the music, some staring into the fire. He said, "After it happened, I thought to myself: *The angels are lucky. I must be losing my wits*. I forgot my sword mid-draw. Just stood there with my mouth hanging open, feeling like my heart had been pulled out through it. Thought I was scraping the bottom of a long life, I did."

He let her process this, and she felt cold and then warm, in waves.

"But it was the same for everyone," said Virko. "It wasn't me, and that's some relief. Something happened to us. Something was done." He paused. "I don't know what, but it's why we're all still alive."

Karou sat back, dazed. How had she not guessed immediately? Nothing like that despair had ever come over her before, not even when she stood ankle-deep in the ashes of Loramendi. And it had come and gone like something passing. A sound wave, or particles of light. Or . . . a burst of magic.

A burst of magic at the precise fulcrum of catastrophe, peeling them back from the edge. And if the White Wolf had risen to his feet and spoken, he had spoken into the silence of its passage, helping to gather them all back to themselves as their souls reeled. But he hadn't done it, hadn't stopped them from killing one another.

Akiva had.

The realization spread through Karou like heat, and before she could even question if she was right, she was sure.

And when Akiva finally did come into the cavern, Karou knew him even from the side of her downcast eyes. Her heart leapt. When she darted a glance to confirm it was him, he wasn't looking her way.

She felt as much as heard the stir in the company around her, though it was a moment before the words came clear.

"It was him," she heard. "He was the one who saved us."

Had someone else figured out what she had?

She swung around to see who had spoken, and was surprised to see the Dashnag boy, who of course was a boy no longer. Rath was his name, and he could know nothing of the pulse of despair; his soul had been in a thurible then. So what was he talking about? Karou listened.

"I'd never have lived to reach the Hintermost," he was telling Balieros and the others with whom he'd been resurrected. "I was moving south with some others. Angels were burning the forest behind us. A whole village of Caprine, and some Dama girls freed from the slavers with me. We were caught in a gully, hiding, and they found us. Two bast—" He stopped and corrected himself. "Two Misbegotten. They were right in front of us. We could hear the aries screaming as they were slaughtered, but the two angels just looked at us, and . . . they pretended not to see us. They let us go."

"Maybe they *didn't* see you," suggested Balieros.

With respect, Rath replied firmly, "They did. And one of them was him." With the jut of his chin, he singled out Akiva. "Eyes as orange as a Dashnag's. I couldn't mistake them."

And all of this Karou heard with that same feeling that the understanding had been there all along, hovering around and ready to land just as soon as she stopped thrashing it away. Of course it wasn't only Ziri whom Akiva had saved in the Hintermost, but slaves and villagers, too, the same fleeing folk whom the Wolf had left for dead by choosing to kill his enemy instead of aid his people.

"Beast's Bane, crusading for beasts?" mused Balieros, leveling a long, speculative look across the cavern, and giving a small smile. "And strangely fold the hours as the end draws near."

Strangely fold the hours. It was a line from a song. All the soldiers knew it. Not exactly hopeful, but appropriate in the context of that scream of magic. *As the end draws near. The end.*

Karou couldn't help herself. She looked at Akiva again. He still wasn't looking back, and it was enough to make her believe that he never would again.

Here they were in the Kirin caves. It was the eve of battle. They'd brought their armies together, which in itself could be counted an unimaginable triumph, but nothing was as they'd dreamt it. They weren't side by side. They couldn't even look at each other.

Karou's heartbeat was playing tricks on her, surging and then shying, like a creature trapped within her. Akiva was surrounded by his own kind, and she was here, with hers, and it seemed that all that was binding them together anymore was a common enemy and the sweet, pure threads of music.

Mik sat on a stone, head bent over his violin, and his song sounded different here than it had in the kasbah. There, it had floated up into the sky. Here, it echoed.

Here, it was trapped, like Karou's heartbeat.

She felt Zuzana's head settle on her shoulder. Issa was on her other side, placid and watchful, and the Wolf was stretched out before her, propped up on his elbows by the fire. He looked relaxed. Still elegant, still exquisite, but absent cruelty, absent menace, as if his stolen body's default expressions were slowly being changed from within. Karou could see the first inklings of a greater beauty beginning to emerge, and she thought of Brimstone's art meeting Ziri's soul. It was nothing to do with Thiago now. That monster was gone forever, and if anyone could purge the taint of him, it was Ziri.

He'd better be careful, though, and not relax too much. Karou took a quick survey of the encircling host, alert especially for Lisseth's unblinking watchfulness. But she didn't see Lisseth. There was Nisk, but not his partner, and Nisk was only staring into the fire.

Karou felt the Wolf's eyes on her, but didn't return his look. Her gaze felt a magnetic pull—across the cavern to Akiva. *Akiva, Akiva.* One more time, she would let herself look. With held breath and, it seemed, a held heartbeat, she made herself pause. It was like an old childhood game of superstition when, exhaling, she thought: *If he doesn't look back this time, I've lost him.*

And the possibility brought on an echo of the earlier despair. *A candle flame extinguished by a scream.*

She lifted her eyes and looked across the cavern. And...

...living fire. That was what his eyes were like, greeting hers: a fuse that seared the air between them. He *was* looking at her. And as far away as he was, and with so much between them—chimaera, seraphim, all the living, all the dead—it felt like touch, that look.

Like the rays of the sun.

They looked at each other. They looked, and anyone might notice. Anyone might see. *Angel-lover. Beast-lover.*

Let them see.

It was madness and abandon, but after everything else, Karou couldn't make herself care enough to look away. Akiva's eyes were heat and light, and she wanted to stay there forever. Tomorrow, the apocalypse. Tonight, the sun.

And finally it was Akiva who broke their gaze. He stood up and quietly spoke to the angels around him, and when he wove his way out of the cavern, lingering a moment in the tall, arched entrance, he didn't look her way again, but Karou still understood. He wanted her to follow him.

She couldn't, of course. She'd be seen. The forward caves were Misbegotten domain, and though Lisseth might not be present—where was she?—there were plenty of other chimaera here keeping an eye on her.

But she had to try. She couldn't bear the thought of Akiva waiting for her and waiting for her. It felt like a last chance.

"I'm going to get some sleep," she said, rising, yawning—it started out fake and quickly became real—and left the cavern by the opposite door as Akiva, the one that led back down to the village.

But as soon as she was out of view, she glamoured herself invisible and passed right back through the cavern, unseen and drifting in a quiet glide over the assembled heads of two armies, her heart pounding, to find Akiva.

29

A Dream Come True

"Things *can* be different," Karou had told Ziri just before the war council. "That's the whole point."

Was that the point? To build a world in which she could have her lover? Seeing the look that passed between her and Akiva across the cavern, Ziri wondered if that was what he'd given up his own life for.

"For all of us," she'd said.

For him, too? What could be different for him? He'd be free of this body someday, in resurrection or evanescence, one way or the other. There was always that to look forward to.

He watched Akiva leave and was unsurprised when, a short while later, Karou left, too. Separately, and by different doors, but he had no doubt that they would find each other. He thought back to the Warlord's ball, all those years ago, and what he'd witnessed then. He'd been just a boy, but it had been as plain as moonlight to him: the way Madrigal's dancing body had curved *away* from the Wolf's but *toward* the stranger's. And even if the full, heady complexity of adult intrigues had been a mystery to him, he'd gotten a sense of it—his first, like a hint of fragrance, exotic, intoxicating...frightening.

Adult intrigues weren't a mystery to him anymore. They were still intoxicating, and still frightening, and watching Karou and Akiva leave, Ziri felt like a boy again. Left out. Left behind.

Maybe he would he always feel that way with her, no matter the age of the bodies they wore.

A figure appeared in the doorway—the one Karou had taken—and for an instant he thought it would be her returning, but it wasn't. It was Lisseth.

Ziri hadn't realized that the Naja wasn't here with the rest of them, and his first, half-formed thought was one of mild self-disparagement. The real Wolf would have known if any of his troops were unaccounted for. But that thought melted away when he caught the look on Lisseth's face. It was an unpleasant face at the best of times, crude and broad and host to a limited repertoire of nasty expressions ranging from sly to vicious, but now she looked...stricken.

The wings of her nostrils flared white, and her lips were pressed to a bloodless crease. Her eyes were unexpectedly unguarded, vulnerable, and there was a stony dignity in the lift of her shoulders, the jut of her blunt chin. She gave him a curt nod, and he rose, curious, and went to her.

Nisk, the other Naja, saw it all, and joined them in the doorway.

"What is it?" Ziri asked.

Her words came out...pinched. She sounded affronted. "Sir, have I done something to displease you?"

Yes, Ziri wanted to reply. *Everything.* But though he strongly suspected that she was the oath-breaker who'd raised hamsas to the

Misbegotten, she had denied it, and he had no proof. "Not to my knowledge," he said. "What's this about?"

"This command should have been mine. I've been waiting for this, and I have more tactical experience. I'm stronger, and when it comes to stealth there's no contest. To not even be told what you were planning—"

"What I was—? Soldier, what are you talking about?"

Lisseth blinked, glanced from him to Nisk and back. "The attack on the seraph, sir. It's under way now."

Did he blanch? Did they see him pale? It was the wrong response. He should have sharpened to cold fury and bared his fangs the instant he realized that his soldiers were, at this very moment, acting without his orders. "This is no plan of mine," he said, and he saw her face transform. Her indignation vanished. With the understanding that he hadn't slighted her, she was her vicious self again. "Take me there," he ordered.

"Yes, sir," she said, turning, and, serpent-smooth, she led the way. Ziri followed, with Nisk coming behind.

Who was it? Ziri asked himself. Lisseth herself with all her acid scrutiny would have been his first guess for a mutineer. Was she? Was this a trap?

Maybe. And yet he had no choice but to follow. Belatedly it struck him that he should have summoned Ten, and it seemed strange to him that the she-wolf hadn't followed of her own accord.

They descended one of the cave system's many down-wending passages, going beyond the ones he knew, deeper and deeper still. Every time they came around a corner with their torches, big pallid insects skittered away ahead of them, squeezing improbably into cracks in the walls. The caverns were pervaded by a heavy, wet-mineral smell, as oppressive a sensory cloak as the wind music was, but as they progressed, new odors filtered through it, traces teased from the darkness. Animal scents, musky and ripe. Chimaera, a group of them. And a cooked-meat scorch, complete with acrid burning hair, that cramped Ziri's gut with foreboding. Any chimaera who had gone to battle against seraphim knew the tang of a burning body.

Ziri's sense of smell in this body was far better than his natural one had been, but he was still learning to unweave the information it gave him and identify the world's many reeks. Its perfumes, too. More smells were bad than good, in his few days of experience, at least, but the good ones were better than he'd ever realized.

Here was one now, weaving through the others like a single gold thread in a tapestry, wisp-thin but bell-bright. *Spice*, he thought. The kind that burns the tongue and leaves in its wake a kind of purity.

Whoever it was—that it was seraph, he was certain—it was all but blotted out by the overwhelming fug of chimaera musks. Ziri experienced a tightening at the base of his skull. Dread. It was dread.

What—and *who*—was he going to find up ahead?

* * *

Karou moved unseen through the passages of her ancestral home. She passed from chimaera domain into seraph. She didn't know where to look for Akiva, but assumed he would make himself easy to find. If she was right, anyway, that he wanted her to find him.

A shiver passed through her. She hoped she was right.

The caverns grew cooler as she moved out toward the entrance hall, and soon she could see her breath cloud before her. One last seraph to get past—it was Elyon, looking weary and hopeless when he thought no one was watching—and she held her breath until he was out of sight so its cloud wouldn't give her away.

There were no other seraphim; they were all together, behind her now. There was only Akiva.

An open door, and there he was. Waiting.

For a moment Karou couldn't move. This was the nearest she'd been to him—and the first time they'd been alone—since...since when? Since the day *he* came to *her* glamoured, beside the river in Morocco, and gave her the thurible that held Issa's soul. She'd said terrible things to him that day—that she'd never trusted him, for a start, what a lie—and she had yet to unsay them.

Still glamoured, she went through the door and saw him raise his head, aware of her. A flush crept up her neck as his searching look swept over her, even if he couldn't see her. He was so beautiful, and so intent. She could feel the heat coming off him.

She could feel the longing coming off him.

"Karou?" he asked, very softly.

She pushed the door closed and released her glamour.

* * *

It was almost a relief to have her anger vindicated. Even on her knees, sick from the sustained assault of close-range hamsas, Liraz was able to think, without passion or triumph, that the world made sense again. This was why the beasts had left her alone that night in the open, when she'd stayed behind with them of her own free will. Because they'd been biding their time.

There were four of them. Three stood with hamsas upheld, assaulting her with magic. The fourth hefted a big, double-sided ax.

Of course, that didn't include the three who lay dead between them—so freshly dead their hearts didn't know it yet and their blood was still escaping in arterial spurts, like water from a hand pump.

"You shouldn't have done that," said the leader of this little band of assassins, stepping over the corpses of her comrades, her wolfish grin unwavering.

Ten.

Liraz didn't know why she should be surprised that Thiago's she-wolf lieutenant was her attacker, but she was. Had she actually begun to believe that the White Wolf had found honor? What idiocy. She wondered where he was now, and why he was missing out on the fun.

"Believe it or not," drawled Ten, "we weren't going to kill you."

"I have to go with *or not* on that." They'd stalked her in the dark, and Liraz had no doubt that her life was at stake.

"Ah, but it's true. We just wanted to play your game."

For a beat, Liraz didn't know what she was talking about. It was hard to think through the thrum and drub of magic, but then it came to her. Her getting-acquainted game. *Which of us killed which of you in previous bodies.* The sickness in her gut deepened, and it wasn't just because of the hamsas. *Of course*, she thought. Wasn't this exactly what she'd imagined would happen? This had been her point, imagining the game, which she'd certainly found no humor in. "Don't tell me," she said. "I killed you once. Or was it more than once?"

"Once was enough," said Ten.

"So what now? Am I supposed to apologize?"

Ten laughed. Her smile glittered. "You should. You really should.

However, since I can't imagine you give apologies, I'll just have your trophies instead. You might still live a long and happy life without them. Probably not, but that's your own affair."

Her hands, she meant. They were going to cut off her hands. Well, they were going to try.

"So come do it," said Liraz, spitting derision.

"There's no hurry," was Ten's reply.

Not for them, maybe. Liraz was getting weaker with every second they held their hamsas out to her, and that was the point. Damned devil's eyes. This was their coward plan: weaken her before they hacked her up.

It wasn't their original plan, but three dead in under a minute had prompted them to reconsider.

Three bodies. A stupid, bloody waste. The sight of them made Liraz want to scream. *Why did you make me do this?*

Ten closed in. Flanking her were two Dracands, lizard aspect, with great ruffs of scaled flesh flaring from their necks like grotesque courtier's collars. Their hands were upheld, hamsas pounding misery into the base of Liraz's skull, and it was taking all of her focus to keep her trembling from entirely overtaking her. She knew she wouldn't be able to for very much longer. Soon, the magic would have her juddering like palsy.

The powerlessness was infuriating, and humiliating, and dire. *Now,* she told herself. If she was to have any chance of getting out of this, she had to act now. The magic of the three pairs of hamsas pulsed at her like sledgehammers.

A single clear thought filtered through her pain: My *hands are weapons, too.*

She lunged.

Ten blocked, catching her by one wrist, and the magic, it *shrieked* into Liraz from the point of contact, screaming sickness into her sinews, her flesh and bone and mind. Relentless. Crashing waves of shuddering. White-hot as flaying. Weakness like a scouring wind. *Godstars.* Liraz thought it would eat her alive, reduce her to ashes or to nothingness.

Ten held her wrist, but Liraz's other hand made it through. She pressed her own palm flat to Ten's chest, screaming back, a wordless roar right in the chimaera's face as . . . the fire stoked. And smoked.

And charred.

The lank gray fur at the she-wolf's chest caught fire. The smell was immediate and foul, and called Liraz straight back to the corpse bonfires in Loramendi. She almost lost her concentration, but managed to just hold on as her hand scorched through the chimaera's fur and into her flesh.

Ten's grimace widened, and she let loose a roar to match Liraz's. They were eye-to-eye and hands to flesh, roaring their fury and agony right in each other's faces until another set of hands seized Liraz and ripped her away, throwing her so hard into a stone wall that she blinked in and out of darkness and found herself flat on her back, gasping.

That was the end of her chance.

In and out of darkness, she felt hands seize her arms before she glimpsed the faces bent over her—the two Dracands. Their mouths were open and hissing, deeply red and reeking, as they muscled her upright once more, the fabric of her long sleeves making a poor barrier between their palms and her flesh.

Her inked flesh, her terrible hidden tally.

Once again she was eye-to-eye with Ten. The she-wolf had lost her grin and was spectacular with hatred—her wolf muzzle ruched in a snarl that no human or seraph visage could ever match for viciousness. She said, "We're not done with the game yet. So far I'm winning, and if you don't have a turn, it's hardly a game, is it? I remember you, angel, but do *you* remember *me?*"

Liraz didn't. All the kills she'd sliced into her arms with campfire soot and a hot knife—at the best of times they were a blur, and now was not the best of times. How many wolf-aspect chimaera might Liraz have slain in the decades of her life? The godstars only knew. "I never said I'd be any good at the game," she choked out.

"I'll give you a hint," said Ten. The hint was a single word, riding a snarl of hate. It was a place.

"Savvath."

The word sliced Liraz's memory open, and blood spilled out. Savvath. It was a long time ago, but she hadn't forgotten it—not the village, or what had happened just outside it. She'd just hidden it from herself, like a torn-out page—except that if it *were* a torn-out page, she'd have burned it.

You couldn't burn memories.

There was the memory of what she'd done to a dying enemy long ago, and there was the memory of how her brothers had looked at her after. For a long time after.

"That was you?" she heard herself ask, her voice hoarse. She hadn't meant to speak. It was the sickness. Her defenses were down. And... it was Savvath. If the great bulk of the obscene hundreds of chimaera Liraz had slain in her life were a blur, that one wasn't, and the simple word, *Savvath*, brought it all back.

But something didn't match. "It *wasn't* you," Liraz said, shaking her head to clear it. "That soldier was—"

Fox aspect, she was going to say, but Ten cut her off. "That soldier was me. It was my first death, did you know that? It was my natural flesh you desecrated, and this, of course, is just a vessel. Your game favors *us*, angel. How could you know who we are by looking? You don't stand a chance."

"You're right," agreed Liraz, and her head felt like a kaleidoscope of ground glass—churning, churning.

"New game," said Ten, taunting. "If you win, you keep your hands. All you have to do is tell me who every single one of your marks is for."

And Liraz imagined telling Hazael she'd solved the puzzle of her recurring dream. *How do you cut off both of your own arms?*

Easy. Give a chimaera an ax.

Because there was no way she was winning this game.

Ten looked to the big beast with the ax and beckoned him forward as she said to the Dracands, "Push up her sleeves."

They obeyed, and Liraz witnessed only the first gut-wrench of their stares—Ten actually *flinched* at the sight of her full tally revealed—and the rest was lost to crashing darkness, like an avalanche of ash, when the Dracands seized her bare arms with their hands. Four hamsas full against her flesh. It almost meant mercy. Liraz saw the nothingness she was to become. She tipped toward it. No seraph could sustain this. She would miss her own death and that wasn't such a bad thing in the end—

It cleared.

No mercy, then. Ten must have ordered the Dracands to keep her conscious, because the avalanche abated and Liraz found herself staring, up close, at the ruined skin of the handprint she'd burned in the center of the she-wolf's chest. It was blistered black and seeping, the char beginning to slough off and reveal the red meat beneath. Hideous.

"Go ahead," Ten commanded in a seethe of malevolence. "I'll make it easier for you. Start at the end and go backward. Surely you remember the recent ones."

Liraz's answering whisper was pathetic. "I don't want to play your game," she said. Something inside her was giving way. Her heartbeat felt like a child's helpless fists. She wanted to be rescued. She wanted to be safe.

"I don't care what you want. And the stakes have changed. If you win, I'll have Rark make a clean cut. If you lose..." She bared and snapped her long yellow fangs in an exaggerated grimace that left no doubt as to her meaning. "Less clean," she said. "*More fun.*" And she seized Liraz's hands and pulled her arms out taut. "Let's start with *me*. Which one, pretty angel? Which mark is mine?"

"None of them," gasped Liraz.

"Liar!"

But it was true. If the Savvath kill *were* inked on her, it would be on her fingers, it was that long ago. But at the end of that day, Hazael had made a point of weighing the tattoo kit heavy in his hand and looking at her—a look too long and too flat for Haz, like she'd changed not just herself that day by what she'd done, but him as well—and then shoving it back into his pack before turning away from her.

Liraz had heard it said that there was only one emotion which, in recollection, was capable of resurrecting the full immediacy and power of the original—one emotion that time could never fade, and that would drag you back any number of years into the pure, undiluted feeling, as if you were living it anew. It wasn't love—not that she had any experience of that one—and it wasn't hate, or anger, or happiness, or even grief. Memories of those were but echoes of the true feeling.

It was shame. Shame never faded, and Liraz realized only now that this was the baseline of her emotions—her bitter, curdled "normal"—and that her soul was poisoned soil in which nothing good could grow.

I can't imagine you give apologies, Ten had said before, and she'd been right, but Liraz thought that she would now. She would apologize for Savvath. If her voice was her own. If it wasn't reeling out of her, rising and falling in a sound that might have been laughter and might—if she weren't Liraz and it weren't unthinkable—have been sobbing.

In truth, it was both. She was going to lose her arms, the clean way or the less clean, and here's where the laughter came in: It was horrific, and it was sadistic, and it was also, literally, a dream come true.

30

Nearer and Touching

First there was no one.

Then the sense of her, nothing Akiva could pinpoint. He just knew he wasn't alone anymore.

Then the door creaked closed and the air gave her up. A glimmer and Karou stood before him like the fulfillment of a wish.

Don't hope, he warned himself. *You don't know why she's come*. But just being this near her, his skin felt alive, and his hands, his hands had their own memories—silk and pulse and flutter—and their own will. He clasped them behind his back to have something to do with them besides reach for her, which of course was out of the question. Just because she'd looked at him back in the cavern—it was *the way* she'd looked, he argued with himself, like she'd given up trying not to—didn't mean that she wanted anything more from him than this temporary alliance.

"Hello," she said. Her gaze dropped to the floor as a blush crept up her cheeks, and Akiva's battle against hope was lost.

She was blushing. If she was blushing…

Godstars, she's beautiful.

"Hello," he said, low and raw, and now his hope exceeded itself. *Say it again*, he willed her. If she did, maybe she remembered the temple of Ellai, when they'd removed their festival masks and seen each other's faces for the first time since the battlefield at Bullfinch.

Hello, they'd said then, like a whispered incantation. *Hello*, like a promise. *Hello*, breath to breath.

The last breath before their first kiss.

"Um," she said now, darting a quick glance up to meet his eyes, then veering it wide again, flushing even deeper. "Hi."

Close enough, Akiva thought, a buoyancy cautiously rising in him as he watched her take a step and then another into this room he'd claimed for himself. They were alone, finally. They could talk, free of the watchful eyes of all their comrades. That she was here at all, it meant something. And with the blaze of the look they'd shared in the cavern, he couldn't help but hope that it meant…everything.

Having hope was like dangling himself over a chasm and putting the rope in her hands. She could annihilate him if she wanted to.

She was looking around, though there wasn't much to see. It was a small chamber, bare but for a long stone slab in its center and a few ledges holding very old candles. The slab was, Akiva supposed, unusual. It was cut more precisely than the rest of the rock surfaces here. It was smooth, its hard corners rare in a world of curves.

"I remember this room," Karou said in a remote voice. "This is where the dead were prepared for burial."

That was vaguely unsettling. Hours Akiva had lain here in his dreaming, in the place inside his pain. He had lain here like a corpse, where how many corpses had lain before him? "I didn't know," he answered, hoping it wasn't offensive, him being here.

She trailed her fingertips over the slab. She was faced away from him, and he watched her shoulders rise and fall with her breathing. Her hair hung in a braid, blue as the heart of a flame. It wasn't neat. The soft hairs at her nape had all come unbound and tufted out like down. Longer loose strands of blue were tucked behind her ears, all except one stray that lay curved against her cheek.

Akiva felt, in his fingers, the desire to brush it back for her. To brush it back and linger, and feel the warmth of her neck.

"We'd dare one another to come in and lie here," Karou said. "The kids, I mean." She made a slow circle around the table, stopping to face him from the far side of it so it made a kind of barrier between them. She looked up at the ceiling. It was high, rising to a peak and funneling to a shaft in the center, like a chimney. "That's for the souls," she told him. "To release them to the sky so they wouldn't be trapped in the mountain. We used to say that if you fell asleep in here, your soul would think you were dead, and up it would go." Akiva heard the smile in her voice just before he saw it flicker over her face, fleet and fond. "So I pretended to fall asleep one time, and I acted like I lost my soul and I made all the other kids help me look for it. All day, all over the peaks." She let the smile come out now, slow, extraordinary. "I caught an air elemental and pretended *it* was my soul. Poor thing. What a little savage I was."

Her face, this face, Akiva realized, was still a mysterious land to him, and the smile almost made her a stranger.

If he'd known Madrigal for a month of nights, he'd known Karou for...two nights? Or was it really one, through much of which he'd slept, and two days in scattered pieces? Their few fraught meetings since, all he'd seen of her was her rage, her devastation, her fear.

This was something else entirely. Smiling, she was as radiant as moonstone.

It struck him with force that he didn't really know her. It wasn't just her new face. He kept thinking of her as though she were Madrigal in a different body, but she was more than that. She'd lived another life since he knew her—in another world, no less. How might it have changed her? He couldn't know.

But he could learn.

The pain of longing felt like a hole in the center of his chest. There was nothing in the worlds he wanted more than to start at the beginning and fall in love with Karou all over again.

"That was a good day," she said, still lost in her long-ago memory.

"How do you act like you've lost your soul?" Akiva asked. He meant it as a lighthearted question about a children's game, but when he heard himself say the words, he thought, *Who knows better than I?*

You betray everything you believe in. You drown your grief in vengeance. You kill and keep killing until there's no one left.

His expression must have betrayed his thoughts, because Karou's smile shrank away. She was quiet for a long moment, meeting his look. Akiva had a lot to learn about her eyes, too. Madrigal's had been warm brown. Summer and earth. Karou's were black. They were sky-dark and star-bright, and when she looked at him like this, piercing, they seemed all pupil. Nocturnal. Unnerving.

She said, "I can tell you how you act when you get your soul *back*," and he knew she wasn't talking about a game now. "You save lives," she said. "You let yourself dream again." Her voice dropped to a wisp. "You forgive."

Silence. Held breath. Beating hearts. Was... was she talking about him? Akiva felt the tilt of the world trying to tip him forward: to be nearer to her—nearer and touching—as though that were the only state of rest, and every other action and movement were geared to achieving it.

She looked down, shy again. "But you know better than I do. I'm just starting."

"You? You never lost your soul."

"I lost something. While you were saving chimaera, I was making monsters for Thiago. I didn't know what I was doing. The same things I hated *you* for doing, but I couldn't see it..."

"It's grief," said Akiva. "It's rage. It makes us into the thing we despise." And he thought, *And I was the thing you despised. Am I still?* "It's the fuel for everything our people have done to each other since the beginning. That's what makes peace seem impossible. How can you blame someone for wanting to kill the killer of their loved ones? How can you fault people for what they do in grief?"

As soon as he spoke the words, Akiva realized it sounded like he was excusing his own vicious grief spiral and its terrible toll on her people. Shame seized him. "I don't mean... I don't mean *me*. What I did, Karou, I know I can never atone for."

"Do you really believe that?" she asked. Her look was sharp, as though she were seeking through his shame for the truth.

Did he really believe it? Or was he just too guilt-ridden to admit he hoped that someday, somehow, he *could* atone? That someday he could feel that he'd done more good than evil, and that by living he hadn't brought his world lower than if he'd never been. Was *that* atonement, the tilt of the scales at the end of life?

If it was, then it might be possible. Akiva might, if he lived many years and never stopped trying, save more lives than he had destroyed.

But that wasn't what he believed, he realized, faced with the sharpness of Karou's question. "Yes," he said. "I do. You can't atone for taking one life by saving another. What good does that do the dead?"

"The dead," she said. "And we have plenty of dead between us, but the way we act, you'd think they were corpses hanging on to our ankles, rather than souls freed to the elements." She looked up at the chimney overhead, as though she were imagining the souls it had conducted in its time. "They're gone, they can't be hurt anymore, but we drag their memory around with us, doing our worst in their name, like it's what they'd want, for us to avenge them? I can't speak for all the dead, but I know it's not what I wanted for you, when I died. And I know it's not what Brimstone wanted for me, or for Eretz." Her gaze was still sharp, still piercing, nocturnal, black. It felt like recrimination—of course she'd wanted him to carry their dream forward, not find a way to destroy her people—so when she said, "Akiva, I never thanked you for bringing me Issa's soul. I... I'm sorry for the things I said to you then—" it struck him with horror. The idea of *her* apologizing to *him*.

"No." He swallowed hard. "There was nothing you said that I didn't deserve. And worse."

Was that pity in her eyes? Exasperation? "Are you determined to be unforgivable?" she asked.

He shook his head. "Nothing I'm doing is for me, Karou, or for any hope I have for myself, of forgiveness or anything else."

And under that black-eyed scrutiny, he had to ask himself: Was *this* true?

It was and wasn't. No matter how much he tried not to hold out hope, hope surfaced, persistent. He had no more control over it than he did over the drone of the wind. But was it the reason he was doing any of this? For the chance of a reward? No. If he knew absolutely that Karou would never forgive him and never love him again, he would still do anything in his power—and beyond his power, it seemed, in the mind-bending light of *sirithar*—to rebuild the world for her.

Even if he had to stand back and watch her walk through it at the White Wolf's side?

Even then.

But . . . he *didn't* know absolutely that there was no hope. Not yet.

* * *

I forgive you. I love you. I want you, at the end of all this. The dream, peace, and you.

This is what Karou wished to say, and it's what she wished to hear, too. She didn't want to be told that Akiva had given up the hope of her, and that whatever his motivation was now, it was no longer the fullness of their dream, which had been not merely peace, but themselves together in it. Had he cut the dream up for kindling? Had *she*? Had it already been fed to the fire?

"I believe you," she said. No hope for himself. It was noble, and it was bleak, and it wasn't the conduit her own unspoken words needed. They were heavy in her, and clinging. How do you just thrust "I love you" out into the air? It needs waiting arms to catch it. At least, right now, Karou's unpracticed, unspoken "I love you" did. After months of its being crushed down into the recesses of her fury and warped out of all natural shape, she could no more blurt it out than she could grab Akiva's face and kiss him.

Kiss him. *That* felt a million miles from possible.

Her eyes did their timid dance of glances again, taking him in in snapshots. A freeze-frame of his face, and then dropping her gaze again to the stone slab or her own hands, she held the glimpse in her mind. Akiva's golden skin, his full lips, his taut, haunted expression and the... *retreat* in his eyes. Back in the cavern, his eyes had reached for her like the rays of the sun. Now they shrank from hers, reticent and guarded. Karou wanted to feel the sun again. But when she lifted her eyes from her restless hands, Akiva was staring down at the stone slab.

Between the pair of them, you'd think this table was one fascinating artifact.

Well. It wasn't only "I love you" that she had come to say. She took a deep breath, and got on with the rest.

* * *

"I need to tell you something."

Akiva looked up again. Instantly, something new in Karou's tone set him on edge. Her hesitation, the catch in her voice. He didn't have to struggle now to keep his hope at bay. Hope deserted him.

What is she going to say?

That she was with the Wolf now. The alliance was a mistake. The chimaera were leaving. He would never see her again.

He wanted to blurt, *I have something to tell you, too,* and keep her from saying whatever it was. He wanted to tell her of his new magic, as yet untested, and ask for her help with it. It's what he'd hoped for, if she actually came here. He wanted to tell her what he'd made possible—for their armies, if not for themselves.

Things change. They can be changed, by those with the will.

Worlds, even. Maybe.

"It's about Thiago," she said, and he felt the cool touch of finality. Of course it was the Wolf. When he'd seen them curved toward each other, laughing, he'd known, but a part of his mind had insisted on denying it—it was unthinkable—and then, when she'd looked across the cavern to him like that, to *him*, he'd hoped...

"He's not who you think," Karou said, and Akiva knew what was coming next.

He braced for it.

"I killed him," she whispered.

...

...

...

Wait.

"What?"

"I killed Thiago. This isn't him. I mean, it's not his soul." She took a deep, dragging breath and rushed on. "His soul is gone. *He's* gone. I've hated letting you think that I...and he...I could never have forgiven him, or..." A quicksilver glance, and, as if she'd read his thoughts: "Or *laughed* with him. And there could never have been peace while he was alive. And this alliance?" Emphatically, she shook her head. "*Never.* He'd have killed you and Liraz at the kasbah."

"Wait," said Akiva, trying to catch up. "Wait." What was she saying? Her words wouldn't settle into sense. The Wolf was dead? The Wolf was dead, and whoever was walking around claiming that title...it wasn't him. Akiva stared at Karou. The idea spun him. He didn't even know what questions to ask.

"I wanted to tell you before," she said. "But I have to be careful. It's all so fragile. No one knows. Only Issa and Ten... and Ten's not really Ten, either... but if the rest of the chimaera found out, we'd lose them like that." She snapped her fingers.

Akiva was still trying to grasp the basic premise.

"They wouldn't follow anybody but Thiago, at least not yet," she said. "That was clear. We needed him. This army did, and our people did, but... we needed a *better* him."

Better.

And Akiva recalled his impression of the Wolf with whom he'd negotiated this alliance. Intelligent, powerful, and sane, that was what he'd thought at the time, never imagining the reason for it.

Finally, the pieces snapped into place and he understood. Somehow, Karou had put a different soul into the Wolf's body. "Who?" he asked. "Who is it?"

A wave of grief passed over her face. "It's Ziri," she said, and when he didn't react to the name, she added, "The Kirin whose life you saved."

The young Kirin, the last of the tribe. So he wasn't dead, not exactly. "But... how?" Akiva asked, unable to imagine the chain of events that had created such a situation.

Karou was silent a moment, and faraway. "Thiago attacked me," she said, reaching up to touch the cheek that had been swollen and abraded when Akiva flew to her in Morocco, he and Liraz bearing Hazael's body between them. She was nearly healed now. She looked like she might say more about it, but didn't. The press of her lips stilled a trembling, and Akiva remembered his full fury at the sight of her brutalized. His fists remembered it, and his heart and gut remembered, too, the unfathomable look of tenderness that had passed between her and the Wolf that night at the kasbah, and it finally made sense.

It didn't comfort him, though.

"He attacked me and I killed him," she went on. "And I didn't know what to do. I knew the others would make me resurrect him if they found us, and I couldn't face it. If things had been bad before, what would they be like after that? I don't know what I would've done. . . ." She trailed off.

Then her eyes came clear again, focusing keenly on *him*. Improbably, she smiled. It wasn't the radiant unfurling of her last smile, but another species entirely, small and sudden and surprised. "As much as I've thought about it," she said, "I didn't get it, until right now, how it all comes back to you."

"Me?" he asked with a jolt.

"You brought me Issa and Ziri both," she said. "If it weren't for you, I would have had no allies, and no chance."

Again, the weight of her words—of her gratitude—stirred Akiva's deepest shame. "If it weren't for me, Karou, you'd have a lot more allies." *A lot more.* How many corpses weighed in those words? Loramendi. Thousands upon thousands.

"Stop doing that," she said in frustration. "Akiva. I meant what I said, about forgiving. It's the only way forward. When the Wolf was still the Wolf, I tried reasoning with him, that his way was death. He wouldn't hear me. He couldn't. He was too far gone. But I kept finding *your* words in my mouth while I argued with him, and I knew that however far you'd gone, you had come back. And . . . it helped bring *me* back."

His words? Akiva had none now. This was all so far from what he'd feared she was going to tell him that he couldn't get his mind around it.

"You said it depended on us, whether the future would have chimaera in it," she told him. "And it wasn't only words. You saved Ziri's life. If you hadn't, we couldn't be here now. You would be dead, and I...I would be the Wolf's..." She didn't finish. Again, a shadow of horror darkened her look, leaving Akiva to imagine what exactly those simple words—*Thiago attacked me*—encompassed.

The flare of his rage threatened to blind him. He had to force it aside and remind himself, breathing, that the object of it was gone. Thiago couldn't be punished. If anything, this only made the rage hotter. "I wasn't there to protect you," he said. "I should never have left you there with him—"

"I protected myself," Karou cut in. "It was after that I needed help, and Ziri was there, and now we're here, all of us. That's what I'm trying to say."

The horror had left her; the brightness in her eyes was tears, and the curve of her lips was gratitude, and Akiva experienced a surge of self-loathing when he caught himself wondering who the brightness and gratitude were *for*.

He saw again the look of tenderness that had passed between her and the impostor Wolf back at the kasbah, and saw again the way they'd stood together laughing just the day before.

Godstars. He would be dead right now if the Wolf had been the Wolf, and yet he could stand here and worry whether this "intelligent, powerful, sane" Thiago, this heroic Kirin who was Karou's closest ally, was a greater threat to his own hopes than a murdering, torturing maniac had been? There were armies poised to fly, and he was worried about who Karou might *love*?

"But even that's not the end of it," she said. "You brought me Issa, and you can't imagine what else you brought with her, but...Akiva, it made the difference." Her eyes were so bright, their black gloss like a mirror for the fire of his wings. "It's Loramendi. It's... it's not redemption, not completely, but it's a start. Or it will be, when we can get there."

And then she told him about the cathedral.

The magnitude of the news... it struck Akiva dumb and erased all his petty worries.

Brimstone had had a cathedral beneath the city—Akiva hadn't found it when he walked in a daze through the ruins, because it had been buried, its entrances collapsed and disguised. And in it, in stasis, were souls. Souls uncounted. Children, women. The souls of thousands of chimaera who hadn't yet gone beyond hope of retrieval.

Akiva had told Karou, back in Morocco, that he would do anything—that he would die a death for every slain chimaera if it would bring them back. He'd said it in the bleakness of believing the words were hollow, that there was nothing he could ever do to prove that he meant them. But... there was.

"Let me help you," he said at once. "Karou... please. So many souls, you can't do it alone." She'd said it wasn't quite redemption? It was so much closer than he'd ever thought he'd come to it. And if redemption was self-serving, coming as it did ribbon-tied to what he wanted most in life? For once, Akiva's shame wouldn't rise to the bait. He wanted what he'd always wanted, and he'd better just say it, his own worries and fears be damned. Whoever she loved, him or the Wolf or no one, he would find out. "It's all I want, to be beside you, helping you. If it takes forever, all the better, if it's forever with you."

And the stone table was between them, a barrier, but there could be no barrier to the smile that was her answer. It was another new species, and Akiva thought that he could spend a thousand years with her—*please*—and still be discovering new species of smiles. This one was unbearable, sweet as music and heavy as tears. It was all her tension, all her wariness and uncertainty, melting into light.

It was her heart, this smile, and it was for him.

"Okay," she said. Her voice was small, but the word was bright and heavy, like something he could reach for, and hold.

Okay. Okay, he could help her? Okay to forever?

Okay.

If that could have been the end of it. Or the beginning. If they could fly together now to Loramendi. Let forever begin *now*. But of course it couldn't. Karou spoke again, and her voice was still small, still bright and heavy, but if her *okay* had been serene and sun-warmed and smooth as a stone, her next words had thorns.

"If we live that long," she said.

31

THE OPPOSITE OF SURVIVAL

Ziri stood in the doorway. In a glance, he perceived the situation.

Three of his soldiers were dead at his feet. Oora, Sihid, Ves. Wasted flesh, wasted pain, and more blood to walk through. Of those still living, Rark loomed largest, his great ax glinting in the dim, but Ziri's eyes cut straight to Liraz. Her wingfire burned low—it burned *dying* low—but she was still the brightest thing in the room. She was shudder-wracked and waxen white, empty-eyed and hollowed out, and she was... laughing? Crying? A horrible sound. She was hemmed in by chimaera, held up by them, and only their grip could be keeping her upright in such a state—keeping her upright and killing her at the same time.

Could a seraph die from the touch of hamsas? One sight of Liraz, and Ziri thought *yes*. But that wasn't how they meant to kill her. They held her arms stretched out before her, and in that first glance, Ziri thought he understood.

Rark. The ax. They were going to cut off her arms.

But the ax was at rest against Rark's thick shoulder, and . . . the truth came together out of shreds. Sound, sight, odor. The snarl. Slaver strung from yellow fangs, and the reek of triumph. Ten.

That fact hit Ziri like a sucker punch, driving the breath from him. It was *Ten. Oh Nitid, oh Ellai, no.* Of all the soldiers under his command . . . his fellow trespasser, his co-conspirator. The one who knew his secret.

She was poised to lunge. And though her body was more human than not, right now her back humped wolflike above her lowered head, fur bristling at the ridge of her shoulders, and the sound of her growl was animal and guttural—*felt* as much as heard. The room reeked of blood and bowels and burning, hot and close and dead. Corpses and vengeance and no turning back. And Ziri knew what Ten—*Haxaya*—meant to do.

"Stop." It was the White Wolf's voice, smooth and cold as iron, but it was underscored by a horror that was purely Ziri's. This scene would not have horrified the Wolf, who had ripped apart angels with his own sharp teeth. And once the immediate threat was averted and Ten had swung around to face him, Ziri wasn't sure why it horrified *him* as profoundly as it did. He didn't kill with his teeth, but he'd fought alongside many chimaera who did—and with beaks and claws and horns and spiked tails, and any other weapon at their disposal. Against the superior might of the seraphim, it was a matter of survival.

But *this* wasn't. This was the opposite of survival.

This was everything put at risk: the alliance, of course, but the deception, too. Because it was Ten.

Because it was Ten, Ziri stood stiff and silent as Rark and the Dracands spun to face him, too, and Nisk and Lisseth drew up behind him. Because it was Ten, he didn't know what to say. He felt Haxaya peering out at him through the she-wolf's yellow eyes, and there was no fear in her, only a sly and roguish contempt.

I dare you, she might well have said. *Punish me, and I'll punish you. Impostor.*

His heart was pounding. He fought to slow it. The Naja could read heat signatures, as serpents could; Nisk and Lisseth would be able to sense his turmoil, and Thiago simply did not fall prey to turmoil. Ziri forced his features to hold the Wolf's default expression of cool, half-lidded appraisal.

"What is the meaning of this, lieutenant?" he asked, low and deadly calm.

Rark's head gave a small jerk of surprise, and the Dracands, Wiwul and Agwilal, turned hooded looks on Ten. Clearly, she'd told them this was their general's order, and they'd had no reason to doubt her. She was his second in command, his most trusted lieutenant.

Not anymore.

"It's vengeance," said Ten, omitting *sir*. It was stark disrespect, and, he knew, a warning. "This angel is a wicked one. Look at her arms."

He did look, and was sickened by what he saw—by her extraordinary tally, but by her anguish, too. He didn't know Liraz, of course. She was beautiful, but what of that? Most seraphim were. She was also hostile and hot-tempered and at full strength she more than matched Ten for ferocity. But he had seen her broken and mourning, too, holding her dead brother in her arms, all that ferocity stripped away to reveal a raw girl. And he had seen something else in her.

Back at the kasbah, to his surprise, she had asked after *him*—himself, Ziri—in such a way as made clear that . . . she had noticed his absence. That she had even been aware of his existence was a surprise to him, and then, when he'd told her the Kirin soldier was dead, he had seen—he was certain—a flicker of sorrow in her eyes, there and gone again, like something escaped and quickly recaptured.

Of course, that wasn't why he couldn't allow his soldiers to kill or mutilate her in this remote cave—there were a lot bigger and less personal reasons for that. But it might be why a fury was rising in him, as cold as he imagined the real Wolf's anger would be, and quick to extinguish his turmoil under a layer of implacable purpose. His heartbeat evened out to a calm and heavy hammerfall.

"Release her," he said, with a flick of his disinterested gaze in her direction. Her eyes were just whites now, rolling up under her fluttering lashes at the edge of consciousness—or life. "Or she'll be dead before you can explain yourselves."

Wiwul and Agwilal let go of her at once, and she collapsed against the wall, but only partially, because Ten still held her wrists. A direct order ignored, in the presence of others. So she was going to challenge him. "Explain *our*selves?" she asked, mock-innocent with an edge of acid. "What about you . . . *sir*?" This *sir* was worse than none, a bald affront that the Wolf would never abide. "Would you care to explain *your*self?"

He heard the intake of breath from behind him—Nisk or Lisseth, stunned by her insubordination. Rark was staring with tusks agape, and Ziri didn't have to ponder what the real Wolf would do. He knew, and it felt like slipping in blood, to do what the Wolf would. One slip and down you go. The blood coats you. The blood is your life now. But what choice did he have?

His awareness heightened—of the unnatural strength in his borrowed flesh, of the malice and mischief in Ten's eyes, and of the weight of the future bearing down on all of them if she gave him away.

How could she be so stupid?

It felt like whip-crack, the sliver of an instant it took him to reach her. To lay hands to her head, one behind and one to her muzzle.

And snap her neck.

There wasn't even time for surprise. With the sound—it wasn't a *snap* but a grinding and giving way punctuated by a string of firecracker *pops*—her eyes went void. No more malice, no more mischief, no more threat, and though the moment before her muscles fell slack felt long, it couldn't have been more than a second. She fell, and falling, dropped Liraz's wrists at last, and Liraz fell, too, leading with her cheek to the floor as if she'd long ago lost sense of up and down. Ziri absorbed his own flinch at the impact of her landing, and made himself ignore her as she lay there, her wingfire burning ever dimmer and her trembling the only sign that she still lived.

He faced his soldiers and said, as though there had been no interruption to the conversation, "No, I would not care to explain myself." His look dared them to be the next to demand it.

Rark was the first to speak. "Sir, we . . . Ten said it was your order. We would never—"

"I believe you, soldier," he cut in. Rark looked relieved.

It was too soon for relief.

"I believe that you did, in fact, think that I would be *this stupid*." Ziri breathed the last through clenched teeth. "Mere hours until we're to fly, desperately outnumbered, into battle, and you believe that I would rob my army of strength at the time of greatest need." He flung a hand out to the dead he'd stepped over in the doorway. "That I would waste bodies that others paid for with their pain. That

I would risk every plan I have put in place, and for what? For one angel? You think that I'm stupid enough to cast everything away, rather than wait . . . a few hours . . . to engage the *thousand* angels who are the true and immediate threat. Is this supposed to make me feel better?"

No one answered him, and he shook his head in slow disgust. "The order you followed countermanded every order that you have heard from my own lips, and if you had been able to think further than the jut of your own teeth, you would have questioned it. You did this because you wanted to. Maybe we *all* want to, but some of us are masters of our desires, and some are slaves, and I had thought you wiser than this."

Lest Lisseth feel herself clear of his excoriation, he turned to her. "It's a small grace that Ten didn't see fit to invite you on her crusade, as you've left me in no doubt that you would have complied with eagerness. You're spared the sentence of your comrades, but we both know it was only circumstance that saved you, not wisdom."

At the mention of a sentence, Rark, Wiwul, and Agwilal stiffened, and Ziri drew out an uncomfortable silence before putting them out of their misery. "You have lost my confidence," he said, "and are stripped of rank. You will fight in the coming battle, and if you survive, you will tithe pain to the resurrection of your comrades until such a time as I deem your sins purged. Do you accept this?"

"Yes, sir," they said, Nisk and Lisseth, too, five voices blending into one.

"Then get out of my sight, and take those three with you." Oora, Sihid, Ves. "Glean their souls and dispose of their bodies, then wait for me at the resurrection chamber. Tell no one what has happened here. Am I clear?"

Again, a chorus of *yes, sirs*.

Ziri arranged his face in a look of resignation, a subtle lip curl hinting at distaste. "I will take care of these two." Ten and Liraz, one living, one dead. He said it darkly, and let the others imagine what they would. He grabbed Ten by the furred scruff of the neck, and Liraz by one arm, roughly—though he kept her bunched sleeve between his hamsa and her skin—as though both were corpses to be dragged down the passageway like cargo. He wouldn't be able to hold a torch, but with the dim flame of Liraz's wings, he didn't need one.

If she died, he would be in darkness.

And darkness would be the least of his worries.

"Go!" he snarled, and the soldiers went, scrambling for the dead, grabbing them and hauling them, leaving blood streaks in their wake, and it was only after they were gone that Ziri readjusted his hold on Liraz, lifting her easily—and gently—with one arm. It felt wrong and far too intimate to rest her body against his own—*Not my own*, he thought with a shudder—so he kept a space between them, even though it proved awkward as he maneuvered toward the door, all the more so for trying not to hurt her further with his own hamsas.

When he shifted his grip on Ten to navigate the turning, Liraz's head tipped and fell heavily against his, her brow to his jaw, and Ziri felt the fever heat of a seraph's skin for the first time before he eased it away, and he breathed up close the scent that he had followed from afar. The spice note was bright, and like a burst of heat it seared a path for something much more subtle and unexpected—the most secret of perfumes, natural, he had no doubt, and so faint his Kirin nose could never have detected it, not even as close as this. It was barely there at all, but in the hint of its existence it was as fragile as night blossoms—not too sweet but just enough, like the dew on a requiem bud in the palest hour of dawn.

Ziri faced straight ahead and didn't lean or turn to try to breathe it in, but even so, walking in the darkness, dragging a corpse and carrying an angel who would probably gut him for touching her as soon as she recovered—*if* she recovered—that secret perfume made him conscious of the claws on his fingers, the fangs in his mouth, and all the ways he was not himself. He wore a monster's skin, and it felt like a violation to even breathe a woman in through its senses, let alone touch her with its hands.

Still he carried her, and still he breathed—because he couldn't *not*—and he gave thanks to Nitid, goddess of life—and to Lisseth, whose intentions had been far less pure—for leading him to her in time. He only wished he could have gotten there sooner and spared her the unknown depths of damage the hamsas may have worked in her. Could she possibly be well enough to fly with the rest of them in a few hours' time? Unlikely. If there was something he could do for her…

Almost at the moment this thought formed, he reached a branching of the passages and realized where he was, and it was the completion of the thought. If there was something he could do for her, he would.

And there was. And so he did.

He turned and took a secondary passage, depositing the she-wolf's corpse in the entrance to the thermal pools before carrying Liraz to the water's edge. The healing waters—were they only good for scrapes and bruises? Ziri didn't know. He had to shift the angel into both arms to carry her into the pool, and when he lowered her into the water, darkness closed in on him and he knew a moment's panic, thinking that her wings had burned out.

But no. A faint glow lit the water from below; her fire still burned, ember-dim. He eased his hold until he was barely touching her—just his arm beneath the nape of her neck to keep her face above the surface—and he waited, watching her lips and eyelids for some hint of movement. And . . . so gradually he didn't at first notice it, the underwater glow brightened, so that by the time Liraz finally moved, Ziri could make out not just the chalk-green cast of the water and the pink of the hanging veils of moss, but the flush of the angel's cheeks, and the dark gold of her lashes as they fluttered and slowly opened. And fixed on him.

He remembered her words to him back at the kasbah. "We haven't been introduced," he had said, to which she'd replied, in hot rebuke, "You know who I am, and I know who you are, and that will serve."

She *didn't* know, though. And he wanted her to.

"We haven't been introduced," he said again, as she found her footing under the surface of the soft, dark water. "Not really."

32

Cake for Later

"If we live that long."

It wasn't what Karou wanted to say. Not even close. In fact, she didn't want to *say* anything. Akiva stood facing her from across the stone table, his eyes still full of forever, and all she wanted to do was climb up onto the slab and meet him in the middle. But since when did she get to have what she wanted? Akiva wanted to spend forever with her? It was... it was sun flares and thunderclaps inside her, but it was also like a piece of cake set aside for later. A taunt.

Finish your dinner and you can have your cake.

If you don't die.

"We'll live that long," he said, ardent and certain. "We'll survive this. We'll *win* this."

"I wish I could be as sure as you are," she said, but she was thinking: *armies angels portals weapons war.*

"Be sure. Karou, I won't let anything happen to you. After everything, and... *now*... I'm not letting you out of my sight." After a pause and in the midst of a sweet and bashful blush—as if he was still not certain he was reading her right, or that his *now* was what he hoped it was—Akiva added, "As long as you want me with you."

"I want me with you," she said at once. She heard the mix-up of her words—*me with you*—but didn't correct herself. It was exactly what she meant. "But I can't be with you. Not yet. It's already decided. Separate battalions, remember?"

"I remember. But I have something to tell you, too. Or better, to show you. I think it might help." And he sat on the table and swung his legs up, moving to the center and beckoning her to join him.

She did, and felt the temperature rise with his nearness. No more barrier between them. She curled her legs beneath her—the stone was cool—and wondered what this was about. It was no echo of her wanting. He didn't reach for her, but only regarded her with a half-hesitant intensity. "Karou, do you think the chimaera would consent to mixed battalions?" he asked.

What? "If Thiago commanded it, they would. But what does it matter? Your brothers and sisters won't. They were pretty clear on that."

"I know," he said. "Because of the hamsas. Because you have a weapon against which we have no defense."

She nodded. Her own hamsas were flat against the slab; it was becoming second nature to conceal the eyes in the presence of seraphim, to guard against accidental assault, but it was precarious. She said, "Our hands are enemies even if we aren't," and her tone was light but her heart was not. She didn't want any part of herself to be Akiva's enemy.

"But what if they weren't?" he persisted. "I think I could persuade the Misbegotten to integrate. It makes sense, Karou. One-on-one, the Dominion are no match for us, but it's not one-on-one, and even without any unforeseen advantage they may have gained, our numbers are strained. Chimaera in our battalions would not only increase our strength, but decrease the enemy's. And there's the psychological advantage, too. It will throw them off balance to see us together." He paused. "It's the best use of our two armies."

Where was he going with this? "Maybe you should have told Elyon and Orit that," she said.

"I will tell them. If you agree, and . . . if it works."

"If what works?"

Still looking at her with that half-hesitant intensity, Akiva reached out very slowly, and, with one fingertip light against her cheek, hooked a loose strand of her hair and pushed it behind her ear. The tiny touch sparked and blazed, but the spark and blaze were subsumed by a deeper, fuller fire when he brought the whole of his palm against her cheek. His gaze was vivid, hopeful, and searching, and the touch was whisper-light, and it was . . . a taste of the cake Karou couldn't have. It was more than a taunt. It was a torment. She wanted to turn her face and press her lips to Akiva's palm, and then his wrist, to follow the path of his pulse to its source.

To his heart. His chest, his solidity. His arms around her, that's what she wanted, and . . . she wanted movement that spoke to movement, skin to skin and sweat to heat to breath to gasp. *Oh god.* His touch made her foolish. It spliced her right out of real life with its drumbeat of *armies angels portals weapons war* and into that paradise they'd imagined long ago—the one that was like a jewel box waiting for them to find it and fill it with their happiness.

Fantasy. Even if they made it to "forever," it wouldn't be paradise, but a war-ravaged world with much to learn and unlearn. Work to do and pain to tithe and . . . and . . . *And cake*, Karou thought with defiance. There could be life, around the edges. Akiva every day, in work and in pain, yes, but in love, too.

Cake as a way of life.

And she did turn her face, and she did press her lips to Akiva's palm, and she felt a shudder go through him and knew that the distance between them was far less than this arm span of physical space. How easy to tip into it and lose herself in a small and temporary paradise . . .

"Do you remember?" he asked, and his voice was hoarse. "This is the beginning." And his touch traced down her cheek and down her neck, and it was fire and magic, kindling every atom of her. His fingertips stopped at her clavicle and his palm came down to rest, light as a shawl of hummingbird-moths, against her heart.

"Of course I do," she said, as hoarse as he was.

"Then give me your hand." He reached for it and she gave it. He drew it toward himself, and Karou's eyes were on the V of his neckline, the triangle of his chest, and already in her mind she was sliding her hand under the fabric to rest her palm against his heart. . . .

Stop.

Distantly, she recognized the danger and resisted, curling her hand into a fist. "I don't want to hurt you."

"Trust me," he said. His half-hesitation had melted away when her lips touched his palm, and now there was only the intensity, and *the pull*—as if, at this distance, their magnets had engaged and could only be wrenched apart by the most committed resistance. Karou's resistance was not committed. She wanted to touch Akiva like she wanted to breathe. So she let him guide her hand, and when her knuckles brushed his collar, she took over her own part in reenacting the memory—"*We are the beginning.*"—uncurling her fingers and slipping them under the edge of the fabric to his chest. Akiva's chest. Akiva's skin. It was alive under her fingertips and she wanted to follow them with her lips. Her desire was mind-melting, and that was why it took her a long, delirious beat, her hand—her palm—full against his skin, to understand.

Her touch didn't hurt him.

With wonder in her voice, she asked, "Akiva... how?"

His hand covered hers and held it against him, and she felt the heat in her hamsa as she always did in the presence of seraphim, a prickling sensation, but Akiva didn't flinch or recoil or tremble. He smiled. The arm span between them had shortened—from the length of his arm to the length of hers, and he shortened it further, leaning toward her, bowing his head and twisting as he whispered, "Magic," and showed her what he had done.

On the back of his neck was a mark that Karou knew had not been there before. It was low, half-hidden by his collar, but she could see what it was: an eye. A *closed* eye. His own magic to counteract Brimstone's. It wasn't indigo like a hamsa; it wasn't a tattoo, but a scar. "When did you do this?" she asked.

"Tonight."

She traced the fine raised lines of flesh with her fingertip. "It's already healed."

He nodded, settling back and raising his head again. And though Karou had begun to get an inkling of what Akiva might be capable of, it still astonished her. The fact that he had scarred and healed himself in a matter of hours was extraordinary, but it was nothing next to the magic it made. He had effectively negated the chimaera's most powerful weapon—after resurrection, that is, if that could be counted a weapon. Maybe it should have terrified her, but right now, terror wasn't what Karou was feeling.

"I can touch you," she marveled, and she couldn't—or at least *didn't*—resist the urge to further prove it by sliding her palm over the hot-smooth terrain of his chest until she felt as if she were holding his heartbeat in her hand.

"As much as you want," he said, and there was a trembling in him, but it wasn't from pain.

Skin and forever made for a potent combination, and the real reason Akiva had conjured this magic was as good as forgotten, and so was everything else outside the pulse of their two heartbeats—

—until it turned up at the door.

* * *

An unlikelier sight could scarcely have been imagined: shoulder-to-shoulder and dripping wet, stalking through passages with silent purpose and crossing from chimaera domain into seraph by way of a straight shot across the main cavern where nearly everyone was gathered... Thiago and Liraz, dragging the corpse of Ten behind them.

Every voice ceased. Mik had set down his violin some time earlier and was lying with his head in Zuzana's lap until her gasp served to lurch him upright.

Issa had reared high on her coil and looked more than ever like a serpent goddess from some ancient temple, and all around them the chimaera host were rising or half rising, alert and ready to fight should they be called upon. But they weren't. The pair marched past, eyes fixed ahead and expressions matching grim, and were gone again, passing by the seraph guard at the far door without a pause or a word of explanation.

Finding Akiva's door still closed, Liraz gave a chuff of derision and didn't knock but only crashed it open and glared at the sight that greeted them. Akiva and Karou, eyes bleary with desire, facing each other on a stone slab and touching, hands to hearts.

Some would say that Ellai—goddess of assassins and secret lovers—had been afoot this night, gliding through the passages, busy at mischief and narrow salvation. A few moments one side or the other and Liraz might be dead, or Karou and Akiva caught in a deeper compromise than a bleary-eyed desire fugue with their hands to each other's hearts. Another moment, and they might have kissed.

But Ellai was a fickle patroness and had failed them—spectacularly—before. Karou didn't believe in gods anymore, and when the door crashed open, there were only Liraz and the Wolf to blame for it.

"Well," Liraz said, her voice as dry as the rest of her was not. "At least you still have your clothes on."

* * *

And thank god for that, thought Karou, snatching her hand out of Akiva's shirt. Instantly she felt the chill of the chamber. How quickly her body adjusted to Akiva's temperature and made everything else seem cold by contrast. It took a few blinks for her daze to clear, to register the details of wet clothing plastered to skin and the plink of drips, not to mention the waft of sulfur.

Ziri had taken Liraz to bathe at the thermal pools? Well, that was . . . weird. Fully clothed? Okay, that was less weird than the alternative, but it was all just *too* weird, and then the Wolf hefted something across the threshold and everything came into focus.

A corpse. "The oath-breaker," said the Wolf.

Ten. *Haxaya.*

What?

Karou unfurled from her perch on the stone table and boosted off the edge to drop down beside the body. At once she saw the scorched handprint on the she-wolf's chest and looked up at Liraz, who greeted her with a deader-even-than-usual stare.

Akiva joined her beside the body, and in a matter of seconds the corridor was filled with seraphim and also chimaera who'd transgressed the boundary to see what was happening. It was almost funny, that an act of violence like this should in some way be the trigger for the armies' freer intermingling. Almost funny, but so very not.

It was another powder keg, a lit match poised to fall on it. The next few moments were a scramble of questions and answers. The Wolf told them what had happened, maintaining the deception in every detail. Ten had done this. And Ten had died. As for Haxaya, Karou tried to process the fact of her part in it. She had known her well. As Madrigal, she had fought beside her, and trusted her. She was wild but not unpredictable. Not *stupid.* In making her part of the deception, Karou had trusted all their lives to her. "Why would she do it?" she asked, and she didn't expect an answer. She was asking the air, but it was Liraz who answered.

"It was personal," said the angel. She faced Akiva, and something in her dead stare gave way. The change in her in that instant, Karou thought, was like the change that Ziri brought to the Wolf's face, though the reason could of course not be the same. It wasn't somebody else looking out through Liraz's eyes. It was the mask slipping, and that softer, almost girlish face that she revealed was *herself*. She said, "Savvath," and Akiva, letting out a hard breath, nodded understanding.

Karou knew the name. As in: *Savvath, battle of.* It was a village on the western shores of the Bay of Beasts, or it had been, once. It was before her time.

To Thiago, her face angled toward him but her eyes downcast, Liraz said, "What you do with her soul is your affair, but you should know, I don't blame her. I deserved her vengeance."

And Thiago made some reply, but Karou heard it in a state of distraction. Something was tickling at her mind. She kept looking from Ten's body to Liraz, from the scorched black handprint on the she-wolf's chest to the angel's tally, all but concealed by her sleeves, pulled down over the heels of her hands.

Our hands are enemies, even if we aren't, recalled Karou.

And the angels all went quietly home and no one died. The end.

Her heart started to pound. An idea was taking shape. She didn't give voice to it, but let its traceries unfurl, following them and searching for defects, anticipating what the arguments would be against it. *Could it be this simple?* The voices around her muted to a murmur and ran soft under the layer of her thoughts. *It could and should be this simple.* The plan as it stood was worse than complicated. It was messy. She looked around at the gathered faces: Akiva, Liraz, and the Wolf in the room with her, Elyon and Issa in the doorway, and the shifting figures behind them visible only as a shuffle of fire feathers and furred haunches, black armor and red chitin, smooth flesh and rough, side by side.

All ready to fly into battle, to enact for humanity the apocalypse of its dreams and nightmares.

Or maybe not.

It wasn't Akiva or the Wolf who first noticed the change in Karou's manner—the straightening of her posture, the brightness of her exhilaration. It was Liraz. "What's come over *you?*" she asked, in a tone of chagrined curiosity.

It was apt, that it was Liraz. "If you think of a better idea, I'm sure you'll let us know," she'd said at the end of the war council, scornful and dismissive. And now Karou fixed her with the strength of her own certainty. Her desperation had become conviction, and it felt like steel.

"I've thought of a better idea," she said. "Reconvene the council. Now."

Once upon a time,
a girl went to see a monster menagerie

where all the exhibits were dead.

ARRIVAL + 36 HOURS

33

Like an Alien Invasion

"They should treat it like an alien invasion."

Morgan's words kept coming back to Eliza on the plane. Outside the window was a mystery nightscape—a blur of clouds parting now and then to reveal...darkness. Were they over the Atlantic? How crazy to not even know that much for certain. How often did this happen to people, this not knowing where in the world you were?

Eliza shivered and drew her forehead back from the cold windowpane. There was nothing to see out there but cloud tatters and night. If this were a book or a movie, she thought, she'd be able to read the stars and get her bearings. Characters always had just the right random skill set to master the situation at hand. Like, *Thank god for that summer on an uncle's smuggling boat and the handsome deckhand who taught me celestial navigation*. Ha.

Eliza had no random skills. Well, she did a mean horror-movie scream, apparently. Useful, that. Oh, and she was handy with a scalpel. When she'd taught the undergrad anatomy lab back at her university, a student had joked that she probably knew all the best places to stab someone, and she supposed she did, though it was not a skill she had ever had to call upon.

So basically, the sum of her special skills amounted to stabbing with great accuracy while horror-movie screaming. She was practically a superhero!

Oh god. It was the fatigue. She estimated that she was into hour thirty-six of keeping awake—not counting her brief doze in the lab—and it was no easy thing. The soft sounds of Dr. Chaudhary's snores from across the aisle were torture. What would it be like, to be able to nod off without fear?

Who would she be, without the dream? Who was she anyway? Was she "Eliza Jones," whom she had created from scratch, or was she, immutably, that other self, molded by others, and crushed by them, too?

People with destinies shouldn't make plans.

Such were her thoughts when she detected the plane's first pitch of descent. She put her face again to the cold windowpane and saw that the darkness outside was no longer entire. A dawn flush clung to the contours of the world, and... Eliza's brow furrowed. She leaned closer, tried angling her face for a better view. She had never been to Italy, but she was fairly certain that this was not it.

Italy didn't have... a desert, did it?

She glanced at the agents seated several rows back, but their faces gave away nothing.

Jostled by turbulence, Dr. Chaudhary finally woke and turned to Eliza. "Are we there?" he asked, stretching.

"We're somewhere," Eliza replied, and he leaned toward his own window to peer out.

A long look, a lift of his eyebrows, and he settled back into his seat. "Hmm," was all he said, which, in the parlance of Dr. Chaudhary, translated roughly to: *Very strange indeed.*

Eliza felt as if her rib cage had flinched up against her heart. *Where are we being taken?*

By the time the plane's wheels touched down on a desolate stretch of desert runway, the sun had cleared a ridge of mountains and revealed a land the color of dust. The single building that served as a terminal was squat and fashioned seemingly of the same dust.

The Middle East? Eliza wondered. Tattooine? A sign, hand-painted, was illegible in exotic, curling letters. Arabic, at a guess. That probably eliminated Tattooine.

An official in some kind of military uniform stood off to the side of the runway. One of the agents conferred with him and handed him papers. And in the shadow of the dirt building, two more men leaned against an SUV. One was an agent in the requisite dark suit; the other was dark-skinned, in a robe, with a length of brilliant blue cloth wrapped around his head.

"A Tuareg," noted Dr. Chaudhary. "Blue men of the Sahara."

The Sahara? Eliza looked around with new eyes. Africa.

The agents said nothing, only led them to the vehicle.

The drive was long and strange: stretches of perfect featurelessness punctuated by marvelous ruined cities, the occasional laundry line or drift of smoke hinting that they were still inhabited. They passed children riding camels, a flock of walking women in headscarves and shabby long dresses of a dozen sun-bleached colors. At a place as featureless as any other, the vehicle left the road and began to bump and rock uphill, sometimes fishtailing over the scree. Eliza's knuckles were white on the strap above the door, and all thoughts of angels were left behind with the airplane.

This was something else altogether, she suddenly *knew*, with a piercing and utterly unscientific breed of knowing that she thought she'd left behind. A dark foreboding gripped her, unleashed from the closet of memory, of childhood, when she had believed with a child's guilelessness what she had been taught to believe: that evil was real and was watching, that the devil was in the shadow of the yew hedge, waiting to claim her soul.

There is no devil, she told herself, angry. But whatever she'd convinced herself of in the years since she left home, it was hard to believe it now, in light of current events.

The Beasts are coming for you.

"Look." Dr. Chaudhary pointed.

Uphill, stark against the shadow of distant mountains, appeared a fortress of red earth. As they drew nearer, tires grinding over rocks, Eliza saw that more vehicles stood outside its walls, among them jeeps and heavy military transport trucks. A helicopter, off to one side, idle. There were soldiers patrolling, dressed in dusty desert camouflage, and . . . she caught her breath and turned to Dr. Chaudhary. He had seen them, too.

Cutting down a path from the fortress: figures in white hazmat suits.

Alien invasion protocol, thought Eliza. *Oh hell.*

One of the agents made a phone call, and by the time their vehicle came to a stop near the others, a man with a broad black mustache was there to greet them. He wore civilian clothes and spoke with an accent and an air of authority. "Welcome to the Kingdom of Morocco, doctor. I am Dr. Youssef Amhali."

The men shook hands. Eliza merited a nod.

"Dr. Amhali—" began Dr. Chaudhary.

"Please, call me Youssef."

"Youssef. Are you able to tell us why we're here?"

"Certainly, doctor. You're here because I asked for you. We have . . . a situation that exceeds my expertise."

"And your expertise is?" inquired Dr. Chaudhary.

"I am a forensic anthropologist," he replied.

"What kind of situation?" asked Eliza, too quickly, too loudly.

Dr. Amhali—Youssef—raised his eyebrows, pausing to take her measure. Should she have remained the silent assistant, the obedient female? Maybe he heard fear in her voice, or maybe it was just a stupid question, considering his field. Eliza was well aware what forensic anthropologists did, and what must have brought them all here.

And when he lifted his head, just slightly, and sniffed the air, wrinkling his nose in distaste, Eliza smelled it: a ripe rankness on the air. Decay. "The kind of situation, miss, that smells worse on a hot day," he said.

Bodies.

"The kind of situation," Dr. Youssef Amhali continued, "that could start a war."

Eliza understood, or thought she did. It was a mass grave. But she didn't understand why *they* were here. Dr. Chaudhary gave voice to this question. "You're the specialist here," he suggested. "What need can you have of me?"

"There are no specialists for this," said Dr. Amhali. He paused. His smile was morbid and amused, but underlying it Eliza detected fear, and it fed her own. *What's going on here?*

"Please." He motioned them ahead of him. "It's easier if you see them for yourselves. The pit is this way."

34

Things Known and Buried

They were at least twenty minutes doing paperwork, signing a series of nondisclosure agreements that escalated Eliza's anxiety page by page. Another quarter of an hour fumbling into hazmat suits—ratcheting the anxiety up even further—and at last they joined the insectlike parade of white-clad figures on the path.

Dr. Amhali paused at the top of the slope. His voice came out thin, filtered through the breathing apparatus of his suit. "Before I take you any farther," he said, "I must remind you that what you are about to see is classified and highly volatile. Secrecy is paramount. The world is not ready to see this, and we are certainly not ready for it to be seen. Do you understand?"

Eliza nodded. She had no peripheral vision, and had to turn to catch Dr. Chaudhary's nod. Several white figures trouped behind him, and she realized that there were no distinguishing features to any of them. If she blinked, she could lose track of which one was Dr. Chaudhary. She felt like she'd stepped into some kind of purgatory.

It was deeply surreal, and became even more so once the restricted site came into view. Downhill from the kasbah, a rope perimeter enclosed a cluster of acid-yellow hazmat tents. Big, squat generators hummed, snaking power lines into the tents like umbilical cords. Personnel milled about, grublike at this distance in their head-to-toe white plastic.

Farther out, soldiers patrolled. In the sky were more helicopters.

The sun was merciless, and Eliza felt as though her air supply were being syphoned into her mask through a straw. Clumsy and stiff in her suit, she picked her way downhill. Her fear, like her shadow, lengthened before her.

What was in the pit? What was in the tents?

Dr. Amhali guided them to the nearest one and paused again. "'The Beasts are coming for you,'" he quoted. "That's what the angel said." And it seemed to Eliza that in the space of seconds she became just a heartbeat encased in plastic. *Beasts. Oh god, here?* "It would seem that they are already among us."

Among us, among us.

And with a showman's flourish, he whipped back the flap door to reveal...

...beasts.

The word *beast*, Eliza realized slowly, encompassed an extremely broad spectrum of creatures. Animals, monsters, devils, even unspeakable dream-things so terrible they can stop a little girl's heart. These were not the latter. Not by a long shot.

These were not her monsters, and as her heart resumed something like normal beating, she chastised herself. Of course they weren't. What had she been thinking? Or *not* thinking. Her monsters existed on a vast dream plane, at a whole different order of magnitude.

You call these beasts, Youssef? she might have said, laughing in breathless relief. *You don't know from beasts.*

She didn't laugh. She whispered, "Sphinxes."

"Pardon me?" asked Dr. Amhali.

"They look like sphinxes," she clarified, raising her voice but not lifting her eyes from them. Her fear was gone. It had been snatched away and replaced by fascination. "From mythology."

Woman-cats. Two of them, identical. Panthers with human heads. Eliza stepped through the door, immediately feeling a reprieve from the heat. The tent was cooled by a loud AC unit, and the sphinxes were on metal tables set atop drums of dry ice. Their furred, felid bodies were soft black, and their wings—*wings*—were dark and feathered.

Their throats had been cut, and their chests were dark with dried gore.

Dr. Chaudhary stepped past Eliza and removed the helmet of his hazmat suit.

"Doctor," said Dr. Amhali at once, "I must object." But Dr. Chaudhary didn't appear to hear him. He approached the nearest sphinx. His head looked small and disembodied above his suit, and his expression was poised at the edge of skepticism.

Eliza took off her helmet, too, and the stench hit her at once—a much purer form of the smell that had wafted up the hill, but she could see the creatures with much greater clarity. She joined Dr. Chaudhary beside the body. Their escort was agitated, scolding them about risk and regulations, but it was easy to tune him out, considering what lay before them.

"Tell me what you know," said Dr. Chaudhary, all business. Dr. Amhali did, and it wasn't much. The bodies had been found, more than two dozen of them in an open pit. That was what it boiled down to.

"I hoped to dismiss it easily as a hoax," said the Moroccan scientist, "but found that I could not. My hope now, I will admit, is that *you* can."

By way of reply, Dr. Chaudhary only lifted his eyebrows.

"Do they all look like this?" Eliza inquired.

"Not remotely," replied Dr. Amhali, twitching a stiff nod toward a sheet of white canvas humped high over a much greater bulk than the sphinxes.

What's under there? Eliza wondered. But Dr. Chaudhary only nodded and returned his attention to the sphinxes. She joined him, ran a gloved finger over a feline foreleg, then leaned over one dark wing. She lifted a feather with a fingertip and examined it. "Owl," she said, surprised. "See the fimbriae?" She indicated the feather's leading edge. "These flutings are unique to owl plumage. It is what makes them silent in flight. These look like owl feathers."

"I hardly think these are owls," said Dr. Amhali.

Are you sure? Eliza quipped inside her head, *because I heard the owls in Africa have lady heads*. She felt...high. Dread had walked down the hill with her. At the mention of the word *beasts*, it had coiled itself around her and squeezed—the dream, the nightmare, the chasing, the devouring—and now it was gone, leaving relief in its wake, and exhaustion, and awe. The awe was on top: the top scoop in the ice-cream cone. *Nightmare ice cream*, she thought, giddy.

Lick.

"You're right. They are not owls," agreed Dr. Chaudhary, and probably only someone as familiar with his tones as Eliza was could have detected the dryness of sarcasm. "At least, not entirely."

And what followed was a cursory head-to-toe inspection with the aim of ruling out a hoax. "Look for surgical seams," Dr. Chaudhary instructed Eliza, and she did as he asked, examining the places the creature's disparate elements conjoined: the neck and the wing joints, primarily. She couldn't share Dr. Amhali's hope; she didn't want to find surgical seams. If she did, for one thing . . . then where—or *who*—had the heads come from? That would be a horror movie rather than a momentous scientific discovery. And anyway, it was a pointless exercise. She knew that the creatures were real. As she knew that the angels were real.

These were things that she knew.

No, you don't, she told herself. *That's not how it works. You wonder, and you gather data and study it, and eventually you posit a hypothesis and test it. Then maybe you begin to know.*

But she did know, and trying to pretend otherwise was like screaming at a hurricane.

I know other things, too.

And with that, one of the other things . . . presented itself. It was as though a fortune-teller flipped over a tarot card in her mind and showed her this knowledge, this truth that had been lying facedown in there . . . all her life. *Longer. Much longer than that.* It was there, and it was a very large thing to suddenly know. Very large. Eliza took a deep breath, which is not an excellent idea while standing corpse-side, and she had to stagger back, taking a succession of quick, purposeful breaths to clear the miasma of death from her lungs.

"Are you all right?" inquired Dr. Chaudhary.

"Fine," she said, struggling to cover her agitation. She really didn't want him thinking she was squeamish and couldn't handle this, and she really *really* didn't want him wishing he'd brought Morgan Toth instead, so she got right back to work, assiduously ignoring the... tarot card... now lying faceup in her mind.

There is another universe.

That was the thing that she knew. In school Eliza had shirked physics egregiously in favor of biology, and so she had only the most simplistic understanding of string theory, but she knew that there was a case to be made for parallel universes, scientifically speaking. She didn't know what that case was, and it didn't matter anyway. There was another universe. She didn't have to prove it.

Hell. The proof was right here, dead at her feet. And the proof was in Rome, alive. And—

It hit her with hilarity. "They should treat it like an alien invasion," Morgan had said, and he'd been exactly right, the little pissant. It *was* an alien invasion. It just happened that the aliens looked like angels and beasts, and came not from "outer space" but from a parallel universe. With ever-deepening hilarity, she imagined floating this theory to the two doctors beside her—*"Hey, you know what I think?"*—and it was about then that she realized her hilarity was not hilarity at all, but panic.

It wasn't the beasts or the smell or the heat or even her exhaustion, and it wasn't even the idea of another universe. It was the knowing. It was feeling it inside herself—the truth and depth of it buried within her, like monsters in a pit. Only the monsters were dead and couldn't hurt anyone. The knowing could rip her apart.

Her sanity, anyway.

It happened, in her family. "You have the gift," her mother had told her when she was very young and lying on a hospital bed, full of tubes and surrounded by beeping machines. It was the first time her heart had gone haywire and turned into a mass of fibrillating muscle, very nearly killing her. Her mother hadn't held her, not even then. She'd just knelt beside her with her hands folded in prayer, a fervor in her eyes—and envy. Always, after that, envy. "You will see for us. You will guide us all."

But Eliza wasn't guiding anyone anywhere. The "gift" was a curse. She'd known it even then. Her family history was potholed with madness, and she had no intention of being the latest in a string of "prophets" locked away in asylums, ranting about the apocalypse and licking spots on the walls. She'd worked very hard to stifle her "gift" and be who she wanted to be, and she'd succeeded. From teenage runaway to National Science Foundation fellow and soon-to-be doctor? She'd succeeded pretty freaking wildly—in all ways but one. The dream. It came when it wanted, too big to bury, more powerful than she was. More powerful than anything.

But now other things were stirring in her, too, other truths that weren't her own, and it terrified her. Several times she swayed. Her light-headedness had become extreme, and she was beginning to suspect that by going sleepless to deny the dream, she had weakened something else within herself. She breathed in and she breathed out, and she told herself she could control her mind as she controlled her muscles.

"Eliza, are you certain you're all right? If you need some fresh air, please—"

"No. No, I'm fine." She forced a smile and bent back over the sphinx in front of her.

They found they could not satisfy Dr. Amhali's hope. There were no seams to be found, they concluded, and no "made by Frankenstein" patch sewn conveniently onto the back of the necks, either. There was something, though.

Eliza held one of the sphinxes' dead hands in her own gloved one for a long beat, staring at the mark, before speaking. "Did you see this?"

From Dr. Amhali's silent stance, she guessed that he had, and maybe had been waiting for them to discover it. Dr. Chaudhary blinked at it several times, making the same connection that Eliza had made.

"The Girl on the Bridge," he said.

The Girl on the Bridge: the blue-haired beauty who'd fought angels in Prague, hands held out before her and inked with indigo eyes. They'd made the cover of *Time* magazine, and had since become synonymous with *demon*. Kids liked to draw them on with ballpoint pen to act wicked. It was the new 666.

"Are you beginning to understand what this means?" Dr. Amhali asked, very intense. "Do you see how the world will interpret it? The angels flew to Rome; it's all very nice for Christians, yes? Angels in Rome, warning of beasts and wars, while here, in a Muslim country, we unearth . . . *demons*. What do you think the response will be?"

Eliza saw his point, and felt his fear. The world needed far less provocation than actual flesh-and-blood "demons" to go crazy. Still, these creatures ignited a wonder in her, and she couldn't bring herself to wish them fake.

In any case, those were concerns for governments and diplomats, police and military, not scientists. Their work was the bodies in front of them—the physical matter, and that alone. There was much to do: tissue samples to collect and store, along with exhaustive measurements and photographs to take and log as reference for each body. But first, they opted for an overview of the work ahead of them.

"Do all the bodies have the marks?" Dr. Chaudhary asked Dr. Amhali.

"All but one," Dr. Amhali replied, and Eliza wondered about that, but the next creature they saw—the large bulk under the white tarp—did have them, and so did the bodies in the next tent, and the next, so Eliza forgot about it. It was enough to try to process what she was seeing—and smelling—one body at a time. She was nauseated and overwhelmed, her panic never far off—the sense of things known and buried—and she was prey, too, to a peculiar sadness. Going tent to tent like this, seeing this array of unearthly creatures, it felt like a carnival menagerie where all the exhibits were dead.

All were wild amalgams of recognizable animal parts, and they were in successively advanced states of decay. The deeper they had been in the pit, the longer they'd been dead, suggesting that they'd been killed one by one over a period of time, and not all at once. Whatever had gone on here, it hadn't been a massacre.

And then they came to the final hazmat tent, off by itself on the far side of the pit. "This one was buried alone," said Dr. Amhali, lifting the flap for them. "In a shallow grave."

Eliza entered, and at the sight of this final "exhibit" in the dead menagerie, sadness sang in her brighter than ever. This was the one without marks on his palms. He'd been buried with some suggestion of care—not flung into the stinking pit, but laid out and covered with dirt and gravel. A grayish residue of dust clung to his flesh, making him seem like a sculpture.

Maybe that was why she was able to think, right away, that he was beautiful. Because he didn't look real. He looked like art. She could almost have wept for him, which made no sense. If the others were variously "monstrous," he was the most "demonic" or "devilish":

mostly humanoid, with the addition of long black horns and cloven hooves, and bat wings stretched out on the ground on either side of him, at least a dozen feet in span, their edges curling up against the sides of the tent.

But he didn't strike her as demonic. As the angels hadn't struck her as "angelic."

What happened here? she wondered in silence. It wasn't her job to figure that out, but she couldn't help herself. Questions rose in a stir, like startled birds. *Who killed these creatures, and why? And what were they doing in the Moroccan wilderness? And . . . what were their names?*

A part of her mind told her this was the wrong response to seeing dead monsters—to wonder at their names—but this last body especially, with its fine features, made her want to know. The tip of one horn was snapped off, a simple detail, and she wondered how it had happened, and from there it was an easy trajectory to wondering everything else. What had his life been like, and why was he dead?

The men were talking, and she heard Dr. Amhali telling Dr. Chaudhary that the creatures seemed to have been living in the kasbah for some time, and had vacated it only the day before yesterday.

"Some nomads witnessed their departure," said Dr. Amhali.

"Wait." Eliza said. "There were some seen alive? How many?"

"We don't know. The witnesses were hysterical. Dozens, they said."

Dozens. Eliza wanted to see them. She wanted to see them living and breathing. "Well, where did they go? Have you found them?"

Dr. Amhali's voice was wry. "They went that way," he said, pointing . . . *up*. "And no, we have not."

According to the witnesses, the "demons" had flown toward the

Atlas Mountains, though no evidence had been found to back this up. If it weren't for the proof of the story in the form of liquefying monster corpses, it would have been dismissed as ludicrous. As it was, helicopters continued to scour the mountains, and agents had gone by jeep and camel to track down any Berber tribes and herdsmen who might have seen anything.

Eliza stepped out of the tent with the doctors. *They won't find them*, she thought, looking at the mountains, the vision of snow-capped peaks so incongruous in the heat. *There is another universe, and that's where they've gone.*

35

Thrice-Fallen

"*Get. Off.*"

As soon as the door closed behind him, Jael, emperor of the seraphim, gave a savage lurch and twist of his shoulders to dislodge the invisible creature riding on his back.

If Razgut had wanted to stay put, such a maneuver would never have knocked him loose. His grip was strong, and so was his will, and—after a long life of unimaginable torment—so was his pain tolerance. "Make me," he might have snapped, and laughed his mad laugh while the emperor did his worst.

Usually he found it worth the pain to cause others misery, but, as it happened, Jael's foulness superseded even the pleasure of torturing him, and Razgut was happy to oblige. He let go of him and flailed to the marble floor with a thud and gasp, becoming visible at the moment of impact. He pushed himself upright, his atrophied legs splayed to one side. "You're welcome," he said, a parody of dignity.

"You think I should thank you?" Jael removed his helmet and

thrust it at a guard. Only in privacy could the ruin of his face be revealed: the hideous scar that slashed from hairline to chin, obliterating his nose and leaving a lisping, slurping wreckage of a mouth. "For what?" he demanded, spittle flying.

A grimace teased Razgut's own hideous face—a bloated sack of purple, his skin stretched blister-tight. He replied peevishly and in Latin, which the emperor could of course not understand: "For not snapping your neck while I had the chance. It would have been so very easy."

"Enough of your human tongues," said Jael, imperious and impatient. "What are you saying?"

They were in an opulent suite of rooms in the Papal Palace adjacent to St. Peter's Basilica, and had just come from a meeting of world leaders at which Jael had presented his demands. Had presented them, that is, by way of repeating every syllable Razgut whispered in his ear.

"For words," said Razgut, in Seraphic this time, and sweetly. "Without my words, my lord, what are you but a pretty face?" He snickered, and Jael kicked him.

It wasn't a dramatic kick. There was no showmanship in it, only brutal efficiency. A quick, hard jerk, and the steel-enforced toe of his slipper spiked into Razgut's side, deep into the misshapen bloat of flesh. Razgut cried out. The pain was sharp and bright, precise. He curled around it.

Laughing.

There was a crack in the shell of Razgut's mind. It had been, once, a very fine mind, and the crack was as a flaw in a diamond, a seam in a crystal globe. It spidered. It snaked. It subverted every ordinary feeling into some mutant cousin of itself: recognizable, but gone oh so very wrong. When he looked back up at Jael, hatred mingled with mirth in his eyes.

It was his eyes that marked him as what he was. To stand back and look at him in the company of his kin, it seemed impossible that they were of the same race. Seraphim were all symmetry and grace, power and magnificence—even Jael, as long as the center margin of his face stayed covered—where Razgut was a blighted, crawling thing, a corruption of flesh more goblin than angel. He had been beautiful once, oh yes, but now only his eyes told that tale. The almond shape of them stood out as fine in his swollen, bruise-colored face.

The other tell of his ancestry was more dreadful: the spikes of splintered bone that jutted from his shoulder blades. His wings had been torn off. Not even cut, but ripped away. The pain was a thousand years old, but he would never forget it.

"When there are weapons in my soldiers' hands," said Jael, looming over him, "when humanity is on its knees before me, then perhaps I'll value your words."

Razgut knew better. He knew that he was destined to become a bloodstain the instant Jael got his weapons, which put him in an interesting position, being the one charged with getting them for him.

If he was to become a bloodstain whether he failed or succeeded, the question was: Would he prefer to be a quivering and obedient bloodstain, or a willful and infuriating bloodstain who brought an emperor's ambitions crashing down around him?

It seemed an easy decision on the face of it. How simple it would be to humiliate and destroy Jael. It had amused Razgut, in the meeting of great gravity and importance they'd just come from, to think up absurd lines he might feed him. The fool was so certain of Razgut's groveling servility that he would repeat anything. It was a rich temptation, and several times Razgut had chuckled, imagining it.

There is no god, you fools, he might have made him say. *There are only monsters, and I am the worst of them.*

It was fun, holding the cards. For his part, Razgut understood perfectly well that if Jael had come here without him, and addressed Earth in his native tongue, their hosts would have put all their considerable human ingenuity to work coding a translation program and would probably have been able to understand them perfectly well within a week, and even speak back by way of a computer-generated voice.

As one may imagine, he had not explained this to Jael. Better to intercept every syllable, control every phrase. To the Russian ambassador: *Does anyone have gum? My breath is unbelievable.*

Or possibly, to the American Secretary of State: *Let us seal our communion with a kiss. Come to me, my dear, and take off my helmet.*

Now wouldn't *that* be fun?

But he had held himself back, because the decision—to ruin Jael or help him—had profound and far-reaching ramifications quite beyond anything the emperor himself imagined.

Oh. Quite beyond.

"You will have your weapons," Razgut told him. "But we must go carefully, my lord. This is a free world and not your army to command. We must make them *want* to give us what we need."

"Give *me* what *I* need," corrected Jael.

"Oh yes, you," Razgut amended. "All for you, my lord. Your weapons, your war, and the untouchable Stelians, groveling before you."

The Stelians. They were to be Jael's first target, and this was rich. Razgut didn't know what had sparked the emperor's especial hatred of them, but the reason didn't matter, only the result. "How sweet will be the day." He simpered, he fawned. He hid his laughter, and it felt good inside him, because oh, he knew things, yes, and yes, it was good to be the one who knows things. The only one who knows.

Razgut had told his secrets once and only once, to the one whose wish for knowledge had made him a broken angel's mule. Izîl. It surprised Razgut how much he missed the old beggar. He had been bright and good, and Razgut had destroyed him. Well, and what had the human expected: Something for nothing? From scholar to madman, doctor to graverobber, that had been his fate, but he'd gotten what he wanted, hadn't he? Knowledge beyond even what Brimstone could have told him, because not even the old devil had known *this*. Razgut remembered what no one else did.

The Cataclysm.

Terrible and terrible and terrible forever.

It was not forgotten by chance. Minds had been altered. Emptied. Hands had reached in, and scraped out the past. But not Razgut's.

Izîl, old fool, had tried to tell the fire-eyed angel who came to them in Morocco. Akiva was his name, and he had Stelian blood, but not Stelian knowledge, that was clear, and he wouldn't listen. "I can tell you things!" Izîl had cried. "Secret things! About your own kind. Razgut has stories—"

But Akiva had cut him off, refusing to hear the word of a Fallen. As if he even knew what that meant! *Fallen*. He'd said it like a curse, but he had no idea. "Like mold on books, grow myths on history," Izîl had said. "Maybe you should ask someone who was there, all those centuries ago. Maybe you should ask Razgut."

But he hadn't. No one ever asked Razgut. *What happened to you? Why was this done to you?*

Who are you, really?

Oh, oh, and oh. They should have asked.

Razgut told Jael now, "We will bring the humans around, never fear. They're always like this, arguing, arguing. It's meat and drink to them. Besides, it's not these self-important heads of state we care about. This is just for show. While they wag their withered faces at each other, the people are working on your behalf. Mark my words. Already groups will be building up their arsenals, making ready to hand them over to you. It will only be a matter of choosing, my lord, who you wish to take them from."

"Where are all these offers, then?" Spittle flew. "*Where?*"

"Patience, patience—"

"You said I would be worshiped as a god!"

"Yes, well, you're an ugly god," spat Razgut, no model himself of the patience he preached. "You make them nervous. You spit when you speak, you hide behind your mask, and you stare at them like you would murder them all in their beds. Have you considered trying charm? It would make my job easier."

Again, Jael kicked him. It was a brighter stab of pain this time, and Razgut coughed blood onto the exquisite marble floor. Dipping a fingertip into it, he scribbled an obscenity.

Jael shook his head in disgust and stalked over to a table where refreshments were laid out. He poured himself a glass of wine and began to pace. "It's taking too long," he said, his voice a snap of spite. "I didn't come here for rituals and chanting. I came for arms."

Razgut affected a sigh and began to drag himself slowly, laboriously, toward the door. "Fine. I'll go and speak to them myself. It will be faster, anyway. Your Latin pronunciation is appalling."

Jael signaled to the pair of Dominion guarding the door, and Razgut was laughing as they seized him by his armpits and hauled him back, dropping him hard at Jael's feet. He cackled at his joke. "Imagine their faces!" he cried, wiping a tear from one fine, dark eye. "Oh, imagine if the Pope walked in here right now and saw the pair of us in all our magnificence! 'These are angels?' he would cry and clutch his heart. 'Oh, and then what in the name of God are *beasts?*'" He doubled over, quaking with laughter.

Jael did not share his amusement. "We are not a pair," he said, his voice cold and very soft. "And know this, *thing.* If you ever cross me—"

Razgut cut him off. "What? What will you do to me, dear Emperor?" He peered up at Jael and held his gaze. Very steady, very still. "Look and see. Look into me and know. I am Razgut Thrice-Fallen, Wretchedest of Angels. There is nothing you can take from me that has not already been taken, nothing you can do that has not already been done."

"You have not yet been killed," said Jael, unyielding.

At that, Razgut smiled. His teeth were perfect in his awful face, and the crack in his mind showed mad in his eyes. With taunting insincerity, he clasped his hands and begged, "Not that, my lord. Oh hurt me, torment me, but whatever you do, please oh please, don't give me *peace!*"

And spasms of fury moved over Jael's cut-in-half face, his jaw clenched so tight that his scar pulled white while the rest of him flushed crimson. He should have understood, then. This was what Razgut thought, still laughing, as Jael laid into him with the steel-enforced tips of his slippers, giving birth to pain after pain, a whole family of them, a dynasty of hurt. That was the moment that Jael should have grasped, finally, that he was not in control. He couldn't kill Razgut; he needed him. To interpret human languages, yes, but more than that: to interpret *humans*, to understand their history and politics and psychology and devise a strategy and rhetoric to appeal to them.

He could kick him, oh yes, and Razgut would croon to the pain all night long and comfort it like an armful of babies, and in the morning he would count his bruises, and number his spites and miseries, and go on smiling, and go on knowing all the things that no one remembered, the things that should never have been forgotten, and the reason—oh godstars, the most excellent and terrible reason—that Jael should leave the Stelians alone.

"I am Razgut Thrice-Fallen, Wretchedest of Angels," he sang in a patchwork of human languages, from Latin to Arabic to Hebrew and around again, breaking it up with grunts as the kicks came to him. "And I know what fear is! Oh yes, and I know what beasts are, too. You think you do but you don't, but you will, oh you will, oh you will. I'll get you your weapons and I'll get them fast, and I'll laugh when you kill me like I laugh when you kick me, and you'll hear the echo of it at the end of everything and know that I could have stopped you. I could have *told* you."

Don't do this, oh no, not this, he could have said. *Or everyone will die.*

"And I might have," he added in Seraphic, "if you had been kinder to this poor, broken thing."

36

The Only Non-Idiot on the Planet

"Hello, King Morgan," said Gabriel, popping his head into the lab. "And how is the planet's only non-idiot on this fine day?"

"Screw you," replied Morgan, without turning from his computer.

"Ah, excellent," said Gabriel. "I'm having a lovely morning, too." He came into the lab a few steps and looked around. "Have you seen Eliza? She hasn't been home."

Morgan snerched. At least, that was the nearest phonetic case to be made for the sound he ejected from his nose: *snerch*. "Yeah, I've seen her. The sight of Eliza Jones asleep with her mouth open ruined my day."

"Oh," said Gabriel, all helpful good cheer. "No, that probably wasn't it. It was probably already ruined, when you woke up from a dream of having friends and being admired and realized you were still you."

Morgan finally turned around to favor him with a sour glare. "What do you want, Edinger?"

"I thought I said. I'm looking for Eliza."

"Who is clearly not here," said Morgan, swinging back around. He was on the very verge of saying, with all the considerable snideness in his arsenal, that she probably wasn't even in the country, followed up with the charming assessment that her absence likely accounted for the unusual clarity of the air, when Gabriel spoke again.

"I have her phone," he said. "She hasn't been home, and she's gotten about a million messages. I honestly didn't think it was possible to *survive* this long without one's phone. Are you sure she's all right?"

And Morgan Toth's expression changed. He was still faced away, and Gabriel might have caught the reflection of his look in his computer screen if he'd been paying attention, but he never paid very close attention to Morgan Toth.

"She went somewhere with Dr. Chaudhary," Morgan said, and his tone was unchanged, as sour as ever, but there was a slyness in his expression now, and a cool, malicious eagerness. "They'll be right back, if you want to leave it."

Gabriel hesitated. He weighed the phone in his palm and looked around the room. He saw Eliza's sweatshirt slung over a chair by one of the sequencers. "All right," he said finally, walking a few steps to set the phone down next to it. "Would you tell her to text me when she gets it?"

"Sure," said Morgan, and for a second Gabriel hesitated in the doorway, suspicious that the little prig was suddenly being so accommodating. But then Morgan added, "Tell you what. Hold your breath until that happens," and Gabriel just rolled his eyes and left.

And Morgan Toth was remarkably restrained. He waited five minutes, five entire minutes—three hundred tiny stutters of the clock's long hand—before he locked the door and picked up the phone.

37

Preoccupied by Bliss

"Are you sure you can do this?" Akiva asked his sister, his brow creased with concern. They were in the entrance cavern where, just the day before, the armies had very nearly ended each other. The scene before them now was... quite different.

"What, spend several days in the company of your paramour?" Liraz replied, looking up from making an adjustment to her sword belt. "It won't be easy. If she tries to dress me in human clothes, I can't be held responsible for my actions."

Akiva's answering smile was humorless. There was nothing he wanted more right now than to be the one spending several days with Karou—even several such days as these would be, persuading their sadistic, warmongering uncle, quite contrary to his own desires, to go back home. "I'm holding you responsible for more than your actions," he told Liraz. He meant it to sound light.

It didn't. Her eyes flashed angry. "What, don't you trust me with your precious lady? Maybe you should assign an entire battalion to escort her."

Or just go myself, was what he wanted to say. He'd told Karou he wasn't letting her out of his sight, but it turned out he would have to, one last time. They had all agreed to her plan, as bold as it was sly, and his own part, as it had evolved, was considerable, and crucial, but it would keep him in Eretz while Liraz accompanied Karou back to the human world.

"You know I trust you," he told his sister, which was almost true. He did trust her to protect Karou. When he'd asked if she was sure she could do this, he'd meant something else. "When it comes down to it, will you be able to keep from killing Jael?"

"I said I would, didn't I?"

"Not convincingly," Akiva replied.

In the reconvened war council, Liraz had greeted Karou's idea with a bark of incredulous laughter, and then stared around the table at each of them in turn, growing ever more appalled that they appeared to be considering it.

Considering not killing Jael.

Yet.

And when, after much discussion, it had all been agreed, she had fallen into a suspect silence that Akiva interpreted to mean that, whatever she might say now, when she stood before their vile uncle, his sister would do exactly as she pleased.

"I said I would," she repeated with finality, and her look dared him to question her further.

Let's be clear, Lir, he imagined himself saying. *You're not planning to ruin everything, are you?*

He let it drop. "We will avenge Hazael," he said. It wasn't a consolation or a half truth. He wanted it as much as she did.

She gave a sardonic half laugh. "Well. Those of us who aren't preoccupied by bliss might."

Akiva felt a sting. *Preoccupied by bliss.* She made it sound frivolous and worse. Negligent. *Was* it a betrayal of Hazael's memory to be in love? But all he could think, in answer to that, was what Karou had said earlier, about the darkness we do in the name of the dead, and whether it's what they would want for us. He didn't even have to wonder. He knew that Hazael wouldn't grudge him his happiness. But Liraz clearly did.

He didn't respond to her jab. What could he even say? You had only to look around to see the non-frivolity of love. Here in this cavern, this uneasy intermingling of seraphim and chimaera was nothing short of a miracle, and it was *their* miracle, his and Karou's. He wouldn't claim it aloud, but in his heart, he knew it was.

Of course, Liraz had her part in it, too, she and Thiago. That had been a sight to behold: the pair of them standing shoulder by shoulder, knitting their armies together by example. They had negotiated the scheme for mixed battalions, and made all of the assignments themselves. Akiva had marked all two hundred and ninety-six of his brothers and sisters with his new hamsa counter-sigil, and now, right now, before his eyes, the armies were testing their marks on each other.

Pockets of soldiers on both sides held themselves back, but the majority, it seemed, were engaged in a kind of cautious…well, a getting-acquainted game, one far less vicious than Liraz had earlier been subject to.

Akiva watched as his brother Xathanael willed a jackal-headed Sab to show him her palms. She was hesitant, and flicked a glance to the Wolf. He nodded encouragement, and so she did it. She lifted her hands, ink eyes raised right at Xathanael, and nothing happened.

They were standing on the dark stain of Uthem's blood, in the very spot where it had all come so close to breaking apart yesterday, and nothing happened. Xathanael had tensed, but he relaxed with a laugh and gave the Sab a clout on the shoulder heavy enough to seem like assault. His laugh was heavier, though, and the Sab didn't take offense.

A little beyond them, Akiva saw Issa accede to Elyon's invitation to touch him, reaching out to lay a graceful hand atop his scarred and inked one.

There was a potency in the image that Akiva wished he could distill into an elixir for the rest of Eretz. *Some, and then more,* he thought like a prayer.

With that, he sought the glimmer of blue that he was always attuned to and his gaze found Karou, as hers found him. A flash, a flare. One look and he felt drunk with light. She wasn't near. *God-stars, why wasn't she near?* Akiva was fed up with the volumes of air that continued to come between them. And soon it would be leagues and skies between them—

"I'm sorry," Liraz said quietly. "That wasn't fair."

A warmth surged through him, and a proud, protective tenderness for his brittle sister, for whom apologies were no easy thing. "No, it wasn't," he said, striving for lightness. "And speaking of fair, you might have waited a few minutes before barging in earlier. I'm sure we were seconds from kissing."

Liraz snorted, caught off guard, and the tension between them ebbed away. "I'm sorry if my almost *dying* interrupted your almost *kissing.*"

"I forgive you," said Akiva. It was hard to joke about the horror so narrowly avoided, but it felt like what Hazael would do, and that was a guiding principle—what Hazael would do—that seemed always to come out right. "I forgive you *this time,*" he stressed. "Next time, please time your almost dying with more consideration. Better yet, no more almost dying." *Try almost kissing instead*, he thought, *or actual kissing*, but didn't say it, partly because it was impossible to imagine, and partly because he knew it would annoy her. He wished it for her, though—that Liraz might find herself, someday, preoccupied by bliss.

"I'm going to go wash before we leave," he told her, pushing off from the cavern wall where he'd been leaning. Several hours of uninterrupted magic had left his body feeling leaden. He rolled his shoulders, stretched his neck.

"You should go to the thermal pools," Liraz said. "They're . . . fairly wonderful."

He halted mid-step and squinted at her. "Fairly wonderful?" he repeated. He didn't think he'd ever heard Liraz use the word *wonderful* before, and . . . was that a hint of a flush rising to her cheeks?

Interesting.

"The healing water, of course," she said, and her direct, unwavering gaze was too direct and unwavering; she was covering some other feeling with feigned cool, and she was overdoing it. On top of which, there was the flush.

Very interesting.

"Well. No time now," Akiva said. There was water in an alcove just down the passage. "I'll be right over here," he told her, departing. He would have liked to go to the thermal pools—he would have liked to go there *with Karou*—but it was one more item for the wistful list of things to do once his life became his own.

Bathe with Karou.

Heat followed the thought, which, for a wonder, met with no instant barrier of guilt and self-denial. He was so accustomed to running into it that its absence was surreal. It was like rounding a corner one has rounded a thousand times, and finding, instead of the wall one knows is there, an open expanse of sky.

Freedom.

And if they weren't there yet, Akiva was at least free now to dream, and that in itself was a very great thing.

Karou forgave him.

She loved him.

And they were parting again, and he hadn't kissed her, and neither of these things was all right. Even if they hadn't had to hide their feelings from two armies, and even if they might yet have stolen a moment alone, Akiva had a soldier's superstition about goodbyes. You didn't say them. They were bad luck, and a good-bye kiss was just another form of good-bye. A kiss of beginning shouldn't be a kiss in parting. They would have to wait for it.

The passage curved into an alcove, where a channel of frigid water spilled from the rough wall, running along at waist height for several meters in a trough before vanishing again into the rock. Like so many of the marvels of these caves, it seemed natural but probably wasn't. Akiva shrugged out of his sword harness and hung it from a spur of rock, then stripped off his shirt.

He cupped the cold water and brought it to his face. Handful after handful, to his face, neck, chest, and shoulders. He dunked his head into it and straightened, feeling it vaporize against the heat of his skin as it ran down in rivulets between the joints of his wings.

He had agreed to Karou's plan because it was sound. It was clever, and its risks were far less than the previous plan's had been, and, if it worked, the threat of Jael to the human world truly would radically diminish, like a hurricane downgraded to a gust. There would still be Eretz to worry about, but there had always been Eretz to worry about, and they would have prevented their enemy from acquiring, as Karou termed them, "weapons of mass destruction."

Liraz may have mocked her in the first war council, suggesting they simply ask Jael to leave, but that, in essence, was the plan: to ask him to please take his army and go home, without what he came for, thank you, and good night.

Of course, it was the *inducement* that was the crux of the plan. It was simple and brilliant—it was *not* "please"—and Akiva didn't doubt that Karou and Liraz could pull it off. They were both formidable, but they were also the two people he cared most about in the world—*worlds*—and he just wanted to carry them safely forward to the future he imagined, in which no one's life was at stake and the hardest decision of any given day might be what to eat for breakfast, or where to make love.

Liraz was right, Akiva thought. He *was* preoccupied by bliss. He wasn't expecting to have another moment alone with Karou for some time, so when he heard a stir behind him—it sounded like a soft intake of breath—he spun, a surge in his pulse, expecting to see her.

And saw no one.

He smiled. He could feel a presence before him as surely as he had heard a breath. She had come glamoured again, and that meant she had come unobserved. Whatever he'd told himself just minutes ago—how a kiss of beginning should not being a kiss in parting—his resolve couldn't survive the surge of hope. He needed it. It felt unfinished, the understanding that had passed between them, hands to hearts. He didn't think he could feel sure of his happiness, or breathe at full depth again, until...and again, astonishingly, there was no barrier of guilt to greet the hope, but only the open expanse of possibilities before them...until he kissed her. Superstition be damned.

"Karou?" he said, smiling. "Are you there?" He waited for her to materialize, ready to catch her in his arms the instant she did. He could do that now. At least, when no one was around.

But she didn't materialize.

And then, abruptly, the presence—there *was* a presence—registered as unfamiliar, even hostile, and there was something else. A feeling came over him—came *into* him—and Akiva experienced an entirely newfound awareness of...of his own life as a discrete entity. A single shining tensity in a warp of many, tangible and... vulnerable. A chill gripped him.

"Karou? Is that you?" he asked again, though he knew it was not.

And then he heard footsteps out in the passage, and in a trice Karou did enter. She wasn't glamoured, but plainly visible—and plainly radiant—and as she drew to a faltering halt, blushing to catch him half-dressed, he saw by her smile that she had indeed come with the same hope that had bloomed in him an instant earlier.

"Hi," she said, voice soft, eyes wide. Her hope was reaching for his, but Akiva felt something else reaching for it, too, and for his life. It was threat and menace. It was invisible.

And it was in the alcove with them.

38

An Excellent Accident of Stardust

In Morocco, Eliza woke with a start. She wasn't screaming, or even on the verge of screaming. In fact, she wasn't afraid at all, and that was rather a nice surprise. She had given in to sleep, knowing that she must—sleep deprivation can actually kill you—and had hoped that either a) the dream might, miraculously, leave her alone, or b) the walls of this place would prove thick enough to muffle her screams.

It would seem that *a* had come through for her, which was a relief, as *b* would clearly have failed. She could hear dogs barking outside, and so it would seem that the walls, thick though they were, would have muffled nothing.

What had woken her then, if not the dream? The dogs, maybe? No. There was something. . . .

Not *the* dream, but *a* dream, something dancing away from her conscious mind, like shadows before the sweep of a flashlight beam. She lay where she was, and there was a moment when she felt she might have captured it, if she'd tried. Her mind was still tiptoeing along the boundary of consciousness, in that state of semi-waking that spins threads between dream and real, and for a moment she felt herself to be a girl who has come down off a porch to confront a great darkness with a tiny light.

Which is a really, really dumb thing to do, so she sat up and shook her head. Shook it all away. *Shoo, dreams. I welcome you not.* There are spikes you can put on window ledges to keep pigeons from landing; she needed some for her mind, to keep dreams away. Psychic mind spikes. Excellent.

In the absence of psychic mind spikes, however, she just didn't go back to sleep. She doubted she'd have been able to anyway, and the four hours she'd gotten were probably enough to stave off death by sleep deprivation for a little while. She swung her feet out of bed and sat up. Her laptop was beside her. Earlier, she'd downloaded the first batch of photos, encrypting them before dispatching them to her secure museum e-mail and then deleting them from the camera.

She and Dr. Chaudhary had started collecting tissue samples from the bodies that afternoon, and would return in the morning to continue. She guessed it would take them a couple of days. With the bizarre composition of the bodies, they needed samples from every body part. Flesh, fur, feather, scales, claws. The rest of their work would happen in the lab, and this brief sojourn would feel like a dream. So quick, so strange.

And what would their findings tell them? She couldn't begin to hypothesize. Would they be composites of different DNA? Panther here, owl there, human in between? Or would their DNA be consistent, and only expressed differentially, in the same way a single human genetic code could express as, say, eyeball or toenail, and every other thing that made up a body?

Or...would they find something stranger yet, stranger by far, unlike anything they knew in this world? A shiver shot through her. This was so big, she didn't even know where in her head to put it. If she were allowed to talk about it, if she could call Taj right now, or Catherine—if she even had her phone—what would she say?

She rose and went to the window for a glimpse of the view. It opened onto an interior courtyard, though, nothing to see, so Eliza pulled on her jeans and shoes and crept out the door.

Creeping, surely, was unnecessary. If she'd been in a big, bland mega-hotel, she'd have felt wrapped in anonymity and sallied blithely forth to go where she wished. But this was not a big, bland mega-hotel. It was a kasbah. Not *the* kasbah, but a kasbah-turned-hotel not too far from the site. Okay, so it was a couple of hours' drive, actually, but in this landscape, that seemed like nothing. If you kept going down the highway right over there, you'd hit the Sahara Desert, which was the size *of the entire United States*. In that context, a couple of hours' drive could be classed as "not too far."

The kasbah was called Tamnougalt, and in spite of having been greeted at the gate by unsmiling children making stabbing gestures with pointed sticks, Eliza kind of loved it. It was this mud city in the heart of a palm oasis, the bulk of it a deserted ruin with just the central part restored, and not to any kind of grandeur. It still looked like sculpted mud—if *fancy* sculpted mud—and the rooms were comfortable enough, with very high beamed ceilings and wool rugs on the floors, and there was a rooftop terrace overlooking the waving tops of the palm trees. Last night, when she'd eaten dinner up there with Dr. Chaudhary, she'd seen more stars than she ever had in her life.

I've seen more stars than anyone alive.

Eliza stopped walking and closed her eyes, pressing her fingertips against them as if by doing so she could tame the stir within her. Conjure some psychic mind spikes and skewer some freaking dream pigeons.

I've killed *more stars than anyone will ever see.*

Eliza shook her head. Traceries of the familiar terror and guilt were slicking into her conscious mind. It made her think of the pale, desperate roots that force their way out through the drainage holes in potted plants. It made her think of things that cannot be contained, and she didn't care for this thought at all. *Ignore it*, she told herself. *You've killed nothing. You know this.*

But she didn't. All of a sudden she was "knowing" things, experiencing highly unscientific feelings of conviction about big cosmic questions like the existence of another universe, but certainty of her own innocence was not among them—at least, not in that deeply resonant way. The voice of reason was starting to seem flimsy and unconvincing, and that probably wasn't a good sign.

Step by heavy step, Eliza climbed the stairs back up to the terrace, telling herself that it was just stress, and not madness. *Still not crazy, and not going to be. I've fought too hard.* Emerging into the night air, she felt a surprising chill and heard the dogs more clearly, barking away down in the hardscrabble terrain.

And she saw that Dr. Chaudhary was still sitting where she'd left him hours earlier. He gave a little wave.

"Have you been here all this time?" she asked, walking over.

He laughed. "No. I tried sleeping. I couldn't. My mind. I keep thinking of the implications."

"Me, too."

He nodded. "Sit. Please," he said, and she did. They were silent a moment, surrounded by the night, and then Dr. Chaudhary spoke. "Where did they come from?" he asked. It was a rhetorical question, Eliza thought, but it was followed by a pause long enough that she might hazard a guess, if she dared.

Morgan Toth would dare, she thought, and so she replied simply, "Another universe." *Trust me. It's a thing I know; it was lying around my brain like litter.*

Dr. Chaudhary's eyebrows went up. "So quickly? I had thought, Eliza, that perhaps you believed in God."

"What? No. Why would you think that?"

"Well, I certainly don't mean it as an insult. *I* believe in God."

"You do?" It surprised her. She knew that plenty of scientists believed in God, but she'd never gotten a religious vibe from him. Besides, his specialty—using DNA to reconstruct evolutionary history—seemed particularly at odds with, well, Creationism. "You don't find it difficult to reconcile?"

He shrugged. "My wife likes to say that the mind is a palace with room for many guests. Perhaps the butler takes care to install the delegates of Science in a different wing from the emissaries of Faith, lest they take up arguing in the passages."

This was unaccountably whimsical, coming from him. Eliza was astonished. "Well," she ventured, "if they were to bump into each other right now, who would win?"

"You mean, where do *I* think the Visitors have come from?"

She nodded.

"I am obliged to say first that it is possible they came from a lab. I think we can rule out surgical hijinx based on our examinations today, but might not someone have managed to *grow* them?"

"You mean, like, in a supervillain's lair inside a volcano?"

He laughed. "Exactly. And if it were only the bodies—the 'beasts,' as it were—then this theory might seem to have some merit, but the angels, now. They're a bit more complex."

Yes. The fire, the flying. "Have you heard," Eliza asked, "that facial recognition databases got no hits on any of them?"

He nodded. "I did. And if we consider, prematurely, that they might indeed be from . . . somewhere else, then our contenders are?"

"Another universe, or . . . Heaven and Hell," Eliza supplied.

"Yes. But what I find myself thinking, out here, staring at the stars . . . 'Gazing' is too passive, don't you think, for stars like this?"

Very whimsical, Eliza thought, nodding agreement.

"And perhaps it's the guests in the palace mingling—" He tapped his head to clarify what "palace" he meant—"but I find myself thinking: What does that mean? Might they just be two ways of saying the same thing? Suppose 'Heaven' and 'Hell' are just other universes."

"*Just* other universes," Eliza repeated, smiling. "And the Big Bang was *just* an explosion."

Dr. Chaudhary chuckled. "Is another universe bigger or smaller than the idea of God? Does it matter? If there is a sphere where 'angels' dwell, is it a matter of semantics, whether we choose to call it Heaven?"

"No," Eliza replied, swiftly and firmly, a bit to her own surprise. "It isn't a matter of semantics. It's a matter of motive."

"I beg your pardon?" Dr. Chaudhary gave her a quizzical look. Something in Eliza's tone had hardened.

"What do they want?" she asked. "I think that's the bigger question. They came from somewhere." *There is another universe.* "And if that somewhere has nothing to do with 'God'"—*It doesn't.*—"then they're acting on their own behalf. And that's scary."

Dr. Chaudhary said nothing, but returned his gaze to the stars. He was quiet long enough that Eliza was wondering whether she'd smacked down his newfound loquacity when he said, "Shall I tell you something strange? I wonder what you'll make of it."

The horizon was paling. Soon the sun would rise. Seeing it from here, such a horizon, and such a sky, it really made you mindful of being plastered by gravity to a giant, hurtling rock, and from there it was a hopscotch to picturing the immensity that surrounded it: the universe, too big for the mind to compass, and that was only the one universe.

Too big for the human *mind, perhaps.*

"You know of Piltdown Man, of course," said Dr. Chaudhary.

"Sure." It was maybe the most famous scientific hoax in history—a supposed early human skull unearthed in England about a hundred years ago.

"Well," said Dr. Chaudhary, "it was in 1953 that it was proved a fake, and the year is important. With all the haste of shame, it was removed from the British Museum, where for forty years it had served as erroneous 'evidence' of a particular wrongheaded view of human evolution. Only a few years later, in 1956, another discovery was made, in the Patagonian Andes. A German amateur paleontologist discovered a cache of..." Here he paused for effect. "Monster skeletons."

And...it all went screwy for Eliza, somewhere in there. Dream siege, and a failure of psychic mind spikes. Dr. Chaudhary had said he was going to tell her something strange, and even as she swerved into some kind of altered state, she had the clarity to understand that the monster skeletons were the relevant fact here, not the site. But it was there that her mind took her.

To the Patagonian Andes.

As soon as he said it, she saw them: mountains that were pitched and pointed, sharp as teeth honed on bone. Lakes, absurd in their purity of blue. Ice and glacial valleys and forests dense with mist. Wildness that could kill, that *did* kill, but hadn't killed her, because she was not easily killed and had survived so very much worse already—

She had been turned inward somehow, like a dress pulled inside out, and she was still sitting there with Dr. Chaudhary, and she could hear what he was saying—about the monster skeletons, and how in the days of scorn after Piltdown they'd been nothing but a joke, even though they were a joke that rather defied explanation—but his words were as a rushing of water over a streambed, and the streambed was a thousand polished stones, a *thousand*-thousand, and they gleamed beneath the surface, beneath *her* surface, and they were her and more than her. *She* was more than her, and she didn't know what that meant but she felt it.

She was more than herself, and she could see the place Dr. Chaudhary was talking about—not the monster skeletons unearthed there, but the land and, most of all, the sky. She was leaning back and looking up and she saw the sky above her now and the sky above her then—*What then? When?*—and it was with the grief of mourning that it came to her that it was denied her.

The sky was denied her, then and now and forever.

She felt the tears on her cheeks right as Dr. Chaudhary noticed them. He was still talking. "The Museum of Paleontology at Berkeley has the remains now," he was saying. "As much for curiosity as scientific merit, but I have a feeling that is going to change.... Eliza, are you all right?"

She swiped at the tears but they kept falling and she couldn't speak.

For a vertiginous moment, staring up at the stars—not gazing, but staring—she felt the scope of the universe around her, so vast and full of secrets, and she sensed the presence of more and greater beyond that... and *beyond* beyond, and then beyond even that, and somehow the unknowable depths within herself corresponded to the unknowable scope without, and... there *wasn't* another universe.

There were many.

Many beyond many, unknowably.

I've seen them, thought Eliza. *Knew* Eliza. Tears were streaming down her face now, and she finally understood the nature of the dream, and it was worse, so much worse than she'd even feared. It wasn't prophecy. They'd had that wrong all along. It wasn't the end of the world she was seeing.

At least, not the end of *this* world.

The dream wasn't future, but past. It was memory, and the question of how Eliza could possibly have such a memory was overshadowed by what it meant. It meant that it couldn't be stopped. It had already happened.

I've seen other universes. I've been to them.

And I destroyed them.

39

Scion

Sirithar had drawn her to him like a musk, through passages of wending stone within the mountain fastness of a dead people, and thus had Scarab, queen of the Stelians, found the magus she had come to kill.

She had hunted him halfway around the world and here he was, alone in a close and quiet place. With his back to her, he was stripped to the waist and scooping water from a channel in the cavern wall, cupping it to his face, to his neck and chest. The water was cold and his flesh was hot, so steam rose from him like mist. He dipped his head into the flow, scrubbing his fingers through his hair. His fingers were tattooed, and his hair was dense and black and very short. When he straightened, water sluiced down the back of his neck, and Scarab noticed the scar there.

It made the shape of a closed eye, and though she felt power in the mark, she was unfamiliar with the design. It was not from the *lexica*. Like the world-wind and the despair, she supposed that this was his own creation, though it had not been wrought of stolen *sirithar* or she would have felt the tremor of its making. Still, *sirithar* clung to him, electric. Like ozone, but richer. Heady.

Here stood the unknown magus who plucked at the strings of the world and who, if they didn't stop him, would destroy it. She had assumed that she would feel a corruption on him, and that her soul would cry to the killing like lightning to a rod, but nothing here was as she had expected. Not the mixed company of seraphim and chimaera, and not him.

—Will you do it, my lady, or shall I?

Carnassial's voice came into her head with the intimacy of a whisper. He was several paces behind her—glamoured, as she was—but his mind brushed hers like the stir of breath against her ear. Tickle and heat and even a trace of his scent. It was deeply real.

And deeply presumptuous.

She delivered her response and felt him flinch away.

—What do you think? she returned. Those were her only words, but there was more to her reply.

Telesthesia was an art form more akin to dreaming than speaking. The sender entwined sensory threads, with or without words, to form a message that keyed to the receiver's mind at every level: sound and image, taste, touch, smell, and memory. Even—if they were very good at it—emotion. A sending from a master telesthete was an experience fuller than reality: a waking dream delivered on a thought. Scarab was not a master telesthete by any stretch, but she could twine several threads into her sending, and she did now. The flexion of cat's claws and the sting of nettles—Eidolon had taught her that one—declared to Carnassial: *Back off.*

Did he think that because she had made him the gift of her body for her first dream season, he could touch her mind uninvited?

Men.

A single dream season was a single dream season. If she chose him again next year, that might begin to mean something, but she didn't suppose she would. Not because he hadn't pleased her, but simply this: How could she know his worth if she had no one to compare him to?

—*Forgive me, my queen.*

From a respectable remove came this sending, more like an approximation of his physical distance, and it was stripped of scent and stir, as was right. She could feel a wisp of penitence, though, and that was a fine flourish. Carnassial wasn't a master telesthete, either—it would be a long time before either of them could hope to achieve mastery; they were both very young—but he had the makings of one. Not for nothing had Scarab chosen him for her honor guard—and not for his lutenist fingers, either, that had learned to play her with such ardor in the spring, or for his deep bell laughter, or for his hunger that understood her own and spoke to it, not unlike a sending, at every level.

He was a fine magus, as were the rest of her guard, but none of them—none of them—pulsed raw power like the seraph before her now. Her eyes swept down his bare back, and she felt the tug of surprise. It was a warrior's back, muscled and scarred, and a pair of swords hung crossed in their harness from a jut of stone to his right. He was a soldier. She had gleaned this much in Astrae, where the folk spoke of him with acid fear, but she hadn't fully believed it until now. It didn't fit. Magi didn't use steel; they didn't need it. When a magus killed, no blood flowed. When she killed *him*, as she had come here to do, he would simply . . . stop living.

Life is only a thread tethering soul to body, and once you know how to find it, it is as easily plucked as a flower.

So do it, she told herself, and she reached for his thread, conscious of Carnassial behind her, waiting. "Will you do it or shall I?" he had asked her, and it galled. He doubted that she could, because she never had. In training, she had touched life threads and let them sing between her fingers—the fingers of her *anima*, that is, her incorporeal self. It was the equivalent of laying a blade to an opponent's throat in sparring. *I win, you die, better luck next time.* But she had never severed one, and doing so would be the difference between laying a blade to an opponent's throat and laying his throat *open*.

It was a very great difference.

But she could do it. To prove herself to Carnassial, she had an inspiration to perform *ez vash*, the clean slash of execution. An instant and it would be done. She wouldn't feel the stranger's thread or pause to read anything of it, but only scythe it with her *anima*, and he would be dead without her ever having seen his face or touched his life.

She thought of the *yoraya* then, and a feeling of reckless might flowed through her.

It was only a legend. Probably. In the First Age of her people, which had been far, far longer than this the Second Age and had been ended with such brutality, Stelians had been very different than they were now. Surrounded by powerful enemies, they had lived ever at war, and so a great deal of their magic had been concentrated on the war arts. Tales were told of the mystical *yoraya*, a harp strung with the life threads of slain foes. It was a weapon of the *anima* and had no substance in the material world; it could not be found like a relic or passed on as an inheritance. A magus made his own, and it died with him. It was said to be a reservoir of deepest power, but darkest, too, achievable only by killing on a staggering scale, and the playing of it was as likely to drive its maker mad as it was to strengthen him.

When she was a little girl, Scarab used to scandalize her nursemaids by plotting her own *yoraya*. "You will be my first string," she had once said, wickedly, to an *aya* who had dared to bathe her against her will.

The same words came into her head now. *You will be my first string*, she thought to the scarred and muscled back of the unknown magus before her. She reached out with her *anima* to perform the execution, and a horror washed through her, because she had meant it, just for a moment.

"Take care what desires you mold your life and reign to, princess," the *aya* had said to her beside the bath that day. "Even if the *yoraya* were real, only someone with many enemies could ever hope to achieve it, and that isn't what we are anymore. We have more important work to do than fight."

Work, yes. The work that was the shape of their lives—and the thief of it. "Not that anyone thanks us," Scarab had replied. She had been a small child then, and more intrigued by stories of warfare than the Stelians' solemn duty.

"Because no one knows. We don't do it for thanks, or for the rest of Eretz, though they benefit as well. We do it for our own survival, and because no one else can."

She may have stuck her tongue out at her *aya* that day, but as she grew up, she had taken the words to heart. She had even, recently, declined a tempting invitation of enemyhood from the fool emperor Joram. She might have had a harp string of him, but instead she had only sent a basket of fruit, and now he was dead anyway—at this magus's hand, if the stories were true—and . . . it was as it should be.

She didn't want enemies. She didn't want a *yoraya*, or war. At least, so Scarab tried to convince herself, though in truth—and in secret—there was a voice within her that called out for those things.

It filled her with dread, but it thrilled her, too, and her dark excitement was the most dreadful thing of all.

Scarab did not perform *ez vash*. Realizing she was trying to prove herself to Carnassial, she rebelled against the idea—it was *he* who must prove himself to *her*—and besides, she wished to see this magus's face and touch his life, to know who he was before she killed him. It was no small thing to draw down *sirithar*. It was no *good* thing, but it was without doubt a *great* thing, and she would know how he had done it when all knowledge of magic in the so-called Empire of Seraphim was lost.

So instead of slashing the thread of his life, Scarab reached for it with her *anima*, and touched it.

And gasped.

It was a very small gasp, but it was enough to make him turn.

—*Scarab*. Carnassial's sending was sheathed in urgency. *Do it*.

But she didn't, because now she knew. She had touched his life and knew what he was before she even saw his face, and then she did see his face and so did Carnassial, and though he did not gasp, Scarab felt the ripples of his shock as they merged with her own.

The magus called Beast's Bane, who drew down *sirithar* and so could not be permitted to live, and who was a bastard and a warrior and a father-slayer, was also, impossibly, Stelian. His eyes were fire—they were searching the empty air where Scarab stood unseen—and that was enough to know for a certainty, but she knew something more about him, which she pushed, fumblingly, toward Carnassial in the simplest of sendings—no sense or feeling, just words.

She sent it to the others, too, who were out in the caverns and passages trying to form an understanding of what was happening in this place. She sent it to Spectral and Reave, that is, but caught herself before releasing, so abruptly and inadequately, this news to Nightingale, to whom it would mean . . . very much.

Scarab waited, breath held, as the magus scanned the air where she stood. And though she knew he couldn't see her, she read his certainty of her presence in the steadiness of his gaze, and his reaction was another surprise in a layering of surprises.

Confronted with the certainty of an invisible presence before him, he showed no alarm. His expression didn't harden, but softened . . . and then—confounding Scarab to her core—he smiled. It was a smile of such pure pleasure and gladness, such breath-catching, unabashed happiness and light, that Scarab, who was a queen, young and beautiful, and had been smiled at by many a man, flushed to be the focus of it.

Except, of course, that she wasn't.

When he spoke, his voice was low and sweet and rough with love. "Karou? Are you there?"

Scarab flushed deeper and was glad of invisibility, and glad she'd pushed Carnassial back from her mind a moment earlier so that he couldn't feel the flare of heat this stranger's smile had sparked in her.

His beauty—it was of the sort that made you fall very still and conserve your awe like a held breath. His power was part of it—the raw, wild musk of *sirithar*, forbidden and damning; just to breathe him in was an indulgence—but it was his happiness that pierced, so intense that she experienced it as much with her heart as with her eyes.

Godstars. She had never felt happiness like what she saw in him in that moment, and she was sure she'd never inspired it, either. Her first night with Carnassial in the spring, when the rituals and dance had ended and they had at last been left alone, she had felt his hunger and delight before he even touched her. It had felt like something real then, but, quite suddenly, it didn't anymore.

This look was so much more than that, and the pierce became an ache as Scarab wondered: Who was it for?

Sendings pulsed back to her from Reave and Spectral, and from Carnassial, too—not Nightingale, whom she had still not told—and for an instant they overwhelmed her. Reave and Spectral were older, more practiced magi and telesthetes than she and Carnassial were, and one of their sendings—the two arrived together and tangled, so that Scarab couldn't say which was whose—conveyed a reaction of staggering shock that actually made her blink and take a step back.

He spoke again, his brow creasing in uncertainty as his smile faltered. "Karou? Is that you?"

—Someone is coming.

Carnassial's words, and on the heels of his sending, Scarab heard footsteps in the passage and moved swiftly to one side, which brought her up against Carnassial in a corner of the chamber. She felt him stiffen at the contact and draw immediately away—afraid of angering her with unsolicited touch, she supposed—and she was sorry for the loss of his solidity in the depth and breadth of this stunning strangeness.

Then a figure came into view.

She was a girl of around Scarab's own age. She was neither a seraph nor one of the chimaera the seraphim here mingled with.

She was . . . alien. Not of this world. Scarab had never seen a human, and though she knew what they were, the actual sight of one was blinkingly curious. The girl had neither wings nor beast attributes, but instead of seeming like lack, this simplicity of form came across as a kind of stripped-down elegance. She was slender, and moved with the grace of a duskdeer drawing its first substance together out of midsummer shade, and her prettiness was of such a curious flavor that Scarab couldn't say whether it was more pleasing or startling. She was cream-colored, and as black-eyed as a bird, and her hair was a shimmer of blue. *Blue*. Her face, like her lover's, was flushed with joy, and dappled with the same sweet and tremulous shyness as his, as though this were something new between them.

"Hi," she said, and the word was a wisp, as soft as the brush of a butterfly's wing.

He didn't answer in kind. "Were you just here?" he asked, looking past her and around her. "Glamoured?"

And this clicked into place for Scarab. Sensing a presence, the magus had thought it was this girl, invisible, which meant that the human could do magic.

"No," was her answer. She looked tentative now. "Why?"

His next move was very sudden. He took her arm and pulled her to him, placed her behind him, and faced outward, peering into the emptiness of the chamber that was, of course, not empty at all. "Is someone there?" he demanded, in Seraphic this time, and when his eyes raked Scarab now, they held only what she had expected to see before: suspicion and the low burn of ferocity. Protectiveness, too— for the pretty blue alien he sheltered with his body.

With his body, Scarab noted with curiosity, but not with his mind. He put up no shield against *anima* but only stood there, strong and fierce, as though that made any difference. As though his life thread and his lover's weren't as frail as gossamers glinting in the ether, as easily severed as spidersilk.

—*Are we going to kill him?* came Carnassial's sending, unadorned by any tone or sensory threads to hint at his own opinion on the matter.

—*Of course not*, Scarab replied, and she found herself unaccountably angry at him, as though he'd done something wrong. *Unless you'd like to explain to Nightingale that we found a scion of the line of Festival and severed his thread.*

As she almost had. She shuddered. To prove that she could kill, she had almost killed *him*.

A scion of the line of Festival. These were the words she had sent to Carnassial and Reave and Spectral but not yet to Nightingale—Nightingale who had been First Magus to Scarab's grandmother, the previous queen, and who had twice sat *veyana* in grief and survived. No one else in the Second Age had survived *veyana* twice, and Nightingale's first sitting had been for Festival.

Her daughter.

Scarab might be queen, but she was eighteen years old, untried, and out of her depth. She'd come hunting a rogue magus, hoping to make her first kill, but what she'd found here was much bigger than that, and she would need the counsel of all her magi, Nightingale most of all, before she decided anything.

—*Then we should go*, Carnassial sent, ignoring her last barbed message. *Before* he *kills* us.

It was a good point. They really had no idea what he was capable of. So Scarab, taking a last deep breath of the electric musk of the stranger's power, retreated.

40

Assume the Worst

In fascination, the Stelians watched the unfolding of the next hour in the caves, and they learned many things, but many more things remained baffling.

The magus went by the name of Akiva. Nightingale scorned to call him by it, because it was an Empire name, and a bastard's no less. She called him only "Festival's child," and kept her sendings uncharacteristically austere. She was one of the finest telesthetes in all the Far Isles, an artist, and her sendings were generally effortless layers of beauty, meaning, detail, and humor. The absence of all of it now told Scarab that Nightingale was overwhelmed with emotion and intent on keeping it to herself, and she couldn't blame her, and since she couldn't *see* her—the five of them maintained their glamours, of course—she couldn't begin to tell how the older woman was grappling with the abrupt existence of this grandson.

Or with what his existence suggested about the fate of Festival, so many years a mystery.

It was within Scarab's rights as queen to touch her subject's minds, but she wouldn't intrude in something like this. She only pushed a simple sending of warmth to Nightingale—an image of one hand holding another—and kept her focus on the activity around her.

Preparations for war? What was this? A rebellion?

It was very strange, drifting among these soldiers who had been for so long mere archetypes in the stories she was raised on. Warnings, really, was what they had been, these kin from the far side of the world. Locked in war, century after century, all their magic lost, they were a cautionary tale. *We are not that* had been the tone of Scarab's education, with their fair-skinned cousins serving as example—at a distance—of everything they eschewed. The Stelians had ever held themselves apart, shunning all contact with the Empire, refusing to be drawn into their chaos, leaving them to burn off their noxious idiocy in their wars on the far side of the world.

And if chimaera burned and bled for it from the Hintermost to the Adelphas? If an entire continent had become a mass grave? If the sons and daughters of a whole half world—seraphim included—knew no life but war, and had no hope of better?

It is nothing to do with us.

The Stelians shouldered their solemn duty, and it was as much as they could bear. Only the great rending drag on *sirithar* that had sucked at the skies of the world had drawn Scarab so far from her isles, because that *was* to do with them, in the deadliest way imaginable.

Find the magus and kill him, restore balance and go home. That was the mission.

And now? They couldn't kill him, so they watched him, and he was a part of something very strange indeed, and so they watched that, too.

And when the two rebel armies, uneasily intermingled, gathered into battalions and left the caves, the five unseen Stelians followed them. South over the mountains and with a westward veer they flew, and they were three hours in the sky before they set down in a kind of crater in the lee of a sharkfin peak.

Three chimaera were waiting there—scouts, Scarab soon determined, making her silent way around the crowd to stand in the shadow of the wolf-aspect general called Thiago.

"Where are the others?" he asked the scouts, who shook their heads, somber.

"They haven't come," said one.

At the general's side—and this was curious—stood not a lieutenant of his own race, but a severe seraph soldier of more than common beauty, and it was she whom he looked to first to say, "We have to assume the worst until we know otherwise."

What worst? wondered Scarab, almost idly, because this was all so very abstract to her. She was a huntress and had marshaled stormhunters from the brink, and she was a magus and a queen and the Keeper of the Cataclysm, and she may have dreamt in childhood of scything the life threads of enemies to build a *yoraya*, but she had never been to war. Once her people had been warriors, but that was in another age, and when Scarab, from her place of isolation in the Far Isles, shrugged off the fates of millions with disdain for the foolishness of warmongers, she did so without ever having seen a death in battle.

That was about to change.

* * *

"But why is *Liraz* coming with us? Why not Akiva?" Zuzana asked. Again.

"You know why," replied Karou. Also again.

"Yes, but I don't care about any of those reasons. I only care that I'll have to spend time with her. She looks at me like she's planning to yank my soul out through my ear."

"Liraz couldn't yank your soul out, silly," said Karou, to assuage her friend's fear. "Your brain, maybe, but not your soul."

"Oh, well then."

Karou considered telling her how Liraz had kept her and Mik warm the other night in their sleep, but thought that if it got back to Liraz, she actually *might* yank out some brains. So instead she said, "Do you think I wouldn't rather be with Akiva, too?" and this time maybe a little bit of her own frustration sounded in her voice.

"Well, it's nice to hear you finally admit it," said Zuzana. "But a little Machiavellian maneuvering would not go amiss here."

"Excuse me? I think I've been pretty damn Machiavellian," said Karou, as though it were an insult not to be borne. "There is the matter of hijacking an entire rebellion."

"You're right," Zuzana allowed. "You are a conniving, deceitful hussy. I stand in awe."

"You're sitting."

"I sit in awe."

Here they were, back at the crater where they'd spent their cold night. They'd just arrived and soon they would be on their way again, toward the Bay of Beasts and the portal. At least, a few of them would, and Akiva was not part of that few. Karou had been trying to be cool about it, but it was hard. When her plan had come clear to her—when she was back in Akiva's chamber with Ten dead at her feet, and her mind had raced through the scenario—it had been Akiva she imagined by her side, not Liraz.

But once she'd presented the idea to the council, she'd begun to realize that her plan was really only one slice in the much greater strategic pie, and that if they went forward with it, Akiva, as Beast's Bane, would be needed here.

Damn it.

And so it was: Liraz would accompany her instead of Akiva, and it was just as well. The chimaera would have questioned Thiago sending Karou off through the portal with Akiva, and there was still the deception to manage. There was *too much* to manage, blast it.

At least once she got through the portal, Karou told herself, she wouldn't have the entire chimaera army watching her every move.

Of course, in the absence of Akiva, there would be no moves to worry about them watching.

"We all have our parts to play," she told Zuzana and Mik, by way of reminding herself. "Getting Jael out is just the beginning. Quick and clean and apocalypse-free. Hopefully. Once he's back in Eretz, he still has to be defeated. And, you know, the odds aren't exactly in our favor."

That was putting it mildly.

"Do you think they can do it?" asked Mik. He was looking at the soldiers coming in to land in the crater, chimaera and seraphim together. They'd made for an arresting sight in the sky, bat wings mixed with flame ones, all of them moving in the same smooth rhythms of flight.

"*We*," Karou corrected. "And yes, I think we can." *We have to.* "We will."

We will defeat Jael. And even that was just a beginning, really. How many damned beginnings did they have to get through before they made it to the dream?

A different sort of life. Harmony between the races.

Peace.

"Daughter of my heart," Issa had told her, back at the caves. With the exception of a few, such as Thiago, those of the chimaera who couldn't fly had stayed behind, and, in parting, Issa had recited Brimstone's final message for Karou. "Twice-daughter, my joy. Your dream is my dream, and your name is true. You are all of our hope."

Your dream is my dream.

Yes, well. Karou imagined that Brimstone's vision of "harmony between the races" probably involved less kissing than hers did.

Stop mooning about kissing. There are worlds at stake. Cake for later; emphasis: later.

It should have happened when she'd followed Akiva into the alcove—dear gods and stardust, the sight of his bare chest had brought back very...warm...memories—but it hadn't happened, because he'd become agitated, insisting there was someone or something there with them, unseen, and had proceeded to search for it with a sword in his hand.

Karou didn't doubt him, but she hadn't sensed anything there herself, and couldn't imagine what it might have been. Air elementals? The ghosts of Kirin dead? The goddess Ellai in a bad mood? Whatever it was, their brief moment alone together had come to an end, and they hadn't been able to say good-bye properly. She thought it might have made parting easier, if they had. But then she recalled their predawn good-byes in the requiem grove years ago, and how hard it had been, every single time, to fly away from him, and she had to admit that a good-bye kiss doesn't make things any easier.

And so she focused her mind on her task and tried not to look for Akiva, who was somewhere on the opposite side of the cluster of soldiers coming in to land.

This was the plan:

Instead of going through the portal to attack Jael in unfamiliar territory, Thiago and Elyon would take the main force of their combined armies north to the second portal and be there to greet Jael when Karou and Liraz sent him home.

And here things became interesting. They didn't know yet where Jael had his troops staged, and couldn't predict what they would find at the second portal, up in the Veskal Range north of Astrae. They would take it as it came, but they anticipated, of course, a vast force. Ten-to-one ratio if they were lucky, worse if they were not.

So Karou had given them a secret weapon. A pair of them.

There they were, sitting quietly by themselves, apart from and above the mass of soldiers, on the rim of the crater, looking down. As Karou watched, Tangris lifted one graceful panther paw and licked it, and the gesture was purely cat in spite of the fact that the face—and tongue—were human. The sphinxes were alive again.

Karou had given the rebellion the Shadows That Live. She had deeply mixed feelings about it. It had provided a pretext for resurrecting the sphinxes, Tangris and Bashees—and Amzallag along with them, since his soul was in the same thurible and she defied anyone to argue with her about it—and that was good. But she'd always had a horror of their particular specialty, which was to move unseen, in silence, and slay the enemy in their sleep.

Whatever their gift or magic, it transcended silence and slyness. It was as though the sphinxes exuded a soporific to ensure their quarry didn't awaken, no matter what was done to them. They didn't even wake up to die.

Maybe it was naive to hope that a bloodbath could be avoided at this stage, but Karou *was* naive, and she didn't want to be responsible for any more bloodbaths.

"The Dominion are irredeemable," Elyon had told her. "Killing them in their sleep is a greater mercy than they deserve."

No one ever learns anything, she'd thought. *Ever.* "The same would be said of the Misbegotten by anyone in the Empire. We have to start being better than that. We can't kill *everyone*."

"So we spare them," Liraz had said, and Karou was primed for more of her icy sarcasm, but, to her surprise, none was forthcoming. "Three fingers," she'd said, and she was staring at her own hand, turning it over and back again. "Take the three middle fingers of a swordsman's or archer's dominant hand and they're useless in a fight. At least, until they can train in the use of their other hand, but that's a problem for another day." She looked straight into Karou's eyes and lifted her brows as if to say, *Well? Will that do?*

It...would. They'd all agreed to it, and Karou had had time in flight to register the strangeness of mercy—for Dominion, no less—coming from Liraz. And this on the heels of her puzzling response to Ten's attack. "I deserved her vengeance," she had said, angerless. Karou didn't want to know what she deserved it *for*; it was enough to marvel at the end of a cycle of reprisals. How seldom it happened, in a long-standing war of hatred, that one side said, "Enough. I deserved that. Let it end here." But in effect, that was what Liraz had said. "What you do with her soul is your affair," she had also said, leaving Karou free to glean Haxaya's soul from the she-wolf body that should never have held it to begin with.

She didn't know what she would *do* with it, but she had it, and now Liraz had not only proposed sparing the Dominion soldiers their lives, but even a usable portion of their hands. They might not be drawing bowstrings or swinging swords again in a hurry, but they'd be much better off than if their whole hand was severed at the wrist. It was more than mercy. It was *kindness*. How odd.

So that was settled. The Shadows That Live would, if they could, disable the soldiers guarding Jael's portal, or as many of them as they could.

As for Akiva, he would fly due west to Cape Armasin, which was the Empire's largest garrison in the former free holdings. His role—and it could make all the difference—was to seed mutiny in the Second Legion, and attempt to turn at least a portion of the Empire's might against Jael. While the Dominion forces were elite, aristocratic, and would fight to protect the privilege they were born to, the soldiers of the Second Legion were largely conscripts, and there was reason to believe that their hearts weren't in another war—especially a war against the Stelians, who weren't beasts but kin, however distant. Elyon thought that Akiva's reputation as Beast's Bane would count for something in the ranks, on top of which, he'd proven himself persuasive with his brothers and sisters.

Karou had need of persuasion, too, to urge Jael to leave, but it was a particular breed of "persuasion" that Liraz could manage as well as Akiva, and so it was arranged.

"I'm going to go find out what the scouts have to say," she told Mik and Zuzana, dropping her gear with a thud and rolling her shoulders and neck. She was passingly bothered by the fact that there had been only three scouts waiting for them: Lilivett, Helget, and Vazra. Ziri had dispatched four pairs of scouts, and each pair was to have sent one soldier to rendezvous here and make report on any seraph troop activity around the bay.

So there should have been four.

Probably just late, Karou told herself, but then she heard the Wolf tell Liraz, "We have to assume the worst."

And so she did.

* * *

And . . . so it was.

41

Unknowns

There were just so many unknowns. From their perch in the Adelphas, the rebels were blind. Up here it was all ice crystals and air elementals, but a world lay beyond the peaks, full of hostile troops and slaves in chains, shallow graves, and the blowing ash of burned cities, and it was all as a play behind a closed curtain to them.

They didn't know if Jael had sent troops to hunt them down.

He had.

They didn't know if he had found and secured the Atlas portal since they passed through it.

He hadn't, yet, but even now his search patrols were crisscrossing the Bay of Beasts, searching.

They didn't even know if he'd returned to Eretz, victorious or otherwise, and they had no way of knowing that Bast and Sarsagon, the unrepresented pair of scouts, had been captured within hours of their dispatch from the crater a day and a half earlier.

Captured and tortured.

And the rebels didn't know and couldn't have begun to imagine that, on the far side of the world, the sky had been twilight-dark for more than a day—a strange and ruthless dark that had nothing to do with the absence of the sun. The sun still shone, but it peered out of the inky indigo like a burning eye from the shadow of a cloak. Its light still fell on the sea and the speckling of green isles. Colors were still tropics-bright—all but the sky itself. It had sickened and blackened, and the stormhunters still wheeled in it, their screams gone hoarse and horrible, and the prisoners in their unprisonlike room watched it out their window and shuddered in nameless horror, but they couldn't ask any questions of their captors, because their captors didn't come to them. Not Eidolon of the dancing eyes, not anyone. No food was brought, or drink. Only the basket of bloodfruit remained, and none had grown hungry enough yet to contemplate it. Melliel, Second Bearer of that Name, and her band of Misbegotten brothers and sisters were seemingly forgotten, and, looking out their barred window, they could only imagine that it meant the end of the very world.

Scarab and her four magi *were* aware of the state of their home sky. Sendings had come to them, even here, and they felt the disaster as a slackness of their own *anima*, as though their souls shrank from the shadow of annihilation.

But if they sensed the annihilation that was nearer at hand—much nearer—they did nothing to warn the host in whose midst they invisibly mingled. Perhaps it was apathy bred of centuries of reclusion. They'd been taught that these folk were fools, and that they deserved their wars. To take it a step further, there was a certain sense in the Far Isles that the wars served a grim good: That by occupying itself killing and dying *here*, the Empire couldn't muster itself to bother the Stelians with its stupid hostilities.

And if there was a grandiosity in the Stelian belief that, above all, *they* must not be bothered, it was a well-deserved grandiosity.

They must not be bothered.

At all costs, the Stelians must be left in peace. Scarab knew, from halfway around the world, what Melliel and the others abandoned in their cell beneath that unnatural dark did not: that Eidolon of the dancing eyes was one of many who strove against the sickened sky, holding the seams of their world intact. That she didn't have time for prisoners now, or for anything else.

And of course it's possible that the five fire-eyed interlopers didn't feel the ambush gathering just out of sight—though it seems unlikely that the collective breath passing in and out of thousands of enemy lungs could go unremarked by magi of such exquisite sensitivity. In any case, they didn't warn the rebels.

They watched.

Scarab's sending to the others was plainthought, without sensory threads or any effort at feeling. *It is nothing to do with us*, she sent.

It had always been true before. She could have no way of knowing how deeply *un*true it was today, or what it was this peculiar ragged hybrid army stood against, or what would be the fallout if they failed.

There were just so many unknowns.

ARRIVAL + 48 HOURS

42

The Worst

The first awareness is a sensation in the spine. Karou feels it and looks to Akiva, across the crowd of soldiers. At the same moment, he looks to her. A crease knits his brows.

Something—

And then, just like that, the sky betrays them. It's low and bright—a lucent, backlit mist, just as it was when they came from the portal. But this time it isn't stormhunters that drop from above.

It's an army.

Many.

The angels are fire, and they are legion, wing to wing, and so the sky has become fire. Bright and alive. But the daylight is brighter and they're blotting it out—so many—and so a tangled darkness falls on the host below.

Shadows, chased by fire.

Very fast. All very, very fast.

It begins.

The crater is a ragged bowl, and the Dominion are as a lid of fire, and they are many and many, wing to wing and swords drawn, and when they plummet in a single breath's span, there is no getting out, and no getting around them.

Nor is there any hesitation from below. Everything that had almost happened in the Kirin caves happens now, unchecked and with whip-crack quickness. Swords: unsheathed; palms: upraised. The effect of the hamsas is instantaneous. Like grass rippled by a wind, the attacking ranks sway away, and in the moment's reprieve this gains the rebels, they surge to greet the ambush, roaring. They don't wait to be pinned between fire and stone but leap—launch—and meet the emperor's troops in the air with a sound like fists smashing on fists.

Many fists against fewer, perhaps, but the fewer have magic.

At the first touch of shadow, Akiva reaches for *sirithar*—

—and is thrown to his knees as though clapped by thunder—thunder as a weapon, thunder in his head—and he's ringing with it, and tilting, and someone catches him. It's the Dashnag who isn't a boy anymore. Rath. His hand is huge on Akiva's shoulder. The same shoulder once savaged by a chimaera, another chimaera now steadies, and there is no *sirithar*, only the clash of blades, and then the boy Rath lunges into battle and Akiva surges to his feet and draws his swords, and he can't see Karou...

...and Karou can't see him, and she can't stop to look. There's Zuzana and Mik and an angel is coming at them and she won't be able to get there in time. She's opening her mouth to scream when she sees Virko. He pounces.

Rends.

The angel becomes pieces and Karou has her crescent-moon

blades in her hands and it's dance, cutting her way through the enemy to reach her friends.

Akiva tries for *sirithar* again, and again thunder invades his head and drives him to his knees.

For the merest instant, he has the impression of a cool hand pressed to his brow, soothing and then gone. All around him is glitter and clash and snarl and stab and teeth and grunt and stagger. Magic is denied him. All he can do is get to his feet and fight.

Zuzana has closed her eyes. Reflexive reaction to dismemberment. You could go your whole life without finding out how you'd react to seeing limbs torn off in front of you, but now Zuzana knows, and she knows the coursing terror of "all this war stuff," and she decides at once that *not* seeing what's happening is worse than seeing it and so she opens her eyes again. Mik is right at her side, and he's beautiful, and Virko is crouched before her, planted there, and he's terrible, and he's beautiful, too. The spikes at his neck have flared wide. She didn't know they did that. They'd lain sleek, almost, like porcupine quills at rest but bigger, sharper, and with serrated edges, but now they're all fanned out and bristling and he looks twice his size. It's like a lion's mane made out of knives.

And then Karou is there with blood on her blades and Virko is folding his spikes back down—they interweave, Zuzana sees, and the elegance of it . . . the symmetry almost overwhelms her with its perfection, and that's the thing that she'll remember most, not the dismemberment, her mind is already pulling a curtain on that, but the symmetry—and Virko's spikes aren't padded now with a smelly blanket, and there's no harness to hold on to when when Mik boosts her up, but Zuzana's not afraid, not of this. In the middle of this very bad dream, she's glad to have a friend with a lion's mane made of knives. Mik mounts behind her and Virko's muscles bunch beneath them. He gives a great, labored heave and they leave the ground and then . . . vanish.

Ziri sees Virko wink out—gone—and Karou is turning, searching. Not for him; Ziri knows that, and he minds less than he did before. A great gust that can only be the draft of Virko's invisible wingbeats blows her hair back like a battle standard, silken blue and streaming, and in the screaming maelstrom of battle, she is surrounded by a curious cushion of stillness.

Because she's being protected, Ziri sees, by both chimaera and Misbegotten. Because she's the resurrectionist, and because she has another, more immediate job to attend to. The realization kicks him forward. Whatever happens here, Karou's plan must go ahead. Jael must be stopped.

Ziri looks for Liraz and she's there, and so is Akiva. They're fighting back-to-back, lethal. Akiva wields a pair of matched swords, Liraz a sword and an ax, and her smile seems a third weapon, almost. It's the same smile from the war council, where she'd scoffed at the odds of the fight. "Three Dominion to one Misbegotten?" she'd said, with eagerness. And Ziri sees that before him: three to one and more. And more, and more, but something's happening. There's Nisk and Lisseth. Astonishingly, they're backing Akiva and Liraz up. Each has a blade drawn but a hamsa outheld, too, and against the pulse of weakness, the Dominion can't match the speed and force of the pair of Misbegotten.

Ziri feels a lift of hope. It's a hope he knows well and despises: the ugly, black hope that one might, by killing, stay alive awhile longer.

Kill or die, no other choice.

Bodies litter the crater and more are falling. Ziri has a flash image of how it will be filled with corpses as though the mountains have cupped their hands to offer up the dead to Nitid, goddess of tears and life, and to the godstars, and to the void.

The bodies are chimaera, too, and Misbegotten, and then—

—a second darkness falls.

Overhead, a second sky of fire is falling, wing to wing to wing, and even the ugly, black hope can't outlast this. Another wave of Dominion as great as the first, and today Nitid is the goddess of nothing but tears.

"Karou!" he calls, and it doesn't surprise him anymore to hear the Wolf's tenor come from his own lips—a voice to cut through battle clangor and rally tired soldiers to keep on, and keep on, as though life is a prize to be won by bloodletting. Kill and kill and kill to live. How many, and for how long? It's just a calculus in the end, and though the real Thiago had surmounted impossible odds in battle, none of them had been *this* impossible.

And besides, he isn't Thiago.

He calls out orders; chimaera and Misbegotten alike take heed. By the time he reaches Karou, there's a buffer of soldiers forming with Karou, Akiva, Liraz, and Thiago at its center.

"You two need to go," the Wolf says. His voice is raised above the chaos, and his eyes are intent but not cold, not mad. This White Wolf will tear out no throats with his teeth today. "Get clear of this. Use the glamour. You have a job to do."

Karou objects first. "We can't leave you now—"

"You have to. For Eretz." *For Eretz.* It's understood that this means: *If not for us.*

Because we'll be dead.

"I'll only go if you designate a safety," Karou says in a choked voice. "Someone. Anyone."

Someone to wait out the killing in safety and come back to glean souls after it's all over. It's pointless. Now that the seraphim know about resurrection, they take measures to prevent it. They burn the dead, and guard the ashes until evanescence is certain. But Ziri nods anyway.

It's time to part. The reluctance that envelops them all is a complex web—a cat's cradle of loves and longings and . . . even the earliest tender unfurlings of a possibility so remote it should have been laughable. Ziri glances to Liraz as she glances to him, and both look swiftly away again: Ziri to Karou, Liraz to Akiva. A second only—an eternity—do they permit themselves for farewells. They wish pointless wishes, and let their *what-ifs* fall to the ground with the corpses.

In the legends, chimaera were sprung from tears and seraphim from blood, but in this moment they are, all of them, children of regret.

As Karou and Akiva begin to turn toward each other for their last look, both their faces falling blank with unfathomable loss—*no please no not now please oh*—the Wolf speaks up. "Akiva," he says. "Take them. Get them to the portal. See to it."

Akiva blinks twice rapidly. He doesn't want to refuse, but he's going to. He should be *here*, fighting—

"It may be guarded," says the Wolf, anticipating his argument. "They may need help." The battle around them is reaching a fever pitch. "Go!"

Akiva nods, and they go.

It's Liraz's gaze that Ziri holds as they vanish. There's no period of transparency, only a sudden lurch from *there* to *not-there*, and at the hard and final edge of *there*, Liraz wears no killing, cutting smile, no scorn or coldness or lust for vengeance. Her features are soft with sorrow and her beauty takes his breath away.

And then she's gone. Within the center of the sphere of soldiers, the White Wolf is left alone. *Lucky Ziri*, he thinks, gutted, hollowed. *Not today, and not tomorrow.*

He looks up. The passage of armies has chased back the mist and he sees ranks of soldiers.

And soldiers, and soldiers, and soldiers.

He laughs. He gathers his stolen body, bares his fangs, and leaps.

He *climbs* them. They're thick enough; they make it easy. He has only to leap and catch one in the air and, catching, kill him. Leap to the next as the body falls. To the next, to the next, until the ground is far below and they're tangling their wings in a rush to escape him. Still more are closing behind, and he has no shortage of prey. No shortage of blood to spill, and his laughter sounds like choking.

He is the White Wolf.

And Liraz is flying, fast, racing toward the portal. The battle rings behind her, and then fades into the rushing of the air, the air that's stinging her eyes. That's all it is, the sting: the air, and speed.

"We haven't been introduced. Not really." That was what he'd said to her in the thermal pools before giving her his secret like a knife. *You could kill me with this. But I trust that you won't.*

Trust. Did she trust him because he'd saved her life, or because he'd trusted her with his secret, or both? Seeing him fight, his style was efficiency with panache; he was brutal and graceful, but it was nothing like the grace she'd beheld in the Hintermost when he wore his true body and danced the Kirin spin of crescent-moon blades.

They had seemed an extension of himself. These swords didn't. This body didn't, either. Since he told her who he is, his White Wolf form has seemed to her like a costume, as though he might unfasten it and step out, long and lean, dark and horned and winged. In her mind's eye, he's a silhouette. She only ever saw him at a great distance, and doesn't even know what his true face looked like.

She wishes she did.

And in the next second the wish seems stupid and petty. What does it matter what his face looked like before? Behind her he could be dying—again and forever. What does "true" even mean when it comes to a face? Only souls are true, and when you spill them to the air they melt away, as Haz's had, and countless others, and the loss... *The loss.* Liraz clutches her hand to her stomach. Fires go out, and the world grows dim.

How could it have taken her so many years to feel the preciousness of life?

They fly, and it's long minutes at speed before they leave the mountains behind them and course out over the dark water of the bay. It looks like a sea from here, haze shrouding the horizons and the land that hems it in. Karou finally spots Mik and Zuzana on Virko, ahead. The humans are trying to maintain the glamour but it flickers, unreliable, and a Dominion patrol has spotted them. They're closing in.

Virko wheels and dips. He makes it. He soars through the cut and vanishes in a ripple, and then Karou, Akiva, and Liraz arrive at the flapping loose edges of the slash in the sky, and instead of darting straight through, Karou spins toward Akiva. They've let go of their glamours, and when she looks at him, the impossibility of good-bye overwhelms her anew—and worse than before, so much worse, coming in the crush of peril. How can she leave him like this?

"Go!" Liraz screams at her. "Go *now*!"

Karou grabs Akiva's hand. Helpless, she tries to forge a final moment with him. A look at least, if not words, if not more. Something to remember. His hand is so warm, and his eyes are so bright—but haunted. He looks aggrieved, heartsick, furious and ready to curse the godstars. He squeezes her hand. "We'll be okay," he says, but it's with desperation. He wants to believe it but doesn't, quite, and if he doesn't then Karou can't, either.

Oh god, oh god. She wants to drag him through the portal with her and never let him go.

Liraz is still screaming at her and the sound fills Karou's head, fills her with panic—and *anger*—and Akiva touches her elbow, urging her through, and that's it. She feels the tatter of the sky brush against her face and she's not in Eretz anymore, and Liraz's screams—"Go! Go!"—ring in her head, stoking her panic. She flushes with fury, ready to hate her, if only for a moment, absolutely ready to tell her to *shut up*, and she swings around to face the portal to wait for her—

—as, on the other side, Akiva turns away from it. He's empty. He's just watched Karou disappear, and he turns to meet his sister's eyes one last time before she follows. *Take care of her*, he wants to say but won't. *And of yourself. Please, Lir.* And their eyes do connect for an instant.

"The urn is full, my brother," she says.

Urn? Akiva blinks, once; then he remembers. Hazael had told him that. Akiva is the seventh bearer of his name; six Akivas dead before him meant the cremation urn was full. "You have to live," Hazael had said, silly and matter-of-fact.

Hazael who had died, while Akiva lived.

Akiva's thoughts are fractured. The Dominion will be on them in seconds. He sees them as hurtling shapes behind Liraz. There's a thrum of frenzy that his sister's screams—"Go! Go! Go!"—have built in him, but still the thought finds purchase: that he's never seen her look more alive than she does right now. There's purpose and energy and resolve in her expression. She's focused; she's *alight*.

And then her feet connect with his chest.

Heart-bruising, rib-jarring, breath-stealing force. All his air and his thoughts are driven out in a rush, and he's reeling, unmoored. He can't breathe and can't see.

And when he catches himself he's through the portal.

It flares into flame, and Liraz is on the far side. She's burning it shut. Akiva thinks he hears a shiver of steel—sword on sword—in the instant before the connection between the worlds is lost.

The slash in the sky is cauterized like a wound. Liraz is still in Eretz and Akiva is here in her place. With Karou.

43

Fire in the Sky

And silence.

It wasn't really silence. There was fire and wind, crackle and whisper, and the rasp of their own hard breathing. But it felt like silence in their shock, and they all squinted in the face of the blaze. It flared hot and sudden and died quickly, and there was no smoke and no smell. It was just over, and whatever it was that had burned—whatever held the worlds distinct—it gave off no residue of ash or fume. The portal was simply gone.

Karou scanned for a sign that it had been there. A scar, a ripple, a ghosted image of the slash, but there was nothing at all.

She turned to Akiva.

Akiva. He was here. *He* was here, and not Liraz. What had just happened? He hadn't looked to her yet; his eyes were horror-wide as he stared at the new absence in the sky. "Liraz!" he called, hoarse, but the way was closed. Not just closed. Gone. The sky was just the sky now, the thin atmosphere above these African mountains, and that anomaly that had made Eretz seem like... like a neighboring country on the other side of a turnstile... it was over, and now Eretz seemed very, very far away, impossibly and fantastically far, like an imaginary place, and the blood that was being shed there—

Oh god. The blood was not imaginary. The blood, the dying. And it was so quiet here, nothing but the wind now, and their friends and comrades and... and *family*, every remaining Misbegotten soldier, Akiva's blood brothers and sisters, they were fighting in another sky, and there was nothing to be done about it.

They'd left them there.

When Akiva did turn to her, he looked stricken. Pale and disbelieving.

"What... what happened?" Karou asked him, moving toward him through the air.

"Liraz," he said, as though he were still trying to understand. "She pushed me through. She decided..." He swallowed. "That I should live. That *I* should be the one to live."

He stared at the air as if he could see through it to the other world—as though Liraz were just on the other side of a veil. But with the portal gone, it had become all at once unfathomable how it had ever existed at all. Where *was* Eretz, and what magic had brought it within such easy reach? Who had made the portals, and when, and how? Karou's mind defaulted to her picture of the known cosmos, starting with planets revolving around a star—a hugeness that was insignificant within a vastness that was incomprehensible—and she couldn't fathom how Eretz fit into that picture. It was like dumping two jigsaw puzzles in a pile and trying to piece them into one.

"Liraz can handle that patrol," she told Akiva. "Or at least glamour herself and get away."

"And go where? Back to the massacre?"

Massacre.

There was a sensation, in the core of her body, like screaming. Her heart and gut screamed; it scoured through her. She thought of Loramendi, and shook her head. She couldn't go through it again, flying back to Eretz to find nothing but death waiting for her. She couldn't even contemplate it. "They can win," she said. She wanted Akiva to nod, to agree with her. "The mixed battalions. The chimaera will weaken the attackers, and you said..." She swallowed. "You said the Dominion are no match for the Misbegotten."

Of course, that wasn't what he'd said. He'd said that *one-on-one* the Dominion were no match for them. And that hadn't been one-on-one, not by a long shot.

Akiva didn't correct her. Neither did he nod or assure her that everything would be fine. He said, "I tried to reach *sirithar*. The... power source. And I couldn't get it. First Hazael died because I couldn't, and now everyone will—"

Karou shook her head. "They won't."

"I began this, all of it. I convinced them. And *I'm* the one alive?"

Karou was still shaking her head. Her fists were clenched. She hunched in the air and held them tight against her middle: that pit below the inverted V of her rib cage. That was where she felt the hollowness and gnawing—like hunger. And there *was* hunger. She was underfed and too thin, and her own body felt insubstantial beneath her fists right now, like she'd been whittled down to essentials. But this hollowness and gnawing were more than hunger. They were grief and fear and helplessness. She'd long since given up believing that she and Akiva were the instruments of some great intention, or that their dream was planned or fated, but she found now that she still had it in her to be outraged at the universe. For not caring, for not helping. For, as it seemed, working against them.

Maybe there *was* an intention. A plan, a fate.

And maybe it hated them.

It was just so quiet, and the others were so very far away.

She thought of the Dashnag boy from the Hintermost, and of the Shadows That Live and Amzallag, whom she had just restored to life—Amzallag, who had hopes of gleaning his children's souls from the ruin of Loramendi—and all the others, and most of all, she thought of Ziri, bearing up under his burden, shouldering the deception alone now in the absence of Issa, Ten, and herself. Dying as the Wolf.

Evanescing.

He'd given everything, or would soon, while she was here, safe... with Akiva. And her emotions were a poisonous brew in the pit of her empty, empty stomach, because deep down, unspeakably, under all the horror and turmoil, there was at least a shred of... dear god, surely it wasn't *gladness*. Relief, then, to be alive. It couldn't be wrong, to be relieved to be alive, but it felt wrong. So very, very cowardly.

Akiva's wings were fanning slowly to keep him aloft. Karou just hovered. Behind them, Virko was flying short back-and-forths with Mik and Zuzana on his back.... *Oh*. Karou did a double take. Virko. He wasn't meant to stay here; he couldn't pass for human, not even close. He was to have set Mik and Zuze down and circled back to the portal. But Karou's thoughts skipped over him for now. Akiva was looking at her, and she was sure he was feeling the same poisonous mix of relief and horror that she was. Worse, because of Liraz's sacrifice. "She decided," he'd said. "That *I* should be the one to live."

Karou shook her head yet again, as if somehow she could shake out every black thought. "If it were *you*," she said, looking right into his eyes, "if it were *you* on the other side right now, like it almost was, I'd believe you were okay. I'd *have* to believe it, and I have to believe it now. There's nothing we can do."

"We could go back," he said. "We could fly straight for the other portal."

Karou didn't have an answer for that. She didn't want to say no. Her own heart lifted at the idea, even as her reason told her it was untenable. "How long would it take?" she asked after a pause. From here to Uzbekistan, and then, on the other side, from the Veskal Range back to the Adelphas.

Akiva's jaw clenched and unclenched. "Half a day," he said, his voice tight. "At least."

Neither of them said it aloud, but they both knew: By the time they could get back, the battle would be over, one way or another, and they'd have failed in their task here on top of everything. It wasn't a failure they could afford.

Hating to be the voice of sense in the face of grief, Karou asked, cautiously, "If it were Liraz here with me, and you were there, what would you want us to do?"

Akiva considered her. His eyes burned out of hooded shadows, and she couldn't tell what he was thinking. She wanted to reach for his hand like she had on the other side, but it felt wrong, somehow, like she was using her wiles to persuade him to give up something intensely important. She didn't want that; she couldn't make this decision for him, so she just waited, and his answer was heavy. "I'd want you to do what you came for."

And there it was. It wasn't even a real choice. They couldn't reach the others in time to make a difference, and even if they *could* reach them, what difference could they hope to make? But it felt like a choice, like a turning away, and in Karou, like a bloodstain, bloomed the earliest apprehension of the guilt that was to haunt her.

Did I do enough? Did I do everything I could?

No.

Even now, barely this side of catastrophe and the battle still under way in the other world, she could already taste the way that it would taint any happiness she could hope to find or make with Akiva. It would be like dancing on a battlefield, waltzing around corpses, to build a life out of this.

Look out, don't step there, one two three, don't trip on the corpse of your sister.

"Um, guys?" It was Mik's voice. Karou turned to her friends, blinking back tears. "I'm not sure what the plan is," Mik said, his voice tentative. He looked pale and stunned, as did Zuzana, gripping Virko tight and in turn gripped by Mik. "But we need to get out of here. Those helicopters?"

This was a jolt to Karou. *Helicopters?* She saw them now, and heard what she should have noticed sooner. *Whumpwhumpwhump . . .*

"They're coming this way," said Mik. "Fast."

And so they were—several, converging on them from the compass points. *What the hell?* This was no-man's-land. What were helicopters doing here? And then she got a very bad feeling.

"The kasbah," she said, a new horror dawning. "Damn it. The pit."

* * *

Eliza was . . . not quite herself today. She was faking it well enough, she thought, taking a swig of tea. She had her family to thank for that ability. *Thank you*, she thought, with the special bile reserved for them, *for the complete disconnection of my emotions from my facial muscles. It comes in so handy for pretending I'm not losing my mind.* After years of concealing misery, shame, confusion, humiliation, and fear, she could pretty much walk through life like a blank, her facade imperturbable, a thing scarcely animate.

Except when the dream took her over, of course. Then she was animate, all right. Hoo boy. And last night, up on the roof terrace...or was it this morning? Both, she guessed. It had gone on long enough to straddle the dawn. She just hadn't been able to stop crying. She hadn't even been asleep this time, and still it had found her. "It." The dream. The *memory*.

A storm had moved through her, entirely impervious to her will, and the storm had been grief, unfathomable loss, and the full intensity of the remorse she'd come to know so well.

With the fading of the stars and the break of day, Eliza's storm had passed. Today she was the ravaged landscape it had left behind. Waters subsiding, and ruin. And...revelation, or at least the cusp of it, the corner. This is what it felt like: detritus washed away, her mind a floodplain, clean and austere, and at her feet, just visible, a corner, protruding from the earth. It could be the corner of a trunk—pirate's treasure or Pandora's box—or it could be the corner of...a rooftop. Of a buried temple. Of an entire city.

Of a world.

All she had to do was blow away the dust, and she would know, or begin to know, what else lay buried within herself. She could feel it there. Burgeoning, infinite, terrible and wondrous: the gift, the curse. Her heritage. Stirring. She'd poured so much of herself into keeping it buried, sometimes it felt like any energy she might have had for joy or love or light went there instead. You only had so much to give.

So . . . what if she just stopped fighting and surrendered to it?

Ay, there's the rub. Because Eliza wasn't the first to have the dream. The "gift." She was only the latest "prophet." Only the next in line for the asylum.

That way madness lies. She was feeling quite Shakespearean today. The tragedies, of course, not the comedies. It didn't escape her that when King Lear made that statement, he was already well on his way to crazy. And maybe she was, too.

Maybe she was losing her mind.

Or maybe . . .

. . . maybe she was finding it.

She was in possession of herself for now, at any rate. She was drinking cold mint tea up at the kasbah—not the hotel kasbah, but the beast-mass-grave kasbah—and taking a break from the pit. Dr. Chaudhary wasn't very talkative today, and Eliza flushed to remember the awkwardness with which he'd patted her on the arm last night, at a total loss in the face of her meltdown.

Damn it. There really weren't all that many people whose opinions mattered deeply to her, but his did, and now this. Her mind was circling back to it yet again—another rotation on the shame carousel—when she noticed a commotion rippling through the assembled workers.

There was a kind of makeshift refreshment station set up in front of the massive, ancient gates of the fortress: a truck serving tea and plates of food, a few plastic chairs to sit on. The kasbah itself was cordoned off; a team of forensic anthropologists was going over it with fine-tooth combs. Literally. They had found long azure hairs in one of the rooms, apparently—the same room in which they'd found, scattered across the floor, a peculiar assortment of *teeth* that had led to speculation that "the Girl on the Bridge" and the "Tooth Phantom"—the silhouette caught on surveillance cam at Chicago's Field Museum—might be one and the same.

The plot thickened.

And now, something else. Eliza didn't see where it began, the commotion, but she watched it move from one cluster of workers to the next by way of gesticulations and loud, fast chatter in Arabic. Someone pointed to the mountains. Up, into the sky above the peaks—in the same direction that Dr. Amhali had pointed when he'd said, wryly, "They went that way."

They. The living "beasts." Eliza drew a hard breath. Had they found them?

She made out the glint of aircraft moving in the distance, and then, at her right, a couple of men disengaged from the general mass of people whose function she couldn't determine—there were a lot of men here, and most of them didn't appear to be doing anything—and made for the helicopter that was at rest on a piece of flat terrain. She kept watching, her tea forgotten in her hand, as the rotors began to spin, picking up speed until billows of dirt were kicking their way toward her and the helicopter lifted up and flew. It was loud—*whumpwhumpwhump*—and her heart was pounding as she scanned the faces of the people around her. She felt handicapped by the language barrier, and very much an outsider here. Surely someone spoke English, though, and this was a small enough feat of courage to perform. With a deep breath, Eliza threw her paper cup in a bin and approached one of the few female workers on-site. It only took a couple of questions to ascertain the source of the commotion.

A fire in the sky, she was told.

Fire? "More angels?" she asked.

"*Insha'Allah*," the woman replied, gazing into the distance. *Allah willing.*

Eliza recalled Dr. Amhali saying, the day before, "It's all very nice for Christians, yes?" "Angels" in Rome, "demons" here. How neat, how tidy for the Western worldview, and how wrong. Muslims believed in angels, too, and Eliza gathered that they wouldn't mind getting some for themselves. For her own part, she had a presentiment that they were better off without them, and she had to wonder—especially in light of what she was beginning to believe—why the prospect of angels frightened her more than the prospect of beasts.

44

This Just In

The seraphim had had the advantage of staging their arrival. They brought their own musical accompaniment, had costumes made for the occasion, and calculated their destination for effect. And even if they hadn't managed all of this, they were beautiful and graceful. Centuries of beneficent mythology anticipated them. They could scarcely have gone wrong.

The "beasts" made their debut with somewhat less aplomb. Their clothing was wrinkled and dark with dried blood, their music was chosen for them by sensationalistic television producers, and their beauty and grace were somewhat lacking.

On account of their being dead.

Two days after the angelic leader's stunning proclamation of "The Beasts are coming for you"—two days of riots and suicide pacts and mass baptisms in overcrowded churches, two days of furrowed brows and hemming and hawing on the part of a closed council of world leaders—a news bulletin preempted a preempt and exploded in the collective human consciousness with as much force as the Arrival had, if not more.

"This just in."

The media was already operating at a pretty fevered pitch—it was hummingbird-metabolism journalism: *fast fast fast*, and voracious. The many flavors of fear were seasoned liberally with glee; such times as these were the stuff of broadcasters' dreams. *Be afraid. No. Be* more *afraid! This is not a drill.*

In that context, the delivery of the latest "this just in" stood apart for its solemnity and gravitas.

The story was broken by the highest-paid news anchor in the world, a kind of human comfort food delivered nightly to American living rooms, year after year, his youthful face changeless save for a subtle lengthening effect brought on by a slow-climbing hairline. He had dignity, and not just the faux kind created by a real-or-fake sprinkling of salt in his pepper, and, to his credit, if it hadn't been for his willingness to use his clout in the service of journalistic ethics, things could have been far worse.

"My fellow Americans, citizens of Earth..." Oh, to be able to say that, *Citizens of Earth!* Lesser broadcasters trembled with envy. "This station has just come into possession of evidence that appears to validate the Visitors' claims. You know what claims I mean. Early independent inquiry suggests these photographs are legitimate, though as you'll see, many questions arise to which we do not yet have answers. I warn you. These images are not suitable for children." Pause. Millions leaned forward, breath held. "They may not be suitable for *anyone*, but this is our world, and we cannot look away."

And no one did, and very few sent their children from the room as, without further preamble, he showed the pictures in silence.

In living rooms across the nation, and in bars and offices and dorm commons and fire stations and the basement laboratories of the National Museum of Natural History and everywhere else, when the first image appeared, brows furrowed.

This was the grace period—the furrowing of brows, the knee-jerk disbelief—but it didn't last long. Knee-jerk disbelief had, over the past forty-eight hours, been knuckled under by credulity. Many people were newly learning how to *believe*. And so, swiftly and in a great wave, viewer cognition swept from *What the hell?* to *Oh my god*, and panic on Earth met its new high-water mark.

Demon.

It was Ziri, though of course no one knew his name, or wondered at it, the way Eliza had.

The personals ad Zuzana and Mik had composed for the Kirin in flight was something along the lines of: "Heroic sweetheart currently occupying smoking-hot maniac body in order to save the world. Would sacrifice everything for love, but hopefully won't have to. I really deserve a happy ending."

In a fairy tale, Zuzana had argued, he would get one for sure. The pure of heart always prevail. There was, between her and Mik, a fairy-tale promise: that when he had performed three heroic tasks, he could ask for her hand. She'd meant it in jest, but he'd taken it to heart, and was only one task down out of three—though secretly Zuzana accepted his fixing the air-conditioning in their last hotel room as a heroic act and counted it.

Ziri's sacrifice of his born flesh absolutely qualified as heroism, but life so very much is not a fairy tale, and furthermore, it sometimes goes out of its way to prove just how *un*-fairy-tale-like it can be.

As now.

Far away, something happened. It was a connection no one would or could make, in either world. What happened in Eretz, happened in Eretz, and the same went for Earth. No one was auditing the time lines for coincidence. But this... it almost suggested a synchronism between the worlds.

At the same moment that the image of Ziri's discarded Kirin body made its debut on human airwaves—the same moment *exactly*—in Eretz, a Dominion blade... pierced him through the heart.

If there *were* other worlds beyond these two, maybe they were linked, and maybe echoes of his story were playing out in all of them, shadows of shadows of shadows of shadows. Or maybe it was just coincidence. Brutal. Uncanny. While the image of Ziri's corpse burned itself into the human consciousness—*demon!*—he died again.

The pain was far worse this time, and no one was there to hold him, and there were no stars to look at, either, as life ebbed. He was alone, and then very quickly he was dead, and no one was near with a thurible. He'd promised Karou he would name a safety, but he hadn't. There just hadn't been time.

And now there never would be.

When Karou had felt Ziri's soul unskinned, back at the pit, when it had brushed against her senses, she had felt in it a rare purity—the high, surging winds of the Adelphas Mountains; *home*—and it was fitting that that was where he shed the White Wolf's hated body and slipped free of the clashing swords and howling all around him. There was no sound, in this state. Only light.

And Ziri's soul was home.

"Ladies and gentlemen," said the anchorman from his desk in New York City. His voice was very grave, without a hint of morbid delight. "This body was unearthed only yesterday from a mass grave at the edge of the Sahara Desert. It is one of many corpses found, no two alike, and none alive. It is unknown who killed them, though preliminary estimates put the deaths at as recently as three days ago."

More corpses, and of all the many pictures taken at the site—by Eliza—this array seemed curated for maximal horror: the most gruesome of the slashed throats, close-ups on the most monstrous jaws, studies of decomposition and curdled faces, eyes collapsing into sockets. Bloated tongues.

In fact, Morgan Toth had forwarded only the grimmest of her shots to the network—directly from her e-mail account, of course. There had been a poetry and poignancy in many of her pictures of the dead beasts; dignity. These he had left out.

Leaning against a doorjamb in the museum sublevels now, he observed the reactions of his colleagues with a supercilious smirk. *I did this*, he thought, enjoying himself immensely. And of course, the best was yet to come. He didn't trust the idiots at the news station to put two and two together regarding the identity of their source, so he'd attached a helpful message. That had been the best part, he thought. Giving public voice to Eliza's private torment.

Dear Sirs and Madams, he had written, as her.

Oh, Eliza. He was feeling something like tenderness for her. Pity. Really, so much made sense now that he knew who she was. Of course, the only breed of pity Morgan Toth was capable of generating was the sort a cat might feel for the mouse between its paws. *Oh, you little thing, you never had a chance.* Sometimes cats grow bored, and allow their prey to feeble themselves to safety, but they never do it out of mercy, and Morgan wasn't getting bored anytime soon.

Dear Sirs and Madams, he had typed. *You may remember me.*

Seven years I have been lost, and while on the surface, the path that I have taken in that time may seem surprising, I assure you it has all been part of a greater plan. God's plan.

Just a couple of days ago she had said to him, with insupportable condescension, "There aren't many things that people will gladly kill and die for, but this is the big one."

No, Eliza, Morgan thought now. This *is the big one. Enjoy.*

In the service of His will, he had written to the station, *I would gladly kill and die, and so gladly, too, do I defy the efforts of our government and others to conceal from the people the truth of this unholy ignominy.*

Ignominy was a good word. Morgan worried that he'd made Eliza sound too smart, but consoled himself that it couldn't be helped.

I couldn't sound stupid if I tried.

His colleagues were pressed in so close to the TV screens that he couldn't see the images, but that was fine. He'd had leisure to study them up close—*thank you, thank you, Gabriel Edinger, and thank you, naive Eliza, for not passcode-locking your phone*—and he had no doubt that after today it would be *he* and not she who would be continuing this momentous work with Dr. Chaudhary. As soon as Eliza's name came out, her time would be up.

So get to it, he thought, beginning to lose patience with the broadcast. *Enough with the rotting monsters.* He knew the rest was just a postscript, that it was the "demons" that mattered, and as to who had leaked the pictures to the press, the world wouldn't especially care. But Morgan needed the last piece of this puzzle to fall into place, and so when, at last, he heard the famous anchorman say, in a bemused voice, "As for the *source* of these startling images, well, it provides the answer to another mystery many of us had given up hope of ever solving. It's been seven years, but you'll remember the story. You'll remember this young woman."

And now Morgan Toth did elbow his way into the throng of scientists. He wasn't going to miss this. There on the TV was the picture that had had its time in the limelight. Seven years ago the story had come and lingered unsolved before finally frittering away into the sad land of cold cases, and Morgan could have kicked himself for not putting two and two together the first moment he met Eliza Jones. But how could he have recognized her as the girl in this picture? It was a terrible shot. Her eyes were downcast, and there was a motion blur, and anyway, he'd written her off as dead. They all had.

The headline summed it up: CHILD PROPHET MISSING, BELIEVED MURDERED BY CULT.

Eliza Jones, a prophet. Morgan's first thought—well, his first coherent thought, after concussive astonishment had given way to the first of many waves of mirth—had been to get business cards printed for her, leave them somewhere for her to find. *Eliza Jones, prophet.* And of course he couldn't leave out the best part. Oh boy. The thing that elevated this story to its special pinnacle of Crazytown. No, really. It was the mansion on the hill overlooking Crazytown. It was "my crazy can beat up your crazy" kind of crazy. Blindfolded. With one hand tied behind its back.

Or one *wing.*

Oh god. Morgan had actually fallen out of his chair, laughing. His elbow still smarted as a reminder. Eliza Jones's charming family cult? These were no run-of-the-mill "chosen ones," not they. Their spectacular difference?

They claimed to be descended from an angel.

DESCENDED FROM AN ANGEL.

It was the best thing Morgan Toth had ever heard.

Eliza Jones, Prophet
1/512th Angel (give or take)

That's what the business cards were going to say. But then he'd seen what she'd e-mailed to herself from Morocco and gotten a better idea. It was playing out now.

"We all prayed for her seven years ago," said the highest-paid news anchor in the world. "Known to us then only as Elazael, she was believed by her . . . church . . . to be the incarnation of an angel of that same name who fell to Earth a thousand years ago. It's quite a story, and it's not over. In an unexpected turn of events, ladies and gentlemen, the young lady is not only alive and living under an assumed name, she is a scientist in the nation's capital, on track to earn her doctorate. . . ."

And Morgan didn't hear the rest, because someone gasped, "It's Eliza!" and then the others erupted in a frenzy.

And that was all right. *Frenzy all you want, my fine idiots. Frenzy away*, thought Morgan Toth, strolling back to his lab. *It's good to be king.*

45

Cats out of Bags

The next fluttering of commotion to sweep through the kasbah had a different feel from the start. No *Insh'Allahs* or gazing skyward this time. There was disbelief, rancor, and . . . they appeared to be looking at . . . *Eliza.*

Eliza had had a problem with paranoia all her life. Well, for a good chunk of her life, it hadn't even been paranoia, but the foregone expectation of rote persecution: simple and nasty and certain. People *were* looking at her, and they *were* judging her. Back home in Florida, in a small town in Apalachicola National Forest, everyone had known who she was. And after she ran away, well. Then it was the chill at the nape of her neck, the dread of being found or recognized, the always looking over her shoulder.

That had gradually faded—never completely—but when you lived with a secret, the paranoia was never far beneath the surface. Even if you'd done nothing wrong (which in her case was debatable), you were guilty of having the secret, and any searching glance cast your way took on this ominous meaning.

They know. They know who I am. Do they know?

But they didn't. They never knew. At least, they never had before, and for that, Eliza had a particular perversity of the church to thank. They shunned "graven images"—not just of God and their "fore-mother," but of the prophets as well, and after Eliza's first vision, no more pictures of her were taken. Not that there were many before that. Her family wasn't exactly preserve-memories-for-posterity kind of people. They were more like prepare-for-Armageddon, guns-in-a-bunker kind of people. The photo used on the news had been taken by a tourist passing through Sopchoppy—that was the actual name of the town near which their church compound stood—who, alerted by a local, had snapped a picture of "those angel-cult freaks" when they came in for supplies.

"Those angel-cult freaks" had been a local story for decades, but had only exploded nationally when Eliza disappeared. Her mother—the "high priestess"—only reported her missing weeks after the fact, desperate enough for help finding her lost prophet to go to the officials she scorned as idolaters and heathens. Of course, it had looked fishy, and society is not predisposed to give cults the benefit of the doubt. The headline had snagged the national imagination like a briar: CHILD PROPHET MISSING, BELIEVED MURDERED BY CULT.

That'll do it.

Eliza could have cleared them at any time. She could have come forward—she was in North Carolina by then—and said, "Here I am, alive." But she hadn't. There was no pity in her for them. None. Not then, not now, not ever. And, as a body was never found—though it was looked for, assiduously, for months—eventually the law had had to leave them alone. Lack of evidence, they'd cited, though this had swayed neither public opinion nor the minds of the investigators. It was a sordid affair, and you had only to look into the eyes of the mother, they said, to know the worst. One of the detectives had gone so far as to state, on camera, that he had interrogated the Gainesville Ripper in his career, and he had interrogated Marion Skilling—her name, it was not lost on the tabloids, contracted to *Marion's killing*—and they gave you the same sense in your soul of pitching headlong into a dark hole.

"I find it difficult to sleep, knowing that woman is free in the world."

A sentiment shared wholeheartedly by Eliza.

The upshot was, the girl Elazael must certainly be buried somewhere in the vastness of Apalachicola Forest. There was not an iota of doubt.

At least, not until today.

"Eliza, come with me, please."

Dr. Chaudhary. He was rigid. Behind him, Dr. Amhali was... worse than rigid. He was livid. He was breathing like a cartoon bull, Eliza thought, her mind taking refuge in inanity even as she understood what must be happening, at long last, after seven years of dreading it.

Oh god, oh god.

Oh godstars.

Another tarot card turned over in her mind and gave that to her. *Godstars*. It tickled her memory, but she couldn't stop to consider it, not just now. "What's the matter?" she asked, but Dr. Chaudhary had already turned and walked away, fully expecting her to follow.

And they were in the middle of nowhere, in a hot, killing land, at the center of a military perimeter. What else could she do?

* * *

The cat was out of the bag. The corpses were out of the pit. Karou hadn't even considered this possibility. It felt like a violation, as if her home had been invaded.

Some home, she thought. She had been deeply miserable here. It was a chapter of her life she had no wish to revisit, and yet she couldn't help circling nearer, peering down at the figures moving beneath her. She passed in front of the sun and saw her own shadow—tiny with distance—hover and flitter like a dark moth among the folk down below. She could disguise herself, but not her shadow, and someone—a young black woman—caught sight of it and looked up. Karou moved back, drawing her shadow-moth away with her.

She could smell the rankness of the chimaera corpses even from up here. This was bad. Her whole plan of avoiding a conflict that would pit "demons" against "angels" was up in smoke. Or rather, stupidly, *not* up in smoke. "I should have burned them," she told Akiva, whose presence she felt by her side as heat and the stir of wingbeats. "What was I thinking?"

"I can burn them now," he offered.

"No," she said, after a pause. "That would be worse." If all the corpses were to suddenly combust? No matter that it was seraphim who commanded the fire to do such a thing, it would look... infernal. "There's no undoing this. We just get on with it."

He didn't answer right away, and his silence was heavy. It was a mercy they couldn't see each other, because Karou was afraid of the pain she would find in Akiva's eyes, as they moved further into their purpose here, obeying their heads and not their hearts. They would return to Eretz when they had done their part here, and not before. And what would they find when they did?

There was an odd feeling of half death settling over her with the realization that the best they could hope for now was not very much at all, even if they succeeded here and drove Jael, weaponless, back to Eretz. What then, for themselves? There wasn't even a future of tithing and bruises now, life squeezed in around the edges, and stolen tastes of "cake" to sweeten a difficult life. Cake for later, cake as a way of life. All of that was gone, smothered by a falling sky, shadows chased by fire: an enemy that was, simply, as Karou had known all along, too great to defeat.

How had she managed to hope otherwise?

Akiva. He had persuaded her. A look from him, and she'd found herself ready to believe in the impossible. It was a good thing that she couldn't see him now. If his belief had kindled hers so completely, what would the sight of his despair do to her, or hers to him? She thought of the despair that had surged through them all in the cave and wondered: Had it been Akiva's own? Did such darkness exist in him?

"How?" he asked. "How do we find Jael?"

How? That was the easy part. Bless Earth for telecom. All they needed was Internet access and an outlet to charge their phones so she could call some contacts. Mik and Zuze would probably like to let their families know they were okay, too. The two of them were on the ground now with Virko, a couple of miles away, hiding in the shadow of a rock formation. Even in the shade it was dangerously hot. Deadly hot, in fact, and they needed water. Food, too. Beds.

Karou's heart hurt. Contemplating even these bare thresholds of life felt like unspeakable luxury. But it's a different matter to take care of loved ones' needs than it is to take care of one's own, and for that reason she considered seeking food and rest. Zuzana hadn't spoken a word since they came through the portal. Her first close encounter with "all this war stuff" had taken a toll on her, and the rest of them weren't much better off.

"There's a place we can go," Karou told Akiva. "Let's go get the others."

46

Pie and Dandelions

"How could you think . . . how could you think I would do this?"

Eliza was aghast. It was so much worse than she'd feared. She'd guessed that Dr. Chaudhary had found out who she was, and oh, he had, but that wasn't the extent of it, and this . . . this . . .

It could only be the work of that weasel, Toth. No. *Weasel* did not begin to express the depravity of Morgan Toth now.

Hyena, maybe: carrion-eater, grinning jut-toothed over the carnage he had wrought.

She didn't know how he had found out about her—*People with secrets*, she recalled with a shudder, *shouldn't make enemies*—but she did know that only he could have accessed the encrypted photos. Did he even know what he had done by exposing this gravesite to the world? The real question was: Did he even care? He'd been smart, though, and kept himself invisible in all of it. She could just imagine him, flipping his bangs off his too-high forehead as he set catastrophe in motion.

Dr. Chaudhary took off his glasses and rubbed the bridge of his nose. A stalling tactic, Eliza knew. They had come into the nearest of the tents at the bottom of the hill, and the death smell was ripe around them, even in the chill of the refrigerated air. Dr. Amhali had shown her the broadcast on a laptop, and she was still trying to process it. She felt sick. The pictures. *Her* pictures, seen like that, without proper context. They were horrific. What was the response, out in the world? She remembered the chaos in the National Mall two nights ago. How bad was it now?

When Dr. Chaudhary lowered his hand, his look was direct even if his eyes were slightly unfocused without his glasses. "Are you saying you *didn't* do it?"

"Of course I didn't. I would *never*—"

Dr. Amhali butted in. "Do you deny that they are your photographs?"

She swung to regard him. "I took them, but that doesn't mean that I—"

"And they were sent from your e-mail."

"So it was hacked," she said, an edge of impatience coming into her voice. It was so obvious to her, but all the Moroccan doctor could see was his own fury—and his own culpability, since he was the one who'd brought them here to drag his country into infamy. "That message was not from me," said Eliza, stalwart. She turned back to Dr. Chaudhary. "Did it sound like me? *Unholy ignominy*? That's not . . . I don't . . ." She was floundering. She looked at the dead sphinxes behind her mentor. Never had they seemed unholy to her, and never had the angels seemed holy, either. That wasn't what was going on here. "I told you last night, I don't even believe in God."

But she could see the shift in his eyes, the suspicion, and realized belatedly that reminding him of last night might not be the best strategy. He was looking at her as if he didn't know her. Frustration welled up in her. If she'd merely been framed for leaking the photos to the press, he might have believed in her innocence and been willing to support her. If she hadn't had an apparent depressive episode on the roof terrace and cried enough tears to flood a desert. If she hadn't been unmasked as a dead child prophet. *If if if.*

"Is it true, what they're saying?" Dr. Chaudhary asked. "Are you . . . her?"

She wanted to shake her head. She wasn't that blurry girl with the downcast eyes. She was not Elazael. She might have changed her name more decisively when she ran away and shed that life, but in some way, "Eliza" had felt true to her. It had been her name of secret protest as a child, the inner "normal" she'd clung to in games of pretend and mental escape. Elazael might have to kneel in prayer until her knees were white-hot, or chant until her voice was as rough as a cat's tongue. Elazael might be forced to do many things—many and more—that she did not want to do. But Eliza?

Oh, she was outside playing. Normal as pie and free as dandelions. What a dream.

And so she'd kept the name, and lived it as best she could: pie and dandelions. Normal and free, though in truth it had always felt like an act. Still, from the age of seventeen on, it was Elazael who was the secret self locked inside, and Eliza who lived in the open—like the prince and the pauper who switched places: the one elevated, the other dispossessed. Of course, the prince and the pauper, she was reminded now, had eventually changed back. But that wasn't going to happen to her. She would never be Elazael again. But she knew that wasn't what Dr. Chaudhary meant, and so, reluctantly, she nodded.

"I *was* her," she corrected. "I left. I ran away. I hated it. I hated *them*." She took a deep breath. *Hate* wasn't the right word. There *wasn't* a right word; there wasn't a big enough word for the betrayal Eliza felt, looking back at her childhood with an adult understanding of just how seriously she'd been abused and exploited.

From the age of seven. Home from the hospital with a pacemaker and a new terror so big it blotted out even her fear of her mother. From the first moment her "gift" made itself known, she had become the focus of all the cult's energies and hopes.

The constant touching. So many hands. No sovereignty over her own self, ever. And they'd confessed their sins to her, begging forgiveness, telling her things no seven-year-old should ever have to hear, let alone punish. Her tears were collected in vials, her fingernail clippings ground into a powder and mixed into the communion bread. And her first menstrual blood? She had to avert her thoughts from that. It was still too sharp a shame, though it was half her life ago. And then there was sleep.

At twenty-four years old, Eliza had still never spent the night with a lover. She couldn't bear to have anyone in the room with her. For ten years she'd been made to sleep on a dais in the center of the temple, the congregation clustered around its base. Dear god. The wheezing and weeping, snoring, coughing. Whispering. Even, sometimes, in the dead of night: rhythmic, tandem panting that she hadn't understood until much later.

She would never be able to scrape away the memory of the collective, unwelcome breathing of dozens of people surrounding her in the night.

They'd been waiting for the dream to visit her. Hoping for it. Praying. Vultures, hungry for scraps of her terror. If they couldn't have the dream for themselves, they wanted to be near it. As though her screams might impart salvation, or better yet, as though maybe, just maybe, it might burst free of her—the dream, the monsters, *terrible and terrible and terrible forever, amen*—and pour forth its annihilation, to the woe of sinners everywhere, and the glorification of the chosen: themselves.

As though Eliza might be the actual fount of the apocalypse.

Gabriel Edinger had gotten nightmare ice cream, and she had gotten *that*.

"I still do. I still hate them," she said now, maybe a little too fervently. Dr. Chaudhary had put his glasses back on, and his eyes were wary behind them. When he spoke, his voice had the stilted delicacy reserved for talking to those of unsound mind.

"You should have told me," he said, with a glance at Dr. Amhali. He cleared his throat, evidently uncomfortable. "This could be considered a . . . a conflict of interest, Eliza."

"What? There's no conflict. I'm a scientist."

"*And* an angel," said the Moroccan doctor with a sneer.

Who sneers? wondered Eliza, fadingly. She'd thought it was something only book characters did. "We aren't . . . I mean *they* aren't. They don't claim to *be* angels," she said, unsure why she was making any explanations on their behalf.

"Pardon me, of course not." Dr. Amhali was all chill sarcasm. "*Descendants of.* Oh, and incarnations of, let's not forget that." He stabbed her with a pointed look. "Apocalyptic visions, my dear? Tell me, do you still have them?" He asked it as though it were worse than absurd, as though the very notion profaned decent religion and must be punished.

She felt herself diminishing, shrinking in the face of double accusation and scorn. Disappearing. She wasn't Eliza, right now, in this tent, in the eyes of these men. She was Elazael. *I'm not her, I'm me.* How desperately she wanted to believe it. "I left all that behind," she said. "*I left.*" The last part was emphatic, because it still seemed simple to her. *I left. Doesn't that mean something?*

"It must have been very difficult for you," said Dr. Chaudhary.

It wasn't that it was the wrong thing to say. Under other circumstances, this conversation might have led there: to his legitimate pity in the face of her tale of hardship. Damn straight it had been difficult for her. She'd had nothing, no money or friends, no worldliness at all. Nothing but her brain and her will, the first woefully neglected—she hadn't been given an education—and the second so often punished that it had become stunted. Not stunted enough. *Kiss my will*, she might have said to her mother. *You will never break me.*

But under *these* circumstances, and in the tone in which he said it—that stilted delicacy, that patronizing indulgence—it wasn't the *right* thing to say, either. "Difficult?" she returned. "And the Big Bang was just an explosion."

She'd said that to him last night, in jest. She'd smiled ironically and he'd chuckled. She meant it in the same spirit now... well, sort of... but Dr. Chaudhary raised his hands in a calming gesture.

"There's no need to get upset," he said.

No need to get upset? No *need.* What did that even mean? No *reason*? Because it seemed to Eliza that she had plenty of reasons. She'd been framed and she'd been outed. Her hard-earned anonymity had been snatched from her, her professional credibility from this moment forward would be entangled with the history that she'd fought so hard to hide, not even to mention this vicious allegation and the damage it could do to her, the legal ramifications of breaking her nondisclosure agreements, and . . . hell, the violent fallout on the world. But the most immediate reason was taking shape in this hazmat tent, in the company of two presumptuous men bent on treating her like their cardboard cutout of a long-lost victim.

Reflexively she glanced at the laptop screen that had shown her her undoing. It was frozen on that old photo of her, with its same old caption. CHILD PROPHET MISSING, BELIEVED MURDERED BY CULT.

"I'm not upset," she said, taking a series of measured breaths.

"I don't blame you for who you are, Eliza," said Anuj Chaudhary. "We can't change where we come from."

"Well, that's big of you."

"But perhaps it's time now to seek help. You've been through so much."

And that's when things started to go sideways. He still had his hands upraised in that let's-not-do-anything-rash manner, and Eliza just stared at him. What was that all about? He was acting like she was hysterical, and for a second, it made her doubt herself. Had she raised her voice? Was she wide-eyed and nostril-flared, like some kind of lunatic? No. She was just standing there, arms at her sides, and she would have sworn by anything worth swearing on—if there *was* anything worth swearing on—that she didn't look crazy.

She didn't know how to react. It brought on a bizarre feeling of helplessness to face such an exaggerated response. "What I need help with," she said, "is proving that I didn't do this."

"Eliza. Eliza. It doesn't matter now. Let's just get you home, and worry about that later."

Her heartbeat started to pound in her ears. It was anger, it was frustration, and it was something else. Free as dandelions, she remembered. Normal as pie. Well, maybe not normal. Maybe not ever, but she would be free. She looked at her mentor, this dignified man of rare reason and intellect who stood to her as a kind of paragon of human enlightenment, and she felt his hypocrisy weighed against her truth—her own new knowing—and there was no contest. "No," she said, and she heard her tone, which had gone soft and slippery with her own shame, slough off all weakness. "Let's worry about it *now.*"

"I don't think—"

"Oh, you think plenty. But you're wrong." A flick of her hand toward the laptop and all it stood for with its freeze-framed news broadcast. "Morgan Toth did this. Look into it. The truth is so far beyond him, I wouldn't expect him to get it. He might be smart, but he's a shallow pond. *You,* though." Again he tried to interject, and again Eliza silenced him. "I expected more from you. You've got *gods* strolling the hallways of your 'mind palace'." She put good, fat air quotes around that. "And they're trying not to bump into the... what was it? The delegates of Science, so they can keep it cordial in there. That's how open-minded you are, right? And now you've *seen* angels, and you've *touched* chimaera." *Chimaera.* The word came to her the same way *godstars* had: a card flipped upside. "You know they're real. And you know—surely you know—that, wherever they came from, *they've been here before.* All our myths and stories have a real, physical origin. Sphinxes. Demons. Angels."

He was frowning, listening.

"But the idea that *I* could be descended from one? Now *that's* crazy! Ship Eliza home, get her some help, and for heaven's sake, keep her the hell out of my mind palace!" She laughed, mirthless. "You don't serve my kind in there, isn't that it? Whoever heard of a black angel, anyway? And *a woman* to boot. This must be so difficult for *you,* doctor."

He shook his head. He looked pained. "Eliza. That's not it."

"I'll tell you what 'it' is," she said, but she held on to it, for a second, wondering if she was really going to do it. Tell it. Here. To these hypocritical, doubting men. She looked from one to the other, from Dr. Chaudhary's pained dismay and . . . embarrassment, for *her*—for her delusion, her sad display—to Dr. Amhali's trembling contempt. Not the greatest audience for a revelation, but in the end it didn't matter. Eliza's new certainties had grown beyond concealing.

"My family," she said, "are miserable, vicious, pitiless people, and I will never forgive them for what they did to me, but . . . they're right." She raised her eyebrows and turned to Dr. Amhali. "And yes, I do still have visions, and I hate them. I didn't want to believe any of it. I didn't want to be part of it. I tried to escape from it, but it doesn't matter what I want, because *I am*. Funny, isn't it? My fate, it's my DNA." Back to Dr. Chaudhary. "This should keep the delegates of Science and Faith busy arguing in the halls. I *am* descended from an angel. It's my goddamn genetic destiny."

47

The Book of Elazael

There was nothing for it, after that. After they perp-walked her through the site, every set of eyes drilling into her, malicious and condemning. After they put her in a car and slammed the door and ordered her returned to Tamnougalt to await her escort home. It was a couple of hours' drive, the sere pre-Saharan landscape of the Drâa Valley surrounding her in all directions, and she had nothing to occupy her but her strange coursing exaltation and outrage.

Well, nothing but that and . . . all the things known and buried.

All the many stirring things. A corner protruding from a floodplain—maybe a cask or maybe a world. All she had to do was blow away the dust. Eliza started laughing. There, in the backseat of the car, laughter poured from her like a new language. Later, when the government agents came to fetch her, the driver would report it, as preamble to explaining what happened after.

When she *stopped* laughing.

* * *

Back in the "good old days" when she'd had nothing to worry about but building a monster army in a giant sandcastle in the wilderness, Karou had periodically driven a rusty truck over rutted earth and long straight roads to reach Agdz, the nearest town where she might, with her hair covered by a hijab, pass unremarked while buying supplies. Bulk bags of couscous, crates and crates of vegetables, chewy, hardscrabble chickens, and a king's treasury of dried dates and apricots.

She looked down on Agdz now, from the sky. Unremarkable. She passed over it, feeling the pull of the others in her wake, and kept going. Their destination lay a little farther on, and was somewhat more remarkable. She spotted the palm grove first, an oasis, the green as surprising as spilled paint on brown ground. And there, within: crumbling mud walls so like the crumbling mud walls they'd just left behind. Another kasbah. Tamnougalt. It had a hotel, Karou remembered, the sort of sprawling out-of-the-way place that would allow for a quiet interlude for their small, strange band, while not so out of the way that they wouldn't find what they needed.

"We can get ourselves together here," she said. "They should have Internet and outlets. Showers, beds, water. Food."

Their tiny shadow-moths grew larger as they dropped down to meet them, and they set themselves down in the shade of the palms and released their glamours. Karou took in the sight of her friends first. Zuzana and Mik looked weak and dehydrated, sweaty and showing signs of sunburn—*Note to self: You can sunburn while invisible*—but the worst was the strain etched into their expressions, and a disturbing laxness about their eyes that made them look unfixed, not fully present. Shell-shocked.

What had she done, bringing them into war?

She looked to Virko next, still afraid of what she would see in Akiva's eyes. Virko, who had been a lieutenant of the Wolf, and one of those to leave her alone at the pit with him. The only one to look back, true, but he had left all the same. He had also saved Mik's and Zuzana's lives. He was stalwart and weathered, well accustomed to the rigors of flight and battle—no sunburn for him or fatigue, but the strain was there in his face, and the shock. And still the shame, Karou saw. It had been there since the pit, in every glance.

She gave him a look that she hoped was focused and clear, and she nodded. Forgiveness? Gratitude? Fellowship? She didn't quite know. He returned the nod, though, with a solemnity that was like ceremony, and then, finally, Karou turned to Akiva.

She hadn't really looked at him since the portal. She had seen him, in brief moments unglamoured, and she had been, every second, attuned to his presence, but she hadn't *looked*, not at his face, not into his eyes. She was afraid, and...she was right to be afraid.

His pain was undisguised, so raw it made her own pain sing straight to the surface, pure enough for tithing, but that wasn't the worst part. If it was only pain, she might have found a way to go to him, to reach for his hand as she had on the other side of the portal, or even for his heart, as she had in the cave. *We are the beginning.*

But...*the beginning of* what? Karou wondered, desolate, because there was rage in Akiva's eyes, too, and an implacability that was unmistakable. It was hatred, and it was vengeance. It was terrifying, and it froze her in place. When she had first lain eyes on him in the Jemaa in Marrakesh, he had been absolutely cold. Inhuman, merciless. What she had seen on him then was vengeance as habit, and fury cooled by years of numbness.

Later, in Prague, she had seen his humanity return to him, like a thaw releasing a heart from ice. She hadn't been able to fully appreciate it at the time, because she hadn't understood what it meant, or what he was coming back *from*, but now she did. He had resurrected himself—the Akiva she had known so long ago, so full of life and hope—or at least, he had begun to. She still hadn't seen him smile the way he had back then, a smile so beautiful it had channeled sunlight and made her feel drunk with love, at once light-headed and firmly, perfectly, gratefully connected to the world—earth and sky and joy and *him*. Everything else had paled beside that feeling. Race was nothing, and treason just a word.

She had just begun to feel that smile was possible again, and the feeling of effortless rightness, too, but, looking at Akiva now, it felt very far away again, and so did he.

As she understood it, there had been several thousand Misbegotten soldiers as recently as last year, and the final berserk push of the war had reduced that number to those she knew from the Kirin caves. Akiva had endured that, survived it, and then he had endured and survived the death of Hazael, and now he was here, safe, while possibly—probably—he lost all the rest.

What Karou saw in him was vengeance still molten, and it was wrong, it wasn't where they were supposed to be, but it felt... inevitable. Brimstone had told her, just before her execution, "To stay true in the face of evil is a feat of strength," but maybe, thought Karou, sick at heart, it was just too much to expect. Maybe that strength was too much to ask of anyone.

The feeling of half death was with her still. She felt flattened out, or hollowed out. Again.

She turned to her friends and, with effort, spoke almost evenly. "Could you two go in and get a room? Maybe it's best if the rest of us aren't seen."

She thought—hoped—Zuzana might make some sarcastic comment to that, or suggest riding right up to the gate on Virko-back or something, but she didn't. She just nodded.

"Do you realize," asked Mik, in a bald effort to jostle some Zuzana-ness back into Zuzana, "that our three wishes are about to come true? I don't know if they'll have chocolate cake here, but—"

Zuzana cut him off. "I'm changing my wishes anyway," she said, and counted them off on her fingers. "One: for our friends to be safe. Two: for Jael to drop dead, and three . . ."

Whatever she meant to say next, she didn't manage it. Karou had never seen her friend look so lost and fragile. She cut in. "If it doesn't include food," she reminded Zuzana gently, "it's a lie. At least, so I've been told."

"Fine." Zuzana took a deep breath, centering herself. "Then I could really use some world peace for dinner." She was all dark-eyed intensity. Something was lost in her. Karou saw it and mourned. War does that, nothing for it. Reality lays siege. Your framed portrait of life is smashed, and a new one thrust upon you. It's ugly, and you don't even want to look at it let alone hang it on the wall, but you have no choice, once you know. Once you really know.

And who was Zuzana going to be, now that this knowledge was hers?

"World peace for dinner," mused Mik, scratching his beard stubble. "Does that come with fries?"

"It freaking *better*," said Zuzana. "Or I will send it freaking *back*."

* * *

The angel's name was Elazael.

The church founded by her descendants—and they preferred the term *church* to *cult*, naturally—was called the Handfast of Elazael, and every girl child born in the bloodline was christened Elazael. If, then, by puberty, she had not manifested "the gift," she was rechristened by another name. Eliza had been the only one in the last seventy-five years to hold on to it, and she had often thought that the worst thing of all—the cherry on the cake of her awful upbringing—was the envy of the others.

Nothing glitters in the eyes like envy. Few could know this as profoundly as she did. It had to be something special to grow up knowing that any given member of your large extended family would probably kill and eat you if it meant they could have your "gift" for themselves, Renfield-style.

The Handfast was matriarchal, and Eliza's mother was the current high priestess. Converts were called "cousins," while those of the blood—venerated even if they didn't have "the gift"—were "the Elioud." It was the term, in ancient texts, for the offspring of the better-known "Nephilim," who were the first fruit of angels' congress with humans.

It was notable that in Nephilim scripture, both biblical and apocryphal, all the angels were male. The Book of Enoch—a text that was canon to no group except the Ethiopian Jews—tells of the leader of the fallen angels, Samyaza, ordering his hundred and ninety-nine fallen brethren to, essentially, get busy.

"Beget us children," he commanded, and they complied, and no mention was made of how the human women felt about this. Unsurprising in writings of the era, the mothers had all the agency of petri dishes, and the progeny that sprang from their wombs—accompanied by, one surmised, extreme discomfort—were giants and "biters," whatever that meant, whom God later bade the archangel Gabriel to destroy.

And maybe he did. Maybe they had existed, all of them: Gabriel and God, Samyaza and his crew and all their enormous biting babies. Who knows? The Elioud dismissed the Book of Enoch as absurd, which was kind of the pot calling the kettle black, Eliza had always thought, but wasn't that what religions did? Squint at one another and declare, "My unprovable belief is better than your unprovable belief. Suck it."

More or less.

The Handfast had its own book: the Book of Elazael, of course, according to which there weren't two hundred fallen angels. There were *four*, two of whom were female, one of whom mattered. Victims of corruption in the highest rank of angels, they were maimed and cast unjustly out of Heaven a thousand years ago. What had become of the three other Fallen, or whether they did any begetting of their own, was unknown, but Elazael, for her part, by way of congress with a human husband, was fruitful and multiplied.

(As a side note, it said a lot about Eliza's insular childhood and early education—or lack thereof—that she was a teenager before she learned that the governing body of the United States was called "Congress." In her world, it meant the act that leads to "begetting."

Coupling. Loin fruit. *Doing it.* As a consequence, *congress* still sounded sexual to her every time she heard it—which, living in Washington, D.C., was often.)

In the Book of Elazael, unlike in the patriarchal Book of Enoch, or Genesis for that matter, the angel wasn't the *giver* of seed, but the receiver. The angel was mother, was *womb*, and, credit nature or nurture, her offspring weren't monstrous.

At least not physiologically.

The Book of Elazael wasn't written down until the late eighteenth century—by a freed slave named Seminole Gaines who married into the matrilineal clan and became its most charismatic evangelist, growing the church, at its height, to number nearly eight hundred worshippers, many of whom were also freed slaves. Of the angel Elazael herself, he wrote that she was "ebon-dark, and the quicks of her eyes white as starfire," though, living eight hundred years after she did, he was hardly an unimpeachable source. Beyond that obviously massive heresy—a black mother angel; no, even better: a *fallen* black mother angel—the book was actually pretty orthodox, derivative enough that it could almost have been the result of an epic session of magnetic poetry, Bible edition.

You know, if magnetic poetry had existed in the late eighteenth century. Or refrigerator doors.

In any case, what Eliza wanted to know about her heritage would not be found in the Book of Elazael. At least, not that edition. The real book of Elazael was within her.

She...contained it. Not in her blood, though only those of the blood had it. It was, in fact, encoded on the thread of her life, that tether hooking soul to body that would be found on no anatomy chart ever drawn in this world. She didn't know that, even as she fell headlong into it, in the backseat of a car on a long, straight road.

Right into the heart of the madness that had claimed each and every "prophet" to come before her.

48

Hungry

There were no french fries to be had at Tamnougalt, and, in what Zuzana considered a blatant breach of hospitality laws, there was no chocolate, either—except in liquid form, that is, and hot chocolate just wasn't going to cut it right now. But if she was back to her old self enough to crave these things, she was *not* back to her old self enough to complain about them.

And I never will be again, she thought morosely, sitting in the shade on the rooftop terrace of this new kasbah. Well, not new, obviously. New to her. It was strange to see people ambling around in their cool leather slippers, at home in this place that reminded her so much of "monster castle." Just add a few homey flourishes, like Berber drums and some big woven cushions laid out on dusty rugs, fat candlesticks bearing years of wax drippings. Oh, and electricity and running water. Civilization, of a sort.

Though Zuzana rather doubted that any running water *ever*

would be able to compete with the thermal pools at the Kirin caves for awesomeness. After Karou had left her and Mik alone in there, they had indulged in a daydream of bringing people to the caves from Earth—not rich adventure tourists, either, but people who needed and deserved it—to "take the healing waters." They'd be carried on the backs of stormhunters, and sleep on fresh furs in the old family dwellings. Candlelight and wind music, a banquet under the stalactites of the great cavern. Imagine, being able to give that experience to someone. And Zuzana didn't even like people! It had to be Mik's good nature rubbing off on her, whether she wanted it to or not.

They had the rooftop terrace to themselves for the moment. The others were down in the room, hiding out, sleeping, and doing research. Mik and Zuzana had taken it upon themselves to procure food, and so here they were, menus spread before them on plastic tablecloths.

They hadn't talked at all about the battle. What was there to say? *Hey, Virko sure tore that angel apart, huh? Like he was slow-cooked chicken, ready to fall off the bone*. Zuzana didn't want to talk about that, and she didn't want to talk about the other things she'd seen as they made their escape, or to compare notes and know whether Mik had seen them, too. It would make them more real, if he had. Like seeing Uthem, whose revenant necklace she had strung herself, set upon by a half-dozen Dominion. And Rua, the Dashnag who had carried Issa through the portal. How many others?

"You know what?" Zuzana said. Mik looked up questioningly. "I am too going to complain. Why even bother living if you can't complain about the absence of chocolate? What kind of life would that be?"

"A pale one," said Mik. "But what absence of chocolate? What's wrong with this?" He was pointing at the menu.

"You better not be messing with me."

"I would never joke about chocolate," he said, hand to heart. "Look. You're missing a page."

And she was. And there it was, in black and white on Mik's menu, spelled out, as every item was, in five languages, as if *chocolate* were not universally understood:

gateau au chocolat
torta di cioccolato
pastel de chocolate
schokoladenkuchen
chocolate cake

But then the waiter came to take their order, and when she said, "First we'll have the chocolate cake, and we'll just eat it while you're making the rest, so bring that first, okay?" he told them—with what struck Zuzana as an entirely inadequate display of regret—that they'd run out.

. . . white noise . . .

But this was when Zuzana felt the nature of the change within herself for a certainty, because it wasn't a big deal. Her lines of context had been redrawn, and the one for "Big Deal" had been scooted *way the hell* back. "Well, that's a bummer," she said. "But I guess I'll survive."

Mik's eyebrows lifted.

They ordered and asked that the food be brought straight to their room—and the waiter triple-checked the quantity of kebabs and tagine, flat bread and omelettes, fruit and yogurt. "But it is enough for... twenty people," he pointed out several times.

Zuzana regarded him levelly. "I'm *very* hungry."

* * *

Eliza wasn't laughing anymore. She was... speaking. Sort of.

The driver was on his phone, shouting over the sound of her voice even as he sped down the long, straight highway. "Something's wrong with her!" he yelled. "I don't know! Can't you hear her?" Twisting his arm around to hold the phone nearer to her raving, he lost his grip on the steering wheel momentarily, swerving onto the shoulder and back with a squeal of rubber.

The girl in the backseat was sitting ramrod straight, eyes glazed and staring, speaking without cease. The driver didn't recognize the language. It wasn't Arabic or French or English, and he would have known German or Spanish or Italian to hear them, too. This was something other, and unutterably alien. It was fluting and susurrous and wind-borne, and this young woman, held rigid in the grip of some... fit... was spouting it like she was possessed, her hands moving back and forth in dreamlike underwater motions.

"Do you hear that?" the driver shouted. "What should I do with her?"

He was glancing manically back and forth between the road and the sight of her in his rearview mirror, and it took... three, four, five of these quick back-and-forths before he finally craned his head around in disbelief to confirm that he was really seeing what the rearview mirror was telling him.

Eliza's hands sculled lightly back and forth in the air as though she were floating.

Because she was.

He slammed on the brake.

Eliza slammed into the seat backs in front of her and crumpled to the floor. Her voice cut off and the car fishtailed, humping up onto the shoulder with a violent jouncing that ricocheted Eliza's inert body between the seats for a long, angry moment as the driver tried to wrest the vehicle back onto the road. He did, at last, and screamed to a halt, jumping out into the cloud of dust he'd made to wrench open her door.

She was unconscious. He shook her leg, panicking. "Miss! Miss!" He was just a driver. He didn't know what to do with madwomen, it was far beyond him, and now maybe he'd killed her—

She stirred.

"*Alhamdulillah*," he breathed. *Praise God*.

But his praise was short-lived. No sooner did Eliza push herself upright—blood was streaming from her nose, garish and slick, over her mouth and down her chin—than she lapsed straight back into that otherworldly raving, the sound of which, the driver would later claim, tore at his very soul.

* * *

"Rome," said Karou, as soon as Zuzana and Mik came back into the room. "The angels are in Vatican City."

"Well, that makes sense," Zuzana replied, choosing not to give voice to her first thought, which had to do with the happy prevalence of chocolate in Italy. "And have they gotten hold of any weapons yet?"

"No," said Karou, but she looked worried. Well. Worried was one of the things she looked. Add to the list: overwhelmed, exhausted, demoralized, and...lonely. She had that "lost" posture again, her shoulders curled forward, head lowered, and Zuzana did not fail to note that she was turned away from Akiva.

"The ambassadors and secretaries of state and whatever have all been talking each other to death," Karou elaborated. "Some in favor of arming the angels, some opposed. Apparently he hasn't made the greatest impression. Still, private groups are lining up to pledge their support, *and* their arsenals. They're trying to get access to make offers, but have so far been denied—at least, officially. Who knows who might have bribed a Vatican insider to get word to Jael. One of the groups is this angel cult in Florida that apparently has a stockpile of weapons at the ready." She paused, considering her words. "Which doesn't sound scary at all."

"How did you find all this out?" Mik marveled.

"My fake grandmother," Karou answered, indicating her phone, plugged into the wall. "She's very well connected." Zuzana knew about Karou's fake grandmother, a grand Belgian dame who'd had Brimstone's trust for many years, and who was the only one of his associates with whom Karou had a real relationship. She was stupendously rich, and though Zuzana had never met her, she felt no warmth for her. She'd seen the Christmas cards she sent Karou, and they were about as personal as the ones from the bank—which was fine, whatever, except that Zuzana knew that her friend craved more, and so she wanted to neck-punch anyone who disappointed her.

She only half listened while Karou told Mik about Esther. She watched Akiva instead. He was sitting up on the deep ledge of the window, the shutters drawn behind him, his wings visible, drooping and dim.

He met her eyes, briefly, and after she got past the first jolt she always got from looking at Akiva—you had to battle your brain to convince it he was real; seriously, that's what it was like, looking at Akiva; her brain wanted to be all *Pshaw, he's obviously Photoshopped*, even when he was right in front of her—a dragging sadness seized her.

Nothing could ever be easy for these two. Their courtship, if you could even call it that, was like trying to dance through a rain of bullets. Now that they'd finally come to the brink of an understanding, grief dragged a new curtain between them.

You can't drag the curtain back. Grief persists. But you can crash through it, can't you? If they had to suffer, Zuzana wondered, couldn't they at least suffer *together*?

And when the knock came at the door—their food—she thought that maybe she could help. At least with physical proximity.

"Just a minute," she called out. "You three, into the bathroom. You don't exist, remember?"

There followed a brief whispered argument that they could simply glamour themselves, but Zuzana would hear none of it. "Where would they put the food, with an enormous chimaera taking up half the floor, an angel perched on the window ledge, and a girl on the bed? Even if you're invisible, you still have mass. You still take up space. Like, *all* the space."

And so they went, and if the room was small, the bathroom was much more so, and Zuzana saw fit to arrange them within it as she chose, pushing Karou by the small of the back and then giving Akiva an imperious look and toss of her head that said, *You next*, and she pressed them together into the shower and shut them in. It was the only way Virko could fit into the room, too. It was all perfectly reasonable.

She closed the bathroom door. They'd have to take it from there. She couldn't do everything for them.

49

An Offer of Patronage

"Patience, patience."

Thus had Razgut counseled Jael half a day earlier. *Patience*. Even then, he'd been feeling the pinch of *im*patience himself. Now, with two full days gone by since their arrival, it was more of a stab. He'd belittled Jael for his expectations, but secretly he was beginning to worry.

Where were all their offers of patronage? Had he miscalculated? This was all his own plan. Only arrive in glory, he had said, and they will fall all over themselves to give you what you want. Oh, not the presidents, not the prime ministers, not even the Pope. They would roll out every red carpet, yes. There would be no shortage of bowing and scraping, but the powers that be would have to practice caution when it came to arming a mysterious legion. There would be scrutiny. Oversight.

Committees.

Oh, give me a half-mad butcher of a tyrant, thought Razgut, at his wit's end. *Only save me from committees!*

But while presidents, prime ministers, and popes entertained them, the quicker, darker currents of the world's will should have been shaping themselves into action. Private groups, the crazy ones, the hellfire chasers, the doomsday gloaters. They should have been lining up, sending offers, paying bribes, getting word to the angels no matter what it cost them. *Take us! Take us first! Burn the world, flay the sinners, only take us with you!*

The world was rife with them, even on a normal day, so where were they all? Had Razgut misjudged humanity's love affair with the end of the world? Was it possible this pageant would not play out quite so easily as he had thought?

Jael had been in foul humor, pacing the suite of magnificent rooms, alternating cursing with icy silence. He kept the cursing low, to his credit, doing nothing "un-angelic" that might ruffle the feathers, so to speak, of their pious hosts. He played his part whenever called upon: the diplomatic posturing, the feasting, the dazzling. The Catholic Church seemed determined to match pageant with pageant, and certainly their costume collection won the day. If Razgut had to endure one more ceremony clinging to Jael's back and listening to an old man in a fancy gown drone in Latin, he thought he might scream.

Scream and let himself be seen, just to spice things up.

So it was with a churning gutful of...hope...that he observed the curious shuffle-dance of faintheartedness being performed in the doorway by one of the Papal Palace servants.

A step forward, a step back, arms aflutter, chickenlike. The man was one of the few approved to enter their chambers and see to their needs, and he had until now kept his eyes fixed on the floor in their "holy" presence. Razgut had thought, on several occasions, that he could probably release his glamour and not even be noticed. That was the level of discretion these servants displayed. They were very nearly ghosts, though the thought of such an afterlife made Razgut bilious.

Or perhaps it was the prodigious output of the Papal Palace kitchens doing that.

He had not indulged in so much rich food in many a century, and found it interesting that the discomfort of his overtaxed intestines had not yet induced him to reduce his intake. Perhaps soon.

Or perhaps not.

The servant cleared his throat. You could almost hear his heartbeat from across the room. The Dominion guards remained motionless as statues, and Jael was in his private chamber, resting. Razgut considered speaking up. Would a disembodied voice really be the oddest thing that happened to this man all day? But he didn't have to. The man managed to summon some spine and mince forward, drawing an envelope from the pocket of his starched and immaculate coat and laying it down upon the floor.

An envelope.

Razgut's field of vision narrowed in on it. He knew what it must be, and his hope sharpened.

Finally.

Jump forward one minute, though—the servant gone, Jael summoned, and Razgut visible, splayed across the refreshment table with the envelope in his hand—and he gave no hint of his own very deep relief and curiosity. He only peeled a slice of paper-thin prosciutto free of its fellows and made sure to give audible proof of his delectation.

"Well, what does it say?"

Jael was impatient. Jael was imperious. Jael was, thought Razgut, at his mercy.

"I don't know," he replied casually, and also truthfully. He hadn't opened it yet. "It's probably a fan letter. Possibly an invitation to a christening. Or a proposal of marriage."

"Read it to me," Jael commanded.

Razgut paused as though he were thinking up a reply, and then he farted. Squinching up his face, he did so with effort. The reward was slight in resonance but grand in aroma, and the emperor was not amused. His scar went white in that way it had when he was extremely put out, and he spoke through clenched teeth, which, on a positive note, *did* help contain the flying spittle.

"Read it to me," he repeated in his deadly quiet voice, and Razgut judged himself to be one step removed from a beating. If he did as he was bid now, he might spare himself some hurt.

"Make things easy for me," Jael had said, "and I'll make things easy for you."

But where was the fun in *easy*? Razgut crammed as much prosciutto into his mouth as he could while he still had the chance, and Jael, seeing what he was about, ordered the beating with a dull twitch of his head.

They both knew it wouldn't yield a result. This was just their routine now.

And so the beating was given and received, and later, when Razgut's new injuries were seeping a fluid that wasn't quite blood onto the fine silk cushions of a five-hundred-year-old chair, Jael tried again.

"When we get to the Far Isles," he said, "and when the Stelians lie shattered in the streets but before we have crushed them utterly, I could demand a boon of them. Everyone grovels at the end."

Razgut's smile was a diabolical thing. *Until you come up against Stelians, perhaps*, he thought, but did not disabuse the emperor of his fantasies.

"If," Jael continued, visibly struggling to maintain a semblance of grace—a mask that fit him very ill—"if... *someone*... were to make his best efforts to be accommodating between then and now, I might be persuaded to ask that boon on his behalf. It is not beyond Stelian arts, I wager, to... repair you."

"What?" Razgut sucked himself upright, his hands flying to his cheeks in his best impression of a beauty queen hearing her name called. "*Me?* Truly?"

Jael was not so big a fool as to miss that he was being mocked, but neither was he fool enough to show his frustration to the Fallen thing. "Ah, my mistake. I thought that would interest you."

And it might have, but for one critical point. Well, two critical points, the first of which was really all that mattered: Jael was lying. But even if he hadn't been, the Stelians would never grant a boon to an enemy. Razgut remembered them from the time before, and they were not foes to be taken lightly. If—and this was a difficult thing to picture, if simply because it had never happened—they ever found themselves overpowered, they would self-immolate before surrendering.

"It's not what I would wish for," said Razgut.

"What, then?"

When Razgut had bartered with the blue lovely for a way back to Eretz, his wish had been simple. To fly? Yes, that was part of it. To be whole again. Not so simple, for more than his wings and legs had been ravaged and he knew that he was, in the most important ways, irreparable. But his true wish, his soul's bedrock, was simple. "I want to go home," he said. His voice was stripped of mockery and sarcasm and his usual nasty delight. Even to his own ears, he sounded like a child.

Jael stared at him, blank. "Easily done," he said, and for that, more than anything Jael had ever said or done to him, Razgut wanted to snap his neck. The void within him was so immense, the weight of it so obliterating, that it sometimes took his breath away to remember that Jael had no knowledge of it at all. No one did.

"Not so easily," he said. If there was one thing Razgut Thrice-Fallen knew beyond a shadow of a doubt, it was this: He could never go home.

More to conceal his own distress than out of any desire to stop torturing the emperor, he unfolded the letter. *What does it say?* he wondered. *Who is it from? What kind of offer?*

Is it almost time?

It was a bittersweet thought. Razgut knew that Jael would kill him the second he no longer needed him, and life, even at its most wretched, does get its hooks in you. With maddening exactitude and the slowest movements he could produce with his shaking fingers, the exiled angel made a show of flattening out the pages.

Confident script, he saw, ink on good paper, in Latin. And then, finally, he read out Jael's first offer of patronage.

50

Happiness Has to Go Somewhere

They were very near, and the situation was absurd. Too absurd, when it came down to it. The shower knob was digging into Karou's back, the feathers of Akiva's wings were actually caught in the door, and Zuzana's contrivance was clear. It was sweet but awkward—*extremely* awkward—and if it was meant to enflame anything, only Karou's cheeks obliged. She blushed. The space was so small. The bulk of Akiva's wings forced him to bend toward her, and by some maddening instinct, both obeyed the impulse to preserve the wisp of space between them.

Like strangers in an elevator.

And weren't they strangers, really? Because the pull between them was so strong, it was easy to fall into thinking they knew each other. Karou, who had never believed in such things before, was willing to consider that in some way their souls *did* know each other—"Your soul sings to mine," he had told her once, and she could swear that she had felt it—but they themselves did not. They had so much to learn, and she so badly wanted to learn it, but how do you do that, in times like these? They couldn't sit on top of a cathedral, eating hot bread and watching sunrises.

This wasn't a time for falling in love.

"Are you two all right in there?" asked Virko. His voice was cast low, not quite a whisper, and Karou imagined the hotel clerk hearing it and wondering who was hiding in the bathroom. With that, the scenario hit a new level of absurdity. In the midst of everything that was going on and the great weight of the mission they were on, they were squished into a bathroom, hiding from a hotel clerk.

"Fine," she said, sounding choked, and it was such a lie. She was anything but fine. It struck her that even to say so in that offhand way was . . . glib. Careless. She hazarded a glance at Akiva, afraid that he could think she meant it. *Oh sure, fine, and nice weather we're having. What's new with you?* And it was a fresh scrape of anguish to see, again, the pain in his eyes, and the anger. She had to look away. *Akiva, Akiva.* Back in the caves, when their eyes had at last met across the breadth of the great cavern—across all the soldiers between them, both sides, and the weight of their treacherous enmity, across the secrets they both carried, and the burdens—even at such a distance, their look had felt like touch. Not so now. A wisp of space between them only, and the meeting of their glances felt like . . . regret.

"Children of regret," she said aloud. Well, she whispered it, and stole another look up at him. "Do you remember?"

* * *

"How could I forget?" was Akiva's answer, an ache in his heart and a scrape in his voice.

She had told him the story—she, Madrigal—the night they fell in love. He remembered every word and touch of that night, every smile and gasp. Looking back at it was like peering down a dark tunnel—all his life since—at a bright place of light on the far side, where color and feeling were amplified. It seemed to him that that night was a place—*the* place—he'd kept all his happiness, bundled up and stowed away, like gear he'd never need again.

"You told me it was a terrible story," she said.

It was the chimaera legend of how they'd come to be, and it was nothing less than a rape myth. Chimaera were sprung of the tears of the moon, and seraphim from the blood of the brutal sun. "It *is* terrible," Akiva replied, hating it even more now than he had then, in light of what Karou had endured at Thiago's hands.

"It is," Karou agreed. "And so is yours." In the seraph myth, chimaera were shadows come to life, wrought by huge world-devouring monsters who swam in darkness. "But the tone is right," she said. "I feel like both now: a thing of tears and shadow."

"If we're going by the myths, then I would be a thing of blood."

"And of light," she added, her voice so soft. They were almost whispering, as though Virko couldn't hear every word, just on the other side of this glass partition. "You were kinder to yourselves in your legend than we were," Karou continued. "We made ourselves out of grief. You made yourselves in your gods' image, and with a noble purpose: to bring light to the worlds."

"A black job we've done of it," he said.

She smiled a little, and gave breath to a rueful laugh. "I won't argue with that."

"The legend also says that we'll be enemies until the end of the world," he reminded her. When he'd told her that story, they'd been entwined, naked and supple after love—their first, their first lovemaking—and the end of the world had seemed as much a myth as the weeping moons had.

But Akiva could almost feel it now, pressing down on them. It felt like hopelessness. At what point, he wondered, was there nothing left to save?

"That's why we made up our own myth," said Karou.

He remembered. "A paradise waiting for us to find it and fill it with our happiness. Do you still believe that?"

He didn't mean it the way it came out: harsh, as though it were nothing but the fool fantasy of new lovers tangled in each other's arms. It was himself he wanted to chasten, because he *had* believed it, as recently as yesterday, when Liraz had accused him of being "preoccupied by bliss." She'd been right. He'd been imagining bathing with Karou, hadn't he? Holding her against him, her back to his chest, just holding her and watching her hair swirl on the surface of the water.

Soon, he'd thought, *it will be possible*.

Flying away from the caves this morning, seeing their armies mixed and moving in effortless flight together, he'd imagined a lot more than that. A place that was theirs. A...a home. Akiva had never had a home. Not even close. Barracks, campaign tents, and, before that, his too-brief childhood in the harem. He'd actually let himself picture this simple thing, as though it weren't the biggest fantasy of all. A home. A rug, a table where he and Karou could eat meals together, chairs. Just the two of them, and candles flickering, and he could catch her hand across the table, just to hold it, and they could talk, and discover each other layer by layer. And there would be a door to shut out the world, and places to put things that would be theirs. Akiva could scarcely conjure what those things might be. He'd never owned anything but swords. It said so very much that, to flesh out his picture of domestic life, he had to draw from the old, rotted artifacts in the Kirin caves where once upon a time his people had destroyed hers.

Plates and pipes, a comb, a kettle.

And . . . a bed. A bed and a blanket to cover them, a blanket that was theirs together. There was something in the thought of this simple, simple thing that had crystallized all of Akiva's hope and vulnerability and made him able to see and believe, truly, that he could be a . . . a *person*, after the war. It had seemed to him, this morning, in flight, almost within reach.

He hadn't bothered dreaming of where this home would be, or what you would see when you walked out the door, but now when he imagined it, that was *all* he saw: what lay outside the quiet little "paradise" of his daydream.

Corpses were strewn everywhere.

"Not a paradise," Karou said, faltering, and she flushed and briefly closed her eyes. Akiva, looking down at her, was caught by the sight of her lashes, dusky and trembling against the blue-tinged flesh around her eyes. And when she opened her eyes, there was the jolt of eye contact, the pupil-less black sheen of her gaze, depthless, and all her worry was there, and pain to match his own, but also strength.

"I know there's no paradise waiting for us," she said. "But happiness has to go somewhere, doesn't it? I think Eretz deserves some, and so . . ." She was shy. There was still the space between them. "I think we should put ours there, and not in some random paradise that doesn't really need it." She hesitated, looked up at him. Looked and looked, pouring herself out through her extraordinary eyes. For him. For him. "Don't you?"

* * *

"Happiness," he said, his voice holding the word so gently, a tinge of disbelief in his tone, as though happiness itself were as much a myth as all their gods and monsters.

"Don't give up," Karou whispered. "It isn't wrong to be glad to be alive."

A silence, and she could feel him struggling to find words. "I keep getting second chances," he said, "that aren't rightly mine."

She didn't answer right away. She knew what guilt he shouldered. The magnitude of Liraz's sacrifice shook her to her core. After another long, deep breath, she whispered, hoping it wasn't the wrong thing to say, "It was hers to give," feeling that it was a gift not only to Akiva but to herself.

And, if Brimstone was right, that hope was the only hope, and that the two of them were, somehow, hope made real, then it was a gift for Eretz as well.

"Maybe," he allowed. "You argued before that the dead don't want to be avenged, and that may be right, sometimes, but when you're the one left alive—"

"We don't know that they're—" Karou broke in, but couldn't even finish the sentence.

"Life feels stolen."

"*Given.*"

"And the only response that makes sense to the heart is vengeance," he said.

"I know. Believe me. But I'm hiding in a shower with you instead of trying to kill you, so it would seem that the heart can change its mind."

A ghost of a smile. That was something. Karou returned it, not a ghost but a real smile, remembering every beautiful smile of his, all those lost, radiant smiles, and making herself believe that they weren't forever ended. People break. They can't always be fixed. But not this time. Not that.

"This isn't the end of hope," she said. "We don't know about the others, but even if we did, and even if it *was* the worst...*we're still here, Akiva.* And I'm not giving up as long as that much is true." She was serious. Fervent, even, as if she could force him to believe her.

And maybe it worked.

There had always been, from the first—at Bullfinch, in the smoke and fog—an amazement in the way Akiva looked at her, his eyes held wide to take her all in. Afraid to blink, almost to breathe. Something of that amazement came back to him now, and his steeliness and the implacability of his rage surrendered to it. So much of expression is the muscles around the eyes, and Karou saw the tension there let go, and it triggered a relief in her that may have been vastly disproportionate to the small change that brought it about. Or maybe perfectly proportionate. This was no small thing. If only it were that easy to let go of hate. Just relax your face.

"You're right," Akiva said. "I'm sorry."

"I don't want you to be sorry. I want you to be...alive."

Alive. Heart-beating, blood-moving alive, yes, but more than that. She wanted him to be eyes-flashing alive. Hands-to-hearts and "we are the beginning" alive.

"I am," he said, and there *was* life in his voice, and promise.

Karou was prey, still, to flashes of remembering him through Madrigal's eyes. She had been taller in that body, so the sightline was different, but this moment still struck a direct link to memory: the requiem grove for the first time, just before their first kiss. The blaze of his look and the curve of his body toward her. That's what struck the vibration between then and now, and time cast a loop that brought her heart back to its simpler self.

Some things are always simple. Magnets, for example.

It took hardly any movement at all. It wasn't the requiem grove, and it wasn't a kiss. Karou's cheek was just of a height to let it rest against Akiva's chest, and she did, finally, and the rest of her body followed her cheek's good example. The damned wisp of space was abolished. Akiva's heart beat against her temple, and his arms came around to hold her; he was warm as summer, and she felt the sigh that moved through him, loosening him so that he could meld more fully to her, and she sighed her own loosening sigh and met his meld. It felt so good. *No air between us*, thought Karou, *and no more shame. Nothing more between us.*

It felt so good.

She traveled her hands around him so that she could hold him even closer, even tighter. Every breath she took was the heat and scent of him, remembered and rediscovered, as she remembered and rediscovered his solidity, too—the realness that somehow came as a shock, because the impression of him was so...unearthly. Elemental. *Love is an element*, Karou remembered from a long, long time ago, and she felt like she was floating. To the eye Akiva was fire and air. But to the touch, so *there*. Real enough to hold on to forever.

Akiva's hand was moving down the length of her hair, again and again, and she could feel the press of his lips to the top of her head, and what filled her wasn't desire, but tenderness, and a profound gratitude that he lived, and she did, too. That he had found her, and that he had found her *again*. And...dear gods and stardust... yet *again*. Let that be the last time he ever needed to come looking for her.

I'll make it easy for you, she thought, her face pressed to his heartbeat. *I'll be right here*.

Almost as if he heard—and approved—he tightened his arms around her.

When Zuzana opened the bathroom door and called out, "Soup's on!" they slowly disengaged and shared a look that was...gratitude and promise and communion. A barrier was broken. Not by a kiss—not that, not yet—but touch, at least. They belonged to each other to hold. Karou carried the heat of Akiva on her body as she stepped out of the shower. She caught sight of the pair of them in the mirror, framed there together, and thought, *Yes. This is right*.

One last look passed between them in the mirror glass—soft and glad and pure, if far from free of their sorrow and pain—and they followed Virko into the bedroom, where an astonishing wealth of food was spread over the floor like a sultan's picnic.

They ate. Karou and Akiva kept within easy touching distance of each other, which Zuzana noted with an approving and ever-so-slightly smug eyebrow.

They had just begun to make a dent in the array of dishes when they heard the shouting, coming from outside.

Car doors slammed, and two male voices vied with each other, angry. It could have been anything, just some private dispute, and would not have caused the five of them to rise to their feet—Akiva first of all—and move en masse to the window. It was the third voice that did that. It was female, melodic, and distressed. It was caught up in the hostility of the other two like a bird in a net.

And it was speaking Seraphic.

51

Abscond

They had no view of the commotion from their window, so Karou and Akiva glamoured themselves and went out. Mik and Zuzana followed, visible, leaving Virko in the room.

The argument was under way in the front court—the dusty domain of kasbah children who pushed one another around in a wheelbarrow and glared at hotel guests—and there was no mistaking the source of the conflict. A young woman sat half in and half out of the open door of a car, and she seemed to have little awareness of herself or her surroundings.

Her face was blank and bloodied. Her lips were full. She was deep brown and smooth-skinned, and her eyes were unnerving: pretty and too light, too wide open, and the whites so very white. Her arms slack in her lap, she rested on the seat's edge, head tilted back as impossible streams of language flowed from her bloodied mouth.

It took the mind a moment to sort it out. The blood, the woman, and the two languages, loud and at cross-purposes. The men were arguing in Arabic. One of them had apparently brought the woman here and was keen to ditch her. The other was a hotel employee, who, understandably, was having none of it.

"You can't just dump her here. What happened to her? What's she saying?"

"How should I know? Some Americans will be coming for her soon. Let them worry."

"Fine, and in the meantime? She needs care. Look at her. What's wrong with her?"

"I don't know." The driver was surly. Afraid. "She's not my responsibility."

"And she's mine?"

They went on in this vein while the woman went on in...quite a different one. "Devouring and devouring and fast and huge, and *hunting*," she said—*cried*, in Seraphic—and her voice was mournful and sweet and drenched in pain, like an otherworldly *fado*. A soul-deep, life-shaping lament for what is lost and can never return. "The beasts, the beasts, the Cataclysm! Skies blossomed then blackened and nothing could hold them. They were peeled apart and it wasn't our fault. We were the openers of doors, the lights in the darkness. It was never supposed to happen! I was chosen one of twelve, but I fell all alone. There are maps in me but I am lost, and there are skies in me but they are dead. Dead and dead and dead forever, oh godstars!"

Hairs raised on Karou's neck. Akiva was beside her. "What's happening to her?" she asked him. "Do you know what she's talking about?"

"No."

"Is she a seraph?"

He hesitated before again saying no. "She's human. She has no flame. But there's something. . . ."

Karou felt it, too, and couldn't name it, either. Who was this woman? And how was she speaking Seraphic?

"Meliz is lost!" she keened, and the hairs stood up on Karou's arms. "Even Meliz, first and last, Meliz eternal, *Meliz is devoured*."

"Do you know who that is?" Karou asked Akiva. "Meliz?"

"No."

"What is going on here?"

Karou snapped around at the sound of Zuzana's voice and beheld her, most excellent rabid fairy, cutting to the chase. She marched right up to the men, who blinked down at her, probably trying to reconcile her steely tone to the tiny girl before them—at least until they got a healthy dose of her *neek-neek* look. They broke off arguing.

"She's bleeding," Zuzana said—in French, which, due to Morocco's colonial past, was the European language most readily understood here, even before English. "Did *you* do this to her?"

Her voice held a glint of outrage, like a knife not yet fully unsheathed, and both men hastily proclaimed their innocence.

Zuzana was unmoved. "What's wrong with you, just standing here? Can't you see she needs help?"

They had no good answer for that, and no time to make one anyway, because Zuzana—with Mik's assistance—was already taking charge of the young woman. Each at an elbow, they eased her up to a stand, and the men only watched, silenced and chastened, as they led her away between them. There was no break in her flood of Seraphic—"I am Fallen, all alone, I break me on the rock and I will never again be whole. . . ."—and no flicker of focus in her striking eyes, but her feet moved and she made no protest, and neither did the men, so Zuzana and Mik just *took* her.

And a couple of hours later, when the Americans in dark suits came to claim her, the hotel clerk led them first to Eliza's room and then—finding it emptied of both person and possessions—to the rooms of the small fierce girl and her boyfriend who had, between them, ordered half the food in the kitchen. They knocked on the door but got no answer, and heard no movement within, and when they let themselves in, it wasn't really a surprise to find the occupants gone.

No one had seen them leave, not even the kasbah kids playing in the courtyard that was the only way to reach the road.

Come to think of it . . . no one had seem them *arrive*, either.

They'd left nothing behind but thoroughly empty dishes and—this would be one for the conspiracy theorists—several long blue hairs in the shower where an angel's hand had stroked a devil's head, locked in a long—and so very long-awaited—embrace.

Once upon a time . . .
A journey began,

that would stitch all the worlds together with light.

ARRIVAL + 60 HOURS

52

Gunpowder and Decay

It was like Christmas for Morgan Toth—in the greed-and-presents sense of the holiday, not the birth-of-Christ sense, of course. Because really.

The text messages on Eliza's phone were getting crazier and more desperate by the hour. It was some kind of nutjob extravaganza delivered right to him, and he wished, almost, for a partner in crime—someone to marvel, with him, that there were such people in the world! But there was no one he could think of who, if he told them what he'd done, would not quail in self-righteous horror and probably call the police.

Morons.

He needed a groupie, he thought. Or a girlfriend. Wide eyes and awe. "Morgan, you're so *bad*," she would coo. But bad in a good way. Bad in a very, very good way.

The phone buzzed. It was Pavlovian at this point: Eliza's phone buzzed and Morgan virtually salivated in anticipation of not-to-be-believed, someone-*must*-be-yanking-my-chain crazy-time. This message did not disappoint.

Where are you, Elazael? The time for petty squabbles is past. Now you must see that you can't run away from who you are. Our kin have come to Earth, as we have always known they would. We have made overtures. We have offered ourselves to them as helpmeets and handmaidens, in ecstasy and servitude. The day of Judgment draws nigh. Let the rest of this blighted world serve as fodder for the Beasts while we kneel at the feet of God. We need you.

Gold. Pure gold. *Ecstasy and servitude.* Morgan laughed, because that pretty well summed up what he wanted in a girlfriend.

He was tempted to write back. So far he had resisted, but the game was getting a little stale. He reread the message. How did you engage with insanity like this? They'd made overtures, it said. What did that mean? How had they managed to offer themselves to the angels? Morgan knew from previous texts that the sender—who he gathered was Eliza's mother, a real piece of work—was in Rome. But as far as he knew, the Vatican was virtually keeping the Visitors prisoner, which was pretty hilarious. He imagined the Pope standing on the dome of St. Peter's with a giant butterfly net: *Caught me some angels!*

After much deliberation, he typed a reply.

*Hi, Ma! I've had a new vision. In it, we *were* kneeling at the feet of God, so that's good. Phew! But . . . we were giving him a pedicure? Not sure what it means. Love, Eliza.*

He knew it was too much, but he couldn't help himself. He hit send. In the ensuing silence he began to fear that he'd killed the joke, but he shouldn't have worried. This was no fragile specimen of crazy he was dealing with. It was hearty.

Your bitterness is an affront to God, Elazael. You have been given a great gift. How many of our ancestors perished without seeing the holy faces of our kin, and yet you can find it in you to laugh? Will you choose to stay and be devoured with the sinners when the rest of us rise to take our place in the—

Morgan never got a chance to finish reading the message, let alone fire off another response.

"Is that Eliza's phone?"

Gabriel. Morgan whirled around. How had the neuroscientist managed to sneak up on him? Had he forgotten to lock the door?

"Jesus, it is," said Gabriel, looking stunned and disgusted. Morgan did wonder about the stun. Edinger despised him. Why should this come as a surprise? And what could he say? Caught in the act. Nothing to do but lie.

"She gets a new text message every thirty seconds. Someone's obviously desperate to find her. I was just going to reply to whoever it is that she's not here—"

"Give it to me."

"No."

Gabriel didn't ask again. He just kicked the leg of the stool Morgan was sitting on hard enough to swipe it right out from under him. Morgan windmilled and fell hard. What with all the impact and pain and fury, he didn't even realize he'd relinquished the phone until he was back on his feet, batting his bangs out of his eyes.

Damn. Edinger held the phone. His looked of stunned disgust had only deepened.

"It was you, wasn't it?" Gabriel said, suddenly realizing. "It was all you. Jesus Christ, and I gave you the means. I gave you her phone."

Morgan's fury turned to fear. It was like antiseptic hitting pus: the seethe, the bubbling, the burn. "What are you talking about?" he asked, feigning ignorance, and feigning it poorly.

Edinger slowly shook his head. "It was a game to you, and you've probably ruined her life."

"I didn't do anything," Morgan said, but he was unprepared to defend himself. He hadn't thought...He hadn't thought about getting caught.

How could he not have thought?

"Well. I can't promise I'll ruin *your* life," Gabriel replied. "Honestly, that's a bit of a commitment. But I can promise you this. I will make sure everyone knows what you've done." He held up the phone. "And if it *does* ruin your life, I won't be sorry about it."

* * *

Another letter. The third. The same servant brought it, and Razgut knew by the envelope that it was from the same sender as the previous two. This time, he didn't bother playing any games with Jael. As soon as the servant—Spivetti was his name—was gone, he seized it and ripped it open.

He had taken special care crafting his last two replies. They had almost felt like love letters. Not that Razgut had ever written a love letter, mind.... Well, no, that wasn't strictly true. He had, but that was in the Long Ago, and it may as well have been a different being entirely who had penned a sweet farewell to a honey-colored girl. He had *looked* like a different being, that was sure. He had still looked like a seraph, and his mind had still been a diamond without flaw, uncracked—and the pressure it takes to crack a diamond!—and unfurred by the molds and filths that claimed it now. It was so very long ago, but he remembered writing that letter. The girl's name was lost to him, and her face, too. She was just a golden blur of no consequence, a hint of a life that might have been, had he not been Chosen.

If I don't return, he had penned in a fine but eager script, forward-tilting, before leaving for the capital, *know that I will carry the memory of you with me through every veil, into the darkness of every tomorrow, and beyond the shadow of every horizon*.

Something like that. Razgut remembered the feeling that went into it, if not the precise words, and it wasn't love, or even the most surface-skimming truth. He'd simply been hedging his bets. If he *wasn't* chosen—and what were the chances that he would be, out of so many?—then he could have gone home and pretended relief, and the honey-colored girl would have consoled him in her silkiness, and maybe they even would have married and borne children and lived some kind of drab-happy life in the undertow of his failure.

But he *had* been chosen.

O glorious day. Razgut was one of twelve in the Long Ago, and glory had been his. The day of the Naming: such glory. So much light in the city as had dazed the night sky, and they couldn't see the godstars but the godstars could see them, and that was what mattered—that the gods see them and know: They were chosen.

The openers of doors, the lights in the darkness.

Razgut never went back home, and he never saw the girl again, but look. He hadn't lied to her, had he? He was remembering her now, beyond the shadow of a horizon, in the darkness of a tomorrow he could never have imagined.

"What does she say?"

She.

Jael's voice broke into Razgut's reverie. This letter, it was from no silken girl but a woman whom he had never seen—though her name was not unknown to him—and there was no sweetness in her, none at all, and that was all right. Razgut's tastes had matured. Sweetness was insipid. Let the butterflies and hummingbirds have it. Like a carrion beetle, he was called to sharper scents.

Like gunpowder and decay.

"Guns, explosives, ammunition," Razgut translated for Jael. "She says that she can get you anything you need, and everything you want, as long as you agree to her condition."

"Condition!" Jael hiss-spat. "Who is *she* to name conditions?"

He'd been like this since the first letter. Jael had no appreciation for a strong woman, except as something to break and keep breaking. The idea of *a woman* making demands? A woman whom he was in no position to humble? It infuriated him.

"She's your best option is who she is," replied Razgut. It was one of many possible answers, and the only one Jael needed to hear. *She's a vulture. She's fetid meat. She's black powder waiting to ignite.* "No one else has managed to bribe their way to you, so here is your choice, today: Keep courting these dour-mouthed heads of state and watch them mince through the minefield of public opinion, fearing their own people more than they fear you, or make this simple promise to a lady of means and have done with all of that. Your weapons are waiting for you, emperor. What's one little condition next to that?"

53

Eyebrow Master Class

When Mik and Zuzana stepped into the lobby of the St. Regis grand hotel in Rome, several conversations ceased, a bellhop did a double take, and an elegant matron with a silver bob and surgical cheekbones raised a hand to her pearls and scanned the lobby for security.

Backpackers did not stay at the St. Regis.

Ever.

And *these* backpackers, they looked . . . well, it wasn't easy to put into words. Someone extremely insightful might say they looked as though they had been living in *caves*, and then been through a *battle*, perhaps even ridden here astride a *monster*.

In fact, they had flown by private jet from Marrakesh, but one could be excused for not guessing as much; leaving Tamnougalt in such a hurry, they hadn't had a chance to take advantage of the shower, and they had no clean clothes between them, and it's likely that neither had ever been quite this unsightly in their entire lives.

It was presumed, by patrons and staff, that they were going to ask to use a restroom—as, every once in a while, this did happen, the underclasses being ill-educated in *the rules*—and then most likely filth it up by bathing themselves in the sink. Wasn't that what these people did?

The doorman who had admitted them kept his eyes fixed on the floor, aware that he had committed a cardinal sin in allowing hoi polloi to breach the perimeter. No doubt, in bygone days, guards had been put to death for just this offense. But what could he do? They claimed to be guests.

Behind the reception desk, the clerks exchanged gladiatorial glances. *Do you want to take them, or shall I?*

A champion stepped forth.

"May I help you?"

The words spoken may have been: *May I help you*, but the tone was something more along the lines of: *It is my unbearable duty to interact with you, and I intend to punish you for it.*

Zuzana turned to meet her challenger. She saw before her a young Italian woman, mid-twenties, sleekly attractive and just as sleekly dressed. Unamused. Nay, *unamusable*. The woman's eyes did a quick flick up and down, flaring with something like indignation when they arrived at Zuzana's dust-caked zebra platform sneakers, and her mouth puckered into a little knob of distaste. She looked rather as though she were preparing to remove a live slug from her arugula.

"You know," observed Zuzana, in English, "you'd probably be a lot prettier if you didn't make that face."

The face in question froze in place. A nostril-flare suggested that offense was taken. And then, as though in slow motion, one of the woman's fine, plucked eyebrows ascended toward her hairline.

Game. On.

Zuzana Nováková was a pretty girl. She'd often been compared to a doll, or to a fairy, not just because of her slight stature but also her fine, small face—a happy blending of angles and arcs set under skin clear as porcelain. Delicate chin, rounded cheeks, wide glossy eyes, and, though she would annihilate anyone for suggesting it, somewhat of a Cupid's bow mouth. All of this cuteness, it was one of nature's great bait and switches, because... that wasn't all there was to Zuzana Nováková. Not even a little bit.

Deciding to take her on was akin to a fish deciding idly to gobble up that pretty light bobbing in the shadows and then—*OH GOD THE TEETH THE HORROR!*—meeting the anglerfish on the other side.

Zuzana didn't eat people. She withered them. And there in the sparkling marble, crystal, and gilded lobby of one of Rome's most exclusive luxury hotels, in just under two seconds, Zuzana's eyebrow taught a master class. Its rise was something to behold. The sweep of it, the arch. Contempt, amusement, amused contempt, confidence, judgment, mockery, even pity. It was all there, and more. Her eyebrow communicated directly with the Italian woman's eyebrow, somehow telling it, *We have not stumbled in here to bathe in your sink. You have miscalculated. Tread lightly.*

And the eyebrow conveyed the message to its owner, whose mouth promptly lost its slug-in-the-arugula pucker, and even before Mik interceded to say, mildly, almost apologetically, "We're staying in the Royal Suite?" she was tasting the first sour hint of her mortification.

"The... *Royal* Suite?"

The Royal Suite at the St. Regis had hosted monarchs and rock legends, oil sheiks and opera divas. It cost nearly $20,000 a night during ordinary times, and these were *not* ordinary times. Rome was currently center of the world's attention, filled to the rafters with pilgrims, journalists, foreign delegations, curiosity-seekers, and crazies, and there simply were no vacancies. Families were renting out balconies and cellars—even rooftops—at a premium, and the already overtaxed police were having a time breaking up pilgrim camps in the parks.

Zuzana and Mik didn't know how much this was costing Karou—or her fake grandmother, Esther, or whoever was footing the bill. Ordinarily, such extravagance would have made them feel awkward and small, peasants in the presence of gentry. Indeed, it would make them feel exactly as this woman had intended them to feel. But not today. In light of recent experience, these insulated, rarified people put Zuzana in mind of expensive shoes kept in their box the three hundred and sixty-two days of the year when they weren't being worn. Wrapped in tissue, safe from harm, and all they knew of life was gala events and the inside of the box. How dull. How dumb. By contrast, the grime of her journey, the outré inappropriateness of the state of her, it felt like armor.

I earned this dirt.

Respect. The dirt.

"That's right," she said. "The Royal Suite. You'll be expecting us." She shrugged her backpack off and let it fall to the floor, its pores emitting a satisfying puff of dirt on impact. "It would be great if you could take care of that," she said, yawning. She raised her arms straight up in the air to stretch out her shoulders, less because they needed it than because this would reveal her pit stains in their full glory. There were, she knew, actual concentric circles stained into them from multiple sweatings. They looked like tree rings and were queerly meaningful to her. She had produced them by living through a dark fairy tale that... that others may *not* have lived through.

This shirt would never be washed.

"Of course," said the woman, and her voice was the shed hull of a voice now. It was funny, watching her struggle against her overwhelming facial impulses to purse her lips or frown, wrinkle her nose or practice that half-lidded, steely *I judge you and find you wanting* look that chic Italian women so excel at. She was diminished. Her amateur eyebrow had slunk back to its resting place, where it stayed during the remainder of their transaction, an apostrophe humbled to a comma. In next to no time, Mik and Zuzana were being led to an elevator. Subsequently elevated. Ushered down a preposterously plush hallway. To be reunited with the rest of their party.

54

Fake Grandmother

For practical purposes, they had parted at Ciampino Airport on the outskirts of Rome, where the jet chartered by Esther had set them down. Zuzana and Mik had disembarked from the flight—the only passengers on the manifest—and gone through the Customs and Immigration lines like human beings while the others did a vanishing act right out the door of the plane. They'd headed straight for the hotel as the crow flies, while Mik and Zuze took a cab to meet them there.

In the living room of the suite, awaiting their arrival, Karou was tucked up on a sofa of embroidered lime floral silk. On the gilded table before her rested a map of Vatican City, an open laptop, and a towering sculpture of real fruit, pineapple included—as if you could just pick that up and take a bite. Karou kept eyeing the grapes, but was afraid of touching them and toppling the whole extravaganza.

"Take them if you want them," said her fake grandmother, Esther Van de Vloet, who sat beside her, stroking, with one bare foot, the muscled back of the massive dog stretched out before her.

Esther, though magnificently wealthy, was not of the breed of magnificently wealthy older women to preserve their youth by way of a doctor's knife, or keep a joyless diet for the sake of bony elegance, or wear stiff designer clothes better suited to mannequins.

She was dressed in jeans with a tunic dress she'd picked up at a street market, while her white hair was secured in a slightly messy chignon. She was no ascetic, as was evidenced by the pastry in her hand and the comfortable curvature of hips and breasts. Her youth—or, more accurately, her seeming age of *seventy*, when she was, in fact, well into her thirteenth decade—was preserved not by surgery or diet but by way of *a wish*.

A bruxis, that most powerful of wishes, dearly paid for, and only once in a lifetime. And what most of Brimstone's traders spent their bruxes on was just this: long life. It was not known precisely how long was long. Karou knew one Malay hunter who had been going on a spry two hundred last she'd seen him. It seemed to come down to a matter of will. Most people grew tired of outliving everyone. For Esther's part, she said she didn't know how many more generations of dogs she could bear to bury.

The current iteration were still young and in the prime of health. They were called Traveller and Methuselah, for the horses, respectively, of generals Lee and Grant. All of Esther's mastiffs were named after warhorses. This was her sixth pair, and she had finally deigned to honor the Americans.

Karou eyed the fruit tower. "But it probably took someone hours to build that thing."

"And we've paid well for their labors. Eat."

Karou took some grapes and was glad that the sculpture didn't topple.

"You will have to learn to enjoy money now, my dear," said Esther, as though Karou were an initiate into this life of luxury, and she her guide. In addition to other Karou-related favors Esther had performed for Brimstone over the years—enrolling her in schools, faking identity documents for her, etcetera—she'd been instrumental in setting up her many bank accounts, and surely knew Karou's net worth better than Karou did herself. "Lesson one: We don't worry about how our fruit sculptures are built. We just eat them."

"I won't have to learn, actually," said Karou. "I'm not staying here."

Esther glanced around the room. "You don't like the St. Regis?"

Karou followed her glance. It was an assault on the senses, as though the designer had been charged to manifest the concept of "opulence" in four or five hundred square feet. High, coved ceiling trimmed in coffered gold. Red velvet drapes that belonged in a vampire's boudoir, gilded everything, a grand piano with tiered silver dishes of biscotti set out on its gleaming lid. There was even an enormous tapestry of a coronation hanging on the wall, some king or other kneeling to receive his crown. "Well, *no*," she admitted. "Not especially. But I mean Earth. I'm not staying."

Esther favored her with a slow blink, perhaps taking that instant to imagine leaving behind such a fortune as was Karou's. "Indeed. Well. Considering the piece of paradise in there"—she nodded her head toward the adjacent sitting room—"I can't say I blame you." Esther was... impressed... with Akiva. "Oh my," she'd whispered when Karou had introduced them. She said now, "Not that I would know, but I suppose one would give up a great deal for love."

Karou had said nothing about love, but she couldn't say she was surprised to find out it was obvious. "I don't feel like I'm giving anything up," she said honestly. Her life in Prague was already as remote as a dream. She knew there would be days when she missed Earth, but for now, her mind and heart were wholly engaged in the affairs of Eretz, its shrouded present—*Dear Nitid, or godstars, or anyone, please let our friends live*—and its tenuous future. And yes, as Esther intimated, Akiva was a big part of it.

"Well. You can enjoy wealth for now, at least," said Esther. "Tell me the bath wasn't lovely."

Karou conceded that it had been. The bathroom was larger than her entire Prague apartment, and every square inch of it marble. She'd just emerged; her hair was damp and fragrant on her shoulders.

She took up the map, flattening it out on the couch between them. "So," she said, "where are the angels being housed?"

Karou's plan was ultimately very simple, so there wasn't much she needed to know beyond where to find Jael. Vatican City might be small as sovereign nations go, but it made for a hell of a scavenger hunt if you just showed up there and started going through rooms.

Esther stabbed a bitten nail at the Papal Palace. "Here," she said. "The lap of luxury." She knew which windows would give the closest access to the Sala Clementina, the grand audience hall Jael had been given for his personal use, and she knew where the guards were likely to be stationed, both the Swiss Guards and the angels' own contingent. Her finger dragged over to the Vatican Museum, too, where the bulk of the host were quartered in a wing of ancient sculpture where once upon a normal life, Karou had whiled away an afternoon sketching.

"Thanks," said Karou. "That's a big help."

"Of course," said Esther, settling back into the prissy sofa. "Anything for my favorite fake granddaughter. Now tell me, how *is* Brimstone, and when is he reopening the portals? I really miss the old monster."

Me, too, thought Karou, her heart instantly icing over. She'd been dreading this moment the whole journey here. On the phone, she hadn't been able to bring herself to tell the truth. The manner of Esther's greeting had been so unexpectedly effusive—"Oh thank god! Where have you *been*, child? I've been worried sick. Months, and no word from you at all. How could you not call me?"—that it had thrown Karou for a loop. She'd acted like a real grandmother, or at least how Karou imagined a real grandmother might act, spilling emotion willy-nilly, whereas before she'd always seemed to dole it out like allowance: on a schedule, and with some measure of reluctance.

Karou had decided to tell her the hard news in person, but now that the time had come, suitable words failed to line themselves up in her brain. *He's dead.*

There was a massacre.

He's . . . dead.

The knocking, just at that moment, felt like providence. Karou leapt up. "Mik and Zuze," she said, and jogged toward the door. The suite was so sprawling, you really had to jog in order to answer the door in a timely fashion. She did, throwing it open. "What took you so long?" she demanded, sweeping her friends together into a slightly smelly hug. Their smell, not hers.

"Two hours to get here from the airport," said Mik. "This city is mad."

Karou knew that it was. She'd had an aerial perspective of the great, pulsing ring of humanity that had collected around the closed-off perimeter of the Vatican. Even from the air, she'd heard their chanting, but couldn't make out the words. From the air, it had reminded her, unsettlingly, of the way zombies in movies press in on human enclaves, trying to get in. And the rest of the city, while not quite as... *zombic*, was close. "I hope you at least got some more sleep in the cab," she said.

They had, all of them, gotten a few hours of much needed sleep on the plane. Karou had lain her head on Akiva's shoulder, and drifted off to memories of his bare skin against her own. Her dreams had been... more energizing than restful.

"A little," replied Zuzana. "But what I really want is a bath." She stepped back and gave Karou a quick scan. "Look at you. A couple of hours in Italy and you're a fashionista. How'd you get new clothes already?"

"That's what happens here." Karou led them inside. "When you get to Hawaii, they give you flower leis. In Italy, it's perfect clothes and leather shoes."

"Well, 'they' must have been on break when *we* got here," Zuzana returned, gesturing to herself. "To the horror of everyone down in the lobby."

"Yikes." Karou cringed to imagine it. "Were they bad?" She'd been spared the scrutiny herself, having arrived glamoured, and by way of the sky and the balcony, not the street and the lobby.

Mik said, "Zuze has been having glare duels."

Zuzana cocked an eyebrow. "You should see the other guy."

"I have no doubt," said Karou. "And 'they' weren't on break. They were just waiting for you here. Esther got us all new clothes."

As she said this, they stepped into the living room. "I sent a shopper out for them, in fact," said Esther, in her singsong Flemish accent. "I hope everything fits."

She rose and came forward. "I've heard so much about you, dear," she said warmly, reaching out to enfold Zuzana's hands in her own. She was, in that moment, very much the picture of a grandmother.

Esther Van de Vloet, however, was nobody's grandmother. She had no children and next to no maternal instincts. Playing the role of "grandmother," she'd been more of a political ally to Karou than an emotional one. In her life, the old woman had midwifed countless diamonds into the possession of the ultrarich, and into the possession of Brimstone, too, dauntlessly doing business with humans and non-humans alike—and *sub*humans, too, as she called the more nefarious of Brimstone's traders, with whom she maintained a global information network. She traveled in elite circles as well as shadowy ones—she'd told Karou on the phone that she had a cardinal in one pocket and an arms dealer in the other, and no doubt she had more pockets besides. And she was revered as a nearly mystical figure, first for her mysterious preservation—she'd been tickled to hear a rumor that she'd sold her soul for immortality—as well as for several impossible favors she was rumored to have performed for highly placed people.

Impossible, that is, unless you happened to have access to magic.

"I've heard so much about you, too," said Zuzana, and Karou saw the glint in her eye that was either a matador sizing up a bull or a bull sizing up a matador. She wasn't sure which, but Esther had it, too. The look that passed between the two women was mutual regard for a worthy adversary, and Karou was glad they *weren't* adversaries, and that they were both on her side.

There was a brief spell of chitchat. The size of the dogs. Room service. The state of Rome. Angels.

It was when Esther said, "I'm just glad Karou had the good sense to come to me," that a slight nostril flare turned Zuzana's expression more bull than matador.

"She came to you once before," Zuzana said, casual with an undercurrent of blame. Karou knew what she was getting at, and tried to intercede.

"Zuze—" she began, but her friend talked over her.

"And I've been curious ever since. When Karou came to you for wishes…" She tilted her head and gave the older woman a *let's be honest* look. "You held out on her, didn't you?"

Esther's smile winked out, her face going smooth and masklike and wary. Not so grandmotherly now.

"No, Zuze," Karou said, putting a hand on her friend's back. They'd argued about this before. "She didn't. She wouldn't." When the portals had burned, last winter, and she'd been desperate to find her chimaera family—desperate for gavriels that could carry her and the thing Razgut up to the sky portal and into Eretz—Karou had gone to Esther first. Esther had said that she had no wish stronger than a lucknow, and Karou had believed her, because why would she lie?

"I did," said Esther, solemn and…contrite? Karou stared at her.

Did she mean that she *had* held out on her? "What?" she asked, confused.

"Well, I'm sorry to say it, dear, of course, but I didn't really believe that you would find him. I'm a greedy old woman. If they were the last wishes I was ever going to get, I had to guard them, didn't I? I can't tell you how happy I am that I was wrong."

Karou's stomach turned over. "You weren't," she said.

Esther cocked her head, puzzled. "I wasn't what?"

"You weren't *wrong.* I didn't find Brimstone. He's dead." She laid it out flat, no emotion in her voice, and watched Esther's face drain of color.

"No, oh no. No," she murmured, her hand going to her mouth. "Oh, Karou. I didn't want to believe it." Her eyes filled up with tears.

"You didn't tell her yet?" Zuzana asked.

Karou shook her head. So much for breaking it to her gently. Esther had lied to her. When the portals had just burned and she didn't know *anything,* when she was battered and bruised from near-death encounters with both Akiva and Thiago, and no gentle treatment from Brimstone himself, she had gone to her for help. She'd been at the lowest point in her life so far, never mind that she was to sink steadily lower and *oh so very much* lower over the next months, she hadn't known that then. She'd trusted Esther, only to find out now that Esther had lied to her face.

She looked genuinely affected, though, and Karou felt some small remorse for telling her so harshly. "Issa's well," she said, to soften the blow, adding a silent prayer that it was so.

"I'm glad to hear it." Esther's voice was tremulous. "And Yasri? Twiga?"

There was no softening that. Twiga was dead. Yasri was, too, though Yasri's soul, like Issa's, had been preserved and left for Karou to find—another hope in a bottle, to relay Brimstone's very important message. Karou hadn't been able to go and retrieve her thurible yet, though she knew where it was: in the ruins of the temple of

Ellai where she and Akiva had spent their month of sweet nights, a lifetime past.

To Esther, she just gave a small head shake. Resurrection was more than she was willing to go into. Esther no more knew what Brimstone had used the teeth for—and the gems that had been her own trade with him—than Karou had known before she broke the wishbone, and she wasn't feeling inclined to be forthcoming just now.

"Very many are dead," she said, trying and failing to keep the emotion out of her voice. "And very many more will die unless we stop these angels and close the portal."

"And you think you can do that?" asked Esther.

I hope, thought Karou, but she said, simply, "Yes."

Zuzana spoke up again, and whether she was matador or bull, she was clear-eyed, fixed, and focused. "Some of those wishes wouldn't be unwelcome now."

"Oh, well," said Esther, flustered. "Now I truly *don't* have any more. I'm so sorry. If I had only known, I might have conserved them better. Oh, my poor dear," she said to Karou, clasping her hand.

Zuzana's mouth was a straight line. "Uh-huh," was all she said.

Perhaps feeling that some social grace was called for to spackle over Zuzana's . . . lack thereof, Mik said, awkwardly, "Well, thanks for the, um, jet. And the hotel and everything."

"You're welcome," said Esther, and Karou felt that the time for introductions and pleasantries—and *un*pleasantries—had come to an end. There was work to be done.

She turned to her friends. "The bathroom's down the hall. It's not too shabby. Clothes are in the big bedroom. Play dress-up."

Zuzana's brow creased. "And the others?" She hesitated. "Eliza? Is she . . . any better?"

A new tension clenched in Karou. What could she say about Eliza? Eliza Jones. What a strange business it was. They only knew her name because she had ID on her, not because she was capable of telling them. From there, a quick Google search had yielded startling results. *Elazael, descended of an angel.* As crazy as it all sounded—just the kind of thing Zuzana would, once upon a time, have made a T-shirt in mockery of—the fact that she was speaking fluent Seraphic did lend it an undeniable credibility.

As for the things she had *said* in Seraphic, they were surpassingly creepy, and flowed out of her in some kind of fugue. And to Zuzana's question: *Was* she any better? Karou didn't know how to answer. She had tried, back in Morocco, to use her own gift of healing to mend her, but how could she, when she couldn't begin to sense what was broken?

Akiva was trying now, in some way of his own, and Karou had hope, leading her friends to the sitting room door, that she might open it and find the two of them just sitting there, deep in conversation.

"In here," she said, reaching for the doorknob. With a glance back at Esther, she made an effort to smile. She hated tension, and wished, not for the first time, that the older woman was a warmer fish. But she knew, as she had always known, that every time Esther had acted on her behalf—including the year she'd brought her home to Antwerp with her for Christmas, conjuring a magazine-worthy living room full of gifts, including a fantastical hand-carved rocking horse that Karou had had to leave there and had never seen again—she'd been compensated for her trouble.

That wasn't friendship, or family. It was business, and smiles weren't required.

But she smiled anyway, and Esther smiled back. There was sadness in her eyes, regret, maybe even penitence, and later Karou would remember thinking, *Well, that's something at least.*

And it was.

Just not what she thought.

55

Lunatic Poetry

Akiva had descended, many times now, through dark levels of mind to the place where he worked magic, and he was no closer to understanding where it was—internal or external. How deep or distant, or how far it went.

There was that sense—not exact, but near enough—of passing though a trapdoor to another realm, and as he had pushed farther and farther, never meeting any kind of boundary, he had begun to envision an ocean vastness, and then even that was insufficient. Space. Limitless.

He did believe that it was his. That it was *him*. But it seemed to go on forever—a private universe, a dimension whose infinity transcended the notion of "mind" that he'd always held—of thoughts as existing within the sphere of his own head, a function of his brain.

What hugeness was a mind? A spirit? A soul? And if it didn't correlate to the physical space his body displaced, then where was it?

It dizzied him. Each time he emerged, feeling vague and drained, it gnawed at him, his frustration with his own ignorance.

And that was before he attempted entering another person's mind.

He sensed, at the threshold of Eliza's mind, another trapdoor, another realm as expansive as his own, but distinct from it. Infinities are not for casual exploration. You could fall and keep falling. You could get lost. She had. Could he draw her back out? He wanted to try. For her, because the idea of such helplessness appalled him and he wanted to rescue her from it. And for himself, too, because of her ceaseless, plaintive streams of language. It was *his* language, curiously both familiar and exotic—Seraphic, but spoken in tones and patterns he had never heard, and…godstars, *the things she was saying…*

Beasts and a blackening sky, the openers of doors and the lights in the darkness.

Chosen. Fallen.

Maps but I am lost. Skies but they are dead.

Cataclysm.

Meliz.

"Lunatic poetry," Zuzana had dubbed it, and it was both: poetic and lunatic, but it struck a resonance within Akiva, like a tuning fork that matched his own pitch. It meant something, something important, and so he crossed from his own infinity to hers. He didn't know if this could be done—or, if it could, whether it *should.* It felt wrong, like transgressing a border. There was resistance, but he penetrated it. He searched for her but couldn't find her. He called for her and she didn't answer. The space around him felt different from his own. It was dense and turbid. Kinetic. Aching, uncalm, and afraid.

There was wrongness and torment here, but it was beyond his understanding, and he didn't dare go deeper.

He couldn't find her. He couldn't bring her out. He couldn't. But he tried, tithing his own pain, to soothe her chaos, at least.

When he came back out and opened his eyes, it was with a feeling of reclaiming himself, and he saw that Karou was present, and Zuzana and Mik. Virko, too, though the chimaera had been here all along. And right before him, Eliza. Her manner had quieted, but Akiva saw with his eyes what he'd already known in his heart: that he hadn't fixed her.

He let out a deep breath. His disappointment felt like loss. Karou came to him. She had a decanter of water, and poured out a glass. While he drank, she laid a cool hand to his brow and leaned on the arm of his chair, her hip to his shoulder. And this was an astonishing new threshold of normal—Karou leaning against him—and it lifted his spirits. She'd spoken of their happiness as though it were an undeniable fact, no matter what happened—*apart* from everything else and not subject to it. It was a new idea for him, that happiness wasn't a mystical place to be reached or won—some bright terrain beyond the boundary of misery, a paradise waiting for them to find it—but something to carry doggedly with you through everything, as humble and ordinary as your gear and supplies. Food, weapons, happiness.

With hope that the weapons could in time vanish from the picture.

A new way of living.

"She seems more peaceful," Karou said, studying Eliza. "That's something."

"Not enough."

She didn't say, *You can try again later*, because they both knew there would be no later. Night was falling. They would leave—he and Karou and Virko—very soon, and they wouldn't be coming back here. Eliza Jones, then, must remain lost, and, with her, the "Cataclysm" and all her secrets. The problem was, Akiva sensed a peril in letting it go. "I want to understand what she's saying," he said. "What's happened to her."

"Could you tell anything?"

"Chaos. Fear." He shook his head. "I know nothing of magic, Karou. Not even basic principles. I have a sense that we have, each of us, a..." He groped for words. "A *scheme of energies*. I don't know what to call it. It's more than mind, and more than soul. Dimensions." Still groping. "Geographies. But I don't know the lay of it, or how to navigate it, or even how to *see*. It's like feeling forward in darkness."

She smiled a little, and there was effortful lightness in her voice when she asked, "And how would you know what darkness is like?" Her hand brushed his feathers and they sparked to her touch. "You are your own light."

And Akiva almost said, *I know what darkness is*, because he did, in all the worst senses of the word, but he didn't want Karou to think he was retreating to the bleak state she'd drawn him out of in Morocco. So he held his tongue and was glad he had when she added, so softly he nearly didn't hear, "And mine."

And he looked at her and was filled with the sight of her, and felt, as he had so many times before in her presence—Madrigal and Karou—new life, new growth. Tendrils of sensation and emotion that he had never known before her and never would have without her, and they were something *real*. Roots branching and reaching, past every trapdoor and through any number of dark levels, and the "scheme of energies" that he had described so inadequately—the unknowable dimensions and geographies of self—was changed by it, like a dark quarter of space when a new star bursts into being. Akiva was made brighter. Fuller.

Only love could do that. He caught Karou's hand, small and cool, within his own, and held on to it as he held on to the sight of her. The happiness was there, ordinary equipment, stowed right alongside the worry and sorrow and resolve, and it didn't solve anything, but it lightened it.

"Ready?" he asked.

It was time to go see his uncle.

* * *

They said their good-byes without saying "good-bye," because Akiva told them it was bad luck to do so, like tempting fate. Whatever words they used, there was a shadow over the lot of them, because it was to be no brief parting. Virko, in what would be his last language lesson for a while, taught Zuzana how to say, "I kiss your eyes and leave my heart in your hands," which was an old chimaera farewell and of course led to Zuzana pantomiming a reaction to having a beating heart thrust into her hands.

Esther fussed over them, grandmotherly again and something close to contrite. She made sure they had the map, and knew the way. She asked, concerned, what they intended to do against so many enemies, but Karou didn't tell her. "Not much," was her reply. "Just persuade them to go home."

Esther looked troubled, but didn't press. "I'll order champagne," she said, "to celebrate your victory. I only wish you could be here to drink it with us."

Eliza, all the while, sat staring.

"You'll see to it she gets some help?" Karou asked Zuzana and Mik. "After we're gone?"

Zuzana's face immediately took on a hard set and she wouldn't meet Karou's eyes, but Mik nodded. "Don't worry," he said. "You have enough to worry about."

He understood, if Zuzana didn't, why things had to be this way. He had reminded her himself, several times, on the way here. "Remember how we're not samurai in even the smallest way?" he'd asked. "We can't help with this. We'd only weigh Virko down and get in the way. And if there's more fighting..."

He hadn't elaborated.

"Thank you," Karou said, with one last, helpless look at Eliza. "I know it's a lot to leave you with, but I showed you how to access money. Please, use it. For her, for you. Anything you need."

"Money," Zuzana muttered, as though it were worse than useless, an insult.

Karou turned to her. "If there's anything for you to come back to," she promised, hating the *if* as though the word itself were her enemy, "I'll find a way to come get you."

"How? You're going to close the portal."

"We have to, but there are more portals. I'll find them."

"What, you'll have time to be hunting for portals?"

"I don't know." It was a refrain. *I don't know what we'll find when we get back. I don't know if there will be any hope left to work with in all the world. I don't know how I'll find another portal. I don't know if I'll be alive. I don't know.*

Zuzana, her hard expression unchanged, tipped her head forward in a kind of slow-motion collision that Karou didn't recognize for a hug until, at the last minute, her friend's arms went around her. "Be safe," Zuzana whispered. "No heroics. If you have to save yourself, do it, and come back here. Both of you. All three of you. We can make Virko a human body or something. Just promise me, if you get there and everyone's..." She didn't say it. *Dead.* "You'll just keep out of sight and come back here and *live.*"

Karou couldn't promise that, as Zuzana must have known, because she didn't give her a chance to answer, but plowed ahead with, "Good. Thank you. That's all I wanted to hear," as though a promise had been given. Karou returned her hug, hating good-byes like she'd hated the *if*, and then there was nothing left to do but go.

56

My Sweet Barbarian

Cleanliness, at last. Mik and Zuzana took turns in the bathroom, so that one of them could sit with Eliza, while also keeping a vigil for breaking angel news. The TV was on low, and Esther's laptop was open with several feeds constantly refreshing, but nothing had happened yet, and wouldn't be likely to for a while

Karou, Zuzana knew, had a stop to make before the Vatican: the Museo Civico di Zoologia. It was a natural history museum, and there had been a calm defiance in her when she declared her intention to go there. It had half broken Zuzana's heart, knowing what it was for—to replenish her store of teeth, in case souls had been saved, at least, in the battle—and that she wouldn't be there to help, whatever it was they found when they got back to Eretz.

Damned helplessness. Zuzana sensed a T-shirt design coming on.

BE A SAMURAI.

BECAUSE YOU JUST NEVER KNOW WHAT'S BEHIND

THE FREAKING SKY.

No one would understand it, but who cares? She'd just glare at them until they went away. That worked in almost any situation.

No, she chided herself. It did not. Because if it *did*, there would be no need to be a samurai, would there?

She looked at Eliza, beside her, and sighed. Eliza didn't seem to need or register company, but the idea of leaving her alone in the corner like a piece of softly murmuring furniture just didn't sit right. Zuzana was no nurse, and had no instincts for it, but she was mindful that the young woman needed someone to take care of her basic human needs for her—food and drink just for starters—and she was more docile now, at least, whatever Akiva had done. Less agitated, and that made it easier.

What they were going to do about her after today, Zuzana couldn't think about right now. Tomorrow was soon enough. When all the tension of today was a thing of the past, and they'd had a full night's sleep in an actual bed, and a meal that had never even been on the same continent as couscous.

Tomorrow.

But for now, it was good to be clean. It felt like rebirth—Venus emerging from a layer of crud—and the clothes Esther's shopper had chosen were elegant and understated, of fine materials and nearly a perfect fit. Zuzana's filthy stuff, zebra sneakers included, she'd stacked neatly and wrapped in several layers of plastic bags; it felt like a betrayal, especially after her old shoes sat next to her new ones on the floor and she got the idea that they were being forced to train their replacements. *She scuffs a bit*, they'd tell the new leather numbers, fond tears seeping from their rheumy old-shoe eyes. *And she stands on tiptoe a lot, so be ready for that.*

"Sentimental of you," Mik had commented when she came back into the sitting room and shoved the bundle into her backpack.

"Not at all," she'd airily declared. "I'm saving them for the Museum of Otherworldly Adventure that I'm going to found. Exhibit title: 'What not to wear camping in freezing mountains while forging an alliance between enemy armies.' "

"Uh-huh."

Mik, taking his turn in the bathroom, felt no such sentimentality for his dirty clothes. He was happy to drop them in the trash, though before he could do that, he fished furtively into the pocket of his old jeans and withdrew...

...the ring.

The maybe-silver, maybe-antique ring he'd been in the act of purchasing when the world went crazy. He turned it over in his fingers, looking at it closely for the first time since. Zuzana was always in proximity (and thank god for that); he hadn't had a chance to take it out. It seemed to him a rough thing now, especially in the context of this ridiculous hotel. Back at Aït Benhaddou it had fit right in: primitive and tarnished, maybe a little lopsided. Here it looked like something that had fallen off a Visigoth's pinkie during the Sack of Rome. Barbarian jewelry.

Perfect.

For my sweet barbarian, he thought, and as he went to tuck it into the pocket of his posh new Italian trousers, he fumbled and it spun from his fingers. It rang against the marble floor and rolled like it was trying to escape. Mik followed, thinking maybe it was real silver after all, because supposedly real silver makes that chime sound, and then it escaped into a three-finger gap beneath the marble vanity.

"Come back here," he whispered. "I have plans for you."

He dropped to his knees to grope for it as, in the sitting room, his sweet barbarian held water to Eliza Jones's ever-murmuring lips to coax her to drink, and, in the smaller bedroom in the back of the suite, with the door closed and music playing to mask her voice, Esther Van de Vloet made a phone call.

It wasn't an easy phone call for her to make, but the most that could be said in her defense was that she had hoped not to make it. She hesitated for a fraction of a second, and though a shadow of her true age may have haunted her face, no indecision did. She forced out a harsh breath and got on with it.

After all, power doesn't maintain itself.

* * *

Karou and her companions cut over the rooftops of Rome, their errand at the natural history museum behind them and only Jael ahead. The night air was thick with Italian summer, the cityscape below them a muted canvas of rooftops and monuments, lights and domes, cut by a snake of dark that was the Tiber River. Honking of horns filtered up as they flew, and traffic whistles, along with snatches of music, and—growing louder the nearer they drew to the Vatican—chanting. It was unintelligible, but followed the rhythm of liturgy.

There was a stink, too—the unmistakable aroma of humans packed too close for too long. Judging by its acrid edge, Karou figured that once pilgrims achieved a spot near the barrier, they didn't want to give it up for something so temporal as bodily function.

Nice.

The news had reported a public health crisis, as people were bringing elderly and infirm loved ones to the perimeter in the hope that the mere proximity of angels might cure their diseases—or, scarcely to be hoped, that the angels might actually come out to bless them. Claims of miracles had been made, and though they were unproven, they nevertheless overshadowed the documented number of deaths resulting from this practice.

Miracles will do that.

Seen from the sky, the Vatican was a wedge—if a lumpy wedge, like a collapsing slice of pie. Within the boundary, its vast circular plaza was its most visible feature, enclosed by Michelangelo's famous curved colonnades. It was incongruously choked with military vehicles, tanks dozing like ugly beetles, jeeps coming and going, even troop transports.

Just beyond the north colonnade lay their destination: the Papal Palace. Karou led the way.

Esther had been able to provide them, thanks to her "pocket cardinal," with the precise location of the chambers Jael had been given for his use, and the three of them swung in a broad circle above the cluster of buildings—the palace was not one, but several, grown together—scanning the rooftops for signs of seraph presence.

They expected guards. Human soldiers were concentrated on the ground—they could see soldiers patrolling with dogs—and certainly at the entrances to the building, both inside and out. But they still expected to find Dominion posted to the rooftop, too, because this was standard operating procedure in Eretz, where an attack was as likely to come from the sky as the ground.

And there they were. Two.

Easy.

"Don't harm them," Karou reminded Akiva and Virko—needlessly, she hoped—and felt them move off. She watched the guards, and saw Akiva's and Virko's moon-cast shadows descend on them. Vividly she recalled the tidal wave of shadow chased by fire that had engulfed the company back in the Adelphas, and felt no pity as the soldiers, in unison, stiffened and then slumped.

Quick blows to the head. They went limp but didn't collapse. Their bodies seemed to drift in slow motion to the rooftop, as Akiva and Virko caught them and laid them quietly down. They'd have goose eggs and headaches later, but no more than that. It wasn't a matter of whether they deserved mercy so much as the parameters of this mission: no blood.

Swift and bloodless, that was the point. No carnage, no crime scene, just persuasion. They should be in and out before these two soldiers even woke up and rubbed their aching heads.

Karou set down lightly and cast a brief glance at one of them. Unconscious, he looked like any number of the Misbegotten from the Kirin caves. Handsome, young, fair. Villain and victim both, she thought, and she recalled Liraz's proposal that fingers be taken instead of lives, and wondered: Was it possible even Dominion soldiers could learn to live in the new world, if ever there was one? Did they deserve the choice? Looking at him like this, to all appearances asleep and innocent, it was easy to think: yes.

Maybe when he woke, his eyes would fill with hate, and he would be beyond hope.

This was a worry for another day. They were here. Jael's windows were in sight. The chanting at the perimeter enclosed them like the roar of the sea, but the effect was a seeming sphere of quiet within.

"I've thought of a better idea," Karou had announced back at the Kirin caves, so certain that this was the way to avoid an apocalypse. A quick and quiet end to this drama. No clash, no weapons, no "monsters."

The angels just melt away.

Simple.

"Okay," she said, pausing to text Zuzana before turning off her phone and tucking it away. "Let's do it."

57

Fed to the Lions

There came a knock at the door of the Royal Suite, and it was not casual. The dogs, Traveller and Methuselah, leapt to their feet, instantly alert.

Zuzana and Mik didn't leap up, but they, too, were instantly alert. They were at the window of the living room now, having transferred from the sitting room on account of the windows on this side facing toward the Vatican. Their eyes were wandering between the TV screen and the slice of sky they had revealed by cranking the red velvet curtains apart, as if something was going to play out on one or the other.

And something *would*, as soon as Karou and Akiva were successful in their mission: The "heavenly host" would rise up into the sky and hightail it the hell back to Uzbekistan and the portal there. *Don't let the . . . uh, sky flap thing . . . hit you on the way out.*

Sky or TV. Where would they see it first?

Zuzana's phone lay on the arm of her chair so she would know at once if Karou called or texted. There had been one message so far.

*Arrived. Going in. *kiss/punch*.*

And so. It was happening. Zuzana couldn't keep still. Sky—TV—phone—Mik, that was the circuit of her glances, with pauses on Eliza, too.

The girl remained subdued and remote, her eyes glassy but not still, not entirely. They'd rest for a time, then flick back and forth, her pupils dilating and shrinking, even when the light was steady. It was as though her mind was participating in a different reality than her body, her eyes seeing different sights, her lips shaping the soft lunatic poetry that Zuzana was glad not to be able to understand. When Karou had translated some of it for her, it had been too eerie for comfort, some kind of horror movie with lots of devouring. And not the kind of devouring that went down between Zuzana and the plate of chocolate-dipped biscotti she liberated from atop the piano.

Okay, exactly that kind of devouring, but from the biscotti's point of view.

KNOCK KNOCK KNOCK.

It was alarming, the force of it. An StB knock—or Stasi, or Gestapo. Pick your secret police. It had a *they come for you in the night* weight to it—and . . . nobody sashays blithely to answer a *they come for you in the night* knock.

Except that Esther did. She'd been in the bedroom in the back; they hadn't seen much of her since the others left. She came forth now, still barefoot and striding calmly through the living room without a sideward glance. As she vanished down the corridor to the door, dogs flanking her, she said, "You should gather your things now, children."

Zuzana's gaze flew to Mik, and his to her. Her heartbeat seemed to lurch to its feet with the same swiftness as the mastiffs had, and then she herself followed suit, jumping up. "What?" she asked at the same moment Mik said, "Jesus."

"Jesus *what?*"

"Get your stuff," he said. "Pack your bag." And Zuzana still didn't know what was happening, but then there were men coming in, two of them, large and in fine suits, and they had wireless com things hooked onto their big, dumb ears and Zuzana's first thought was *Holy, they really* are *secret police*, but then she spotted the crest embroidered on their coat pockets, and her fear transformed to the first simmer of outrage.

Hotel security. Esther was throwing them out.

"All right," said one of the men. "Let's go. It's time for you to leave."

"What do you mean?" Zuzana faced them down. "We're guests."

"Not anymore you're not," said Esther from the doorway. "I tolerated you for Karou's sake. And now that Karou . . . Well."

Zuzana swung toward her. The old woman was leaning there with her arms crossed and her dogs pacing around her. There was a look of predatory calculation in her eyes, and Zuzana's immediate impression was that a snake had swallowed the downy-haired grandma and somehow *become* her. The liveried hotel thugs weren't a step into the room before the weight of what this meant slammed down on Zuzana.

Karou.

"What have you done?" she demanded, because if Esther was throwing them out, it meant that she anticipated having no further contact with Karou—not just tonight, but ever.

"Done? I've just alerted the management that I find myself overrun with uncouth young people. They knew at once who I meant. It seems you made quite an impression downstairs."

"I mean, what have you done *to Karou*?" She hurled the words and started to hurl *herself*, and in that moment she could have believed that she *was* a *neek-neek*, sting and all, and woe to lion-sized dogs and beefy bullies who stood in her way.

She was a *neek-neek* that was easily captured in midair, however, the nearest bully hooking her wrist with a practiced grab and holding tight. "Let go of me!" she snarled at him, and tried to thrash her arm free.

No luck there. His grip was ridiculous, like he spent all his spare time squeezing one of those stupid rubber balls, but then Mik lunged in and grabbed the hand that held her. "Let go of her," he demanded, and, in an uneven match of violin player versus brute, he tried to peel back the thick ugly fingers from Zuzana's wrist. No luck there, either; Zuzana was able to register, just barely, through her outrage, how humiliatingly un-samurai-like the pair of them were at this moment. With his free hand, the guard easily shoved Mik down the corridor to the front door—so much for getting their stuff—and Zuzana after him. Her wrist throbbed where he'd held her, but that was scarcely noteworthy in the tornado of rage and worry that had become her mind.

Refusing to be herded, Zuzana broke aside, darting around the guard to come face-to-face with Traveler and Methuselah, barring the way to their mistress. The dogs regarded her. One of them lifted the lips from his teeth in a bored kind of growl, as if to say, *See these here choppers?*

I've seen scarier, she wanted to tell them. Hell, she wanted to bare her teeth right back, but instead, she just held her ground and lifted her eyes to Esther. The look on the old woman's face—stony apathy—was scarcely human. This wasn't a person, Zuzana thought.

This was greed wearing skin. "What did you do? What did you do, Esther? What. Did. You. Do."

Esther breathed out a sigh. "Are you an idiot? What do you think?"

"I think you're a backstabbing sociopath, that's what I think."

Esther just shook her head, a blaze of scorn displacing her apathy. "Do you suppose I wanted it this way? I was happy with the way things were. It's not my fault Brimstone is dead."

"What does that have to do with anything?" Zuzana demanded.

"Come now. I know you're not the little doll you look like. Life is choices, and only fools choose their allies with their heart."

"*Choose their allies*? What is this, *Survivor*?" Zuzana was overcome with disgust of her own. Esther had "chosen" the angels, clearly. Because Brimstone was dead, and she was looking only to her own advantage. In that moment, and knowing what she did about Esther's true age, she had a flash of insight about her. "You," she said, and her disgust made a thick coating around the word. "I bet you were a Nazi collaborator, weren't you?"

To her surprise, Esther laughed. "You say that like it's a bad thing. Anyone with sense would choose to live. Do you know what's foolish? Dying for a *belief*. Look where we are. Rome. Think of the Christians fed to the lions because they wouldn't renounce their faith. As if their god wouldn't forgive them their desire to live? If you have no more self-preservation instinct than that, maybe you don't *deserve* life."

"Are you kidding me? You're going to blame the Christians, not the Romans? How about they just don't throw them to the goddamn lions in the first place? Don't delude yourself. You're the monster here."

Esther, abruptly, had had enough. "It's time for you to go now," she said, brisk. "And you should know that upon her decease, all of Karou's assets go to her next of kin." A thin and joyless smile. "Her devoted grandmother, of course. So don't bother trying to access those accounts."

Upon her decease, upon her decease. Zuzana wouldn't hear it. Her mind batted the words away.

Esther motioned to the hallway and the knob-knuckled paws of the security guards hoisted them toward it. "You can keep the clothes," Esther added. "You're welcome. Oh, and don't forget the vegetable."

Vegetable.

She meant Eliza. All this while, Eliza had remained quiet. She was catatonic, and Esther was going to throw her out on the street, and Mik and Zuzana, too, with nothing.

Upon her decease. The tornado had gone from Zuzana's mind, leaving whispers in its wake. What had happened? *Could they be . . . ?*

Shut up.

"Let me get our bags, at least," Mik asked, sounding so calm and reasonable that Zuzana was almost incensed. *How dare he be calm and reasonable?*

"I gave you a chance," said Esther. "You elected to stand here insulting me instead. As I said before, life is choices."

"Let me at least get my violin," he pleaded. "We've got nothing, and no way to get home. At least I'll be able to play in a piazza for train fare."

The mental image of them panhandling must have appealed to her sense of class stratification, not to mention degradation. "Fine." She flicked her wrist, and Mik took off down the hall, fast. When he came back he was holding his violin case in his arms like a baby, not swinging it by its handle. "Thank you," he actually said, as if Esther had done them a kindness. Zuzana glared at him.

Had he lost his mind?

"Get Eliza," he said to her, and she did, and Eliza came along like a sleepwalker. Zuzana halted just once, to face Esther across the living room.

"I've said this before, but I was always kidding." She wasn't kidding now. She'd never been more serious. "I will get you for this. I promise you."

Esther laughed. "That's not how the world works, dear. But you can try, if it makes you happy. Do your worst."

"Wait for it," Zuzana seethed, and the security guard shoved, and she was propelled down the passage, Eliza at her side, and out into the grand hall to the elevator. Subsequently *de*-elevated. And, at last, frog-marched through that gleaming lobby, subject to stares and whispers and, most stingingly, the haughty amusement of her eyebrow challenger—who again dared, in light of this shift in circumstances, to raise one of her overplucked, starved-looking amateur brows in a crude but effective *I told you so*.

The burn of mortification was like passing through a field of nettles—a thousand small pains merging into a haze—but it was nothing next to Zuzana's heartsickness and panic at the thought of their friends, even now at the mercy of their enemies.

What was happening to them?

Esther must have warned the angels. What had they promised her? Zuzana wondered. And more important, how could she and Mik prevent her from getting it? How? They had *nothing*. Nothing but a violin.

"I can't believe you thanked her," she muttered as they were shoved through the doors and out into the street. Rome came crashing in on them, its vitality and sultry air a marked change from the artificial calm and cool of the interior.

"She let me get my violin," he said with a shrug, still holding it to his chest like it was a baby or a puppy. He sounded . . . pleased. It was too much. Zuzana stopped walking—they had no destination but "away" anyway—and swung to face him. He didn't just *sound* pleased. He looked it. Or keyed-up, at least. Practically vibrating.

"What's with you?" she asked him, at a loss and ready to just sit down and cry.

"I'll tell you in a minute. Come on. We can't stay here."

"Yeah. I think that's been established."

"No. I mean we can't stay anywhere that she can find us, and she *will* come looking. *Come on.*" There was urgency in his voice now, puzzling her even more. He hooked his arm around her to steer her, and she drew Eliza along with them—a dreamlike figure who seemed, almost ethereally, to drift, and the crowd subsumed them, parade-thick and easy to get lost in. And so the human density that they'd earlier cursed became their refuge, and they escaped.

58

The Wrong Ugliness

All was as it should be. The heavy window shutter was unlatched, as promised, and now Karou had only to get it open in silence. It wanted to creak; its resistance dared her to push it faster and let it squeal. It had been a while since she'd lamented the lack of the "nearly useless wishes" she used to take for granted—scuppies she'd plundered from a teacup in Brimstone's shop and worn as a necklace—but she found herself wanting one now. A bead between her fingers, a wish for the window's silence.

There. She didn't need it. It took patience to open a window with such excruciating slowness while her heart thundered, but she did it. The chamber was open to them, dark but for a rectangle of moonlight stretched out like a welcome mat.

They passed inside one by one, their shapes cutting the moonspill to shards. It re-formed in its entirety as they stepped out of the way. They paused. There was a sense of letting the darkness settle, like water sinking beneath oil.

One last breath before approach.

The bed looked out of place. This was a reception hall, the most famous in the palace. The bed had been brought in, and you had to give them credit for finding a Baroque monstrosity that almost held its own in the fanciful chamber. It was a big four-poster, carved with saints and angels. Twisted blankets traced a form. The form breathed. On the bedside table sat the helm Jael wore to conceal his hideousness from humanity. He shifted slightly as they watched, turning. His breath sounded even and deep.

Karou's feet weren't touching the floor. It wasn't even conscious, this floating; her ability had become natural enough now that it was simply part and parcel of her stealth: Why touch the floor if you don't have to?

She moved forward, gliding. Akiva would go around to the far side of the bed, and be ready.

This moment would be the most tenuous: waking Jael and keeping him silent while they offered up the "persuasion" that was the crux of Karou's plan. If it went smoothly, they could be back out the window and away inside of two minutes. She held a wad of burlap in her hand to stifle any sounds he might make before they had a chance to convince him he'd do better to lie quiet. And, of course, after that, to muffle his sounds of pain.

Bloodless didn't mean painless.

Karou had never seen Jael, though she thought she could imagine his unique brand of ugliness well enough from all the reports she'd heard of it. She was braced for it, when the sleeping angel stirred again and knocked his pillow askew. She was expecting ugliness, and ugliness was what she got.

But it was the wrong ugliness.

Eyes flew open from feigned sleep—fine eyes in a ravaged face, but there was no slash, no scar from brow to chin, only a bruise-colored bloat and depths of depravity deeper even than the emperor's. "Blue lovely," said the thing, with a throat-rattling purr.

Karou never had a chance with the wad of burlap. She moved fast, but he had been lying in wait—*expecting her*—and she wasn't yet near enough for her lunge to smother his cry.

Razgut had time to shriek, "Our guests have arrived!" before she caught his foul face under the rough weave of the burlap and shut him up. He sputtered to silence but it didn't matter. The alarm was sounded.

The doors crashed open. Dominion flooded in.

59

Self-Fulfilling Prophecy

In the Royal Suite of the St. Regis, Esther Van de Vloet stood in the doorway to the bathroom, her pace arrested mid-step by the sight of... of a violin, lying in the tub.

A violin, lying in the tub.

A violin.

...

...

...

Her cry was guttural, a croak almost, as a toad in extremis. Her dogs flew to her, upset, but she shoved them violently away, threw herself to her knees, and reached, groping, up and into the hollowness beneath the marble vanity.

All disbelief, she groped and reached, too frantic even to curse, and when she cried out again, collapsing back on the marble floor, it was an inarticulate torrent of pure emotion that flowed from her.

The emotion was unfamiliar to her. It was defeat.

* * *

In under an hour, Zuzana had perfected the art of the angry sigh. The sky remained resoundingly empty, and that wasn't a good sign. Enough time had passed since Karou, Akiva, and Virko left the St. Regis for them to have routed Jael, but there was no evidence of it, and Zuzana's phone screen remained as blank as the sky. Of course she'd texted warnings, and had even tried calling, but the calls went straight to voice mail and it reminded her of the awful days after Karou left Prague—and left Earth—when Zuzana hadn't known if she was alive or dead.

"What are we going to do?"

They'd ducked into a narrow alley, Mik acting strangely furtive, and Zuzana seated Eliza on a stoop before slumping down beside her. This was one of those intensely Italian nooks—tiny, as if once upon a time all people had been Zuzana's size—where medieval nudged up against Renaissance on the bones of ancient. On top of which some knob had contributed twenty-first century to the party by way of sloppy graffiti enjoining them to "*Apri gli occhi! Ribellati!*"

Open your eyes! Rebel!

Why, Zuzana wondered, *do anarchists always have such terrible handwriting?*

Mik knelt before her and laid his violin case on her lap. As soon as he released it, its weight sunk into her.

Its... *weight*? "Mik, why does your violin case weigh fifty pounds?"

"I was wondering," he said, instead of answering. "In fairy tales, are the heroes, um, ever... thieves?"

"Thieves?" Zuzana narrowed her eyes in suspicion. "I don't know. Probably. Robin Hood?"

"Not a fairy tale, but I'll take it. A noble thief."

"Jack and the Beanstalk. He stole all that stuff from the giant."

"Right. Less noble. I always felt bad for the giant." He flicked open the clasp on the case. "But I don't feel bad about this." He paused. "I hope we can count this as one of my tasks. Retroactively."

And he flipped up the lid and the case was filled with . . . medallions. *Filled*. They varied in size from a quarter's span to a saucer's, in an array of patinas of bronze from brassy bright to dull dark brown. Some were entirely engulfed in verdigris, and all were roughly minted and graven with the same image: a ram's head with thick coiled horns and knowing, slit-pupiled eyes.

Brimstone.

"So," said Mik in a faux-lazy drawl, "when fake grandma said she didn't have any more wishes? She lied. But look. Self-fulfilling prophecy. Now she really doesn't."

No One Dies Today

The doors crashed open. Dominion flooded in.

Karou's first impulse was to reach for pain to tithe for a glamour, and the pain was all too easy to find, because Razgut caught her wrist in his crushing grip and held her, so that it didn't matter.

Visible or not, she was caught.

She flickered in and out, struggling with the Fallen. His chuckling sounded like a purr, and his grip was unbreakable. She had her crescent-moon blades to fall back on, but they had determined to shed blood only as a last resort, and so her hand paused on her hilt as she watched the soldiers, implacable and many, swords drawn and faces blank, file into the room. Once again, as had happened and happened over these past days, the turn of time went thick as resin. Viscous. Sluggish. How much can happen in a second? In three? In ten?

How many seconds does it take to lose everything you care about?

Esther, she thought, and in the midst of her frantic scuffle she was bitter but unsurprised. They had been expected here. This wasn't the personal guard of six that Jael kept to guard his chamber. Here were thirty soldiers at least. Forty?

And there. Through the open doors, unhurried, to take up a position behind a deep buffer of soldiers, sauntered Jael. Karou saw him before he saw her, because he was looking straight ahead, unwavering. His ugliness was all she'd heard and more: the knotty rope of scar tissue and the way the wings of his nostrils seemed to creep out from beneath it like they were trapped there—as trampled mushrooms going softly to rot. His mouth was its own disaster, collapsing in on scraps of teeth, his breath coming and going through it like the squelch of steps in mud. But that wasn't the worst thing about the emperor of seraphim. His expression was. It was intricate with hate. Even his smile was party to it: as malicious as it was exultant.

"Nephew," he said, and the single wet word was layered with enmity and triumph.

* * *

Jael peered out between the shoulders of his soldiers at Akiva. Beast's Bane, so-called, whose death he'd first argued for when the fire-eyed bastard was just a brat crying himself to sleep in the training camp. "Kill him," he'd advised Joram then. He remembered the taste of those words in his mouth—keenly, because they'd been among the first he spoke when the bandages were removed from his face. The first he'd *tried* to speak, anyway, when it was agony, his mouth a red, wet wreck, and the revulsion he saw in his brother's eyes—and everyone else's—had still had the power to shame him. He had let a woman cut him. Never mind that he lived and she didn't. He would wear her mark forever.

"If you're smart, you'll kill him now," he'd told his brother. Looking back, it was so clearly the wrong tactic. Joram was emperor, and did not respond well to commands.

"What, still trying to punish her?" Joram had scoffed, dragging the specter of Festival between them. Both of them had tried and failed to humble the Stelian concubine; she might be dead, but she had never broken. "Killing her didn't scratch the itch, you have to have the boy, too? What, do you think she'll know it somehow, and suffer more?"

"He's her seed," Jael had persisted. "She was a *spore*, drifted here. An infection. Nothing safe can grow of her."

"*Safe*? What use have I for a 'safe' warrior? He's *my* seed, brother. Do you mean to suggest that my blood isn't stronger than some feral whore's?"

And there was Joram for you: blind, incurious. The lady Festival of the Far Isles had been many things, but "whore" wasn't one of them.

"Prisoner" wasn't, either.

However she'd come to be in the emperor's harem, and *why* ever she had chosen to stay, it could not believably have been against her will. She was Stelian, and though she'd never revealed it, Jael was certain that she'd had power. The design, he had always thought, must have been her own. So... why would a daughter of that mystical tribe have put herself in Joram's bed?

Slowly, Jael blinked at Akiva. *Why indeed?* You had only to look at the bastard to see whose blood was stronger. Black hair, tawny skin—not as dark as Festival's had been, but closer to it than to Joram's fair flesh. The eyes, of course, were purely hers, and sympathy for magic? In case there had still been doubt.

Joram should have listened to his brother. He should have let him exercise his wrath in whatever way he saw fit, but instead he'd mocked him and banished him to eat his meals alone, saying he couldn't bear the sucking sounds he made.

Well, Jael could afford to laugh about it now, couldn't he? And make all the sucking sounds he liked while doing so.

"Beast's Bane," he said, stepping forward but not too far forward, keeping a thick barrier of his soldiers in place, two score Dominion between himself and the intruders, and ten of them wielding the very special weapons that had subdued Akiva so spectacularly before: bare hands.

Not their own, of course. Withered and mummy-brown, some clawed, all inked with the devil's eyes, they held them out before themselves, the severed hands of chimaera warriors.

At the sight of them, the beast by Akiva's side emitted a growl low in his throat. The ruff of spikes at his neck lifted, bristling, and opened like a deadly flower. He seemed to double in size right there, becoming a battlefield nightmare, all the more terrible for the stark contrast between himself and this ornate room he suddenly seemed to fill.

It chilled Jael. Even safe behind his barricade of flesh and living fire, and even expecting it—thanks to the warning of that monstrous woman who was to be his human benefactor—the sight appalled him. Not the chimaera itself, but seraph and chimaera standing together? The beasts had been his brother's crusade. Jael had his sights set on a new enemy, but nevertheless, the alliance he saw before him here marked a thousand years turned inside out—a cancer that must not be permitted to spread through Eretz.

When he returned, he would crush any sign of it. The rest of the rebellion must be crushed already, he thought with satisfaction. Why else would these three come to him alone, without an army at their back? He wanted to laugh at them for fools, but he saw how narrow his salvation had been and a shudder stopped him cold. If not for the woman's warning, he would have been asleep in that bed when they slipped through the window.

Too close. Only luck had given him the upper hand this time. He wouldn't be so careless again.

"Prince of Bastards," he continued, feeling as though he were performing a rite many years delayed: the purging of Stelian infection, the eradication of Festival's last trace and whatever she had meant by bringing it forth. "Seventh bearer of the cursed name Akiva." Here he paused, speculative. "No Misbegotten ever bore that name to manhood before you. Did you know that? Old Byon the steward, he gave it out of spite. Wanted your mother to beg him not to. Any other woman in the harem would have, but not Festival. 'Scribble whatever you like on your list, old man,' she told him. 'My son will not be tangled in your feeble fates.' "

He studied Akiva closely, scanning for a reaction. "Brave words, no? And how many deaths have you eluded, all told? The curse of your name, and the several deaths I carved out for you. How many more?"

It seemed to him that Beast's Bane stiffened then. Jael sensed a wound. "Others die, but you live?" he probed. "Perhaps you've turned the curse outward. *You* don't die. Everyone near you does instead."

Akiva's jaw was hard-clenched. "It must be a terrible burden," Jael pressed, shaking his head in mock pity. "Death looks for you and looks for you, but he can't *see* you. *Invisible to death*, what a fate! Finally, he grows weary of the search and takes whoever is near at hand." He paused, smiled, and tried to sound warm and genuine as he said, "Nephew, I have good news for you. Today we break the curse. Today, at last, you die."

* * *

Even braced for the sight of his uncle, Akiva was unprepared for the visceral assault of reliving this moment, and it caught him like a fist to the heart. It was an echo of the Tower of Conquest, when, just like this, Jael and his soldiers had seized control of the room.

"Kill everyone," Jael had said on that day, and, expressionless, his soldiers had complied, gutting counsellors, butchering the big brute Silverswords that Hazael and Liraz had taken such care to disarm without hurting. They had even cut down the bath attendants. It had been a literal bloodbath, emperor and heir discarded in a pool of red. Blood on the walls, blood on the floor, blood everywhere.

The voice, the face, the number of soldiers. Akiva could guess, by the still-healing abrasions on their faces, that some of these men had been at the tower and survived its explosion. In addition to swords, they even leveled at him the same vile weapons that they had surprised him with on that bloody day.

And Jael's greeting was the same, too. Oh, that slurp of a voice. "*Nephew.*" He had said it then to Japheth, the witless crown prince, just before he slew him. Now it was all for Akiva, and was followed by a hissed litany of his many names.

Beast's Bane. The Prince of Bastards. Seventh bearer of the cursed name Akiva.

Akiva listened in silence, hearing them all and wondering: Were any of them *him*? What had his mother meant, that he wouldn't be tangled in their feeble fates? It made him feel as though even "Akiva" weren't his true name, but just another Misbegotten accessory, like his armor or his sword. His name, like his training, was something imposed on him, and hearing Festival's reaction to it, he wondered: Who else was he? What else?

And the first answer that came to him was simple, as simple as what he had come here to do, as simple as his desires.

I am alive.

He remembered the moment—and it seemed very long ago but wasn't—when he had lain on his back in the training theater at Cape Armasin, an ax—Liraz's ax—embedded in the hardpan just inches from his cheek. He'd believed Karou was dead, and then and there, breathing hard and looking up at the stars, he had accepted life as a medium for *action*. Something to wield like a tool. One's own life: an instrument for the shaping of the world.

And he remembered Karou's plea from just the day before, when they were crushed into that tiny shower. "I don't want you to be sorry," she had said. "I want you to be . . . *alive*."

She'd meant something more than life as a tool. Something about the way she'd said it, Akiva had known that, to her, in that moment, life was *hunger*.

And whatever his name, whatever his past or ancestry, Akiva *was* alive, and he was hungry, too. For the dream, for peace, for the feel of Karou's body pressed against his, for the home they might share, somehow, somewhere, and for the changes they would see—and cause—in Eretz for decades to come.

He was alive and intent on staying that way, so while his uncle taunted him, probing for a weak spot—it wasn't enough to kill; he had to torment—Akiva heard what he said, but none of it touched him. It was like threatening darkness at the break of day.

"Today we break the curse," said Jael. "Today, at last, you die."

Akiva shook his head. Passingly he wondered if he should be pretending weakness he didn't feel. In Joram's bath, these gruesome hand "trophies" had given the Dominion the advantage they needed to subdue Akiva, Hazael, and Liraz. Tonight things were different. No rush of weakness assaulted him. He experienced only a sensation of awareness in the new scar at the back of his neck as his own magic met it and turned it aside. He remembered the feeling of Karou's fingertips tracing the mark, so lightly, when he had shown it to her, and he remembered the press of her palm against his heart, no magic screaming into his blood, and no sickness, only what the touch itself intended.

He was aware of her flickering glamour and her struggle with the thing Razgut. He wanted to surge toward her, smash the bloated purpled face and free her, even twist off that vile stringy arm if he had to. And he wanted to back the creature into a corner and fire questions at him, too. *Fallen.* What did it mean? He'd had the chance to ask him once before and had thrown it away, and now wasn't the time, either. He knew Karou could manage the creature.

His own true adversary stood before him. "Not today," Akiva told Jael. The first words he'd spoken since coming into this room. "No one dies today."

Jael's laugh was as nasty as ever. "Nephew, look around. Whatever you meant by creeping to my bedside in the night"—and here he diverted his attention for the first time from Akiva to glance at Karou, and an appreciative light came on in his eyes—"and I expect that it is *not* the more pleasant of several possible explanations...." He paused. Smiled. "I would expect it to run counter to my own intentions."

He was enjoying himself. This was an echo of the Tower of Conquest for him, too, so much so that he was failing to notice the critical difference: Akiva wasn't trembling under his assault of magic. "It does," Akiva acknowledged. "Though I doubt it's what you expect."

"What?" Mockery. Hand to his chest. "You mean you *haven't* come to kill me?"

He spoke it like a good joke. Why else, indeed, would they have come? Akiva's reply was mild. "No. We haven't. We've come to ask you to leave. Leave just as you came, with no blood spilled, and carrying nothing from this world back with you. Go home. All of you. That's all."

"Oh, that's all, is it?" More laughter, spit flying. "You make demands?"

"It was a request. But I am prepared to demand."

Jael's eyes narrowed, and Akiva saw the mockery transform first to incredulity and then to suspicion. Did he begin to sense that something was wrong? "Can you count, bastard?" Jael was trying to hold on to his mockery. He wanted this to be funny, but an edge to his voice betrayed him, and when his eyes swiveled suddenly like they were on casters, Akiva saw that he was doing an accounting of his own, and trying to believe in the strength of his position. "You are two against forty," he said. *Two*. He discounted Karou. Well, Akiva wasn't going to correct him. It wasn't his uncle's only error; it was only the most obvious. "However strong you are, however cunning, it's numbers that matter in the end."

"Numbers do matter," Akiva conceded, thinking of shadows chased by fire, and the tangled darkness of the ambush in the Adelphas. "But other factors sometimes turn the tide."

He didn't wait for Jael to ask what those other factors might be.

Only a fool would ask—what could the answer be, but a demonstration?—and Jael was not a fool. So before the monstrous emperor could command his soldiers to strike first, Akiva spoke. "Did you think," he asked, "that you could ever surprise me again?"

After that came one word only. It was a name, in fact, though Jael wouldn't know it. And for an instant, his brow furrowed with confusion.

An instant only. Then the tide turned.

61

Superpowers Willy-Nilly

"Now, let's not be hasty," said Mik, holding one of the saucer-broad wishes in his hand. "What exactly *is* a samurai, really? Do you think that's something we should know before we wish it?"

"Good point." Zuzana held a matching wish on her own palm. It dwarfed it, and weighed even more than it looked like it should. "It might turn us both into Japanese men." She squinted at him. "Would you still love me if I were a Japanese man?"

"Of course," said Mik, without missing a beat. "However, as cool a word as *samurai* is, I don't think it's what we really mean. We just want to be able to kick ass, right?"

"Well, definitely don't phrase it *that* way. We'd probably just become highly skilled at kicking people in the ass. *Don't turn your back on them,*" she intoned. "*They never miss.*"

Wording was important when it came to wishing. Fairy tales could tell you that, even if Karou herself hadn't, plenty of times. Zuzana had wished on scuppies before, but she'd never held a true wish in her hand, and the weight of it cowed her. What if she messed up? This was a gavriel. A mess-up could be severe.

Wait. Back up. This was *a gavriel.*

Of which there were *four* in Mik's violin case.

The case sat at Zuzana's feet now. She was still in awe of Mik, swiping the mother lode of wish stashes right out from under Evil Esther's nose. *The sweetness.* Had she noticed yet? How frenzied was she? And did revenge even count if you didn't get to see your enemy's anguish?

It definitely counted as one of Mik's tasks, anyway, though they were in disagreement as to which. Zuzana said it was the third and last, because she was still counting his getting the air conditioner working back in Ouarzazate. He said that didn't count—not by a million miles, because it had been in his own self-interest, so that he could pounce on her—and he still had one task to go. Zuzana could only argue up to a point before it would begin to seem like she was begging him to just propose marriage already, so she let him have it his way. Besides, their hands were a little full right now: the sky still ominously empty, and her phone silent to match. They didn't know what they could or should attempt. With flight and fighting skills, could they help? What could they do that Akiva, Virko, and Karou couldn't? Zuzana didn't suppose you could wish for battle experience and strategic good sense. Could you?

And there was Eliza to think of, too. Even if they glutted themselves on wishes, gifting themselves superpowers willy-nilly and soaring off to save the day, they couldn't just leave her sitting here, could they?

Hey, wait.

Zuzana looked at Eliza, then at Mik. She perked an eyebrow. Mik looked at Eliza, too. "Well, yeah. Of course," he said at once.

And so, quickly, feeling the press of time and need, they formulated the best words they could think of for the mending of a young woman whose ailment was a mystery to them. In a reverent hush, Zuzana spoke them to the gavriel in her hand. It felt almost as though she were talking to Brimstone.

"I wish that Eliza Jones, born Elazael, will be granted full power over herself in mind and body, and be well." Something possessed her to add at the end, "May she be her best possible self," because it seemed, in that moment, to be the truest of all wishes—not a betrayal of self that came from coveting others, but a *deepening* of self. A ripening.

When a wish exceeds the power of the medallion it's made on, nothing happens. Like, if you held a scuppy and wished for a million dollars, the scuppy would just lie there. Mik and Zuzana didn't know if what they were asking was within the realm of a gavriel's power. So they watched Eliza closely for some small sign that it might be taking effect.

There was no small sign.

That is to say . . . the sign was not small.

Not even a little bit.

62

The Age of Wars

The word that Akiva spoke was *Haxaya*, and Jael might have had no notion what it meant, or even that it was a name, but the result was clear enough.

One second.

The air beside him was empty and then it wasn't, and the shape that filled it—a streak of fur and teeth—was in motion. He saw it and it hit him. Two halves of the same second. He was dragged swiftly backward.

Two seconds.

His soldiers were all before him. They only turned when he felt the steel against his flesh and gasped, and by the time their heads craned around, he was in the doorway on his knees, a blade to his throat and his attacker behind him, out of their reach.

A caterwaul went up. It matched the roil of outrage in Jael's head, but it wasn't coming from his own lips. He didn't dare scream, not with the press of the blade. It was the Fallen who screamed, writhing on the bed, still struggling with the girl.

Three seconds.

The blade bit. Jael thought his throat was slashed and he panicked, but he could still breathe. It stung—just a cut. "So sorry," came a voice—a feminine whisper close to his ear. The blade was sharp and she was not careful with it. Another sting, another cut, and a laugh from over his shoulder. Throaty, amused.

All that his men had had time to do was swing their heads around to stare. The space in between seconds was strung with their shock and clotted with Razgut's cries. "No no no!" The fallen thing's voice was dark with fury. "Kill them!" he raged. "Kill them!"

As though following his command, one of the soldiers made a move toward Jael, raising his sword toward the chimaera who held him. Her arm tightened around Jael. Her claws sank into his side, through his clothing and into his flesh, and her knife sank a little deeper, too.

"Stop!" he cried. To her, to his men. He was not pleased to hear that it sounded like a yelp. "Stand down!" And he was trying to think what to do—five seconds—but he had sent every soldier before him as a buffer and kept none behind. By pulling him into the doorway, his attacker gave herself the whole wall as barrier—and his body as barrier, too, and behind her there was nothing but an empty room. No one could get to her, and this was Jael's own fault, for hiding behind a wall of soldiers.

"How easily comes the blood," she said. Her voice was animal, guttural. "I think it wants to be free. Even your own blood despises you."

"Haxaya," said Akiva, warningly—and now Jael understood that the word was a name—"Our imperative was no blood."

It was too late for that. Jael's neck was slick with it. "He squirms," was Haxaya's response.

Razgut was still wailing. The girl was free of him now, standing at the bastard's side, the three of them abreast: human, seraph, beast, the three he'd been alerted to expect, and what of this fourth he hadn't looked for? How had it happened? *How?*

When Akiva spoke again it was to Jael, casually, as if picking up a dropped thread of conversation. "Other factors," he said, his voice damnably smooth and certain. Other factors may turn the tide, he had said a moment before. "Such as placing special value on one life above others. Your own, for example. If numbers were all that mattered, you could still win here. Not you personally. You would die. You would die *first*, but your men might take the day, if they decided not to care whether you lived." He paused, let his gaze move over them, as though they were entities capable of choice, and not mere soldiers. "Is that what you want?"

Who was he asking, him or them? The idea that they could answer, that *they* could choose *his* fate, appalled Jael. "No." He found himself spitting out the word in haste, before they might venture another response.

"You want to live," Akiva clarified.

Yes, he wanted to live. But it was unthinkable to Jael that his enemy would permit him to. "Don't play games with me, Beast's Bane. What do you want?"

"First," said Akiva. "I want your men to lay down their swords."

* * *

Karou had had enough of Razgut's purring chuckle and his sweating hand clenched around her wrist, and so at the moment that Akiva pronounced Haxaya's name, she dropped an elbow hard into the thing's eye socket and pivoted, using the instant of his sharp surprise to wrench free. Even so, she almost didn't break away. Sweat-slicked though it was, his grip had the crushing power of talons, and her skin, when she braced a foot against the bed frame and pulled with everything in her, came away gouged and bleeding. But it came away, blessedly, and she was free.

Razgut was holding his eye and screaming—"No no no!"—and the other eye was open and wild, rolling and malevolent, as Karou paced backward, away from him, drawing her moon blades now as she took up a position by Akiva's side. She on one side, Virko on the other, watching Haxaya subdue the monster Jael.

Haxaya, alive again, and—thanks to teeth pilfered from the Museo Civico di Zoologia—in her proper fox aspect, lithe and very fast.

She wasn't part of the plan. Not initially. Back in the caves, when the idea had first taken shape in Karou's mind, Haxaya's corpse—or Ten's corpse, most recently vacated by Haxaya's soul—had been its inspiration, but Karou had not in any way intended her to play a part in its fulfillment. She had gleaned the soldier's soul with the thought to decide later what to do with it. The thurible was a small one, and she'd hooked it to her belt and forgotten to place it with the others before leaving the caves. Serendipity? Fate? Who knew.

Whichever it was, it was how, earlier this evening, after getting an unsettling vibe from Esther, Karou had thought to give the fox chimaera a chance to redeem herself.

They had hoped not to need a shadow soldier here. They had hoped, even as they slipped through the window, fracturing the moonspill not three times but four, that the plan might play out its simplest variant. It hadn't.

But they weren't so stupid as to have come unprepared.

"Can we trust her?" the three of them had asked themselves. As Haxaya's was the only soul in their keeping, she was the only candidate for the job.

"It was personal," Akiva had repeated Liraz's words. The Battle of Savvath, and whatever Liraz had done there to take such vicious vengeance in her stride. When it came down to it, they thought that Haxaya would be able to appreciate the gravity of the mission they were on now, and the stakes, and play her part. And so, it seemed, she was—with the exception of scorning the no-blood imperative, though perhaps that was well played. Jael was white and wide-eyed, and his voice shook as he issued the command to his soldiers to lay down their swords.

"Back up," Akiva instructed them, and they did, parting warily to draw back against the walls of the chamber. It was hard to think of them as individuals, as mindful creatures with souls. Karou made herself look at their faces in turn, to try to see them as *real*, as citizens of her world who had been made and trained into what they were now and who might—if Akiva could, if Liraz could—*un*make themselves, *un*train themselves.

She couldn't see it. Not yet. But she could hope.

Not for Jael. He could be no part of the future they were building. Akiva advanced toward him. Karou, blades drawn, guarded his right side, and Virko his left. They were nearly finished here.

"Listen to me," Akiva told the soldiers. "The age of wars is over. For those who return and shed no more blood, there will be amnesty." He spoke as though he had the power to make such promises, and, listening, even knowing the full bleakness of their own uncertainty, Karou believed in him. Did the Dominion? She couldn't tell. They were silent by training, and Jael was silenced by Haxaya's knife. Razgut alone was unsilent.

"The age of wars?" he parroted. He was at the edge of the bed, one useless leg dangling over the side, a limp curl of a thing. The eye that Karou had sunk her elbow into was swelling shut, but the other was still incongruously fine, almost pretty. There was madness in it, though. So very black. "And who are *you* to end an age?" he growled. "Were *you* chosen of all your people? Did you kneel before the magi and open your *anima* to their sharp fingers? Have *you* drowned stars like they were babies in a bath? *I* ended the First Age, and I'll end the second, too."

And with that, he hefted a knife none had seen, and hurled it at Akiva. No one moved. Not in time.

Not Karou, whose hand flew out too late, as though she might catch the knife out of the air or at least deflect it, but it had already passed her by.

Not Virko, who stood on Akiva's other side.

And not Akiva. Not a hairsbreadth.

And Razgut's aim was true.

The blade. What Karou saw was peripheral. If her hand couldn't catch the blade, her head couldn't turn fast enough to see it enter Akiva's heart. His heart that she had pressed palm and cheek to, but not yet her own heart, not her own chest to his, or her lips to his, or her life to his, not yet. The heart that moved his blood, and that was the other half of her own. She saw from the corner of her eye, and it was enough. She *saw.*

The blade entered Akiva's heart.

63

At the Edge of a Knife

Ice and ending. The instant froze, impossible. Unthinkable. True.

Your entire being can become a scream. At the edge of a hurled knife, that fast. Karou's did. She wasn't flesh and blood in that instant but only air rushing in to gather for a scream that might never end.

64

Persuasion

An angel lay dying in the mist. Once upon a time.

And the devil should have finished him off without a second thought.

But she hadn't. And if she had? Karou had wondered it a hundred different ways. She'd even wished for it, in her blackest grief at the kasbah, when all she could see was the death that had come of her mercy.

If she'd killed Akiva that day, or even just let him die, the war would have ground on unbroken. Another thousand years? Maybe. But she hadn't, and it hadn't. "The age of wars is over," Akiva had just said, and even as Karou saw what she saw and no possibility of mistake, and even as her whole being gathered itself into a scream, her heart defied it. The age of wars was over, and Akiva would not die like this.

The blade entered his heart.

But Karou's scream was never born. Another took its place, but first: a sound. A fraction of an instant after the knife sunk into Akiva's chest . . . a *thunk*. It wasn't a flesh sound. Karou's head completed its turn and her gaze scribbled a wild pattern, taking in what she saw.

There stood Akiva, unmoved.

No stagger step, no blood, and no knife hilt protruding from his heart. Frantic, Karou blinked, and she wasn't the only one, though none could experience the same despair she had felt an instant earlier or the joy that overtook her now when she spotted the blade, sunk into the wall beyond Akiva. None could know quite the same flavor of wonder as she did, either, as the truth took shape, but everyone in the chamber tasted some version of it.

Haxaya spoke first. "Invisible to death," she murmured, because there was no mistaking what had just happened. Akiva hadn't moved, and the trajectory didn't lie.

The knife had passed through him.

It was Karou's gaze he held in that moment, and she saw that he was half-stunned, half-haunted. She wanted to ask him: Had he done this? He must have. No one knew, not even he, what he was capable of.

Razgut had collapsed, wailing and beating his fists to his own brow. Two strides and Karou was to him, yanking him to the floor, checking the bedclothes for more weapons. The Fallen didn't even seem to register her presence.

The Dominion looked wary but wonderstruck, too, in the presence of Akiva, and Karou didn't think she needed to worry about any strikes coming from them now. She didn't relax, though. Akiva's life had flashed through her peripheral vision in a streak. She was ready to be out of here, and all that remained was persuasion. Her plan, in all its simplicity.

At last they came to it.

Once more, Akiva faced his uncle. Jael was quiet, his face pinched and pale as his horrendous mouth quivered. In the face of such power, he had lost even the courage to sneer.

Akiva had never even drawn his swords, and so his hands were free. He reached toward his uncle now and laid one flat upon his chest. The gesture looked almost friendly, and Jael's eyes were swiveling in their sockets again, trying to grasp what was happening to him. It didn't take long.

Karou watched Akiva's hand, and she remembered the moment, in Paris, when she had come to Brimstone's doorway, out of sorts from dragging elephant tusks across the city, and had seen, for the first time, a handprint scorched into the wood. When she'd traced it with her finger, ash had flaked and fallen. And she remembered Kishmish charred and dying in her hands, his heartbeat slowing from panic into death, and how the wail of fire sirens had peeled her out of her grief—out of that grief and into a greater one, as she had raced from her apartment and through the streets to Brimstone's door to find it engulfed in flame. Blue fire, infernal, and in its nimbus, the silhouette of wings.

All around the world, at the same moment precisely, dozens of doors, all marked with black handprints, had been devoured by the same unnatural fire.

Akiva had done it. All seraphim were creatures of fire, but igniting the marks from afar was a working of his own, and had made it possible for him to destroy every last one of Brimstone's doorways in an instant, cutting his enemy off without warning.

When Karou had seen the blistered skin on Ten's corpse back at the Kirin caves, the mark of Liraz's hand scorched clearly into her chest, this had been her thought.

Smoke effused from beneath Akiva's palm. Jael likely smelled it before he felt the heat eating through his clothing, though perhaps not, as he wore not armor but the pageant robes he'd dreamt up to awe humanity. Whatever it was, the heat or the smoke, Karou saw the understanding light his eyes, and the panic as he struggled to get out from under that pressing hand. She hoped Haxaya wouldn't slit his throat by accident.

His scream was a wavering wail, and Karou watched him as Akiva stepped back. There it was: burned into Jael's chest, reeking and charred, the black already peeling away to reveal the raw meat beneath. A handprint in flesh.

Persuasion.

"Go home," said Akiva. "Or I will ignite it. Wherever you are, wherever I am. It doesn't matter. Unless you do as I say, I will burn you to nothing. There won't even be ash to show where you stood."

Haxaya let Jael go and stepped aside. Her knife wasn't needed any longer, and she wiped the blade clean on the emperor's own white sleeve. He slumped as if his legs couldn't hold him, pain and rage and impotence congealing on his countenance. He seemed to be grappling with his situation, trying to understand all that he had lost. "And what then?" he finally burst out. "When I'm back in Eretz wearing your mark? You'll just burn me then. Why should I do what you want now?"

Akiva's voice was steady. "I give you my word. Do this. Go home now. Take your army with you and nothing else. Make no chaos. Just go, and I will never ignite the mark. I promise you that."

Jael gave a disbelieving snort. "You promise. You'll let me live, just like that."

Karou watched Akiva as he made his reply. He'd kept calm from the first moment Jael burst into the room, and had managed to conceal the depths of hatred this man stoked in him. "That's not what I said."

Was he thinking of Hazael? Of Festival? Of a future they were in the process, even now, of averting, when guns would have reshaped Eretz into something even more brutal than its citizens had yet known?

"I won't *burn* you." He let his opinion of his uncle show on his face. "That's my only promise, and it doesn't mean you get to live." He let his uncle's foul imagination do the work. "Maybe you'll have a chance." A thin smile. "Maybe you'll see me coming." He leaned into the silence and let it lengthen, and then, just like that, he vanished. "But probably not."

Karou followed his lead and vanished, too. Virko and Haxaya an instant later, as Akiva threw his glamour over the pair of them. Jael and the Dominion saw shadows move toward the window and then those were gone and there was nothing left here but a broken emperor's raw breathing, a mad monster's ragged sobbing, and two score soldiers standing quiet, not knowing quite what to do with themselves.

65

Chosen

He was one of twelve in the Long Ago, and glory had been his.

* * *

She was chosen one of twelve. *Oh, glory.*

* * *

Out of thousands did they rise, candidates come from every reach of the realm, young and full of hope, full of pride, full of dreams. So beautiful they were, all of them, and strong and of every hue from palest pearl to blackest jet, and reds and creams and browns and even—from the Usko Remarroth, where it was ever twilight—*blue*. This was what seraphim were then: a world's richest offering, as jewels shaken out on a tapestry. Some came clad in feathers and others in silk, some in dark metals and some in skins, and they wore gold, and they wore ink, and their hair was braids or it was curls, it was golden, black, or green, or it was scraped to the scalp in a pattern of flame.

Razgut would not have been noted in the throng—not for his garb, which was fine but plain, or his color, which had never seemed drab to him until that day. Mid-beige, he was, and his hair and eyes were brown. He was beautiful, too, then, but they all were, and none more striking than Elazael.

She was out of Chavisaery, whence the darkest tribes of seraphim hailed. Skin as black as a raven's wing at the umbra of eclipse, and her hair was featherine, the soft rose of sunrise, and falling in pale shoals about her dark shoulders. A white stripe painted on each cheek, a dot above each eye, and her eyes themselves: They were brown, not black, lighter than the rest of her and startling. And the whites. There never fell a purer snow than the whites of Elazael's eyes.

Every tribe had sent their best.

All but one. One hue was absent from that crowd: There were no fire eyes in that massing of their world's brightest youth. The Stelians alone opposed this choosing and all it meant, but no one cared. Not then. That day they were forgotten, dismissed. Even shunned.

Later, that would change.

Oh godstars, would it change.

Only the magi knew what they were looking for, and they didn't tell. They tested, and the tests were arcane, and every day saw fewer candidates remaining—hope, pride, and dreams, sent back where they came from, no glory for them—but some lasted. Day by day, they rose while others fell, until they were twelve before the magi, and the magi, at last, smiled.

That day the twelve bid farewell to the lives they had known and became Faerers, the first and only. They were halved to two sixes, two teams for two journeys. They went into training to prepare for what lay ahead, and who they were at the end was not who they had been. Things were...done to them. To their *anima*—the incorporeal selves that are the true totality for which bodies were only as icons fixed in space. The magi were always striving and delving, and of the Faerers they shaped something new. It was fitting, for their work was new, and it was great.

The Faerers were chosen to be explorers, the lightbearers of their people, to voyage through all the strata of the Continuum that was the great *All*. The Magus Regent of the College of Cosmology had explained it to them:

"The universes lie one upon the next as the pages of a book. But in the Continuum, every page is infinite, and the book has no end." That was to say, each "page" extended infinitely along the plane of its existence. One could never hope to come to a universe's edge. They had none. An explorer traveling along a plane would fly forever and find nothing to come up against. Planets and stars, yes, worlds and vacuum, on and on and no boundary at all. Nothing to *cross*.

It was necessary to push *through*. Not along the plane, but right into it. Like the nib of a pen jammed right through the page to write itself onto the next. The magi had learned how to do it, after thousands of years of study, and such was to be the work of the Faerers: to press through, and write themselves and their race onto each new world as they met it.

One Six in one direction, the other in the opposite. For the rest of their lives the distance between the teams would grow—to the greatest distance, no less, that had ever been achieved between members of their race or any other. This was the pinnacle of achievement of a very, *very* old world: no less than to map the totality of the great All and stitch the fullness of the Continuum together with their light. To open doors and go, and go, universe to universe to universe. To know them, and by knowing, in some fashion *claim* them.

Each Six would be everything to one another—companions and family, defenders and friends, and lovers, too. They were charged, in addition to their prime directive, to bear heirs to their knowledge. They were three and three, men and women, and that was how the magi had framed the directive: not to beget "children" but "heirs to their knowledge."

They were to be the birth of a tribe, something more than their people had ever been before. Elazael and Razgut were of the same Six, with Iaoth and Dvira, Kleos and Arieth, and their direction was set. Another night of blazing light to draw the eyes of the godstars to them. For the glory of all seraphim, this great deed before them, a spreading of wings that would never be forgotten, a departure that would echo through time, and then one day unimaginable, so far was it in the future, they or their descendants would come back home. To Meliz.

Meliz, first and last, Meliz eternal. The home world of the seraphim.

They would be remembered forever. Venerated. Heroes of their people, the openers of doors, the lights in the darkness. All would be glory.

Oh, spite. Oh, misery. Laughter that gnaws like a bellyful of teeth. That wasn't what happened. No, and no, and no, and no forever.

The Cataclysm happened.

* * *

It was the dream, simply and purely and terribly.

Watch the sky.

Will it happen?

It can't. It mustn't.

It did.

Not every stratum of the Continuum was fit to be opened, and not every world in the infinite layering was hospitable to light, as the Faerers learned, to their very great despair.

There was darkness unspeakable, and monsters vast as worlds swam in it.

They let them in. Razgut and Elazael, Iaoth and Dvira, Kleos and Arieth. They didn't mean to. It wasn't their fault.

Except that of course it was their fault. They cut the portal, one too far.

But how were they to have known?

The Stelians warned them.

But how were they to have known to listen to the Stelians? They were too busy being chosen, oh, glory.

Oh, misery.

And how many portals had they cut by then? How many worlds had they "stitched together with their light"? How many laid open to the Beasts and left unprotected as they wheeled and fled, again and again? They sealed the portals as they raced back toward Meliz in panic and despair. Each portal in turn they closed behind them and then watched the Beasts sunder it and keep coming. They couldn't hold them out. They hadn't been taught how to do that, and so, world by world, page by page in the book that was the great All: darkness. Devouring.

Nothing worse had ever been done, by accident or design, in all of time, in all of space, and the guilt was theirs.

And finally there were no worlds left between the Cataclysm and Meliz. Meliz first and last, Meliz eternal. The Faerers came home, and the Beasts came behind them.

And devoured it.

66

So Much More Than Saved

Eliza woke from the dream to find herself still dreaming. She'd been very deep, she was aware, and supposed she must be emerging through *layers* of dreams, like climbing up out of the earth, out of one of those open-pit mines that are like hell made real, and each level bringing her nearer to waking.

It had to be a dream, though, if only because it defied reality.

She was sitting on a step. Real enough, so far. A girl was beside her: small but not a child. A teenager, doll-pretty and wide-eyed. Staring at her.

With an audible gulp, the girl swallowed, and said, in hesitant, accented English, "Um. I'm sorry? Or... you're welcome? Whichever one seems... appropriate... to you?"

"I'm sorry?" said Eliza. She meant it in the vein of: *What?* What did the girl mean? But she seemed to take it as an answer to her question.

"Sorry, then," she said, deflating. Her eyes were held wide and unblinking. Eliza shifted a glance to the young man by her side. Matching wonder in his eyes, she saw. "We didn't mean to," he said. "We didn't know . . . *that* . . . was going to happen. They just . . . grew."

The wings, he meant: dream wings growing from Eliza's dream shoulders. Awakening—if you could call the passage from one dream to the next awakening, which she supposed you really couldn't, much as it felt like it—she had been aware of the change in herself, without visual confirmation or even surprise, as is the way with dreams. She turned her head now to see what it was she already knew.

Wings of living fire. She shifted her shoulders, feeling the play of new muscles there as the wings responded, flexing and dropping a pretty rain of sparks. They were the most beautiful things Eliza had ever seen, and awe bloomed in her.

This was a much better dream than she was used to.

"Sorry about your shirt," said the girl.

At first Eliza didn't know what she meant, but then she realized it hung loose and tattered, as though the wings had torn it when they grew. It hardly seemed consequential, except for one thing. It was an unexpected detail, for a dream.

"How do you feel?" asked the young man, solicitous. "Are you . . . back?"

Back? Back where, or . . . back *from* where? Eliza realized she had no idea where she was. What was the last thing she remembered? Being in a car in Morocco, in disgrace.

She looked around now and beheld a twist in a narrow alley that could almost have been a stage set. Cobblestones and marble, iconic red geraniums lined up on a window ledge. Laundry lines roped overhead. Everything said "Italy" as clearly as Eliza's glimpse of desert out the airplane window had said, "*not* Italy." An old man in suspenders even leaned heavily on his cane, frozen as still as a cardboard cutout, staring at her.

It was like a tingling, at first, the presentiment that this was not a dream. The old man's cane had duct tape wrapped around the handle. One of the geranium plants was dead, and there was litter, and noise. Tinny horns just out of sight, a brief canine quarrel, and some kind of muffled drone lying over it all: a hive sound of many distant voices. The blares and dents of the world, intruding in a dream? That was when Eliza began to understand.

But to understand her situation truly, she had to listen inward.

The sensation of stirring within her had gone still. The things known and buried, they weren't trying to dig themselves out anymore. It took her a moment to understand why, and it was so simple. They were no longer buried.

They were known.

Eliza understood what she was. This realization was the mental equivalent of a slow-motion clip played in reverse: A great mess lifts itself off the floor and flies upward to arrange itself on a tabletop. Tea unpuddles and siphons itself into cups midair to land neatly on a tray. Books leap from a jumble, flapping their covers like wings, and rise to roost in a stack.

Sense out of madness.

It was all there, and it was still terrible—*and terrible and terrible*—but it was quiet now, and it was hers. She was saved.

"What did you do to me?" she asked.

"I don't know," said the girl, worried. "We didn't know what was wrong with you, so we just made this broad kind of wish in the hope that the magic would know what to do."

Magic? Wish?

"I know what was wrong with me," Eliza said, realizing it was true. There was an explanation for the things known and buried, and it was *not* that she was an incarnation of the angel Elazael.

Elation and devastation fused to become a new emotion, unnameable, and she didn't know how to react to it. She knew what had been wrong with her, and it was not the thing she'd most feared. "It wasn't me," she said aloud, and this was the elation. The guilt from the dream was not, and never had been, and never would be, her own.

But the Cataclysm was real. She understood it fully now, and this was the devastation.

Her hands went to her head, holding it, and it felt familiar under her fingers—*I'm me, Eliza*—but on the inside, it, and she, encompassed a vast new territory.

The young man and woman were watching her with furrowed brows, probably wondering if she was crazier now than she'd been before. She wasn't. She knew this absolutely. Her brain, her body, her wings felt as finely calibrated as one of nature's perfect creations. A double helix. A galaxy. A honeycomb. Entities so improbable and uncanny that they made you dream that Creation had a will and a wild intelligence.

It didn't.

It wasn't that she understood. No one ever could. But... she knew the source.

Of everything.

It was among the things known and no longer buried, all of them part of her now, orderly and intertwined, and it was so beautiful she wanted to worship it, even though she knew it had no consciousness. It would make about as much sense as worshiping the wind. She saw that magic and science were heads and tails of the same bright coin.

And she beheld Time itself laid open before her, unzipped like a strand of DNA. Knowable. Possibly even navigable.

Her mind trembled at the brink of this new vastness. She was saved, she had thought, moments ago. She saw now that she was more than saved. So much more than saved.

"So," she said, trying not to cry as she fixed her saviors with all the warmth her eyes could bestow. "Who *are* you guys?"

67

A Spray of Sparks

Karou followed Akiva away from the Papal Palace, and they were glamoured, so when she came to him it was clumsy. But only for the first surprised seconds.

She didn't even mean to do it. Well, it's not that it was an accident. They didn't stumble against each other with their faces. It was only that her body didn't run it by her brain first.

She knew where he was by heat and airflow, and she meant to follow him to the cupola of St. Peter's. From there, the four of them planned to watch Jael's exodus and escort the Dominion army unseen all the way back to Uzbekistan, and through to Eretz.

But a part of Karou was still poised at the edge of that hurled knife, hearing the scream she had almost become. She couldn't *see* Akiva, to reassure herself that he was well, and so she couldn't catch her breath. They had no victory to celebrate yet except for being alive, and that was all she could bring herself to care about in the moment it took her to catch up to him. They were over the plaza,

Michelangelo's colonnades curving beneath them like outstretched arms.

Karou reached for where Akiva's shoulder might be and got wing instead. A spray of sparks, and he turned into her touch, startled by it, so she careened into him and he caught her against him, and that was all it took.

Magnets collide, and swiftly align.

Her hands found his face, and her lips followed. She was clumsy, showering kisses of thanks on his invisible face. She was overwhelmed, and her lips landed where they would—on his brow, then his cheekbone, then the bridge of his nose—and in the profound relief of the moment she barely registered the sensation of his skin against hers: the heat and texture—at last—of Akiva against her lips.

She dropped one hand to his heart to be sure it hadn't been some illusion, that he was truly whole and uninjured, and he was, and so her palm, satisfied, joined her other in slipping to where his neck met his jaw to hold his face steady and gauge the location of his lips.

He didn't wait for her to find them.

A beat of his wings and he surged through the air with such force that she was melded to him more completely even than when they had embraced in the shower, and her face was not against his chest this time, nor her feet planted on the floor.

Her legs twined with his. She smoothed her hands up his neck and into his hair and held his head as she was swept away with him, spiraling.

Finally. Finally, they kissed.

Akiva's mouth was hungry and sweet and rich and slow and hot, and the kiss was long and deep and every other measure of scope there was except for infinite. It wasn't that. A kiss must end for another to begin, and it did, and did again.

Kiss gave way to kiss, and in the eyes-closed, all-consuming world of their embrace, Karou had the sensation that each kiss encompassed the last. It was hallucinatory: Kiss within kiss within kiss, going deeper and deeper and sweeter and hotter and headier, and she hoped that Akiva's equilibrium was guiding them because she'd lost all sense of her own. There was no up or down; there were only mouths, and hips, and hands—

—and *now* she registered the heat and texture of him. The smoothness, the roughness, the realness.

A kiss while flying, invisible, above St. Peter's Square. It sounded like a fantasy but felt so very, very real.

And then a shared smile was shaping their mouths, and laughter came between them. They were breathless with relief—and with simple oxygen deprivation, too, because who had time to inhale? They rested their foreheads together, and the tips of their noses, and paused to let it all sink in. The kiss, their breath, and all that they'd just done.

Human soldiers patrolled beneath them, wondering at a sudden gust of sparks, and Karou and Akiva spun there in the air, held aloft by magic and languid wingbeats, and held together by a pull they'd felt from the very moment of first meeting, on a battlefield long ago.

Karou touched Akiva's heart again, reassuring herself. "How did you do that?" she asked quietly, her head still spinning from the kiss. "Back there."

"I don't know. I never know. It just comes."

"The knife passed right through you. Did you feel it?" She wished she could see him, but since she couldn't, she kept a hand on his face and her forehead to his.

She felt his nod, and his breath brushed her lips when he spoke. "I did and didn't. I can't explain it. I was there and not there. I saw it hit me and keep going."

She was silent for a moment, processing this. "Is it true, then, what Jael said? That you're... invisible to death? I don't have to worry about you ever dying?"

"I don't think that's true." He traced the contours of her face with his lips, as though he could see her like that. "But you would have resurrected me in any case."

Is that what would have happened, if Akiva had died? Or would they have lost control of the situation and all been overpowered? Karou didn't even want to think about it. "Sure," she said with false lightness. "But let's not be casual about this body, okay?" She nuzzled him back. "It may be your soul that I love, but I'm pretty keen on its vessel, too."

Her voice had dropped lower as she spoke, and his response was low and husky in kind. "I can't say I'm sorry to hear that," he said, and brushed his face past hers to kiss a place beneath her ear, sending instant, electric frissons coursing through her body.

She gave a faint murmur of surprise that sounded like the *Oh* in *Oh my*, but without the *my*, and then she saw, over Akiva's shoulder, the ascension of the first ranks of Dominion from the Papal Palace, as Jael's army returned to the sky.

68

Fallen

"It wasn't our fault!" Razgut had screamed when the Faerers were sentenced, but this was a lie. It *was* their fault, and this knowledge made a dimension of grief and guilt in their bodies and minds that supplanted everything else they had ever been or contained.

Home to Meliz, mindless with panic. Raise the alarm. The Six were only four now. Iaoth and Dvira had turned back to fight the Cataclysm and been devoured.

Back to the capital and cry out: *Beasts are coming! Flee! Beasts are coming!*

Some made it out, through a back door, as it were. The worlds were layered, like a stack of pages. The Beasts came from one direction, laying waste to everything in their path. Those who could fled in the other direction, to the neighbor world the other side: Eretz. There was no time to organize an evacuation. Some thousands out of millions made it out. Not even ten thousand, not even as many as that. All the rest were left behind.

The many, the colors. The jewels shaken out on a tapestry. A world's richest offering. Lost.

Many made it all the way to the portal only to be denied. It was small, the cut. Two or three at a time might squeeze through; it was slow, and the Beasts were coming. Screams from on the other side, they echoed in Razgut's ears to this day as the scream of a whole dying world. He remembered how abruptly it had cut to silence, and how some of the last to make it through were still reaching back for loved ones trapped on the other side.

So the portal was closed, but this the Faerers had done dozens of times in their retreat, and it had never held the Beasts out yet. Once wounded, the skin between the worlds never fully healed. It would have failed again, and the Cataclysm would have taken Eretz, too, and then Earth, and every world after, through each portal cut by the second Six, however far they'd voyaged.

But the Stelians were among those who made it out of Meliz, and they were ready. They had always opposed the Faering, and in the years since the Faerers' departure, they had prepared themselves to do what no one else could or would: mend the skin, the veil, the membrane, the energy, the layers of the great All. They closed the portal and kept it closed, and Eretz was saved, and Earth, and all the rest.

It was the Stelians who had saved them.

As for the Faerers: damnation, infamy. And obliteration.

They heard, from their prison cell, what was done to the memories of the survivors. The magi hadn't learned not to meddle. They stole from each seraph the past, not just the Cataclysm but Meliz, too, so that their people could begin a new life. So that the people, Razgut understood, wouldn't wake up one morning and realize where the blame truly lay: with the magi who had dreamt up the Faering in the first place, and had chosen the best of their young folk to see it through. They shared the blame. But not the punishment. Oh no, not they.

Iaoth and Dvira were the lucky ones: swiftly eaten, swiftly dead.

As for the rest, their wings were wrenched off. That was the first thing. Not cut. Not sliced. Pulled. Splintering bone, oh pain, oh pain like nothing they had ever dreamt. Razgut saw the other three maimed alongside him, heavy hands laid to the joints of their beautiful wings, twisting, and their faces twisting, their agony unbearable, and he felt it all. They all did, because of what they were, and what had been done to them. They were linked. What each felt, all felt, oh godstars. And the sum of all their pain, it was too much.

And that wasn't even the worst of it. Imagine. This was only the salt in the wound of their true punishment, which was exile.

And even *that* they might have borne, and made some crippled kind of life in their prison world, Earth, but oh, spite. Oh, misery.

They parted them. Four they were, and there were four portals, too, by ill luck or cruel planning, and they dragged them from one another to the far corners of Eretz, and threw them out. Alone. Wingless. Legs stomped to pulps. They pitched them into another world, four broken creatures, to fall from the skies and shatter against the alien landscapes there, and not even together.

Razgut they carried out over the Bay of Beasts, and it was a beautiful day and the water was green, and there wasn't a cloud in the sky. A beautiful day for agony, and they carried him by his armpits to the edge of that ragged, flapping cut in the sky, and they heaved him through, and he fell.

And fell. And fell.

And didn't die, because of what he was: He was what the tests had proven that long-ago day of glory, and what they had made of him after. He was a Faerer, and he was strong beyond strong, too strong to die of *falling*, and so he lived, if you could call it that, and he never found the others in the world of their exile, though he felt their pain—and their grief and their guilt, fourfold—until it all began to fall away. Across the years he knew it when they died, each in turn. Not how or where, but which, yes, and they who had been part of him were taken, finally and fully—Kleos, Arieth, Elazael, gone one after another—and he was truly alone. He was a small thing adrift in a great absence. He lived with a crack in his mind, a thousand years in exile.

And oh, spite. Oh, misery. He lived still.

* * *

Esther Van de Vloet may have lost possession—temporarily—of her wishes, but her money and influence were untouched, and she didn't lie despairing on the bathroom floor for long. She made phone calls, went online to find photographs of the miscreants—they made it so easy, idiot youth, no sense of privacy—and e-mailed them not to the police, who had their hands full these days keeping hell from breaking loose, but to a private firm who knew her reputation well enough to be at once pleased and dismayed to hear from her.

"They're in Rome," she said. "Find them. Payment will be twofold. First, a million euros. I imagine that will suffice?" Of course it would, they assured her, not *more* pleased by the obscene sum but *less*, sensing, surely, what must come next. "Second," said Esther, "succeed and I won't destroy you."

After that, she paced. Waiting was for soldiers' wives, and she abhorred it. Traveller and Methuselah kept out of her way, bewildered and miserable. The drapes were still yanked wide, not because Esther had any care for the sky, but because they'd been left that way. Her pacing carried her past the windows, but she didn't turn her head. She felt fluorescent with rage. She had been robbed, violated. She had no sense of irony or just desserts. Only tremulous, vision-narrowing, warpath fury.

God knows how many turns she took, pacing past the window, before she finally noticed the change in the sky, and her night went from bad to oh so very very bad.

The angels had risen.

Cries spread through the streets below. Esther wrenched open the glass doors and rushed onto the balcony. "*No.*" She felt her voice in her gut, moanlike, and pulled it up and out, unreeling it in strips, moan by moan, each one the same simple word—"*No. No. No.*"—flayed from her like meat and pulled out raw.

The angels were leaving?

What about *her*? What about their deal? She had given them Karou, and promised so much more—everything they'd need to conquer the world beyond that veil of sky. Arms, ammunition, technology, even personnel. And what had she asked in return?

Not much. Only mining rights. To an entire world. An entire undeveloped world with a slave population already in place, and an army to guard her interests. Esther had made certain that she had no competition, that no other offers reached the angels, and no bribes topped her own. It was the single greatest negotiating coup of all time. Or, it had been, and Esther Van de Vloet had to watch, trembling and speechless, as wings carried it away.

"Not much," Karou had said, evasive. "Just persuade them to go home."

And so, it seemed, they had.

They were gone, and the sky was empty again. Esther fumbled on the TV and watched the helicopter's-eye view along with the rest of the world as the "heavenly host" retraced the journey it had made from Uzbekistan three days earlier.

"The Visitors appear to be leaving," announced the more cool-headed pundits, though it could not be said that cool heads prevailed on this day. "They're abandoning us!" was the more common refrain. It was a turn of events that called for blame. At the angels' first appearance in the sky, the crowds at the Vatican perimeter left off chanting and began to cheer and cry out in ecstasy. But when the phalanxes re-formed and began to move off, cheers turned to wails, and the lamentation began.

The Pope could not be reached for comment.

By the time Esther's phone rang, she had gone far beyond fury to a bright white echoing place that might have been the waiting room to madness. To have come so close to greatness and have it snatched away... But the sound of the ring was like fingers snapping in front of her eyes.

"Yes, what? Hello?" she answered, disoriented. She couldn't have said who she expected it to be. The agency she'd hired to track down the wish thieves would probably have been her guess, and her best hope. The angels had flown. Esther had lost, somehow, and she was not such a fool as to imagine she would get another chance at a power play like this. So when it was Spivetti on the line—the steward who had, at Cardinal Schotte's behest, been doing her bidding inside the Papal Palace—a flare of hope went up in her. Of *salvation.*

"What is it?" she demanded. "What's happened, Spivetti? Why did they go?"

"I don't know, ma'am," he said. He sounded shaken. "But they've left something behind."

"Well?" she demanded. "What is it?"

"I... I don't know," said Spivetti. The man was beside himself, and might have given some rudimentary description had Esther demanded it, but she did not. In her greed, she was already hurtling down the long hallway.

It took her hours to get into the Vatican, through the pulsing, stinking, wailing crowd and the military checkpoints. Hours and dozens of phone calls, favors cashed in and favors promised, and when she finally arrived, disheveled and wild-eyed, she mistook Spivetti's look of horror for a reaction to the sight of her, when in fact it had predated her by some hours, and would linger long after she had gone.

"Take me there," she barked.

And that was how Esther Van de Vloet came at last into Jael's chamber and approached the grand, carved bed. It was dim. Her eyes were scanning for a casket of treasure, maybe, some object of wealth. A message even, a map. She didn't sense the presence until she was practically on top of it, and by then it was too late. The shadows reached for her and they were arms. Spindly and as tough as rawhide, they eased around her, almost caressing. Like a lover settling a shawl down over her shoulders. That thought came and went. The arms tightened and flushed from shadow to flesh, so that Esther Van de Vloet saw, for the first time, the thing that was going to be her companion to the end of her days.

It was both promise and threat when he said to her, in a coarse, chuckling mewl: "You'll never be lonely again."

ARRIVAL + 72 HOURS

69

Don't Let the Sky-Flap Thingy Hit You on the Way Out

On the twelfth of August at 9:12 GMT, a thousand angels vanished through a cut in the sky.

There had been no witnesses to their arrival. Heavenscapes of cumulus clouds had been imagined, rays of light escaping aslant, like a picture from a Sunday school workbook. The truth was less impressive. One by one through a flap. There was almost a livestock quality to it. Sheep to the shearing, cows to the slaughter, on you go. At a rate of approximately six seconds per soldier, it took more than two hours, and this was plenty of time for a cadre of helicopters to amass behind them.

In keeping with their established inability to decide on a course of action regarding the angels, the leaders of the world balked at attempting to send a mission through behind them. *What message would this send? What diplomatic consequences might there be? Whose ass was on the line?*

It took a billionaire independent adventurer to attempt it. Piloting his own state-of-the-art helicopter, he hesitated just long enough to line his craft up with the cut, keeping a fixed visual the whole time. He had begun acceleration when the fire flared.

Fire in the sky.

He kicked aside just in time and had a front-row view of the burn: fast and bright and over, and with it, his chance at his fourth world record. First manned mission to . . . heaven? Who knew?

No one. And now they never would.

* * *

Zuzana, Mik, and Eliza watched the fire in the sky on the TV in a corner bar in Rome, and toasted success with prosecco.

"What do you want to bet Esther never drank that champagne she ordered?" Mik gloated, taking a deep swill of bubbly.

After all their worry and Evil Esther's fell contrivances, Karou, Akiva, and Virko had pulled it off. The angels were out, and they had definitely not been carrying guns.

"In your *face*, fake grandma," Zuzana crowed, but her triumph was chased by sorrow. The portal was closed, and a violin case full of wishes wouldn't get her back to Eretz, where anything could still be happening. There was nothing to do now but keep worrying, and possibly mope.

"What do you want to do?" she asked Mik. "Go home?"

He blew out a breath. "I guess. See our families. Plus, a certain giant, wicked marionette is probably very lonely."

Zuzana scoffed. "He can stay lonely. My ballerina days are over."

"Well. You could make him a wife at least, so he can enjoy his retirement."

At Mik's mention of the word *wife*, something inside Zuzana fizzed. She smothered it with a scowl.

Eliza looked at them, perplexed. "You're going back to Prague?"

Zuzana shrugged, ready to sink into a good, slumpy self-pity jag. *Maybe I'll even cry*, she thought. "What are you going to do?"

"I can tell you what I'm *not* going to do," she said. Her wings were glamoured, which she'd somehow figured out how to do on her own, and her torn shirt didn't even look that weird. It could practically have been fashion. "I'm not going to finish my dissertation. Sorry, *Danaus plexippus*."

"Who?" asked Mik.

Eliza smiled. "Monarch butterfly. That's what I research." She paused, corrected herself. "Researched. I can't go back to that life, not now, as much as I yearn to demolish Morgan Toth with the most excruciating forehead smack of all time. What I want to do?" She looked at them intently, her eyes so big and bright. "Is go to Eretz."

Zuzana and Mik just looked at her. Zuzana cut a significant glance at the TV screen, where they'd all just watched the portal burn.

Eliza, cottoning to this nonverbal language, raised eyebrows and shoulders in a fully committed *Yeah, so?*

Mik released an even breath. Zuzana scarcely dared to hope, but when Eliza started talking again, it wasn't about Eretz.

"Did you know, monarch butterflies migrate five thousand miles, round-trip, every year? No other insect does anything like it. And the most amazing thing about it is that the migration is multigenerational. The ones who return north aren't the same ones that went south the year before. They're several life cycles removed, but somehow they retrace the route."

She was silent for a moment, a weird little smile playing at her lips, like she couldn't tell if something was funny or not. Honestly, Zuzana didn't know what to make of Eliza now that she was non-vegetal. It wasn't just that she was coherent. She was ... more than human, somehow. It wasn't just the wings, either. You could feel it coming off her: this energy, unknowable and crackling. What in the hell had they done to her, with one gavriel?

"I don't really remember how I first got interested in them. It was definitely the migration, though, and it makes so much sense now. I guess I always knew more than I knew I knew, if that makes sense."

"Not really," said Zuzana, flat.

"I'm a butterfly," Eliza said, as if that explained it. "Several life cycles removed. Well, except more than several. A thousand years. I don't know how many generations."

Zuzana frowned, waiting for her to say something that made sense. Mik, though, in much the same blasé way as he'd reacted to Karou telling them, months ago, that she was a chimaera, said only, "Cool."

Eliza laughed, and then she told them about Elazael. The real Elazael, and what she had been and done, and about the dream that had plagued Eliza all her life, and what it meant, and Zuzana had thought she'd lost her capacity for surprise, but she found it again in a corner bar in Rome. No, it wasn't surprise. It was bigger than that.

Zuzana found flummox in a corner bar in Rome. Universes. Many. And split seams in the linings of the space-time continuum. Or something. And angels who were like space explorers without ships, like science fiction but with magic in the place of science.

"The magi did something to the Faerers' minds," Eliza explained. "Their *anima*, actually. It's more than mind; it's self. Part of their duty was to bear children on their journey, who would be born with all their maps and memories...coded into them. Like genetically coded ancestral knowledge. Crazy. So one day they could find the way home."

"And you're one of the children," said Mik.

"Many-greats, or something."

"And you have the maps," he said. "The memories."

Eliza nodded. It was Mik's intensity that clued Zuzana in that something more than storytime was going on here. Maps, memories.

Maps. Memories.

"There's a lot of information in here," Eliza said, tapping her head. "I haven't processed it yet. Throughout my family history there's been madness. I think it's too much for the human mind to take. It's like an overloaded server. It just crashes. I was crashed. You uncrashed me. I'll never be able to thank you enough."

Zuzana's slumpy self-pity jag was already over. She sat up straight. "If you're saying what I think you're saying, you can totally thank us enough."

Eliza skewed her lips into a contemplation pucker. "That depends. What do you think I'm saying?" Mischief gleamed in her eyes.

Zuzana wrapped her hands lightly around Eliza's throat and mimed throttling her. *"Tell. Us."*

"I know another portal," said Eliza. *"Duh."*

70

White No Longer

Jael's wingbeats were clipped with fury, anything but smooth as he returned to Eretz. He practically tore his way through the portal, wishing he could damage it, damage something. *Akiva*. Yes. See the bastard shot full of arrows like an archery-range dummy, dancing from the Westway gibbet for all to come and goggle at.

He looked around uneasily. Damn the bastard, he could be anywhere. Had he preceded Jael through the portal? Would he come behind? By the terms of their agreement, the moment Jael passed back into Eretz, Akiva was free to kill him in any manner *other* than igniting the suppurating handprint on Jael's chest. That left him a lot of options.

And Jael had just as many. More, because he wasn't held back by honor, which does shorten a list of ways to kill your enemy.

It was not lost on him that his very survival depended upon his enemy having honor, but this did not in any way oblige him to play by the same rules. On the contrary, it was critical that he draw first blood. He would not be able to rest until the bastard was dead.

Once through the portal, Jael didn't stay to oversee the tedious return of his army but flew straight on to camp in the center of a phalanx of guards, with archers wide at their flanks in case Akiva should make an appearance.

The landscape here was much the same as the one they'd just left behind: dun-colored mountains and nothing to see. The camp was in the foothills, some half hour distant. In a field of grasses flattened by the wind, rows of tents stood orderly in a rough quadrangle with guard towers at its corners, manned by archers in case of aerial onslaught. It was a skeleton defense. Up here, there was nothing to defend against. The bulk of Jael's forces were deployed south and east, hunting down the rebels.

And how had they fared? He should know soon enough.

Sooner even than expected.

The camp was scarcely in his sights when saw what awaited him on the piked palisade.

* * *

Karou saw it, too, though from a greater distance, and she couldn't stifle her gasp. From the palisade, billowing in the wind, hung a banner that had been white and was now fouled with blood and ash. She knew it at once. Its slogan was clear, even if the wolf-head emblem in its center was...concealed. *Victory and Vengeance*, it read, in the chimaera tongue. It was the White Wolf's gonfalon—not the copy he'd hung at the kasbah but the original, plundered as it must have been from Loramendi after the fall.

But it wasn't the gonfalon that had made Karou gasp. If the banner alone hung here, it might be interpreted as a sign that the White Wolf had conquered and overtaken this camp. But with what dangled in front of it, obscuring the wolf emblem, no such misconception was possible.

Karou thought that she had managed her hope. She'd believed, flying back through the cut, that she was prepared for the possibility—the likelihood—of bad news.

Delusion.

Sometime since leaving their comrades behind, she had begun to believe, without admitting it to herself, that all would be well. Because it had to be. Didn't it?

But it wasn't. All was not well.

Also once white, and white no longer, by a noose around its neck, swung the stained and broken body of Thiago.

And here was the answer, sooner than expected, to the question of what had happened when they left the battle raging in the Adelphas, and made the hard decision to complete their own vital mission before returning.

Did I do enough? Karou had asked herself then, already knowing the answer. *Did I do everything I could?*

No.

And their comrades had lost. And died.

Akiva caught her and held her, and they didn't speak but watched, helpless, moving in the air with the steady tide of Akiva's wingbeats, as Jael landed before the corpse of the White Wolf and laughed.

71

Absence

Karou went to the body, after Jael was gone. Just for a moment, just in case. Drawing close, she remembered the last time this flesh had bled out. Her own small knife had killed him then, and the neat wound was easily knit back up to prepare the vessel for Ziri's soul.

This wound was... not neat.

Look away.

This death had not been easy, and Karou's mind screamed for the brown-eyed orphan who once upon a time had trailed her around Loramendi, shy and gangly as a fawn. Whom she'd kissed once on the forehead, and only remembered it because he'd told her. Blushing.

Ziri. And she knew the feel of his soul from when she'd put it in this body, and hope, hope would just never learn.

Of course his soul would be gone. It could never have survived this long in the open, or such a journey. Of course it had evanesced. But Karou still opened her senses to it, because she couldn't not try.

Did I do everything I could? And still she held her breath, as invisible tears tracked down her invisible cheeks. And still she hoped.

Absence has presence, sometimes, and that was what she felt. Absence like crushed-dead grass where something has been and is no longer. Absence where a thread has been ripped, ragged, from a tapestry, leaving a gap that can never be mended.

That was all she felt.

72

The Several Days' Emperor

Mood incrementally improved, Jael bulled his way toward his pavilion, trailing his retinue of guards. The soldiers in the watchtowers had saluted him on approach, and one leapt down to glide up short and stride at his side.

"Report," Jael barked, removing his helmet and tossing it to him. "The rebels?"

"We trapped them in the Adelphas, sir—"

Jael whirled on him. "*Sir?*" he repeated. He didn't recognize the soldier. "Am I not your emperor as well as your general?"

The soldier bowed his head, flustered. "Eminence?" he ventured. "My lord emperor? We cornered the rebels in the Adelphas. Misbegotten and revenants together, if you can credit it."

Oh, Jael could credit it. He gave out a hiss of a laugh.

"I'm not lying, sir," said the soldier, mistaking him. Again, *sir.*

Jael's eyes narrowed to slits. "*And?*"

"They put up a valiant defense," said the soldier, and Jael read the rest in his smirk. A valiant defense was a doomed defense. It was what he expected, especially after the sight of the White Wolf's corpse, and it was all he needed to know for now. Jael's blood was thrumming with pent-up frustration, and his muscles were rage-tense. He'd been meek as a rabbit—a neutered rabbit—for days in that infernal palace, not daring to injure his reputation by answering his own hungers. And all for what? To be chased away like a skulking dog? He hadn't even dared slay the Fallen for fear of defying the bastard Akiva's prohibition of bloodshed.

He looked around for his steward. "Where is Mechel?"

"I don't know, my lord emperor. Can I assist you?"

Jael gave a grudging grunt. "Send me a woman," he said, and turned to go.

"No need, sir. There's one already in your tent, waiting for you." Still that smirk. "A victory celebration."

Jael hauled off and backhanded the soldier, whose expression scarcely altered as the slap turned his head from east to west. A thread of blood appeared at his lip, and he did nothing to stanch it.

"Do I look victorious to you?" Jael seethed at him. He held up his empty hands. "Do you see all my new weapons? I can scarcely carry them all! *That's my victory!*" He felt his face empurpling and was reminded of his brother, whose rages had been famous, and murderous. Jael prided himself on being a creature of cunning, not temper, and cunning meant killing not in passion but in coolness.

So he just shoved the soldier aside—fixing the smirk in his memory for a more considered punishment later—and marched into his pavilion, tearing at his ridiculous white pageant garb and giving a hiss of pain when he peeled at the place the scorched silk had hardened against the weeping flesh of his wound, reopening it.

He cursed. The pain was a throbbing reminder of his failure and vulnerability. He needed to remember his own might. He needed to get his blood moving, his breath flowing, to prove who he—

He stopped short. The bed was empty.

His eyes narrowed. Where was the woman, then? Hiding? Cowering? Well. His heat rose. That would make a fine beginning.

"Come out, come out, wherever you are," he rasped, turning in a slow circle.

The pavilion was dim, the canvas walls hung with furs to keep out both wind and light. No lanterns were lit. The only illumination came from Jael's own wings…

…and the woman's.

There.

She was not hiding. She was not cowering. She was at his desk. Jael bristled. The wench was sitting at his war desk, languid in his chair, all his campaign charts spread before her as she rolled a paperweight back and forth beneath her palm. Her other hand, he did not fail to note, rested on the hilt of a sword.

"What are you doing?" he growled.

"Waiting for you."

There was no fear in the voice, no coyness or humility. She was backlit by her own wings, and, besides, a shadowy stillness seemed to cloak her, so that Jael could make out only the shape of her as he strode forward, ready to yank her out of his chair by her hair. And that was better than if she were hiding, better than cowering. Maybe she would even resist—

He saw her face, and faltered to a stop.

If he was slow to process the ramifications of this visit it was only because it was unthinkable. He had deployed four thousand Dominion to crush rebels numbering less than five hundred, and they *had*, and they had brought back the White Wolf's body as proof, and besides, *the guards*—

Behind him, the soldier he hadn't recognized spoke from the doorway, having entered without summons or permission. "Oh, I should clarify," he said, smirking away. "I didn't mean a celebration of *your* victory. Sir. But of *ours*."

Jael sputtered.

Drawing sword from sheath in one smooth motion, Liraz rose from her chair.

* * *

"Karou," said Akiva, as they moved silently through the camp.

"Yes?" she whispered. The deserted camp was eerie, but she knew it wouldn't stay this way for long. The troops would arrive soon enough, and then it would be dangerous for them to stay. If they were going to move on Jael, they should do it now.

To her shock, though, Akiva abruptly dropped his glamour.

"What are you doing?" she whispered, alarmed. They were in full view of a guard tower, and Jael's personal escort had scarcely dispersed. They could be anywhere. Why, then, didn't Akiva look concerned?

Why did he look . . . amazed?

"That soldier," he said, indicating the emperor's pavilion, and the guard who had just slipped inside it behind Jael. "That was Xathanael."

* * *

Liraz. Jael had to blink because the queer cloak of darkness shifted and seemed to move with her as she came out from behind the desk. Long legs, long stride, no hurry. Liraz of the Misbegotten came forth with an escort of darkness, and her hands were ink-black with all the lives she had taken, and the darkness that cloaked her had taken as many or more. Moving like mercury, it resolved into forms by her sides.

There were two of them: winged and feline, with the heads and necks of women. Sphinxes, and they were smiling.

"Misbegotten and revenants together, if you can credit it," said the soldier behind him.

"My brother Xathanael," said Liraz, in such a calm way as though she were a hostess here, to make polite introductions. "And do you know Tangris and Bashees? No? Perhaps by their popular name, then. The Shadows That Live?"

This Jael could *not* credit, though he saw it with his own eyes: Liraz, as deadly as she was splendid, standing between The Shadows That Live. *The Shadows That Live.* In a camp like this one, during the chimaera campaigns, there had been no greater terror than these mysterious assassins.

Ice cut through him. It was when he thought to call for his guards that the full realization descended on him, belatedly and like a cage: The camp was taken, and so was he, and by now his guards must be, too.

His guards, maybe, but not his army. Jael's hope rallied. They were his salvation, headed this way, and in numbers to easily overwhelm the paltry force here. Numbers. Let even Akiva strive against such numbers. Jael couldn't fall into the same trap as last time, and let himself be taken as leverage. He eyed the sphinxes. One of them winked at him, and he shuddered.

"A bravura strategy," he said, stalling. "Enemies unite."

"It's your own gift to Eretz," Liraz replied, "and I'll make sure you're remembered for it. 'The Several Days' Emperor,' you'll be called, because that was all the time you had, and yet, in it, you not only dissolved the Empire, you accomplished the extraordinary feat of uniting mortal enemies in a lasting peace."

"Lasting," he scoffed. "As soon as I'm dead, you'll fall right back at each other's throats."

Bad choice of words.

"Dead?" Liraz regarded him with surprise. "Why, uncle. Are you unwell? Planning to die soon?" She had changed. This wasn't the hissing, spitting cat he'd tried to take for his own in the Tower of Conquest. "There's no ride in the world," he'd said then, taunting, "like a storm in fury." Here was no storm, no fury. There was some new quiet in her, but it didn't shrink or wilt her. Rather, it seemed to enlarge her. She was no mere weapon as she was trained to be, but a woman in full command of her power, unbowed and unbroken, and that was a dangerous thing.

Jael strained, listening for some sign that his army was drawing near. She must have noticed. She shook her head ruefully, as though she were sorry for him, then looked a question at the smirker, who nodded.

"Good." She turned back to Jael. "Come. There's something you should see."

Jael didn't wish to see anything she wanted to show him. He thought to draw his sword then, but the sphinx who had winked at him came at him in a blur half-cat, half-smoke, and wreathed around him. A daze overtook him—a sweet, soft stupor—and he missed his chance. Liraz disarmed him as though he were a child or a drunk, tossed his sword aside, and shoved him toward the door and out into the camp.

Before anything else, he saw Beast's Bane dead ahead. Instinctively, he flinched. Come to kill him as he said he would, and Jael's guards were scattered and gone?

But Beast's Bane wasn't even looking at him. "Liraz!" he cried, and there was joy in his voice that should have burned Jael, but he scarcely noticed it, fixing instead on what Liraz had brought him out to see.

Like a storm cloud overhead came the shadow of an army. It was tremendous, spanning the visible sky.

And it wasn't his.

He stared up, head craned back and all else forgotten, trying furiously to calculate the number those ranks represented. They should have had no more than three hundred Misbegotten, even if they had all survived the attack in the Adelphas. Even if...

The smirking soldier. "They put up a valiant defense," he had said, and so it would seem. Of the troops hovering overhead, a fair swath were clad in Misbegotten black. And the rest? Chimaera were among them, yes. They didn't keep the same steady formation as seraphim, but were just what could be expected of them: wild beasts, no uniformity in shape or size or dress. They were a bestiary shaken open, and godstars help the angels who allied with them.

Godstars help the Second Legion, then, for Jael saw, through a haze of fury, that they made up the bulk of this sky-borne force, steel-clad and plain in their standard-issue armor, no colors, no standards, no crests or coats of arms. Only swords and shields. Oh so many swords and shields.

And there, from up the mountains, came his own white-clad

Dominion, overmatched, and caught off guard, and Jael had no choice but to stand on the ground and watch as the two forces faced each other across a gulf of sky. Emissaries ventured out from both sides to meet in the middle and Jael spat in the grass, laughing in the faces of bastards and beasts, and declared, "Dominion never surrender! It is our creed! I wrote it myself!"

Let them fight, he willed now with a fervor that verged on prayer. Let them die, and whether they win or not, take traitors and rebels with them to their graves.

They were too distant for him to see who spoke for them, let alone guess what was said, but the result became clear when the Dominion dropped low in the sky—beyond a rise in the swaying grass and out of his sight—and came to ground in the mode of... surrender.

"Maybe they're not surrendering," said the smirking soldier in false consolation. "Maybe they all just really had to piss."

Jael didn't see them lay down their swords. He didn't have to. He knew he had lost.

His Eminence, Jael Second-born, Jael Cut-in-Half—the Several Days' Emperor—had lost his army and his empire. And surely now his life.

"What are you waiting for?" he screamed, launching himself at Liraz. With a neat step and parry she sent him face-first into the ground, and with one well-placed kick turned him over, gasping, onto his back. "Kill me!" he coughed out, lying there. "I know you want to!"

But she just shook her head and smiled, and Jael wanted to howl, because her smile had... plans in it, and in those plans, he saw, there would be no easy death.

73

A Butterfly in a Bottle

Karou and Liraz met, without prearrangement, to take Thiago's body off the palisade.

There had been a great deal of activity in the camp since the Dominion surrender, and there just hadn't been time to see to it earlier. Reunions and introductions, exclamations and explanations, logistics and strategies to debate and implement, and celebration, too—though cut with a fair portion of grief, because there had been losses in the Adelphas, many of them irretrievable.

There were some thuribles, and Karou had opened every one of them and let the impression of souls brush against her senses, but in none of them had she found what she was looking for.

She came with heavy steps to the body that she had such reason to hate, and found that she couldn't. Was it all for Ziri, her grief, or was some small measure of it for the true Wolf, who, for all his great faults, had given so much—so many years, so many deaths, and so much pain—for his people?

To her surprise, Liraz was there, facing the palisade and the corpse that dangled from it. "Oh," said Karou, caught off guard. "Hi."

No hi in return. "I put him here," said Liraz without turning her head. Her voice was tight.

Karou understood that she mourned him—Ziri—and though she didn't know how it had happened, how any feeling had had time to grow between them, she wasn't surprised. Not by Liraz, not anymore.

"It was for Jael, in case he was suspicious, coming into camp." She cut Karou a tense look. "It wasn't . . . disrespect."

"I know."

This seemed inadequate, so Karou added, softly, "It isn't him. Not in any way."

"I know." Liraz's voice was gruff. They didn't speak again until they'd cut the ropes and lowered the body to the ground. They tore the gonfalon down, too. Those words—*victory and vengeance*—belonged to another time. Karou laid it over the body, a shroud to conceal the desecration of violent death.

"Would you burn it?" she asked. *It*, not *him*, she said, because that's all it was. An empty thing, as a shell left on a beach.

Liraz nodded, and knelt beside it to touch fire to the broad, dead chest. Wisps of smoke curled up around her hand, and—

"Wait," said Karou, remembering something. She knelt, too, on his other side, and reached into the general's pocket. What she withdrew was a small article the length of her little finger. It was black and smooth, coming to a point on one end. "From his true body," she said, and handed it to Liraz. The tip of his horn. "That's all."

Then, he burned. The fire reached high, clean and splendid and unnaturally hot, leaving only ash that the wind carried away even before the flames had died.

Only then did Karou notice the silence that had fallen inside the camp, and turn to the gate to see the host clustered there, watching. Akiva stood in front, and so did Haxaya, and she looked at Liraz, and Liraz looked back, and there was no more enmity between them.

"Come," Akiva said, and he turned the watchers aside, and then it was just Karou and Liraz again. No corpse. Not even ash. Karou lingered. There was a question she wanted desperately to ask, but she fought against it.

"I didn't see him die," said Liraz. She clasped the horn tip in her fist, tight against her ribs.

Karou held her silence, and held a stillness with it, sensing that it was coming: the thing that she wanted greatly to know. "Coming back from the portal, it was chaos. Once, I saw him but couldn't reach him, and when I looked again, he wasn't there. After..." She looked troubled, cast Karou a sidelong glance, and said, plainly, "I don't know how it happened. How we won. There is no explanation. I saw soldiers fall from the sky, no arrows, no injury, and no one near to have hurt them. Others fled. More fled, I think, than fell. I don't know." She shook her head as if to clear it.

Karou had heard much this same account already, from Elyon's initial report to Akiva, seconded by Balieros. A mysterious—an impossible—victory. What could it mean?

"I found his body, finally. It had fallen into a ravine. Into a stream." She cut Karou a glance, and everything about her was wary and on guard. She seemed to be waiting for Karou to say something.

Did she think that Karou would blame her? "It's not your fault," Karou said.

Whatever it was Liraz wanted her to say, that wasn't it. She let out a short huff of impatience. "Water," she said. "Does water, moving water, does it... hasten... evanescence?"

Karou looked at Liraz as her words sank in. Her stillness deepened. She was caught between breaths. This was what she hadn't been able to ask. Did she mean...? So clearly Karou remembered the devastation on Liraz's face when she'd had to tell her, as gently as she could under the circumstances, that Hazael's soul was lost. How, for nothing, she had hauled his corpse through two skies, and how, in the process of bringing him to a resurrectionist, instead cast his soul adrift.

Surely that wasn't why she'd dragged Thiago's body all this way?

Karou's glance flickered to where the corpse had been, which did not go unnoticed by Liraz. "You think I didn't learn?" the angel asked, incredulous.

And with that, Karou almost dared to hope. "Did you?" she asked, and her voice was very small.

Did you learn?

Did you glean Ziri's soul?

Dear gods and stardust, did you?

Liraz started to tremble. "I don't know," she said. "I don't know." Her voice shattered, and just like that she was crying. She fumbled at her belt, and then she was holding something out to Karou with wildly shaking hands. It was her canteen.

"It's not a thurible, but it closes. I didn't have incense, and I couldn't find anyone, not nearby, and I thought it might be worse to wait, but then I couldn't tell if anything happened. I couldn't feel anything, or see anything, so I'm afraid... I'm afraid it was already gone." Now rushing over words, now pulling back in a series of taut silences, and there was a war in her eyes between hope and caution. "I...I sang," she whispered, "if that matters," and Karou felt her heart pulled to pieces. This Misbegotten warrior, fiercest of them all, had crouched in an icy stream bed to sing a chimaera soul into her canteen, because she hadn't known what else to do.

The singing wouldn't have mattered, but she wasn't going to tell Liraz that. If Ziri's soul was in that canteen, Karou would happily learn whatever song Liraz had sung and make it part of her resurrection ritual forever, just so that the angel would never feel that she'd been foolish.

And who knows? Karou thought, reaching for the canteen. *Who really knows? Because I sure as hell don't.*

And her hands were shaking, too, as she twisted the cap loose. She tried to still them against the jug's metal neck, which should have been cool in the mountain air but was warm from resting against Liraz's body.

Then, as delicately as she could with her jittery fingers, she lifted the cap aside.

She strained, listening with her senses. Reaching, hoping. It was like leaning forward and breathing deeply—without leaning, without breathing. Some unknowable part of herself shifted forward, unwound, reached. What had Akiva said? A scheme of energies, more than mind and more than soul. She reached with it, whatever it was, and felt...

...home.

That was what came to her. Her home and Ziri's. Maybe all of theirs now. She would gladly share. They could be a big, crazy tribe, come one, come all, angels and devils at rest and in love, or arguing, or sparring, or learning the violin from Mik, or teaching their half-caste babies to fly on wings that were neither Kirin nor seraph, but some kind of feather-bat-fire wings. Or else it would be like eye color; you'd inherit one or the other. *Was she thinking about babies?* Karou was laughing, and nodding, and Liraz was sobbing and laughing, and they fell against each other, the canteen between them, its precious cap replaced, and their relief was a shared country, because against her senses Karou had felt the stir of stormhunters' wings, and the high roaming wind of the Adelphas Mountains, the beautiful, mournful, eternal song of the wind flutes that filled their caves with music, and also: a note that she didn't remember from before. It was fire, held in cupped hands, and she thought she knew what it meant.

Liraz may have captured Ziri's soul like a butterfly in a bottle, but that was only a formality. It was already hers.

And, clearly, judging by the state of her, laugh-sobbing in Karou's arms, hers was his, too.

74

Chapter One

So. Jael was deposed, and the portals closed with no weapons brought through them to wreak new havoc. The Dominion were vanquished, leaving the Second Legion, or so-called common army, as the dominant force in the land. They were the largest army, and had always occupied a middle ground between the high-bred Dominion and the bastard Misbegotten, and if they had to choose—as they had found themselves in the unthinkable position of doing—they would side with the bastards.

Under the auspices of a commander named Ormerod whom Akiva knew and respected, they had done so, de facto nullifying the Misbegotten death sentence and declaring an end to hostilities.

Declaring an end and *achieving* an end were different animals, and aside from tensions that existed between the seraph armies, the Second Legion were a long way from considering their chimaera foes to be companions in arms. For now, they had grudgingly made the same promise that the Misbegotten had made days earlier, and

Karou hoped it would not have to be tested in the same way. They would not strike first.

A détente is not an alliance, but it's a start.

Elyon, it transpired, had—after the mystifying Adelphas victory—been the one to go to Cape Armasin in Akiva's stead and plead the rebel cause, and he had clearly done well. Now he and Ormerod would escort Jael back to Astrae to begin a new era in his life. From captain to emperor to . . . exhibit.

The Several Days' Emperor was going to star in his own zoo.

No one would have faulted Liraz for killing him, and none would have mourned him. But as she stood over the writhing, screaming heap of him, she had discovered that she lacked the will for it. Not just for the sake of her tally, and to be done with killing, but also for the simple reason that he clearly *wanted* her to.

In the Tower of Conquest, it had been she who'd courted death rather than face the fate he had picked out for her. "Kill me with my brothers, or you'll wish you had," she had spat at him, and he had feigned offense. "You would *die* with them, sooner than scrub my back?"

"A thousand times," she had choked out. And he? He had pressed a hand to his heart. "My dear. Don't you see? Knowing that is what makes it sweet."

Now it was she who knew the sweetness of denying death rather than granting it. "I was thinking," she had mused, standing over him, "that it would do the people good to see with their own eyes the tyranny they've been freed of. It's one thing to hear about the *horror* of you, and another to experience it firsthand."

He'd stopped his writhing to stare up at her, aghast.

"Come and see, this is what an emperor is," she'd said, warming to her idea. Now she was remembering what she had witnessed in the Hintermost, when Jael had skewered Ziri's palms through with swords and force-fed him the ashes of his comrades. "Come and take a peek, see what we've saved you from, and you'll be down on your knees thanking us. And possibly vomiting."

To his savage response—a stream of spittle-flecked invectives and a series of facial contortions that achieved for him new heights of monstrosity—she had replied only, mildly, "Yes, that. Do exactly that when they come to look at you. Perfect."

As for true justice, the Empire had no system in place for it, and none knew how to undertake building one, not to mention a new system of governance to take the place of the wretched one they had just toppled. And then there was the work of freeing the slaves, as well as finding occupation for the many men and women who knew no livelihood but war.

If there was one thing they did know on this night in the foothills of the Veskal Range, it was how much they did *not* know. In essence, they had written "Chapter One" on the first page of a new book, and everything—*everything*—remained to be written. Karou hoped that it would be a long book, and dull.

"Dull?" Akiva repeated, skeptical. They sat together at the edge of the firelight, eating Dominion rations. Karou was intrigued to see Liraz between Tangris and Bashees on the far side, and she thought they were good company for one another.

"Dull," Karou affirmed. History conditioned you for epic-scale calamity. Once, when she was studying the death tolls of battles in World War I, she'd caught herself thinking, *Only eight thousand men died here. Well, that's not many.* Because next to, say, the *million* who died at the Somme, it wasn't. The stupendous numbers deadened you to the merely tragic, and history didn't average in the tame days for balance. *On this day, no one in the world was murdered. A lion gave birth. Ladybugs lunched on aphids. A girl in love daydreamed all morning, neglecting her chores, and wasn't even scolded.*

What was more fantastical than a dull day?

"*Good*-dull," she clarified. "No wars to spice it up. No conquests or slave raids, only mending and building."

"And how is that dull?" asked Akiva, amused.

"This is how," said Karou, clearing her throat and assuming what she intended to be the stuffy voice of history. "Eleventh January, Year of the . . . Neek-Neek. The garrison at Cape Armasin is disassembled for timber. A town is plotted on the site. There is indecision as to the height of a proposed clock tower. Council meets, argues . . ." She paused for suspense, shifting her eyeballs from side to side. "Splits the difference. Clock tower duly built. Vegetables grown and eaten. Many sunsets admired."

Akiva laughed. "That," he said, "is a willful failure of imagination. I'm sure a lot of interesting things happen in this imaginary town of yours."

"Okay then. You go."

"Okay." He paused to think. When he spoke, he approximated Karou's history voice. "Eleventh January, Year of the Neek-Neek. The garrison at Cape Armasin is disassembled for timber. The town plotted on the site is the first of mixed race in all of Eretz. Chimaera and seraphim live side by side as equals. Some even . . ." His words caught, and when he resumed talking, it was in his own voice, if a tender, careful version of it. "Some even live *together*."

Live together. Did he mean—?

Yes. He meant. He held Karou's gaze steady and warm. She had imagined it, or tried to. Living together. It always had the wordless, golden unreality of a dream.

"Some," he went on, "lie together under a shared blanket and breathe the scent of each other in their sleep. They dream of a temple lost in a requiem grove, and of the wishes that were made there . . . and came true."

She remembered the temple grove—every night, every moment, every wish. She remembered the pull of him, like a tide. The heat of him. The weight of him. But not with this body. To this body every sensation would be new. She flushed, but didn't look away.

"Some," he said, soft now, "don't have much longer to wait."

She swallowed, finding her voice. "You're right," she allowed, practically whispering. "That's not dull."

* * *

Not much longer to wait. "Not much" was still longer, though, and for the most part it was tolerable.

Not tolerable: the two nights they spent at the Dominion camp, when Elyon, Ormerod, and a cluster of others, including the bull centaur Balieros—stepping into Thiago's command—kept them engaged in planning until dawn so that Karou, who had determined to steal Akiva somehow into one of the empty campaign tents, never got the chance.

Tolerable: the third morning, leaving—*finally*—because they were leaving together.

There was some consternation about it. Ormerod held that Akiva would be needed in the capital, which had yet to be brought, gently or otherwise, into this new post-Empire era. Akiva replied that they would be better off without the hysteria his presence would ignite. "Besides," he said, "I have a prior commitment."

When his expression softened then, with a look to Karou, the nature of his "commitment" was easily misconstrued.

"Surely it can wait," protested Ormerod, incredulous.

Karou blushed, seeing what they all thought—and they weren't wrong to think it. *Will it ever be time for cake?* Having kissed Akiva at last didn't make the waiting any easier, but had just served to stoke her hunger for him. But that wasn't the commitment Akiva was referring to, anyway. "Let me help you," he had pled back at the caves, when Karou had told him what work lay ahead for her. "It's all I want, to be beside you, helping you. If it takes forever, all the better, if it's forever with you."

It had seemed so far off then, but here they were. Work to do and pain to tithe and cake around the edges.

The edges, she pledged, would be ample. Hadn't they earned it?

Liraz settled the matter by declaring that the chimaera needed a seraph escort anyway in this critical time, when they were still so far from anything like an easy peace, and their mission was one of such importance. She spoke in the same quiet and unnerving way as she had in the war council, and with the same effect: Liraz spoke, and truth was born.

It was a power, Karou thought, looking at her with ever-increasing respect, that the angel hadn't begun to explore. And she liked it a lot better when it was used *for* her, not against her.

And it couldn't be only the sway Liraz held over them, that once the seraphim were made to understand just what mission of importance the chimaera now undertook, they tried to volunteer for it.

It was then, looking around at their faces, that Karou knew her first draught of easy hope for the future of Eretz. As it had before, when Liraz admitting singing Ziri's soul into her canteen, her heart felt pulled to pieces.

Every Misbegotten within earshot volunteered to go to Loramendi, and help with the excavation of souls.

They were all of them warriors; each had their haunting memories, and most, their shames. None had ever had the chance to... unmassacre a city before. In some sense, that was what they would do, unearthing the souls buried in Brimstone's cathedral—those hidden thousands who had chosen their death that day for its hope of rebirth. Brimstone's hope, and the Warlord's: that a girl raised human, with no memory of her true identity and no knowledge of the magic she contained, might somehow, someday, find her way to them and bring them out.

And the heavier hope still: that there could be a world worth bringing them out *to*.

It seemed crazy now, on this side of things, that it could have come to pass, and though Karou stood in the midst of several hundred soldiers of both sides who had had their role in it, it was as though a gleam drew her gaze to Akiva, without whom it never could have. The wishbone. Ziri's life. Issa's thurible. The offer of alliance. All of it. Every step of the way, he had been there. But before, long before, there had been the dream. A "*life* wish," as he had said once. For a different sort of life.

Every once in a while, back in her human life as an artist, it had happened that Karou would do a drawing that was so much better than anything she'd done before that it would stun her. When that happened, she wouldn't be able to stop looking at it. She'd come back to it all day long, and even wake in the middle of the night just to gaze at it, with wonder and pride.

It was like that looking at Akiva, too.

He was as fixed on her as she was on him, and there was hunger where their eyes met. It wasn't passion, simply, or desire, but something bigger that contained those things and many others. It was hunger and satiety at once—"wanting" and "having" meeting, and neither extinguishing the other.

And whether it was Liraz's intervention, or the strength of that look, no one bothered arguing further. And under what chain of command did he fall, anyway? Who could tell Akiva what to do? He would, of course, accompany Karou.

Once upon a time,
there was only darkness.

And there were monsters vast as worlds who swam in it.

75

Want

They were two score Misbegotten and as many chimaera. All the others—the joined force that had so darkened the skies of the Veskal Range—would fly south to introduce themselves to Astrae.

"We'll need thuribles and incense," said Amzallag, who would lead the excavation of Brimstone's cathedral. He had lost his family in Loramendi, and was eager to be off and begin. Shovels and picks, tents and food they liberated from the Dominion camp, but these more specialized supplies would be harder to come by, and so it was decided, for this reason and others, that they would fly first to the Kirin caves, which were, in any case, almost on the way.

Karou was eager to see Issa, and she was conscious, too, that those left behind at the caves hadn't had food to sustain them for long, nor—being wingless, for the most part—the means to leave and seek it.

In addition, though she and Liraz and Akiva had kept this news contained among themselves for now, there was the question of Ziri.

None but they—and Haxaya—knew that a soul had been gleaned from the White Wolf's body, and so Karou had hope that the entire episode of the deception might be swept under the carpet of history. It was Thiago, the Warlord's firstborn, fiercest enemy of seraphim, who had changed his heart and banded together with the Empire's outcast bastards to forge a new way forward. Did that rob Ziri of the glory due him for his very great role in their victory?

Maybe. But Karou thought it would sit just fine with him. Maybe, in time, the truth could even be told. As for the last son of the Kirin, Karou knew they would have to concoct some good story to explain his abrupt return to them, keeping it free of any association with the White Wolf's death. But as his end had been a mystery—he had simply never returned from Thiago's last mission of massacre—and none but Karou had ever seen his body, she thought it could be managed. It seemed right that he should make his reappearance among them at the home of his ancestors—and her own.

Perhaps Karou would even find the time, now, to return to her own childhood village deep inside the mountain.

And there was one more reason for her eagerness to return to the caves, of course—last but not least—and that was their dark and branching ways, where those with a will for it could easily slip away for an hour or three. Or seven.

She had a will for it.

* * *

Liraz had her own sharp hope. It dug at her heart like a spike, and she didn't speak it aloud. She had the horn tip pressed deep in her pocket, but Karou carried the canteen now, and Liraz missed the weight of it at her hip. When would she resurrect him? Liraz wouldn't ask her. It was just that they had never said, outright. At the time, outside the palisade, it hadn't seemed in any way necessary. The tears and laughing! If anyone had tried telling her that she would ever sob into that blue hair... well. She would have given them a very icy look. No more than that, because that would be brutish.

You wouldn't want to be brutish, she imagined Hazael's voice in her head, the lazy, laughing cadence of it. *You'll scare all your suitors away.*

It was a subject only he would have dared to broach. Liraz had never looked at a man—or a woman—not like... *that.* If he'd known that the very thought terrified her, he'd certainly never let on. Always, he had built up her strength.

"Anyone who takes on my sister," he had postured once, all puffed-out bravado, "will have to deal with... *my sister.*" And then he'd dived behind her and cowered.

Haz. And what would he make of her now, pining for... for the air inside a canteen? Was that what this was, pining? She'd witnessed her brothers' passions—so very different, the pair of them. Haz's were mercurial things, frequent, and played for humor. The Misbegotten may have been forbidden the pleasures of the flesh, but it had never stopped him. He'd fallen in love like it was a hobby—and out of it the same way. Liraz supposed that meant it wasn't love.

Akiva, though. Once only, and forever.

Silent, suffering Akiva. Liraz thought that she had never felt a closer kinship with him than she did now. She knew it wasn't because *he* had changed, but *she* had. It was curious. To feel longing like this, with all the fear that went with it. She should have hated it. And part of her did. *Feelings are stupid*, a voice in her still insisted, but it was a diminishing voice. The louder one she scarcely recognized as her own.

I want, it said, and it seemed to come from deep within her, from a place, perhaps, where many things were patiently waiting to be discovered. Real laughter, for one. Haz's kind: tumbling, easy, loose-muscled, and free. Touch, for another, though just the thought of it set her heart racing.

She knew what Haz would say. He'd give her a smug look and say, "You see? There's a *much* better way to get your blood moving than battle." And he would add, she didn't doubt, because he had said it enough times, "And *please* unbraid your hair. It hurts me just to look at it. What did it ever do to deserve such punishment?"

Liraz laughed a little, imagining him, and she might have cried a little, too, missing him, but no one saw, and her tears froze before they hit the mountains, because they had climbed high into the Adelphas now, and she cast Karou a glance, just enough to catch the glint of silver at her hip where the canteen swayed.

When? she wondered.

And *What then?*

* * *

Akiva, for the duration of the journey, felt divided in two.

There was the memory of kissing Karou, and everything he'd said to her, and everything he'd thought but *hadn't* said—which was the far greater portion—and every stir in him, when his eyes traced the lines of her in flight, his hands aching to trace them, too... She should have been all he could think of. They would spend a night at the Kirin caves to break their journey, and he knew that it would not be another night spent apart. They had come to the end of those, at last, and it felt like a bubble inside him, this great pressure in his chest: joy and hunger and a shout building, a wordless cry of gladness ready to burst from him and echo.

He wanted only to set down in the entrance cavern, call hasty greetings to those who awaited them, drop his gear on the ice-rimed floor and let it lie there. Seize Karou's hand, and draw her, running, away with him. Into the caves, and in, and in, and take her, and hold her, and laugh against her neck in disbelief that she was finally his, and that the world was finally theirs, and *this was all he wanted.*

Or rather, it was all that he wanted to want.

But there was an intrusion in his mind. It had been there for some time. Most recently: hearing the accounts of victory in the Adelphas, and seeing the vague puzzlement of those who did the telling. The dream logic of it, and how they all accepted it because it had happened. The way they accepted what had happened in the caves when they first faced one another, blooded, ready to kill and die—and hadn't.

But the intrusion had been there already. When he had reached for *sirithar* in the battle of the Adelphas and gotten thunder instead. And before that, when he had sensed a presence in the cave with him, or thought he had. And even before that, from his first attainment of true *sirithar,* a state of power his mind had no context for and that made him feel, in its aftermath, like an infinitesimal figure pulled along in the wake of some catastrophic force. A flood, or a hurricane. He couldn't control it. Somehow, he could summon it, and that wasn't the same thing at all.

He had spoken to Karou of a "scheme of energies," and that was real—a place that he had navigated, blind, since his first earliest fumblings with magic. He sensed the vastness that was in him, the limitlessness, and was humbled by it, but... this wasn't that.

This was what troubled him most: the suspicion that when he attained *sirithar*—that is, this thing which he had chosen to call *sirithar*, because it was the only word he knew for a state of exceptional clarity—he was not reaching down within himself, but *out*. Beyond. And that what responded—the source of the power—it was not him, and not his.

So... what was it?

76

Waiting for Magic

They were watched for.

Those left at the caves must have kept a sentry always posted to look out for their return, because by the time they drew nigh—cautious, in case anything had gone wrong in their absence—everyone had gathered in the entrance cavern to welcome them, and it felt good. Like coming home.

Karou flew straight into Issa's arms and stayed there long enough that a nest of serpents the Naja had called to herself for company—blind cave snakes from the muggy passages below—wound round her, too, pallid and glimmering, and joined them together.

"Sweet girl," whispered Issa, "all is well?"

"And more than well," Karou said, and flushed with emotion, knowing that this was as close as she would ever come to telling Brimstone that it was begun: the unlikeliest dream, and the sweetest.

After the greetings there was news to share, and much of it, though they kept it as brief as they could. There would have been no natural end to the speculation that followed, but that Issa intercepted a glance between Karou and Akiva.

It was the lit-fuse look, the space between them fairly shimmering with heat, and Issa's lips pressed into a smile. They didn't see her notice it—they didn't see anything but each other—and when she said, "Well, I imagine our travelers are weary," and began to break up the gathering, they didn't guess that it was on their behalf.

Everyone seemed to share the sense of homecoming, even the Misbegotten, and the whole party moved off together, along with those who'd come out to greet them. And when they reached the grand cavern, where the chimaera might have gone on and down toward the village they had formerly occupied, they didn't, but stayed with the angels to prepare a meal together, beneath the stalactites.

Karou wasn't hungry. Not for pilfered Dominion rations, anyway.

A Christmas-morning feeling had come over her. Well, she'd had few enough Christmas mornings in her life. The one with Esther had felt more like a stage play—glittering and special, but as something she was meant to *watch*, rather than participate in. She'd had two with Zuzana's family, and those were much better, and though they hadn't exactly been children, they'd acted like it as much as possible. Holiday rituals in the Novak home were immutable, and even Zuzana's older brother, who had tried so hard to impress Karou with his dubious manliness, had come scampering down the stairs at dawn on Christmas morning to see what magic had happened in the night.

The feeling, it was the sense of waiting drawing to an end. Not dread waiting, but excited waiting of the best kind: waiting for magic.

And the magic Karou was waiting for now, waiting for and reaching for—and she could feel it reaching right back, like a mirror image at the very instant before your fingertips touch their twins in the glass—was of the decidedly *grown-up* variety.

She couldn't stop looking at Akiva. And every time she did, either she found his gaze waiting, or else it sensed hers at once and came around to meet it. Every look was vivid and full and alive. There was laughter in the set of his mouth, because it had become funny, at last, at the tail end of waiting. Only funny because it was almost over, and everything that was...*not them*...was obstacle. It was a tease now, this lingering, a game, to see who could last another minute, and a dance. Their bodies—two in the midst of many—moved to the pull of the same magnet, no matter who stood between them.

Karou felt as though her skin had been awakened. It had been dormant and she hadn't even known it, but since the kiss in the sky—more exactly, when Akiva's lips had touched the place beneath her ear—some switch had been flipped. Small, exquisite currents of electricity were coursing all over her, raising goose bumps, shivers, waves of heat. She couldn't still her hands. The "love chemicals," she knew from her school days: dopamine, norepinephrine. She remembered, in their reading, how one scientist had called them the "cocktail of love rapture" and how she and Zuzana couldn't stop giggling about it. Well, she was flooded with them now. Flushed and trembling, her belly a riot of butterflies. *Papilio stomachus*. Her heartbeat was a tap dance and her breathing was shallow. She tried to draw deep breaths to settle herself, but every one felt like a buoy refusing to sink. The edge of hyperventilating, but in a good way—which sounded stupid but felt like the full spectrum of excitement, from trills of giddiness to the rich and languid bass note of anticipated pleasure, slow and sweet as syrup.

All of which is to say: Karou was on fire.

Akiva caught her eye again. There was the spark and flash. Light and heat, racing up a fuse. No more laughter. She saw that his hands at his sides could not find stillness. He curled them into fists. Uncurled them, but they would not be at peace until they were allowed to do what they wanted and touch her. His whole body was taut. So was hers. They were violin strings, the pair of them, ready to sing.

A question in his eyes, in the tilt of his head, in the set of his shoulders. His whole being was this question.

And the answer was so easy. Karou nodded, and the unknown switch apparently had a higher setting, because she shifted into it. Her skin practically hummed.

Finally. *Finally.*

She turned to slip away down the passage that led to the baths—*the baths?* Where did it come from, this notion? Her face went hot. It was a very fine notion—and, turning, she caught sight of Liraz.

Liraz, standing apart, tall and still and always too damn straight, as though someone—Ellai maybe—had fastened a string to the top of her skull and wouldn't just let her relax. There was her rigidity, and the look of agonized suspense on her face, and Karou's switch, newly discovered, gave a twang. Power cut. Electrical currents nil, skin temperature normalizing, cocktail of love rapture neutralized. No more shivers, and her breath sank back into her like an anchor sliding into the sea.

Jesus, what was wrong with her? She blinked. Ziri's soul was hanging from her belt and she was about to . . . ?

She shook her head, hard, fast, and repossessed herself. Akiva, across the cavern, furrowed his brow. She gave him a helpless look, touched the canteen, and he understood. His gaze flickered to Liraz, who saw everything that passed between them and looked stricken.

They came together at the very door Karou had been headed for, but for a different purpose now, and a different destination.

"It won't take long," Karou said.

"I'll help you," Akiva replied, and she nodded.

She'd been ready for this since before Ziri ever cut his own throat to become the Wolf. When he'd been missing, when all the patrols had come back except his, she'd gathered what she would need, all the components to conjure a Kirin body as strong and true as she could make it. Human and antelope teeth, tubes of bat bone, iron and jade. Even diamonds, preciously hoarded for him alone. They were all tumbled together in a small velvet jewelry pouch with her resurrection gear, packed away down in the cave with the thuribles and incense.

Ingredients for a Ziri.

Well, the one essential ingredient for a Ziri was in the canteen. She wanted, though, to make this new body as close to his true Kirin flesh as possible. Her head snapped up with a thought. "Wait a second," she said, and crossed the cavern to where Liraz stood alone.

"You don't have to, now—" Liraz began.

Karou waved it off. "Do you have that piece of horn I gave you?"

Liraz handed it over, hesitating as though she was sorry to part with it, and Karou found herself hoping, softly and deeply, that this angel's feelings were shared, not just for her sake, but for Ziri's, too, whose loneliness was even deeper than her own had once been. She, at least, had had Brimstone, and the memory of her parents and her tribe. Who had Ziri ever had?

Let this be another improbable, glorious beginning, she thought. "Do you want to come?" she asked, but Liraz shook her head and so she left her there, outside the circle of soldiers, and went to do this one last thing.

77

We Haven't Been Introduced

Liraz couldn't stay in the grand cavern. She felt too transparent, so she wandered and eventually found herself back in the entrance cave. One of the flightless chimaera was standing guard and she took over for him, settling herself on a ledge.

The sun set in due course, and the crescent-moon opening was positioned to catch every ray of it. She watched, and it seemed to melt when it touched the far peaks, spreading molten and golden across the breadth of the horizon. Orange light glazed all the world between, from it to her, and reached behind her, far into the cavern, to light the skims of ice with a blinding shine.

And then it paled and cooled, golds giving way to grays, and it was at that moment of the sky's deepest blue, in the seconds before it eases to full black and sets forth stars, that she heard a tread behind her, and was afraid to turn.

The tread was slow, a sharp *clip, clip*. The ring of hooves. That was her first awareness of him—*hooves*—and she couldn't help herself, it was too long trained into her, and too deep: She felt a surge of misgiving, almost revulsion. He was a chimaera. What had come over her? Just because someone saved your life didn't mean you had to fall in love with him.

Love? Godstars. It was the first time the word had dared to form itself, and only this way, in the negation of it. Still, it hit her in the gut: fear and denial and the urge to flee.

It was a struggle, staying still. She had done nothing, she had to remind herself. Said and encouraged nothing. Not before he died in his Wolf skin, not ever. There was nothing between them to regret or back away from, and no reason to flee. He was only a comrade, only a—

"We haven't been introduced."

Liraz's heart gave a slam. She'd gotten used to the Wolf's voice, but that didn't mean she'd ever liked it. Even when Ziri had spoken to her as himself—the one time only, the two of them chest-deep in the strange soft water of the baths—there had been a roughness to it, like it could turn to a growl at the edge of a breath. It had been a match for his clawed hands, his fanged mouth. Latent brutality.

This voice, though. It was as sonorous as the Kirin wind flutes, effortlessly rich and smooth.

She knew her own part in this dialogue. Finding her voice, and wincing to hear it shake, she replied, "You know who I am, and I know who you are, and—"

"—that *won't* serve." His voice twined with hers, changing the script. And in the lapse after their words, she heard him waiting. How can you *hear* waiting? She didn't know, but you could. She did. He was waiting for her to turn around, and she couldn't put it off any longer.

She turned, and Ziri of the Kirin was before her, and Liraz could scarcely breathe.

He was tall. She'd known that, having seen him fight in the midst of a cluster of Dominion who had looked undergrown beside him. But seeing it at a distance, and seeing it before you and having to tilt your head up are two different experiences. Liraz tilted her head up. And *up*, tracing the length of horns that stretched the effect of his height to extremes. They had to be the length of her arms at least, long and straight, black and gleaming. Intact, she noted, fleetingly—no broken point—and she wondered what had become of that token that had fit just so in her palm.

He was lean, long-muscled, less broad than Akiva or most of the Misbegotten, but this served only to accentuate his height, and his shoulders were anything but narrow. Behind them, his wings were folded. Dark. Liraz could guess at their expansiveness, against the length of him. He was wearing white, and this seemed wrong, and he must have seen a wrinkle at her brow because he plucked at his shirt and said, "The Wolf's. I didn't have anything of... my own. Except"—he smiled and, with both hands, gestured to himself—"all the rest. I guess."

It was the smile. Ziri smiled, and Liraz saw him.

Not hooves, not horns, which she'd been examining in pieces, but his *self*. He was just as he should be, and in every way striking and heart-stopping. His Kirin beauty was of a jagged, wild species. Sharp horns, sharp hooves, and the cut of his wings sharp, too. He was angles and darkness, her opposite—a moon-creature to her sun, a slicing shadow to her glow. But that was all silhouette. It was in his smile, and in his eyes, and in his waiting—he was still waiting—that she saw him, and knew him. Strength and grace and loneliness and longing.

And hope.

And hesitation.

He was standing still to let himself be judged, and it shamed her. She saw it in his stillness. He was afraid that she would think him a beast, and how could she assure him of what she herself, five seconds before, had been uncertain? How could she tell him that he was magnificent, and she was humbled—speechless not with distaste but with awe.

She tried. "I . . . You . . . It's . . ."

Nothing more came. No words. She was failing at this. It was beyond her skill. What had she thought, that she would be able to summon some warmth from within herself, when she'd spent her entire life stifling it? He would think she was disgusted by him, by the way she was acting, stiff as a board, and silent as the godforsaken stalagmites all around her. She had to try harder.

She . . . nodded.

Oh, great. Do that *some more. At least it's one up on the stalagmites.*

She folded one arm across her ribs, tight, and with the other reached up as though to stop herself from nodding, and ended up putting her hand over her mouth, as if to prevent herself even from talking.

Really? Was this really the best she could do? He was watching her tie herself in a knot, hand over her mouth in a gesture that could so easily be misinterpreted, and there came a flicker of uncertainty into his wide, brown—*sweet*, brown—questioning eyes, which drove her to one final, monumental effort.

"I like it," she whispered, and her hand didn't stop her from nodding like a fool, but it did muffle her words, so that Ziri didn't understand.

He inclined his head in query. "What?"

She moved her hand away, and said, as clearly as she could—which wasn't very—"I like it. *You*, I mean." And then she put her hand right back over her mouth and reddened, and was about ready to call on that fell chimaera goddess of assassins to come and put her out of her misery when the flicker of uncertainty vanished from Ziri's brown eyes.

What his smile did then should have irritated her, because it splayed crooked in amusement—at her expense, at her extreme discomposure, and Liraz had never been able to bear teasing—but it didn't stop there. It kept going, his smile, from amused to purely pleased to deeply relieved. It was so lovely that she felt it in her heart.

"Good," he said. "I like you, too."

And she blushed deeper, but he was blushing, too, now, so it wasn't so bad.

No, it was still bad. What now? Was she supposed to string more incoherent sentences together? Maybe she could list all the other things she liked, how she imagined a child might, except that—oh, well, she didn't like many things, so the list would be short, and it would only kill a moment.

She didn't want to kill a moment. She wanted to *live* one. Live *many*.

So how in the name of the godstars do you do *that?* Was it too late to learn?

"Uh," said Ziri. He moved his shoulders, rolling them, and shook open his wings. They flared, seeming in the close space as vast as a stormhunter's, and he said, clearing his throat, "One of the worst things about being the Wolf was not being able to fly. I'm going to, now." He was awkward, his voice halting, as he gestured out through the crescent opening where the time of purest blue had passed to black, and the stars were thick as sugar.

Oh. Okay. Liraz was almost—*almost*—relieved to have this ended, so that she could slink away. Melt. Curse herself. Die a little.

Ziri cleared his throat and looked at her. So earnest. So hopeful. "Do you . . . want to come?"

Flying? That was something she could do. She didn't even have to risk the syllable it would take to say yes. She just had to nod.

78

(Breathe)

Karou combed her hair. Calmly. Well, the calm was an exercise. *(Breathe.)* She laid down the comb. It was a Kirin relic that she'd found: carved bone with a crude silhouette of a stormhunter etched into the handle. She was going to keep it.

(Breathe.)

By the light of a flickering skohl torch, she looked down at herself. She was still in her Esther clothes. They were in a decent enough state, though she didn't like knowing there was Razgut drool on her sleeve. She'd left a few things here in the caves when she went away, but they were dirtier still. She wondered if she would ever again know the simplicity of a closet full of clothes, and the pleasure of choosing an outfit—a *clean* outfit—in which to go and meet her... *what*? What could she call Akiva?

Boyfriend sounded too Earth. *Lover* was affectation, intended to shock. "Have you met my *lover*? Isn't he *divine*?" Nope. That is, *yep*, he was divine. *Nope*, she wasn't go to call him that, even if she was dizzy with the urgency to *make* him that.

(Breathe.)

Partner? Too dry.

Soul mate?

A warmth spread through her. When had it ever been truer than it was for her and Akiva? And yet, as a word, it, too, rang with wan associations. "You like the Pixies? I swear, it's like we're soul mates!"

Well, she didn't have to call him anything right now. She just had to go to him, and she was pretty sure he wouldn't care what she was wearing.

One last breath. Her heartbeat kicked up a notch, getting wind that it was time, really and truly time, at last.

Akiva had helped her conjure Ziri's body. He'd tithed, at his insistence, and he didn't need vises, which was good, because she didn't think she could have touched his bare skin to clamp them on without dissolving back into the state of tremulous hunger that had possessed her in the grand cavern. She'd sunk into her trance state knowing he was there, and then, when it was done—the new body wrought and stretched out on the floor, as yet inanimate—she had come back out of herself to the sight of Akiva watching her. He'd looked kind of dazed with happiness, and immediately the same feeling had bloomed in her.

"That's the longest I've ever been able to look at you," he'd said.

"I thought you were going to watch the resurrection." She gestured to the new body, glorying in the sight of it. It looked almost exactly like Ziri's true flesh had, and she thought that he could pass as his natural self. She'd even left off hamsas, in part because the true Ziri hadn't had them, and in part because she wanted them to become obsolete.

"I meant to watch," Akiva said, abashed, and scratched his fingers through his short, thick hair in that way he had. "I got distracted."

"Well, no fair. I didn't get to look at you back."

"I promise to hold still for you later." Later? *After*, he meant. After they'd had their fill of *not* holding still.

(Breathe.)

"I accept."

And then, and then, oh holy, at last: the smile.

The smile that she had never yet seen with these eyes, but only remembered through Madrigal's. Warm with wonderment, a smile so beautiful it ached. It crinkled his eyes, and shaped his beauty into another kind of astonishing, a better kind, because it was the astonishment of happiness, and that reshapes everything. It makes hearts whole and lives worth living. Karou felt it fill her, dizzy and delirious, and she fell a little deeper in love.

He'd offered to leave her to finish the resurrection alone, and she'd accepted, because she wanted to have a moment with Ziri, as he'd guessed she must. And seeing Ziri's new eyes open—brown, and not ice-blue, and with none of Thiago's arrogance to overcome in letting himself shine through—had been the sweetest moment yet in her career as a resurrectionist. She'd hugged him, and held him, and told him it was all over, he didn't have to hide anymore, and his relief had been so profound it had deepened her already very deep appreciation of what he'd put himself through for all their sakes.

Between them they'd come up with the simplest explanation they could for his absence and return, and then he'd gone. Karou thought that he'd been so happy to be in Kirin form again that he'd just wanted to fly, though maybe he'd sensed her own distraction. Or it could have been the news of who'd been carrying his soul around in a canteen, and was out there in the caverns somewhere, waiting.

Whatever the reason, he'd gone off quickly enough, and here she was, her last duty fulfilled, her time her own. She paused, took a breath. From the pocket of her bag she collected one small thing that she'd been been carrying since the sultan's picnic on the floor of the desert hotel in Morocco, a couple of days past. A whim.

A wishbone. Smiling, she closed it in her hand. From the first night, it had been their parting ritual at the temple of Ellai: to make a wish. She was ready for ritual again, but not the parting part. They'd had enough of that to last them lifetimes.

She went. She walked, holding the wishbone to her heart. Or she started out walking but was soon enough gliding, skimming along, not touching the floor. *One could get lazy*, she thought, but she wasn't especially worried about it. The passages twisted. Her torch flickered green, trailing long and threatening to go out when she went too fast. It was almost used up, but she wouldn't need it, as soon as she was with Akiva.

And she came to the entrance to the bath cavern. There was a laugh in her throat as she rounded the bend, ready to murmur, laughing, *Finally, finally, I thought I might die*, against his mouth, against his throat, hungry and laughing and eager and—

She stopped short.

Akiva wasn't here.

Of course, murmured a tiny, cold voice in her heart.

She smothered it. *Yet*. Akiva wasn't here *yet*. Which was odd, because he'd said he was coming directly. Well, okay. No reason for concern. Maybe he'd gotten lost. No. Karou had more respect for Akiva's resourcefulness than to believe that. Maybe he'd gone to do something, thinking he could still make it back before she did. She *had* gotten here fast; Ziri hadn't lingered.

The water was pale green and steaming, the crystal growths glittered, and the curtains of darkmoss swayed where their longest tendrils trailed in the current. Karou considered slipping out of her clothes and into the water, but only briefly, and not seriously. A feeling of foreboding was working its knuckles into her shoulders. It was a more advanced feeling of foreboding than she was prepared for, and she realized when it hit that she'd been waiting for the other shoe to drop ever since they flew back through the Veskal portal. What other shoe? She didn't know. That cold little *of course* voice didn't know, either. It just knew—*she* just knew, on some level—that it had all been too easy.

It was a sensation in the spine, like she'd gotten just before the Dominion ambush. There was something she was missing.

Yes. *Akiva.* That's what she was missing.

He should be here.

She tried to be reasonable. She'd only been here five seconds; he would come around the corner any second.

But he didn't.

Of course, of course. Did you really think you could have happiness?

Karou's pulse hammered faster and her breathing shallowed, but it was panic barely contained, this time, not desire.

Akiva didn't come.

Karou's torch sputtered and died, and she had no seraph fire to light her passage back. She had to feel her way in darkness, clutching her unbroken wishbone to her heart.

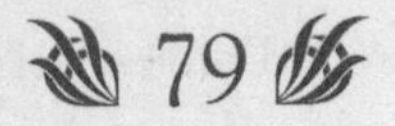

Legends

"Look."

Ziri saw the stormhunter before Liraz did. He didn't point, only breathed the word, not wanting to send it veering in the opposite direction. The creatures could sense the smallest movements from impossible distances. In fact, it was a marvel that it was flying this near them.

It was flying *toward* them.

Liraz did look, and Ziri was caught as much by the play of starlight over the fine planes and curves of her face as by the sight of a stormhunter on a direct path for them. More, in fact, and easily. He watched her watch it, and drew wonder from her wonder.

Until she said, eyes narrowing, "Something's wrong."

He turned, and saw that in the moment that he'd been looking at Liraz, the creature had veered aside, and was no longer on a course for them. It was still distant, and for a beat he didn't see what it was that had alarmed Liraz. It was gliding, tilting on an updraft. It looked glorious.

Ziri squinted. "Is that—?"

"Yes."

Liraz's voice was tense, and for good reason. This was an anomaly akin to . . . well, akin to a Kirin and a Misbegotten going for a starlight fly together. Strange, Ziri thought, was going to have to try harder in the future. Still, it *was* strange.

It was the unmistakable shimmer of seraph wings.

His first thought was that an angel was hunting it, somehow pursuing it. But nothing in the manner of its flight suggested distress. It was just flying, and an angel was flying alongside it.

"Have you ever heard of that happening?" he asked.

Liraz gave a small laugh, barely a breath. "No. I know Joram wanted one for his trophy room. It was a sport, for a while. Every lickspittle lord and lady in the Empire hoped to bring him one, with no luck, and some died trying, and finally he had to call in hunters, trappers. The best. And do you know how many they got?"

It was the most she'd spoken since he found her in the entrance cavern, so disarmingly tongue-tied, and again Ziri found himself pulled to watch her, half forgetting the stormhunter and the mystery of a seraph flying at its side. "How many?" he asked.

"None."

"I'm glad."

"Me, too."

He realized, with a pang of deep sorrow, that though she was directly upwind of him, and the spice scent of her was as bright to his senses as a color, he could no longer detect the other—the secret perfume, so fragile, that hid within it. He had breathed it while carrying her in his arms, but his Kirin senses were duller than the Wolf's had been, and it was lost to him now. Well, he would always remember that it was there. That was something. Being the Wolf had given him that, at least.

They held their position and watched in silence as the stormhunter went on tilting and wheeling, the angel keeping pace with it, sometimes pulling ahead, sometimes falling behind.

"Come on," said Liraz, when it began to put distance between them, heading north. "Let's follow them."

They did, and saw that their path was erratic, carrying them near to cliff faces where the wind funneled and charged, and then up to circle around a minor peak, threading through a terrain of clouds. Eventually they spun and headed, once more, toward Liraz and Ziri.

They watched the stormhunter come, and it was very near before Ziri realized that the figure flying along with it was not its only company. There were figures *riding it*. He hadn't noticed them before because, not being seraphim, they didn't give off light.

"Is that—?" he began, dumbfounded.

"I think it is," breathed Liraz.

It was. And, catching sight of Liraz and Ziri, they gave sharp cries in their strange human language. Ziri could, of course, not understand what they said, but the note of victory was plain, as was the pure, delirious joy.

And who could blame them for it? Mik and Zuzana had tamed a stormhunter. They were going to be legends.

80

A Choice

Akiva didn't know what was happening to him. He was in the bath cavern, heart pounding, waiting for Karou.

And then he wasn't.

Time stuttered.

"There is the past, and there is the future," he had said to his brothers and sisters not long ago. "The present is never more than the single second dividing one from the other."

He'd been wrong. There was *only* the present, and it was infinite. The past and the future were just blinders we wore so that infinity wouldn't drive us mad.

What was happening to him?

He had lost awareness of his body. He was inside that realm of mind, the private universe, the infinite sphere of himself where he went to work magic, but he hadn't come here of his own accord, and couldn't rise back out.

Had he been put *here?*

There was a sense of presence. A feeling that voices were passing just out of reach. He couldn't hear them. He only felt them as ripples skimming at the surface of his awareness. As the drag of fingers on the far side of silk. They were in discord.

Energies vied. Not his own.

His own was coiled, clenched. This was what he knew, this was *all* he knew: He was not where he needed to be. Karou would come and he wouldn't be there. Perhaps it had happened already. Time had come unspooled. Had it been ten minutes? Hours? It didn't matter. Focus. There was only the present. You had only to open your eyes in the right direction to be whenever you wished.

But there were an infinite number of directions and no compass, and it didn't matter because Akiva couldn't open his eyes. He was pressed deep. Contained. This was being done to him.

He was not where he needed to be. He was taken. The impotence of it, and at a moment when his hope had been so full he couldn't contain it. To be crushed down now and robbed of will, when Karou was waiting for him, when they had finally come to a moment that could be *just theirs*. It was unbearable.

So Akiva didn't bear it. He pushed.

At once, the thunder. Thunder as a weapon, thunder in his head. He recoiled from it, but not for long. Thunder is sound, not barrier. If that was all that was holding him, then he wasn't truly held. He gathered every fiber of his strength into a silent roar and pushed, and it exploded in him, merciless, but he was explosive, too, and unflinching.

And he was through it, past it, into silence and the aftershock colors of his violent passage, and... his *self*. He felt himself. His edges where they pressed on rock. He was lying on the ground, and it was not into silence that he had spilled, but only into a pause between voices, the air taut with the tug of their discord.

"It's the wrong way."

It was a woman's voice, strange to him, its inflections softer than the Seraphic he knew, though not altogether unfamiliar.

"We've wasted enough time here." Sharper, this voice, and younger. Also a woman. "Should I have let him keep his appointment? Do you think it would be easier for him to leave *after* having his taste of her?"

"His *taste*? He's in love, Scarab. You must let him choose."

"There is no choice."

"There is. You're making it."

"By letting him live? I should think you'd be glad."

"I am." A sigh. "But it must be *his* decision, can't you see that? Or he'll always be your enemy."

"Don't tempt me, old woman. Do you know what I could do with an enemy like that?"

Another silence fell and echoed, dissonant with shock. Akiva understood that they were speaking of him, but that was all he understood. What choice? What enemy?

Scarab, the one was called. There was something there. Something he should know.

When the other spoke, her voice was thin, rising out of the pit of her shock. "Make a harp string of him, is that what you mean? Is that what you would do with my grandson?"

Grandson. Only for a moment, hearing this, did Akiva think, *It isn't me, then, that they're discussing.* He was no one's grandson. He was a bastard. He was—

"Only if I had to."

"How could you possibly have to?" This came out as a cry. "It's a dark thing that you've begun, Scarab. You must end it. That isn't who we are. We're not warriors—"

"We should be."

Concussions of shock.

"We were," continued Scarab. There was a tone of stubbornness in her, and the willfulness of youth clashing with age. "And we will be again."

"*What are you saying?*" Akiva's defender—his . . . grandmother?—was aghast. Staggered. Akiva knew because he felt her turmoil enter him, and he understood. It entered him and became his own, just as he had pushed his despair into every soldier in the Kirin caves, and it had become theirs. This woman had called him grandson, and there was another vital piece to this puzzle. *Scarab.*

Accompanying the audacious basket of fruit the Stelians had sent to answer Joram's declaration of war had been a note, unsigned but for a wax seal depicting a scarab beetle.

Stelians.

Akiva opened his eyes and came upright in one movement. They were in a cave, and it looked and felt like the Kirin caves, and sounded like them, too, eerie with wind flutes, and he registered relief in the back of his mind. He hadn't been taken away, then. Karou wouldn't be far off. He would be able to find her, and make things right.

The two women were before him, and gave a start at his sudden lurch. It meant something that neither leapt back, nor even stepped back. Scarab's eyes didn't even widen, but only fixed on him and he was still again, held frozen in the act of rising to his feet, and suddenly intensely aware, as he had been before, when he felt an unseen presence in the cave, of the discrete entity that was his life.

And of its fragility.

They held him motionless and stared at him. All he could do, because he couldn't move, and because it was all he wanted to do anyway, was stare back.

He hadn't seen a Stelian since he was five years old and had taken one last desperate look over his shoulder at his mother as he was dragged from her. Here were two women, and the older of them... Akiva couldn't say that she looked like Festival, because he didn't remember his mother's face, but looking at this woman made him feel as though he did. Scarab had called her "old," but she wasn't, nor young, either. Cares had touched her, deepening the set of her eyes, etching the corners of her mouth. Her hair was a braid wound as a crown and shot through with silver bright enough to seem like ornament. In her eyes still echoed tremors of her recent shock, and a deep, a very deep pathos. Toward her, from first sight, Akiva felt kinship.

The other, though.

Her black hair was unbound and wild. She wore a storm-gray tunic that wrapped her slim form in slanting folds, fastening at her shoulder to leave bare her brown arms that were ringed wrist to shoulder with evenly spaced golden bands. Her face was severe. Not like Liraz's, or Zuzana's, made so by expression only, but sculpted for it from the start. Sharp, with the hard, hunting brow of a hawk, shadowing her eyes in a line. The way her cheekbones and jaw cut to edges seemed the work of a chisel, but her mouth was full and dark, her only softness.

Until she smiled at him, that is, and he saw that her teeth were shaved to points.

Akiva recoiled.

He saw then, for the first time, that there were more besides the two women: another woman and two men, for five in all. The others had been silent and remained so, but watched them with burning intensity.

"Clever you," said Scarab, pulling Akiva's attention back to her. And now he saw that her teeth were normal, white and straight. "We mustn't underestimate you, I suppose." She turned on the other woman. "Or did *you* release him, Nightingale?"

Nightingale. She shook her head without once taking her eyes off Akiva. "I did not, Queen." Queen? "But I won't bind him again. This is where we grant him the dignity due his birth and *talk to him*."

"Talk to me about what?" he asked. "What do you want with me?"

It was Scarab who answered, with a dark sideward glance to Nightingale. She was regal in her arrogance, so that Akiva thought he would have known now, if he hadn't already heard, that she was queen. "A choice has been made on your behalf. By me."

"And that is?"

"Not to kill you."

It wasn't a complete surprise, given what he had overheard, but there was a force to it, so bluntly spoken. "And what have I done to call my life into question?" Being certain of his own innocence, he didn't expect the vehemence of her reply.

"*Much*," she snapped, biting a piece off the air. "Never doubt it, scion of Festival. By rights you're dead already."

He tried to rise to his feet, but found himself still constrained. "Can you let me go?" he asked, and to his surprise, she did.

"Because I don't fear you," she said.

He stood. "Why should you? Why should I threaten you, even if I could? How many times have I wondered about the people of my mother's blood? And never once with a thought to *hurt* you."

"And yet no one has come so close to destroying us in over a thousand years."

"What are you talking about?" he burst out. He'd never even been near the Far Isles, nor seen a Stelian. What could he have done?

Nightingale cut in. "Scarab, don't taunt him. He doesn't know. How could he?"

"Know what?" he asked, quieter now, because when they came from Scarab, in anger, the accusations seemed absurd, but from Nightingale, in sadness, they did not. The intrusion in his mind. The tide of power sweeping through him. The way he felt . . . *discarded* after, as though it had used him, and not the other way around. Faltering, he asked, "What have I done?"

81

The Wish Police

What Zuzana actually said, crying out from the stormhunter's back, was, "Oh my god! All mountains look the same!"

They were lost, though it was frankly astonishing that they'd made it this far, to say nothing of the *style* of the journey.

The first was owing chiefly to the maps buried in Eliza's mind, and the second to music, and Mik's having charmed, with his violin—a new and better one than he'd left in Esther's bathtub—a flying creature the size of a small ship. Zuzana had no problem claiming her share of the credit, though. She was confident that her enthusiasm throughout had been the true driving force in this endeavor.

From the moment of Eliza's revelation that she knew another portal—the one her many-greats grandmother had been exiled through a thousand years ago—Zuzana had been ready to go. Never mind that it was *in Patagonia* (wherever *that* was. . . . Oh. Hell. Really, *really* far. *Seriously?*), they had the means to get there.

Wishes were fun.

They were also rare, and irreplaceable, and sacred, having been made by Brimstone, and they were not to be spilled out like pocket change on a candy counter. Besides, Karou was likely to have far greater need of gavriels than they ever could, not that they would do her any good if they couldn't *get* them to her, so the deal they had made amongst themselves was this: They would get them to her. Simple. And they would make every effort to do so without recourse to gavriels. Mik had joked about the "wish police" once, playing Three Wishes back at the caves, and now he teased Zuzana that she had become just that.

"No samurai skills?" He'd made puppy-dog eyes. "Or perhaps some other, more cautiously phrased superpower request?"

"We can get Virko or someone to teach us how to fight," she'd said. "It's a nonessential wish."

"It's a *lazy* wish. That's its appeal. Learning stuff is hard."

"Says the violinist to the artist."

"Right. *Right.*" He'd beamed. "We totally know how to learn stuff." He'd turned to Eliza. "Scientist and smart fellow learner-of-stuff, want to do samurai-monster training with us? We intend to become dangerous."

"I'm in," she'd said, that easy. Eliza Jones was what's known in fruit parlance as: a peach.

Really. If they weren't tied together by a quirk of fate and a crazy shared purpose, Zuzana would still have wanted to be friends with her. That didn't happen often, and she was really, really glad it was the case. If Eliza had been a whiner, or a prima donna, or some kind of *loud chewer* or something, this journey could have been a nightmare.

What it had been, instead, was awesome.

First, getting to Patagonia (which turned out to be in Argentina, mainly, with a slice of Chile thrown in; who knew?). That only required money, which they had no shortage of, on account of Karou's accounts being perfectly in order, apparently unmolested by Evil Esther. *In your face again, fake grandma.* Zuzana had lamented not being able to gloat at least, or better yet make good on her threat, but Mik, for his part, had been sanguine.

"Having to keep her own company for the rest of her life is vengeance enough," he said.

Little imagining.

Eliza, it turned out, had a wicked yen for vengeance, too, which only made Zuzana like her more. She looked so sweet, with those big, beautiful eyes, but she knew how to nurse a grudge. She demurred from wasting a wish on her nemesis, though, who sounded like *such* a rancid little weenie, until Zuzana persuaded her that a shing—of which they had dozens, and which were far too modest to be of any real heroic value to Karou—could still wreak a satisfying morsel of revenge.

She'd told her about Karou's most excellent torment of Kaz, and had her and Mik both in helpless laughter describing the sight of his nude Adonis body doing a spastic itch-dance on the model stand. But it was the companion piece to that revenge—Svetla's ever-grow eyebrows—that had been Eliza's inspiration.

She'd kissed the shing like lucky dice before pronouncing, "I wish that the hair just between Morgan Toth's nose and upper lip will grow in at a rate of an inch per hour, beginning now, ending one month from now."

There was always that moment of wondering if your wish exceeded the medallion's power, but the shing vanished with her last syllable.

"You do realize," Mik had said, "that you just described a Hitler mustache?"

By the glint in her eye, they gathered that she did. The revenge was not complete, however, if the subject didn't know who was responsible, so she'd sent, to his work e-mail, a picture of herself, finger raised to her lip like a mustache. Subject line: *Enjoy.*

"We have to do that to Esther, too," Zuzana had declared. "*Right now.*"

So they did, and began their journey in the best of all possible ways: imagining, in solidarity, the bewildered horror of their enemies.

A long flight, some shopping for cold-weather gear and supplies, a long drive, a long hike—in the snow; damn, it was winter in the Southern Hemisphere—and they were there. Near enough to the portal to contemplate a couple of gavriels for flight. They almost did it, too, but it had become a matter of honor by this point, to preserve them, so Mik said, "Let's just see what's on the other side before we decide. Eliza can carry us."

She did, and that was how they found out what no one in all of Eretz knew:

Where stormhunters nested.

And what none could have guessed:

They liked music.

And it was official: Mik's three fairy-tale tasks were accomplished. And the ring burning a hole in his pocket? The one that had seemed so crude in the light of the Royal Suite's shining marble bathroom?

It happened to look just perfect on stormhunter-back, with a northerly sea rolling beneath them, dotted with icebergs and breaching sea creatures that were not in any way whales. He couldn't go down on one knee without risk of falling off, but that was entirely okay, under the circumstances. "Will you marry me?" he asked.

* * *

The answer was yes.

* * *

"Am *I* glad to see *you*," Zuzana cried now, crowing at the sight of Liraz and Ziri. *Ziri!* Not the White Wolf, but Ziri! Oh. That meant he must have...But it was okay, wasn't it, because here he was in Kirin form again, and he looked pretty nearly exactly the same as he had in his natural flesh. He was smiling broadly, so very handsome, and Liraz at his side was smiling broadly, too, and beautiful, laughing in unbridled amazement, laughing. *Laughing like a person who laughs. Liraz.*

That seemed almost more amazing than showing up on a freaking stormhunter. But wasn't.

Because *nothing* was as amazing as that.

"Can you tell them," Zuzana asked Eliza, after the initial jag of laughing and exclaiming in mutually non-understandable languages had begun to subside, "that we can't find the caves?"

Eliza spoke Seraphic, which was handy, but also mildly irritating, as it undercut any sound argument Zuzana might have made for spending a wish to acquire an Eretz language herself. It would have been Chimaera, though, because come on.

"We'll just have to learn that, too," Mik had said with a sigh that didn't fool her for a second. "Resurrection and invisibility and fighting and now non-human languages, too? What is this, *school?*"

But Eliza wasn't translating, and Zuzana realized she was staring at Ziri agog. *Oh!* Right. His body. She'd seen his body at the pit. That was going to take some explaining. "It's him," Zuzana confirmed. "We'll tell you later."

And so translations were given—to Liraz, who in turn translated to Ziri in Chimaera—and then they were guiding them back south, asking things like where they'd come from and whether the stormhunter had a name, and when Zuzana spotted the crescent, she realized a flaw in her grand vision of sweeping in and bowling everyone over with amazement and tornado-force wingbeats.

The stormhunter—who did not have a name—wasn't going to fit through the crescent. Well, damn.

She had to put a halt to small talk and make herself understood. "We need an audience. This needs to be witnessed, and spoken of far and wide. *Sung.* I want songs to be written about this. Do you mind? Could you go get everyone? And Karou?"

At which point Ziri and Liraz both got all bashful and weird, and Mik suggested, delicately, that perhaps Karou and Akiva were... busy.

Collision of emotions! Thrill at the thought that *at last* Karou and Akiva were "busy"! And injustice, that it should coincide with her own moment of glory. "We can interrupt them for *this*, though, right?" she begged. They were coasting in circles now, forestalling the moment they would have to disembark and enter the caves on foot.

"No," spake Mik, voice of sanity.

"But—"

"*No.*"

"Fine. But I want *someone* to see us."

Everyone saw them. Liraz went to fetch them, and they crowded into the crescent, and there were gratifying gasps and shouts. Zuzana heard Virko's affectionate bellow of "*Neek-neek!*" and then felt, finally, that it was okay to bring this ride to an end.

They brought the huge creature as close as they could to the rock face and jump-scrambled from its back, hugging its vast neck first in thanks and farewell. They supposed it would go now and leave them, but hoped that it wouldn't ("If it doesn't, we're naming it."), and they paused to watch, wistful, as it rose higher and higher until it was just a shape cut from the glittering vault of the sky.

Only then, turning toward the gathered chimaera and seraphim, did they realize that something was wrong. There was a pall over their manner, and... Karou was there. *Not* busy. *Why* not? And why was she standing way back there? And where was Akiva?

Karou gave them a wave, and a brief marveling smile and head shake, and her eyes popped at the sight of Eliza's wings, of course, but even that didn't draw her forward to greet them. She was talking to Liraz, and Liraz was no longer laughing like a person who laughs. She was back to her most terrible self. Tight-lipped and white-nostrilled with ire, more savage than ever the White Wolf had looked.

Zuzana forgot all her glory and rushed to her friend. "What? What what what? God, Karou, *what?*"

"Akiva." So lost. Karou looked so lost. That wasn't how she was supposed to look. "He's gone."

82

Aberration

—There is a reason—

("What have I done?")

—There is a reason for the tithe.

This wasn't speech. What Nightingale conveyed to Akiva, she did so in silence, in sending, and it was more than words. It was memory opened to him, in sound and image, and emotion unfolded for him, in horror and heartache. It was not possible to misunderstand. He stood before Nightingale and Scarab and outwardly he saw them, and the other three behind them. But inwardly, he experienced something else, and shrank from it.

—Be calm. You are my child's child.

Festival. Nightingale gave her to Akiva in a memory so saturated with yearning that he understood, for its duration, what he himself could have no context for: a parent's love for a lost child.

—I wish to know you. To help you, and not to hurt you. And so you must listen to me. You are my child's child, but I never knew of you.

Festival was lost to us. Vanished. Only because you exist do I know what became of her. I know that my beloved daughter was a concubine in the harem of a warmonger who tore half a world apart.

She didn't disguise the desolation this caused her, and Akiva felt himself to be the root of it, as though time worked backward, and he had caused his mother to make the choice that would create him.

—*I also know that this could not have befallen her . . . against her will. She was Stelian, and mine. She was strong. And so she must have chosen this.*

The memories were as seamless as though they were Akiva's own. Running beneath the surface of Nightingale's words: a pure distillation of the woman who had been Festival, beautiful and troubled. Troubled? By a dowser's sense for the veins of fate, and a compulsion to follow them, even into the dark.

—*And so. And so she must have had a reason.*

From Nightingale's mind to Akiva's passed the understanding that for many Stelians, fate was as real as love or fear—a dimension of their life with weight enough to shape it. It was called *ananke*, this sensitivity to the pull of destiny. If your *ananke* was strong, well then, you could follow or resist, but with resistance came an oppressive sense of wrongness that would haunt your every choice.

—*And the reason must be you.*

The memories evanesced, leaving a void, and Akiva bereft in it.

You, you, echoing in the emptiness, and finding other words there, waiting. "My son will not be tangled in your feeble fates." But before he could begin to process this, a new sending bloomed in the space where Festival had been. It was very different: cold, and remote, and immense.

—*The Continuum that is the great All is bound and bounded by energies. We call them veils. They have other names, many, but this is the simplest. They are beyond our compass. They are the first and nest of all things, and this we know: The veils hold the worlds intact, and they hold them distinct. Touching, but separate, as the worlds are meant to be. When you pass through a portal, you're transgressing a cut in a veil.*

Veils, the Continuum, the great All. These were not terms that Akiva had heard, but he was gifted an idea of them, and there was reverence in it bordering on worship. It wasn't a picture or a memory, because that was impossible. No one can have *seen* the Continuum. It was everything. The sum of the worlds.

Until now, Akiva had known of two: Eretz and Earth. In Nightingale's sending, he understood . . . many.

It was dizzying. What he glimpsed in the idea of the Continuum was enough to make him want to fall to his knees. He beheld space, all around him and peeling open. And open, and open, no end to its opening, no limit to its dimensions. Like a god rearing its thousand-thousand heads, one after another after another after another, opening its thousand-thousand mouths to loose a tremendous, world-echoing roar—

—We draw energy from the veils to make magic. They are the source. Of everything. It is no simple matter. Power can't just be taken. There is a price, a trade of energies. This is the tithe.

"The pain tithe," Akiva said. He spoke it, not knowing how to communicate in kind, and saw Scarab's brows knit, while Nightingale's, which had been knit, fell smooth. She regarded him curiously, and her reply imparted gentle pity.

—Pain is one way. The easiest and crudest. The pain tithe is . . . using a plow to pluck a flower. Is it all you know?

He nodded. It was unnerving, this speaking without speaking.

"Not *all*," objected Scarab, aloud. "Or we wouldn't be here."

The way she looked at him, the blame. Akiva began to understand. "*Sirithar*," he said, hoarse.

Scarab's look sharpened. "So you *do* know."

"I know nothing." He said it bitterly, feeling it more keenly than he ever had before.

Sensing his distress, Nightingale came forward. She didn't reach for him but he felt, as he had once before, a cool touch at his brow, and knew it had been she who had prevented him from drawing power in the battle of the Adelphas, and who had, so briefly, soothed him after. In the next instant, he knew something else, and it staggered him: The enigma of the victory in the Adelphas. It had been them, of course.

These five angels had somehow turned the tide against four thousand Dominion. Many times over the past years, Akiva had tried to imagine the magic of his kin, but he had never guessed at such might as this.

Nightingale spoke now aloud, putting no more into his mind, and Akiva was glad of it, especially when he heard what more it was she had to say.

No cool touch could mitigate this.

"'*Sirithar*' is the energy itself, the raw substance of the veils. It is... the shell of the egg, and the yolk, too. It protects and it nourishes. It gives form to space and time, and without it there could be only chaos. You asked what it is you've done. You have taken *sirithar*." She sounded sad. "So much at once that to tithe for it would have killed you hundreds of times over, but it didn't, because you didn't tithe. Child of my child, you gave nothing, only took. It shouldn't be possible, and this is a very grave thing. What Scarab said is true. We tracked you here to kill you—"

"Before *you* could kill *everyone*." This from Scarab. No gentleness from her. It didn't matter.

Akiva was shaking his head. Not in denial. He believed them. He felt the truth of it, and the answer to the question that had been gnawing at him. But he still didn't understand. "I know nothing," he said again. "How could *I* kill—?" *Everyone*.

Nightingale's voice grew hoarse. "I do not understand why *ananke* guided my daughter to the creation of you. Why should the veils give birth to their own destruction?"

Ananke. Echoes and reverberations of fate. "Destruction?" echoed Akiva, hollow. All his life, it had been made clear to him that he was not his own, that he was only a weapon of the Empire, a link in a chain; even his name was only borrowed. And he had broken free, claimed himself. He had claimed his life as a medium for action—action of his own choice—and he had believed that he was finally free.

He didn't understand yet what Nightingale was telling him, or why Scarab held his life in question, but he understood this: All along, he had been ensnared in a far greater web of fate than ever he had ever dreamed.

His heart pounded, and Akiva knew that he was not free.

"It shouldn't be possible to take without a tithe," Nightingale repeated. She said it heavily, significantly, as though to be certain he understood. There was consternation and wariness in her look, and other flickers—blame? Possibly awe? "It *isn't* possible for anyone else," she added, her stare undeviating, and a word came to him—from a sending or from his own mind, he couldn't tell.

Aberration.

"But you've done it three times. Akiva, to take without a tithe thins the veil." Her gaze flickered to Scarab. She swallowed. "By thinning the veils..." She hesitated. This was it, Akiva knew. Here was the truth. It lurked behind her eyes, and it was as deep and bleak as any story ever told. He caught echoes, shreds. He had heard them before. *Chosen. Fallen. Maps. Skies. Cataclysm. Meliz.*

Beasts.

Nightingale tried to shy away from the telling, but Scarab didn't let her.

"You wanted to talk to him, didn't you? So talk. Tell him what it is we do, hour by hour, in our far green isles, and what he has to thank us for. Tell him why we've come for him, and what he nearly brought down on us. Tell him about the Cataclysm."

83

Most Things That Matter

Karou held a gavriel on her palm. Everyone was gathered around her in the grand cavern. Chimaera, Misbegotten, humans. And Eliza, whatever she was now. Karou looked to where the girl was standing back by Virko's side, and she didn't know what Eliza was, but that they shared this: They were neither of them quite human, but something more, and each the only one of her kind.

"What will you wish?" asked Zuzana.

Karou looked back down at the medallion, so heavy in her hand. Brimstone seemed to gaze back at her. It was a crude casting, but it still brought his eyes home to her in a rush, and his voice, so deep it had been like the shadow of sound.

"I dream it, too, child," he'd told her in the dungeon as she awaited execution, and she wished she could show him what was before her now—though no wish could ever accomplish that. *See what we've done.* See how Liraz and Ziri stand side by side. She would bet anything that the skin of their arms, so close to touching, was electrified as her own skin had been earlier, when Akiva was near her. And there was Keita-Eiri, who just a few days ago had been flashing her hamsas at Akiva and Liraz and laughing. She stood beside Orit, the angel from the war council who had glared across the table, arguing with the Wolf about the discipline of his soldiers. And Amzallag, who was ready, in the body Karou had made for him—not massive and gray like his last, or horrifying—to go and draw the souls of his children out of the ashes of Loramendi.

They were solemn and united, comrades who had fought together and survived an impossible battle, and who carried with them the mystery of it, and even more than solidarity. After the Adelphas, there was a creeping sense of destiny.

Destiny. Once again, Karou couldn't shake the sense that, if there was such a thing, it *hated* her.

As to Zuzana's question, what was she going to wish on this gavriel? What could she wish that would bring Akiva back to her, that would quell this vicious feeling stealing over her that they might accomplish everything they had believed they needed to, and still not be allowed to have each other? Brimstone had always been very clear as to the limits of wishing.

"There are things bigger than any wish," he'd said, when she was a little girl. "Like what?" she'd asked, and his answer haunted her now, this gavriel heavy in her hand, and all she wanted was to believe that it could solve her problems. "Most things that matter," was what Brimstone had said, and she knew he was right. She couldn't wish for the dream, or for happiness, or for the world to just let them be. She knew what would happen. Nothing. The gavriel would just lie there, Brimstone's likeness seeming to accuse her of foolishness.

But wishes weren't useless, either, so long as you respected their limits.

"I wish to know where Akiva is," she said, and the gavriel vanished from her palm.

84

The Cataclysm

Nightingale began the telling, but Scarab took it over. The older woman was being too gentle, trying to downplay the horror of a story that was the essence of horror—as though she feared the warrior before her wouldn't be able to bear it.

He bore it. He paled. His jaw clenched so tight that Scarab could hear the creak of bone, but he bore it.

She told him of the hubris of magi who had believed they could lay claim to the entire Continuum, and she told of the Faerers, and how the Stelians alone had opposed their journey. She told of the puncturing of the veils, how the chosen twelve had been taught to pierce the very fabric of existence, a substance so far beyond their ken that they might have been carrion birds pecking at the eyes of god.

And she told him what they had found on the far side of one far distant veil. And unleashed.

Nithilam, they named them, because the beasts had no language to name themselves, only hunger. *Nithilam* was the ancient word for mayhem, and that is what they were.

There was no describing them. No one living had ever seen them, but Scarab felt their presence, less here than at home, but even now. They were always there. They never stopped being there. Pressing, leeching, gnawing.

Being Stelian meant going to sleep every night in a house where monsters ravened on the roof, trying to force their way in. But the roof was the sky. The veil, really, but it aligned with the sky, in the Far Isles where everything was either sea or sky, and so they spoke of it this simply: the *sky* bleeds, the *sky* blooms. It sickens, it weakens, it fails. But it was the veil, made up of incalculable energies—*sirithar*—that the Stelians nurtured, guarded, and fed, every second of every day, with their own vitality.

Such was their duty. It was how they held the portal closed when the Faerers themselves had failed, and it was why their lives were shorter than those of their dissolute cousins to the north, who gave nothing, but only took from this world they had come to for sanctuary and then claimed by force.

Stelians bled energy to the veil that fools had damaged, to hold it against the mindless, battering force of the *nithilam*. The monsters. But they were greater than monsters, so vast and destructive that, to Scarab, only one word would do:

Gods.

Why else did such a word exist, if not to express an unseen immensity like this? As for the "godstars," so long worshiped by her kind, to Scarab they were no more use than a bedtime story. What good were bright gods who only watched from afar while dark gods strove every moment to devour you?

She imagined the *nithilam* as immense black rooting things, and their great mouths—pulsing, cartilaginous suckers—fixed to the veil like glower eels to the flesh of a sea serpent washed up on a beach, pale belly to the sun, dire and dying while its parasites still pulsed. Still sucked. Frenzied at the end to drain every mortal drop.

She didn't tell Akiva that. It was her own nightmare, what she saw when she closed her eyes in the darkness and felt the writhe of them against the veil. She only told him what the myth said, for in the myth was truth: There was darkness, and monsters vast as worlds swam in it.

And when she told him of Meliz, she saw the understanding sweep through him, and then the loss. It was an echo of what she'd seen a short time before, when Nightingale sent to him of Festival. Perhaps the older woman had meant to be kind. Or perhaps she was made blind by the grief of her own loss. It had surprised Scarab to be the one who saw what it did to Akiva, to have his mother given to him in a sending—his *first* sending, and his mind would be scrambling to distance it from reality—and then taken away again so abruptly.

And now Meliz. Meliz, crown of the Continuum, garden of the great All. The home world of the seraphim, and all the grace of its hundred thousand years of civilization. She watched Akiva's face as she simultaneously gave him the undreamable depths of his own history, the greatness of his ancestry, the glory of the seraphim of the First Age, and took it away. Meliz, first and last. Meliz, lost.

She reminded herself of what he was, and hardened herself to the waves of loss and sorrow working through him, each one seeming to rob something vital from him, leaving him... less than she had found him.

Was that what she wished? To diminish him? What *did* she want with him? She wasn't entirely sure. She had hunted him to kill him, but the answer, she knew now, was not that simple.

After the battle in the Adelphas, when she had scythed at life threads of attacking soldiers, gathering them for the beginning of her *yoraya*—that mystical weapon of her ancestors—the thought had settled in her that *his* thread would be its glory. His life to string her harp. His power, under her control.

And maybe that was the answer. Perhaps it had been the end that Festival's *ananke* had impelled her toward all along.

Scarab could wish her own *ananke* to be clearer on the matter.

On one matter, it was very clear. The *nithilam* were her fate.

And she was theirs.

She was always aware of them, but it was when she lay down to sleep, and darkness arched above her, that she felt herself to be facing them across an expanse. Across a barrier, yes, but there had always been—even before there was any sane hope to support it—a . . . premonition of challenge. Of locking into place, might against might, and no more barrier. She their enemy, as they were hers.

She *their* nightmare, as they were hers.

Scarab, scourge of the monster gods. Claimant to all the eaten worlds.

There still wasn't any *sane* hope. Scarab saw that Nightingale sensed what was growing in her—not only the *yoraya* begun, but its purpose—and how she shrank from it in horror. And who wouldn't?

The Stelians had built their life in this new era on the belief that the Cataclysm could not be defeated, but only held back. So they held it. They held it and died too young and without glory. Accepted a duty their forebears would have despised. Cowering and bleeding out their vitality, no thought given to meeting the enemy in battle because the enemy were world-devourers, and Stelians were no longer even warriors.

And because what they risked, if they failed, was...all that remained. *All* that remained. Eretz was the cork to a deluge of darkness that would meet no end. If the Stelians failed, every other world would fall.

None of this did she say to Akiva. By now she had told him everything but his own part in this story. It should have been easy for her to finish. *Look what he has done.* But her voice hid from her. Incongruously, faced with the bleakness she had caused in him, she flashed back to the way he'd smiled—at her but *not* at her—and she remembered the radiance that was in him then, and the joy, and how it had made her reel with discovery, like a novice introduced to the *lexica*, sensing, for the first time, an entire glittering, secret language. She'd seen it again in the bath cavern where he'd waited for...for what she had called, to Nightingale, "his appointment," not wanting to use the real word for what it was. For what the lovely, blue-haired alien stoked in him, and the radiance that was born of it.

Akiva was in love.

It was a pity, but it wasn't her problem. Next to the *nithilam*, it was as a footprint in ash, as fleeting, and as easily brushed away.

Her pause grew too long, and Nightingale, with great grace, tried to take the tale from her like a skein of yarn, to spin this final piece so that she would not have to.

Scarab shook her head and found her voice, and told Akiva the rest herself.

And she felt it in her chest, when he fell to his knees. She thought of Festival, whom she had never known, called to an ugly fate half a world away: to give up her own sanctity to a tyrant king for the sake of bringing this man into being: Akiva of the Misbegotten, who, for some ineffable reason, was powerful beyond all others.

Well, and it was Scarab's own ugly fate to fell him to his knees, but she thought that Festival would have understood. *Ananke* digs grooves so deep you can either follow it or live your life trying to scale the sides and escape. Scarab was not going to try to escape. Always, she had been growing toward this, ever since she heard of a harp strung with taken lives, and before that still, to the earliest moment when energies joined in the making of her. Her path lay before her, and Akiva was entangled in it.

She had come on this journey to hunt and kill a magus.

She would return from it armed to hunt and kill gods.

* * *

Once upon a time, there was only darkness, and there were monsters vast as worlds who swam in it. They loved the darkness because it concealed their hideousness. Whenever some other creature contrived to make light, they would extinguish it. When stars were born, they swallowed them, and it seemed that darkness would be eternal.

But a race of bright warriors heard of them and traveled from their far world to do battle with them. The war was long, light against dark, and many of the warriors were slain. In the end, when they vanquished the monsters, there were a hundred left alive, and these hundred were the godstars, who brought light to the universe.

Akiva tried to remember the first time he'd heard the myth. World-devouring monsters who swam in darkness. Enemies of light, swallowers of stars. Had it been from his mother? He couldn't remember.

Five years only he'd had her, and so many years since to blot them out. It could have come from the training camp, propaganda to build their hatred of chimaera, because that was how the tale had been twisted in the Empire: into an origin myth so ugly it was silly.

He'd told it to Madrigal their first night together, as they lay atop their clothes on a bank of shrive moss, heavy and lazy with pleasure. They'd laughed at it. "Ugly Uncle Zamzumin, who made me out of a shadow," she had said. Absurd.

Or not. Scarab called them by another name than the one Akiva knew, but it made its own sense. As *sirithar* had come to mean, in the Empire, the state of calm in which the godstars work through the swordsman, *nithilam* had been its opposite: the godless, thick-of-battle frenzy to kill instead of die. These names had once meant something about the nature of their world. Somehow, the truth had been lost.

Now Akiva learned that the monsters were real.

That every second of every day they battered at the veil of the world.

That the people who were half his blood lived their lives in devotion to shoring up that veil with their own life force.

And that he... *he*... had nearly torn it wide open.

He was on his knees. He was only dimly aware of getting there. What the Faerers had done was only half a cataclysm. In his ignorance, he had almost finished it.

—*Not just ignorance*, sent Nightingale, to his mind. She settled to her own knees before him, while Scarab stood where she was, unmoved. *Ignorance and power. They're a poor combination. Power is as mysterious as the veils themselves. Yours more than anyone's. We can't take it from you except by killing you, and we don't wish to do that. Nor can we leave you, and hope that you'll contain it on your own.*

And Akiva understood his choice that wasn't a choice. "What do you want from me?" he asked, hoarse, though he already knew.

"Come with us," said Nightingale, aloud. Her voice was soft and sad, but Akiva looked over her shoulder at Scarab, and saw no sadness in her and no mercy. His grandmother added, so softly, "Come home."

Home. It felt like a betrayal even hearing the word, all the more so as he was looking at Scarab when he did. Home was what he would make with Karou. Home *was* Karou. Akiva felt his future unraveling in his hands. He thought of the blanket that did not yet exist, the symbol of his simplest and deepest hope: a place to love and dream. Would they have to rip it in two, he and Karou, and carry their ragged halves with them where their fates were determined to lead them? "I can't," he said, desperate, not thinking what it meant, or that it might be construed as his choice.

Nightingale just looked at him, a twitch of disappointment at the corners of her mouth. As for Scarab, her face gave away nothing, and yet she made the nature of his choice very clear to him, in case he misunderstood. Twice before, he had been overcome by this sudden, intense awareness of his own life. This was the third time, and with it came a sending, cruder than Nightingale's, unmistakably Scarab's, and it wasn't cruel, only pitiless, and he understood that there was no space for pity, not for her. She was queen of a people enslaved by a burden so great that the entirety of the Continuum depended on them. She couldn't waver, ever, and didn't. This was *strength*, not cruelty. Her sending was an image: a shining filament held between two fingers, and the understanding, with it, that the filament was Akiva's life, and the fingers were her own, and that she could end him as easily as snapping.

And would.

But he sensed something else in the sending, and it surprised him. It would be safer for everyone, and easier for her, to kill him now. And not only easier, not only safer. There was something he couldn't quite grasp, there in the image of that shining filament. A harp string. Scarab and Nightingale had argued about it earlier, and Akiva sensed that the queen stood somehow to *gain* by killing him.

But she didn't want to.

"Well?" she asked.

And it was an easy choice. Life, first. You have to be alive, after all, in order to figure out everything else.

"All right," Akiva said. "I'll come with you."

And of course, because Ellai walked here—phantom goddess who had stabbed the sun, and who betrayed more lovers than she ever helped—Karou stepped into the cavern at just that moment, and heard him.

85

An Ending

"Akiva?"

Karou didn't understand what she was seeing. The fulfillment of her wish had been simplicity itself. No sooner had the gavriel vanished than she knew where he was: nearby but hidden, deep in a quarter of the Kirin caves that their party had yet to explore. So she'd guided them here, through many turnings, coming finally around this corner to find... Akiva on his knees.

There were five others, black-haired strangers, and she heard what he said to them but it didn't make sense, and she didn't run to him. She didn't *run*. Her feet never touched stone, but she was there inside a second, drawing him up beside her and looking at him, *into* him. Pouring herself into him, and knowing. At once.

Here was an ending.

He seemed to her a guttered fire, and all things lost and hollow. "I'm sorry," he said, and she couldn't fathom what had happened, in a matter of hours, to do this to him. Where was the waiting gaze, vivid and alive, and the laughter, the tease, the dance, the hunger? What had they done to him? She spun toward the strangers, and that's when she saw their eyes.

Oh.

"What is this?" she asked, and was immediately afraid to hear the answer. She waited for it, though, and it was slow in coming, or else she was misperceiving time again, and then Akiva took her into his arms and pressed his lips to the top of her head, long and lingering. As kisses go, it might have been fine, had it fallen on her lips. As answers go, it was very bad. It was *good-bye*, through and through. She felt it in the rigidity of his arms, the tremor of his jaw, the defeat in his shoulders. She pulled away, out from under the press of his good-bye lips. "What are you doing?" she asked him. Belatedly she processed what she'd heard him say first of all. "Where are you going?"

"With them," he said. "I have to."

She took a step back, glancing once more to this "them." Akiva's people, Stelians. She knew that he had never met any before, and couldn't guess what it meant, that they were here now. The older woman stood nearest, and she was very beautiful, but it was the younger woman Karou couldn't look away from. Maybe it was the artist in her. Sometimes, rarely, you see someone who doesn't look like anyone else, not even a little, and who could never, ever be mistaken or forgotten. That's what she was like, this seraph. It wasn't even beauty—not that she wasn't beautiful, in her sharp, dark way. She was unique, extreme. Extreme angles, extreme intensity, and her regal stance spoke volumes. Here was someone, Karou thought, envious, who had known exactly who she was from the day she was born.

And she was going to take Akiva away with her.

Because whatever this was, not for a second did Karou wonder or fear that Akiva was leaving her by choice. She felt the presence of her own friends and comrades closing the space behind her. All of them were here: Issa, Liraz, Ziri, Zuzana, Mik, even Eliza. Plus two score Misbegotten and more than two score chimaera, all prepared to fight for Akiva when they found him.

Only to find him *not* fighting for himself.

"I have to," he had said.

It was Liraz who responded. "No," she said, in the way she had of laying down a truth and standing over it like a lioness guarding a kill. "You don't." And she drew her sword and faced the Stelians.

"Lir, no." Akiva raised his hands, urgent. "Please. Put that away. You can't beat them."

She looked at him like she didn't know him.

"You don't understand," he said. "In the battle. It was them." He looked to the Stelians, focusing on the older woman. "Wasn't it? You fought our enemy for us."

She shook her head. "No. We didn't," she said, and Akiva blinked in confusion. But then she added, with a gesture to the fierce young woman at her side, "Scarab did."

And no one spoke. They remembered the way their enemies had fallen limp in battle and plummeted from the sky. One woman. One woman had done that.

Liraz let her sword slip back into its sheath.

"Please tell me what's going on," Karou whispered, and when Akiva turned again to the older woman, she thought for the briefest moment that he was ignoring her plea. In fact, he was making a plea of his own.

"Would you?" he asked. "Please?" And Karou had no idea what he meant by it, but was aware that something passed between the two women then: a wordless argument. Afterward she would understand that they'd debated telling them—*sending* them—the answer to her question, and that Nightingale had won. Because afterward Karou would understand all of it.

Into her mind—all their minds—came an experience of sense and feeling so complete it was like living it, and it was nothing Karou wished to live. She knew why Akiva had asked his grandmother—*his grandmother*—to answer them in this way, because no told truth could match this. It enveloped her and entered her: a history of tragedy and unspeakable horror, relentless and complex and yet somehow delivered with the utmost ease. It was simply given to her mind, compressed and precise, like a universe contained within a pearl. Or like memories pressed into a wishbone, Karou thought. But this history was so much deeper and more terrible than her own. It was dreamlike.

Nightmarish.

And she understood what had happened to Akiva since she saw him last, because now she was a guttered fire, too, and all things lost and hollow.

How do you take in something so massive and so hideous? Karou found out. You stand there gasping, and wonder how you ever found it in yourself to imagine a happy ending.

For a long moment, no one spoke. Their horror was palpable, their breathing louder than it should have been. There had been, briefly, in Nightingale's sending, a sensation of great weight and savage, quaking hunger, and now that they knew it, none of them would ever unknow it: the press of the *nithilam* against the skin of their world.

Karou stood but a pace away from Akiva, but it felt like a gulf, already. His own part in the story had been made clear in the sending, and there could be no question: He had to go. The reshaping of an empire had once seemed so huge to them, and now it was only a side note to the question of Eretz's very survival. Karou reeled. Akiva looked into her eyes, and she saw what he wanted to ask but wouldn't, because her own destiny was not some afterthought to pin to his. She couldn't go with him. Without her, there could be no rebirth for the chimaera people.

It was he who was meant to stay with her—"a prior commitment," as he had told Ormerod—but now he couldn't, and their story was, after all, *not* to be the story of all Eretz: seraphim and chimaera together, and a "different way of living." It was only one flutter out of millions within a world besieged, and once more, they were torn apart.

It was Liraz who broke the silence at last. "What about the godstars?" she asked, like a plea. "In the story, they battle the beasts and win."

"There are no godstars," said Scarab, and with her words came a brief, bleak sending: just a sundered sky and the understanding that there was nothing out there in all the vastness to watch over them, and no help coming. For the many gods they had named and worshiped in three worlds and more, when had help *ever* come? Scarab said, in a voice to match her words for bleakness, "And there never were."

It was the worst, the lowest moment of all, and Karou would always remember it as the blackest of shadows—the kind of black that shadows can only achieve when they lie alongside the brightest light.

Because another sending came to them then. It cut through the other, brilliant and blinding. It was *light*, reeling and abundant. A sensation of light. An *army* of light. There were figures limned in it, golden and many, and Karou knew who and what they were. They all knew, though the silhouettes didn't match the myth. This was dream logic, and heart-deep *knowing*. These were the bright warriors.

The godstars.

Karou saw Scarab's head snap up, and Nightingale's, too, and she read their shock and knew that this sending was not theirs, nor the other Stelians', either, who looked as staggered as they did.

So where did it come from?

"*Yet.*"

One word, from behind Karou, from within her own party, and the voice was familiar but too wholly unexpected for her to place it in that first instant. She had to turn and see with her eyes, and blink, and see again, before she could believe it.

"People with destinies shouldn't make plans," Eliza would say later, laughing, but right now what she said was, "There never were godstars *yet*."

Because it was her. Eliza. She came forward, and she was beatific, practically glowing. She had been all but forgotten amid the mingled creatures of this world, and no surprise, because none knew what she was, not really. She had told Mik and Zuzana that she was a butterfly, but they had no context for what this meant—the ramifications of it—and anyway, she was more than that. She was an echo, and more than that, too. She was an answer. Mystery sang from her skin; she was suffused with it like a black pearl. There were no ebon seraphim in this the Second Age; those of Chavisaery had perished with Meliz, and so the Stelians gazed at her, amazed.

She was fixed on Scarab, and Scarab on her. "Who are you?" asked the queen, her severity already softening into wonder.

Eyes bright with invitation, Eliza gave a nod, calling to Scarab to know her—to touch the thread of her life—and Scarab did, with a single fingertip of her *anima*, a featherlight caress that ran the length of it. Eliza shivered. The sensation was new, and gave her goose bumps, and she was able to think that it was funny, that her body should respond in so ordinary a way as goose bumps to the touch of a golden seraph queen at the thread of her very life.

Whatever Scarab read there, they all saw fire dance in her eyes, and she grew beatific, too.

None of them understood it then, except for Eliza and Scarab. Not even Nightingale. But all present in the Kirin caves that night—seraph, chimaera, and human—would ever afterward say that they felt, in that instant, a dark age quietly give way, and a bright one bloom into being. It was an ending overlapped by a beginning, and it was thrilling and confounding, primal and terrifying, electric and *delicious*.

It felt like falling in love.

Scarab took a step forward. All her life she had been haunted by *ananke*, the relentless tug of fate. It had been oppressive, and it had been elusive. It had caused her uncertainty and dread. But never had she experienced the perfect, puzzle-piece fulfillment of it that she did now. Completion. More than that. Consummation.

Ananke went quiet. Her release from it was like the silence when a baby's cries have become unendurable and then abruptly cease.

She stood before this woman—this seraph come from nowhere, of the lost line of Chavisaery whom all Meliz had revered as prophets—and all of Scarab's uncertainty and dread . . . evanesced.

"How?" she asked. How was it possible? Where had Eliza come from? Where had *her sending* come from, and what did it mean?

How? Eliza's gaze flickered to Karou and Akiva, and to Zuzana and Mik, and to Virko, who, she understood, had carried her on his back, away from the kasbah, away from government agents and who knows what else. The five of them had rescued her from infamy and madness, and from a life with no future. Because of them, she was here where she was supposed to be, and oh, she had a future now. They all did, and what a future it was. She took in the rest of the company too, and felt the same fulfillment that Scarab did. This was right. This was *meant*, and it was at once impossible and inevitable, like all miracles.

"I think it's time," was her answer. Spoken with wonder, her words weighed of fate, and even if the company didn't understand, they were unnerved by the gravity of the moment, and held their tongues.

Well. Except for Zuzana. She and Mik clung together, drinking everything in with their eyes and ears, and making sense of it, too—the words, at least—because Zuzana had snuck wishes into her pocket earlier, wish police be damned, and they had no sooner come into the presence of the strangers than she vanished two lucknows, one for herself and one for Mik, gifting them both the language of the angels.

It proved little help in interpreting the moment, though, and so Zuzana ventured to ask, "Um, time for what?"

A ripple of mirth moved through them all—and relief, that someone had given voice to the question they all wanted answered. *Indeed. Time for what?*

"Time for liberation," said Eliza. "For salvation. Time for the godstars."

"They're a myth," spoke Scarab, uncertain and ready to be persuaded. Like the rest of them, she held the vision from Eliza's sending in her mind, and didn't know what to make of it. She only knew that she wanted to believe it.

"They are," agreed Eliza, smiling. Everyone watched her. Everyone listened. How strange, that she should become the nucleus of this moment—this tremendous moment in the story of all their worlds.

"My people understood that time is an ocean, not a river," she said to them all. "It doesn't flow away and pour itself out, done and gone. It simply *is*—eternal and entire. Mortals might move through it in one direction, but that's no reflection of its true nature—only of our limitations. Past and future are our own constructs.

"And as for myths, some are made up, nothing but fantasy. But some myths are true. Some have already been lived. And in the drift of time, eternal and entire, some haven't." She paused, gathering up the words that would make them understand.

"Some myths are prophecy."

A race of bright warriors heard of the nithilam *and traveled from their far world to do battle with them.*

These were the godstars, who brought light to the universe.

Sometime in the midst of this, Karou and Akiva had bridged the space between them. They clung together now, their amazement making the cave reel around them. Their good-bye was not forgotten or evaded. Their fear was gone, but not their sorrow. Whatever happened here tonight, a parting was still before them.

Loramendi waited, all those souls quiet under ash. Karou was still the chimaera's last hope, and Akiva was what he was, unquantifiable and dangerous. But they had seen something in that golden sending, and the new future it laid open was as magnificent as it was appalling.

It was also, somehow, instantly . . . certain. It was as though Eliza's sending had spliced itself into all of their life threads and become a part of them.

There was no stepping back from this.

Ziri had caught Liraz's hand when the first dark sending gripped them, and he held it still. It was the first time either of them had ever held another's hand, and for them alone, the immensity of what unfolded that night was overshadowed by the perfect wonderment of fingers intertwined—as though this was what hands had always been for, and not for holding weapons at all.

Their wonder was also undercut by sorrow, as the understanding grew in them that they were not yet done holding weapons.

Not even close.

Eliza was a prophet, and she was a Faerer, too, and the first was great, because she gifted them this sending and all that it portended, but the second was greater, because she was the fulfillment of her own prophecy. Maps and memories were in her. Elazael of Chavisaery had, so long ago, journeyed beyond the veils and mapped the universes there, and because of what power-drunk magi had made of the twelve, those maps were all Eliza's now, and so were her foremother's memories of the beasts themselves. No one alive had beheld the *nithilam* or traveled the lands they had laid waste, but Eliza contained it all.

If Scarab was going to fight the Cataclysm, she would need a guide. And she was, and now she had one.

And more than a guide. Anyone could see it. Scarab and Eliza were settled fate and halves made whole from the moment they set eyes on each other. Even Carnassial, silent throughout, relinquished his hopes as quietly as he had ever held them.

And as for the rest of them, they'd all seen the silhouettes in the sending, and they all believed it in the way of dreams, without consideration or doubt. "Some myths are true," Eliza had said. "Some have already been lived. And in the drift of time, eternal and entire, some haven't."

And the rest of them knew two things at once: *who* the bright warriors were, and *what* they were.

The "what" was simple, though no less profound for it. They were the godstars, who in the swim of time had not yet come to pass.

And as for the "who"?

The silhouettes were light-drenched, magnificent, and... familiar. They saw *themselves*, each one of them, from Rath the Dashnag boy who was no longer a boy, to Mik, the violinist from the next world over, and Zuzana the puppet-maker. To Akiva and Liraz, who would never lose their longing for Hazael to be among them. To Ziri of the Kirin, lucky after all, and even to Issa, who had never been a warrior before. And to Karou.

Karou who had, a lifetime past, begun this story on a battlefield, when she knelt beside a dying angel and smiled. You could trace a line from the beach at Bullfinch, through everything that had happened since—lives ended and begun, wars won and lost, love and wishbones and rage and regret and deception and despair and always, somehow, hope—and end up right here, in this cave in the Adelphas Mountains, in this company.

Fate took a bow, so neat it all was, but still it stole their breath away to hear Scarab, queen of the Stelians and keeper of the Cataclysm, say, with a fervor that sent tremors up every last spine, including her own: "There will be godstars. And they will be us."

Epilogue

Karou woke most mornings to the sound of forge hammers and found herself alone in her tent. Issa and Yasri would have slipped out quietly before first light to help Vovi and Awar see to the volumes and volumes of breakfast that began their days in the camp. Haxaya was with the hunting party, away for days at a time tracking skelt herds up the Erling River, and who knew where Tangris and Bashees spent their nights.

By the time Aegir's first hammer fell—Karou's alarm clock these days was an anvil—Amzallag's excavation crew would already have eaten and left for the site, and the other work crews would be taking their turn at the mess tent.

Aside from the smiths—and they were forging thuribles now, not weapons—there were fishers, water haulers, growers. Boats had been built and caulked, nets woven. A few late summer crops had been seeded in good land a few miles away, though they all expected hunger this winter, after a year of razed granaries and scorched fields.

Fewer mouths to feed, though, and this was not a silver lining, but a truth that would, nevertheless, help get them through.

The rest concerned themselves with the city. What bones had survived the incineration had been buried first of all, and there was nothing to salvage in the ashes. There would be builders eventually, but for now the ruins had to be cleared, and the twisted iron bars of the great cage hauled away. They were still trying to find beasts of burden enough to accomplish this, and they didn't know what they would do with all the iron once they had the muscle to move it. Some thought that the new Loramendi must be built under a cage as the old had been, and Karou understood that it was too soon for chimaera to feel any safety beneath an open sky, but she hoped that by the time that decision had to be made, they might choose to build a city befitting a brighter future.

Loramendi might be beautiful one day.

"Bring an architect back with you," she'd told Mik and Zuzana, only half in jest, when they left for Earth astride the stormhunter they'd named Samurai. They'd gone back for teeth, primarily, chocolate secondarily—according to Zuzana—and to see how their home world fared in the aftermath of Jael's visitation. Karou missed them. Without Zuzana to distract her, she was always a step away from self-pity or bitterness. Though she was far from alone here—and a million miles from the isolation she'd suffered in the early days of the rebellion, when the Wolf had led them into bloodshed and she'd spent her days building soldiers to resurrect a war—the loneliness Karou knew now was like a blanket of fog: no sun, no horizon, just a continuous, creeping, inescapable chill.

Except in dreams.

Some mornings when the hammer woke her with its first ringing strike, she felt herself drop back into her life from some sweet golden sphere that lost all definition with the flood of consciousness—like vision blurred by tears. She was left with a feeling only; it seemed to her the impression of a soul, as she got when she opened a thurible, or went gleaning over the dead. And though she had never felt *his* soul—as, blessedly, he had never died—it left her awash with a sense of grace, like standing in the sun. Warmth and light, and a feeling of Akiva's presence so strong she could almost feel his hand to her heart, and hers to his.

This morning it had been especially powerful. She lay still, a phantom heat lingering on her chest and palm. She didn't want to open her eyes, but only rise back into the golden sphere and find him there, and stay.

Sighing, she remembered a silly song from Earth about how if you want to remember your dreams, as soon as you wake you should call to them as if they were little kittens. Pretty much the entire song went, "Here kitty kitty kitty kitty kitty kitty kitty kitty kitty kitty . . ." and it had always made her smile. Now, though, the smile was more of a twist, because she so wanted it to work, and it just didn't.

And then, at the flap door of the tent: a softly cleared throat. "Karou?" The voice was pitched low enough not to wake her if she still slept, and when she saw the figure framed in the opening, the dawn sun painting itself along the line of one strong arm as bright as gold leaf on an altarpiece, she was upright like a snapped spring.

Cover thrown aside, to her knees and rising before she realized her mistake.

It was Carnassial.

She couldn't disguise her anguish. She had to cover her face with her hands. "I'm sorry," she said after a moment, pushing it all down deep, as she did every morning, in order to get on with her day. She took her hands away and smiled at the Stelian magus. "It really *isn't* horrible to see you," she told him.

"It's all right." He stepped inside. She saw that he'd brought tea and her morning ration of bread, so that they might start out directly for the site. "It's good to know what it's supposed to look like when someone is happy to see you. Though I don't imagine most people ever get a reaction like that. I never have, but now I'll hold out for it all my life."

"Maybe it's a curse, anyway," said Karou, taking the tea from him. She understood that Carnassial had shared something with the queen, and that it was over now; she suspected it was why he had volunteered to come to Loramendi, instead of returning to the Far Isles with the others. "Or maybe it's like skohl," she said. That was the high-mountain plant whose stinking resin they burned on their torches at the caves. "And only grows in the worst conditions." You'd never find skohl in some sun-dappled meadow, but only on a cliff face, crusted with hoarfrost. Maybe heart-crushing love was the same, and could only grow in hostile environments.

Carnassial shook his head. He didn't really look that much like Akiva, but was mistaken for him constantly here, since Akiva was the only Stelian known to this part of the world.

"He did the same thing, you know," he told her. "The first time we saw him. We'd come to kill him. It would have happened then and there, if he hadn't turned out to be who he is. Scarab made a sound and he turned and fixed on where she was glamoured. And he smiled as though joy itself had just cornered him in the dark." He paused. "Because he thought it was you."

Karou's hand trembled, holding her tea, and she steadied it with the other, to little effect. "When did you get back?" she asked him, changing the subject. He had been to Astrae in his capacity as representative of the Stelian court. Liraz and Ziri had gone, too, to meet with Elyon and Balieros and discuss plans for the coming winter.

"Last night," Carnassial told her. "Some of yours came back with us. Ixander is furious to have missed the chance, in his words, to become a god."

A god. A godstar.

There had been plenty of discussion of what this meant since the night of Eliza's sending, and for the most part, they agreed that by no feasible interpretation were they going to become "gods." There was an extraordinary unity and solemnity among them, though, in accepting their fate. They would play a part in the realization of myth. It might have been a seraph myth before, but now it belonged to all of them. Mortal or immortal was beside the point. A war loomed, of such epic scope as made knees buckle and minds go dim, and *they* were the bright warriors who would banish the darkness.

"I'm going to just go ahead and consider myself a god," Zuzana had said. "You guys believe what you want."

Karou enjoyed the idea that you could "believe what you want," as though reality were a buffet line. If only.

Triple helpings of cake, please.

Carnassial went on about Ixander. "He says by right he should be one of the godstars, since he wanted to return to the Kirin caves with you, but was ordered to Astrae instead. I was afraid he was going to challenge me for my place." He smiled.

Karou found her own smile, imagining the big ursine soldier arguing loopholes with fate. "Who knows," she said. "It's not like we could freeze Eliza's sending and make a list of names." They couldn't see the sending again, either, because Eliza had gone to the Far Isles with the Stelians and Akiva. "Maybe we all saw what we wanted to see."

"Maybe," Carnassial agreed. "I saw you, though."

Karou couldn't reply in kind. She hadn't seen him. She had seen herself in the radiance of that vision, and she had seen Akiva at her side. The sight had been like a buoy to one drowning, and she clung to it still.

She did believe that the time would come when their duties would free them to be together—or at least a time when they could twist and bend and wrestle their duties into alignment. If they were bound to be dutiful fate-slaves forever, then mightn't they at least be dutiful fate-slaves on the same continent, perhaps even under the same roof?

Someday.

And hopefully *before* Scarab's war called them all to meet the *nithilam*.

And when would it? Not soon. This wasn't a confrontation to rush into. The very idea of it had met with violent opposition when the Stelians returned home, according to Carnassial, who received sendings from his people.

The opposition wasn't universal, though. Apparently, many stood with their queen in hoping for a future free of their duty to the veil.

"Have you heard from home?" Karou allowed herself to ask. There had been some messages from Akiva, and she was hoping today might bring another.

Carnassial nodded. "Two nights past. Everyone is well."

"Everyone is well?" she repeated, wishing for Zuzana's eyebrow prowess to express just what she thought of the extent of this news. "Is that seriously all?"

"More than well, then," he allowed. "The queen is home, the veil is healing, and it's nearly the dream season."

Karou understood that the veil was healing because Akiva was no longer draining it, and that ordinary stability was returning, but she didn't know what the dream season was. She asked.

"It's . . . a good time of year," Carnassial replied with a roughened voice, and looked away.

"Oh," she said, not yet understanding. "How good?"

His voice was still rough when he said, "That entirely depends on who you share it with," and this time it was Karou who looked away.

Oh.

She pulled on her boots and gathered her hair back, tying it with a strip of cloth she'd torn from one of her two shirts. Fancy. *Get rubber bands*, she willed Zuzana, wishing for telesthesia of her own.

She was dressed already. This was not a life for pajamas, even if she'd had them. She alternated two sets of clothes, sleeping and waking in one set until it failed the sniff test—though, in all honesty, it was quite the lenient sniff test these days. It was a little funny to imagine the boutique in Rome where Esther's shopper had purchased these, and under what conditions, say, the next shirt in the stack found itself on a normal day. Some Italian girl was wearing it on a moped, maybe, with a boy's arms looped lightly around her waist. Give her an Audrey Hepburn haircut, because why not? Rome daydreams deserved Audrey Hepburn haircuts. One thing was sure: That imagined other girl's shirt might have started out identical to Karou's, but it could bear no resemblance to the ash-darkened, river-wash-roughened, sun-bleached, sweat-stiffened article that Karou wore now.

"Okay," she said, draining her tea and taking the bread from Carnassial to eat en route. "Tell me what's happening in Astrae."

And he did, and the morning air was sweet around them, and there were sounds of laughter in the awakening camp—even children's laughter, because refugees had begun to find them here—and at this time of day, when the land was bathed in the sherbet glow of dawn, you couldn't really tell that the distant hills were colorless and dead. Karou could see all the way to the ridge where the temple of Ellai stood, a blackened ruin, though she couldn't make out the ruin itself.

She had been there to retrieve Yasri's thurible. She'd gone alone, prepared to be cut to the bone by memories of that month of sweetest nights, but it hadn't even looked like the same place. If the requiem grove had regrown since Thiago put it to the torch eighteen years ago, it had been burned again last year, along with everything else. There was no canopy of ancient trees, and no evangelines—the serpent-birds whose *hish-hish* had been the sound track to a month of love, and whose burning screams marked the end of it all.

Well, but *not* the end. More chapters had been written since then, and more would be, and Karou didn't think, after all, that they would be dull, as she had hoped aloud at the Dominion camp that night with Akiva. Not with *nithilam* out there, and a bold young queen gripping fate by the throat.

Karou and Carnassial crested the rise that hid the ruined city from the view of the camp, and there it was before them, no longer quite as it had been when Karou had flown here from Earth months earlier to find it scraped free of all life, no souls to brush at her senses, and no hope. The bars of the cage lay just as they had then, like the bones of some great dead beast, but below them, figures moved. Teams of chitinous, many-legged myria-oxen strained before blocks of black stone that had made up the ramparts and towers of a hulking black fortress. Down under it all, Karou knew, there was beauty hidden. Brimstone's cathedral had been a wonder of the world, a cavern of such splendor it was half the reason he and the Warlord chose to site their city here a thousand years ago.

It was a mass grave now, but from the moment she found out what the people of Loramendi had done at the end of the siege, Karou hadn't thought of it like that. She'd thought of it as Brimstone and the Warlord had intended it: as a thurible, and a dream.

She spent her days here, helping with the excavation, but mostly roaming the dead landscape, senses attuned to the brush of souls, alert for the moment when the shifting of rubble would open a crack to what lay buried beneath their feet. No one else could feel them; only she. Well, she didn't feel them yet, but she would, and she would glean them, every one, and not let a single one slip through her fingers. And then?

And then.

Karou took a deep breath and looked up. The sky would be blue today. Chimaera and seraphim would work beneath it, side by side. Word spread in the south that Loramendi was being rebuilt, and more refugees found them every day. Soon, freed slaves would be coming from the north, most of them born and raised there, in servitude. In Astrae, too, chimaera and seraphim were working together, at labor more suffocating than backbreaking. Making over an empire. What a thing. And on the far side of the world, where hundreds of green islands speckled the sea in queer formations, looking more like the crests of sea serpents than any inhabited land, fire-eyed folk prepared for a sweeter season.

Well, Karou supposed they deserved it. She understood now what work shaped their lives, and what they fed of themselves to the veil that held Eretz intact. She didn't know why they called it the "dream" season, but she closed her eyes and let herself imagine that she could meet Akiva there, if nowhere else, in that golden place inside her sleep, and share it with him.

* * *

Akiva never knew if his sendings reached Karou, but he kept trying, as weeks turned into months. Nightingale had warned him that great distance required a level of finesse he was unlikely to achieve for years. She dispatched some messages on his behalf, but it was hard to know what to put into words. It was feelings he wanted to send—though he was told feelings were master-level telesthesia, and not to expect success—and those could only come from himself.

The Far Isles were strewn across the equator, so the sun set in early evening, at the same hour all year round. It was at the gloaming that Akiva took some time to himself each day to try to send to Karou. For her, on the far side of the world, it would be the hour just before dawn, and he liked the idea that in some way he was waking up with her, even if he couldn't experience it himself.

Someday.

"I thought I'd find you here."

Akiva turned. He'd come to the temple at the top of the island, as he did most evenings, for solitude. One hundred thirty-four days and counting, and this was the first time he'd encountered anyone besides one of the wizened elders who tended the eternal flame. The flame honored the godstars, and the elders refused to acknowledge that their deities did not exist. Scarab didn't press the issue, and the flame continued to burn.

But here was Akiva's sister Melliel, whom he'd found imprisoned here on his arrival. She and the rest of her team had been freed that day, as had a number of Joram's soldiers and emissaries who had been held in separate confinement. All had been given the option to stay or go, and the Misbegotten, having no families to return to, had remained, at least for now.

A few of them, including Yav, the youngest, had powerful incentive in the form of the dream season, which would soon come to its end and quite likely see the introduction of blue eyes to the Stelian bloodline. For her part, Melliel claimed that her reason was the *nithilam*, and to be where the next war would stage. But Akiva thought she looked less martial every day, and he'd noticed that she spent more time singing than sparring. She'd always had a beautiful voice, and now her accent had softened to something close to the Stelians' own, and she was learning old songs out of Meliz, with magic in them.

He greeted her, and didn't ask why she was looking for him. They would see each other at dinner in an hour, and so he thought that if she was seeking him now, it must be to speak in private. If there was something she wanted to say, though, she didn't get to it right away.

"Which one is it?" she asked him, standing by his shoulder and gazing outward with him over the vista. On a clear day, from up here, nearly two hundred islands were visible. Some ninety percent of them were uninhabited, and perhaps scarcely habitable, and Akiva had claimed one for himself. And for Karou, though he never spoke this aloud. He pointed out an island cluster to the west, the sun setting behind it.

"The small one that looks like a turtle," he said, and she made a noise like she had picked it out, though he thought it unlikely. It wasn't one of the sharp-featured islands, all upthrust and ancient lava extrusions, and it wasn't one of the calderas, either, with their perfect hidden lagoons.

"Does it have fresh water?" Melliel asked.

"Whenever it rains," he said, and she laughed. It rained ruthlessly at this time of year—every few hours, a kind of downpour such as they'd never experienced in the north: brief but torrential. The waterfalls that descended from this peak would swell and turn from blue to brown in a matter of minutes, and then shrink back to normal almost as quickly. The air was heavy, and clouds drifted low and slow, burdened by bellies full of rain. One of the eeriest things Akiva had ever seen was the shadows of those clouds hunting across the surface of the sea, looking so much like the silhouettes of submerged sea creatures that at first he hadn't believed they weren't, and was still teased for it.

"Look, a rorqual!" Eidolon would say, pointing at a cloud shadow bigger than half the islands, and laugh at the idea that there could ever be a leviathan so large.

A *nithilam* is what it put Akiva in mind of. They were never very far from his thoughts.

"And the house?" Melliel asked.

He shot her a sideward glance. "It's a stretch to call it that."

It was something, though. Hope kept Akiva sane, and the thought of Karou kept him working, day by day, at foundational lessons in the *anima* that was the proper name for his "scheme of energies," and which was the root not only of magic but of mind, soul, and life itself. Only when it was certain he was master of himself and his terrifying ability to drain *sirithar* would he be free to go where he wished. As for whether Karou might come here and see what he busied himself with in his spare hours, her own duty would keep her away for a long time to come. It was some consolation to him to know that Ziri, Liraz, Zuzana, and Mik were with her, to make sure she took care of herself. And Carnassial, too, who had promised to tutor her in a finer tithe method than pain.

Though somehow the thought of Karou in daily lessons with the Stelian magus was less than pure consolation to Akiva.

"It's coming along, though?" Melliel asked.

He shrugged. He didn't want to tell her that the house was ready, that it had been ready, that every morning when he woke in the longhouse he shared with his Misbegotten brothers and sisters, he lay still for a moment with his eyes closed, imagining morning as it might be, rather than as it was.

"Is there anything you need for it? Sylph gave me a beautiful kettle, and I haven't used it once. You could have it."

It was a simple offer, but it caused Akiva to cut Melliel a suspicious glance. He didn't have a kettle, or much of anything else, but he didn't know how she could know this. "All right, thank you," he said, with an effort to be gracious. Kind as the offer was, it felt intrusive. For the most part, Akiva's life since coming here had been an open book. His routine, his training, his progress, even his moods seemed to be up for general discussion at any time. One of the magi—most often Nightingale—kept contact with his *anima* at all times, a monitoring process that had been compared to holding a thumb to his pulse. His grandmother assured him that no one was reading his thoughts, and he hoped this was true, and he also hoped that in his inexperience he wasn't scattering his attempted sendings like confetti over the entire population.

Because that would be embarrassing.

Anyway, what with feeling like the communal project of the Stelians, he wanted to keep this to himself. He never spoke of it—the island, the house, his hopes—though apparently they knew everything anyway. And of course he had never taken anyone there. Karou would be the first. Someday. It was a mantra: *someday.*

"Good," said Melliel, and Akiva waited a moment to see if she would say whatever she might have come here for, but she was quiet, and the look she gave him was almost tender. "I'll see you at dinner," she said finally, and touched his arm in parting. It was an odd interaction, but he put it out of his mind and focused on shaping the day's sending for Karou. It was only later, when he descended the peak, returning to the longhouse on his way to dinner, that the oddness struck a chord, because more oddness awaited him there, in the thatched-roofed gallery that ran the length of the structure.

He saw the kettle first, and so he understood the rest were offerings, too. He mounted the steps and looked over all these things that hadn't been here an hour earlier. An embroidered stool, a pair of brass lanterns, a large bowl of polished wood full of the mixed fruits of the island. There were lengths of diaphanous white cloth, neatly folded, a clay pitcher, a mirror. He was examining it all in puzzlement when he heard an arrival on wing behind him and turned to see his grandmother descending. She held a wrapped parcel.

"You, too?" he asked her, mildly accusing.

She smiled, and her tenderness was a match for Melliel's. *What are the women up to?* Akiva wondered, as Nightingale mounted the steps and handed him her gift. "Perhaps you should take them over to the island directly," she said.

For a moment, Akiva just looked at her. If he was slow in grasping her meaning, it was only because he kept his hope as carefully contained as his unruly magic. And when he did think he understood her, he didn't speak a word. He only pushed a sending at her that exited his mind like a shout. It was nothing but question, the essence of question, and it hit her with a force that made her blink, and then laugh.

"Well," she said. "I think your telesthesia is coming along."

"Nightingale," he said, tense, his voice little more than breath and urgency.

And she nodded. She smiled. And she sent to his mind a glimpse of figures in a sky. A stormhunter. A Kirin. A half-dozen seraphim and an equal number of chimaera. And with them one who flew wingless, gliding, her hair a whip of blue against the twilight sky.

Later, Akiva would think that it was Nightingale who'd come to give him the news in case, in his joy, he unknowingly tapped *sirithar*. He didn't. They were training him to recognize the boundaries of his own *anima* and hold himself within them, and he did. His soul lit up like the fireworks that had burst over Loramendi long years past, when Madrigal had taken him by the hand and led him forward into a new life, one lived by night, for love.

Now night was coming, and, unwatched for, serendipitous, and sooner than he'd let himself dream, so was love.

* * *

It was Carnassial who had sent ahead to tell of their approach, but the women arranged everything else. Yav and Stivan of the

Misbegotten, and even Reave and Wraith of the Stelians, argued that it was cruel to send Akiva away when they did, but the women didn't listen. They only gathered on the terrace of Scarab's modest cliff-face palace, and waited. By then night was upon them, and one of the quick squalls of ruthless rain was, too, so that the newcomers were landing even before the wing-glimmer of the seraphim among them could be seen in the storm.

They were received without fanfare. The men were separated out like wheat chaff and left where they stood. Carnassial and Reave shared a look of long-suffering solidarity before leading Mik and Ziri, along with Virko, Rath, Ixander, and a few wide-eyed Misbegotten, out of the downpour.

Scarab, Eliza, and Nightingale, meanwhile, guided Karou, Zuzana, Liraz, Issa, and the Shadows That Live through the queen's own chambers and into the palace bath, where fragrant steam enveloped them in what they all agreed was the best of all possible welcomes.

Well, except for one. Karou had scanned for Akiva in those seconds between landing and being spirited away, and she hadn't seen him. Nightingale had squeezed her hand and smiled, and there was some comfort in that, though nothing would be true comfort until she saw him and felt the connection between them unbroken.

She believed it was. Unbroken. Every morning she woke with the certainty of it, almost as though she had been with him in her sleep.

"How is it you've come?" Scarab asked, when they had all disrobed and settled into the frothy water, earthen goblets of some strange liquor in all their hands, its cooling properties offsetting the almost unbearable heat of the bath. "Have you already finished your work?"

Karou was grateful to Issa for answering. She didn't feel up to faking her way through any normal social interaction.

Where is he?

"The gleaning is done," said Issa. "The souls are gathered and safe. But the winter is expected to be difficult, and more refugees arrive every day. It was deemed best to wait until a fairer season to begin the resurrections."

It was a nice way of saying that they'd chosen not to bring the dead of Loramendi back to life just so they could huddle and hunger through a gray season of ice rain and ash mud. There wasn't enough food to go around as it was, or shelter, either. It wasn't what Brimstone and the Warlord had envisioned when they crushed the long spiral stair that led down into the earth, trapping their people belowground. And it wasn't what those who stayed above had sacrificed themselves for, either—that others might one day know life in a better time.

The day had not yet come. The time was insufficiently better.

It was the right decision, Karou knew, but because it freed her to do what she most wanted, she had held herself out of all debate and left the decision to others. She couldn't help but view her own desires as selfish, and all of her hoarded hope as a bounty she had no business carrying away with her around the curve of the world, to spend on just one soul, while so many others lay in stasis.

As though sensing the conflict in her, Scarab said, "It was a brave choice, and I imagine not an easy one. But all will come well. Cities can be rebuilt. It's a matter of muscle, will, and time."

"And on the subject of time," said Nightingale, "how long will you stay?"

Liraz replied, "Most of us only a couple of weeks, but it has been decided"—she gave Karou a stern look—"that Karou should stay with you until spring."

This was Karou's deepest conflict. As much as she wanted it—the whole winter here with Akiva—she couldn't help thinking of the bleak conditions the others would endure. *When the going gets tough*, she thought, *the tough* do not *go on vacation*.

"The health of your *anima* is of paramount importance to your people," said Scarab. "Never forget that. You need to heal and rest."

Nightingale added, "As pain makes for a crude tithe, so does misery yield crude power."

"In happiness," said Eliza, looking as though she knew what she was talking about, "the *anima* blooms."

Issa nodded along with everything the women said, *I told you so* fixed firmly on her face. Of course she'd said the same thing herself, if not in quite the same terms. "It is your duty, sweet girl," she chimed in now, "to be well in body and soul."

Happiness has to go somewhere, Karou remembered, and she settled deeper into the water with a sigh. Some fates were difficult to accept, but this wasn't one of them. "Well, okay," she said, with mock reluctance. "If I have to."

They washed, and Karou emerged from the pool feeling purified in body and spirit. It was good to be cared for by women, and what a group they were. The deadliest of all the chimaera alongside the deadliest of seraphim, with a Naja, a ferocious *neek-neek* in deceptively adorable human form, a pair of fire-eyed Stelians of unfathomable power, and Eliza, who had been the answer. The key that fit the lock. And also, just a really cool chick.

They brushed Karou's hair and twisted it, still damp, into vine-tied coils down her bare back. They brought out light, silken raiments in the Stelian style and held lengths of cloth against her skin. "White won't do for you," said Scarab, tossing a dress aside. "You'll look like a phantom." She produced, instead, a whisper of midnight-dark silk, aglimmer with clusters of tiny crystals like constellations, and Karou laughed. She let it pass through her hands like water, and the past with it.

"What?" asked Zuzana.

"Nothing," she replied, and let them dress her. It was a kind of sari gathered over one shoulder, leaving her arms bare, and Karou almost wished for a bowl of sugar and a puff with which to dust herself. An echo of another first night. The gown was so like the one she'd worn at the Warlord's ball, when Akiva had come to find her.

"Do you want to keep your clothes?" Eliza asked, nudging the discarded pile with her foot.

"Burn them," said Karou. "Oh. Wait." She delved into a trouser pocket for the wishbone she'd carried with her all these months. "Okay," she said. "*Now* burn them."

She felt like a bride as they led her back outside. The rain had stopped, but the night was alive with its memory in drips and rivulets, and with creature trills and honey scents, the air balmy and rich with mist.

And there was Akiva.

Soaked to the skin and haloed in vapor where the heat of his body was cooking away the rain. His eyes were ablaze, he was furious with waiting. His hands shook and clenched, and then stilled when he saw Karou.

Time stuttered, or else it only felt like it did. No use, any longer, for those invasive seconds in which they weren't touching. They'd had too many of them already, and made short work of these final few.

They flew together. Time itself leapt out of the way, and Karou and Akiva were spinning, and the ground was falling away. The island was falling away. The sky drew them up and the moons hid in the clouds, keeping their tears to themselves, and their regret, which belonged to the ended age.

Lips and breath and wings and dance. Gratitude, relief, and hunger. And laughter. Laughter breathed and tasted. Faces kissed, no spot neglected. Lashes wet with tears, salt kissed lips to lips. *Lips*, at last, soft and hot—the soft, hot center of the universe—and heartbeats not in unison but passed back and forth across the press of bodies, like a conversation made up only of the word *yes*.

And so it was. Karou and Akiva held on to each other and didn't let go.

It was not a happy ending, but a happy middle—at last, after so many fraught beginnings. Their story would be long. Much would be written of them, some of it in verse, some sung, and some in plain prose, in volumes to be penned for the archives of cities not yet built. Against Karou's express wish, none of it would be dull.

Which she would have cause to be glad of a million times over, beginning that night.

Flight through sifting mists, hands joined. An island among hundreds. A house on a small crescent beach. Akiva had spoken truly when he told Melliel it was a stretch to call it a house. He'd imagined a door once to shut out the world, but there was no door here, so that the world seemed an extension of the house itself: sea and stars forever.

The structure was a pavilion: a thatched roof on posts, snug against the cliff and sheltered by it, its floor of soft sand, with living vines trailing down from the cliff to make green walls on two sides. That much Akiva had done before today. And there were a table and chairs. Well, they were hewn driftwood, but the "table" had a cloth on it, finer than it deserved. And now a wooden bowl of fruit sat atop that, and a beautiful kettle, too, with a box of tea and a pair of cups. Lanterns hung from hooks, and lengths of diaphanous fabric made a third, gently billowing wall, transparent as sea mist.

Nightingale's gift had been unwrapped and given its proper place, and when Akiva brought Karou to the home he'd made for her—a place out of fantasy, so perfect that she forgot how to breathe and had to learn again in a hurry—his wish had all but come true already.

On the bed: a blanket to cover them, a blanket that was theirs together. And some time in the night they met on it and faced each other across lessening space, knees curled beneath themselves and wishbone held between.

And they hooked their fingers around its slender spurs, and pulled.

THE END

Acknowledgments

An ending is reached. It's deeply satisfying, a little bewildering, and unbelievably sad to be closing this chapter of my life. A trilogy, completed! I'm still dazed. I'm also still waiting for Razgut to show *me* a portal. Because obviously Eretz is real.

What, you think I made this all up?

There is really no way to prioritize the thanks due to so many. I'm bursting with gratitude for all these wonderful people:

Readers! Deepest thanks to all the readers who've been rooting for me, and for Karou, since *Daughter of Smoke & Bone*, and who have kept me company on this entire journey. Thank you for being there, and for being excited, and for waiting. Series readers are the best readers. And thank you to the endlessly entertaining fandom, for art and humor and warmth.

Here it is! I hope you love it.

And thank you to the team at Little, Brown for bending time and space so that I could finish this book the way I wanted and needed to, while still ensuring its timely publication. I'm profoundly grateful for the support. To Alvina Ling for the invaluable editorial feedback and crucial enthusiasm that was like fuel, always just when I needed it. And to Bethany Strout, Lisa Moraleda, Melanie Chang, Faye Bi, Andrew Smith, Victoria Stapleton, Ann Dye, Nellie Kurtzman, Tina McIntyre, Adrian Palacios, Julia Costa, Amy Habayab, Kristin Dulaney, Nina Pombo, JoAnna Kremer, Andy Ball, Christine Ma, Rebecca Westall, Renée Gelman, Tracy Shaw, and Megan Tingley: deepest thanks for creating such an exceptional publishing home.

And since I'm blessed to live in parallel worlds in this regard, to my second, amazing publishing home of Hodder & Stoughton in London: Thank you for always having such big, brilliant ideas, and for believing in me so wholeheartedly. To Kate Howard especially, who crossed an ocean and a continent for Karou, way back in the beginning. You really know how to sweep a writer off her feet! To Jamie Hodder-Williams, Carolyn Mays, Lucy Hale, Katie Wickham, Naomi Berwin, Veronique Norton, Lucy Foley, Fleur Clarke, Catherine Worsley, Claudette Morris, and Linnet Mattey: Thank you!

To Jane Putch, my so-much-more-than-agent: so-much-more-than-thank-you! It's been a crazy year—a crazy five years, on this trilogy!—and I couldn't have done it without you. Not even close. Here's to the past, the present, and the future. Cheers!

And my family. First, to my sister, Dr. Emily Taylor, professor, researcher, and rattlesnake wrangler: Thank you for the science consultations and proofreading. I hope that I got Eliza's work right in the end! (Astute readers may remember a "young blonde herpetologist" who Karou buys teeth from in *Daughter of Smoke & Bone*; that was Emily.) To my parents, Patti and Jim Taylor, for everything and more, and to my brother Alex.

Thank you to Tone Almjhell for the heroic last-minute read and sanity check.

And most of all, always, to Jim, who got me writing after I'd kind of given up—or at least had put it on indefinite hold—all those years ago, and who's been my biggest cheerleader ever since. I'm so lucky. Here's to three hundred more years!

Lastly, to Clementine, who was born a month before Karou (though Karou gestated longer), and who has known her all her life. Thanks for being a little trooper, always, best kid in the world.